P

7/07

DWELLING PLACES

BOOKS BY VINITA HAMPTON WRIGHT

FICTION

Grace at Bender Springs

Velma Still Cooks in Leeway

The Winter Seeking

NONFICTION

Simple Acts of Moving Forward:
A Little Book About Getting Unstuck

The Soul Tells a Story:
Engaging Creativity with Spirituality in the Writing Life

DWELLING PLACES

A NOVEL

VINITA HAMPTON WRIGHT

HarperSanFrancisco
A Division of HarperCollins*Publishers*

HarperCollins books may be purchased for educational, business, or sales promotional use. For information please write: Special Markets Department, HarperCollins Publishers, 10 East 53rd Street, New York, NY 10022.

HarperCollins Web site: http://www.harpercollins.com
HarperCollins®, ▟®, and HarperSanFrancisco™ are
trademarks of HarperCollins Publishers.

Designed by Joseph Rutt

FIRST EDITION

Library of Congress Cataloging-in-Publication Data is available.
ISBN-13: 978-0-06-079080-6
ISBN-10: 0-06-079080-6

06 07 08 09 10 RRD(H) 10 9 8 7 6 5 4 3 2 1

To every family
forced to relinquish
the land called home.

PART ONE

DEVOTION

COMING HOME

Trials dark on every hand, and we cannot understand
All the ways that God would lead us to that blessed
     promised land;
But he guides us with his eye, and we'll follow till we die,
For we'll understand it better by and by.
By and by, when the morning comes, when the saints of
     God are gathered home,
We'll tell the story how we've overcome, for we'll
     understand it better by and by.
                                    — *"When the Morning Comes"*

Rita

In Beulah, Iowa, widow women all over town garden in the clothes of deceased husbands. From a distance, they often look like small-framed men. They keep their husbands' clothes because it's wasteful to throw away hats and shirts that still have wear in them. They wear the clothes in memory of the men they have survived, even after the scent of them has been laundered away.

It was a full year after her husband's death before Rita Barnes could wear his clothes. Nearly ten years have passed since Taylor died, and Rita is stretched out on their double bed this morning, naked, because it was humid last night and because she's sixty-six and does what she pleases. She is mentally searching her pantry for cream-style corn, because her son Mack is coming home from the mental hospital today, and his wife Jodie is cooking a nice dinner for him, and a nice dinner for the Barneses always includes Rita's corn casserole. She's also promised chicken and homemade noodles. It will take some time to make the noodles, so maybe she should haul her bones off the bed now.

She stops at the bathroom, rinses her face, combs her hair, and puts in her dentures. In ten minutes she is at the kitchen table, taking some raisin toast with her coffee along with vitamins. The automatic coffeemaker that Mack and Jodie got her for Christmas five years ago is possibly one of the best gifts of her lifetime. She can go smoothly into her day, not even having to count scoops of coffee but leaving the waking-up process to the drinking itself.

By ten-thirty, the noodles are made and ready to throw in with the chicken, and Rita's house is cleaner than it needs to be. The farmhouse, where Mack's family now lives, is still the family center, just as it was when Rita and Taylor lived there. It turns out that Rita's status as mother of the family was not the main reason her home was the hub all those years. The house itself, large and functional and not very beautiful, is what compels them all to congregate. Rita figured that out a year or so after Taylor's passing, when she moved to town and a smaller place. The kids stop by every day, but they don't circle around and land at her little house in town the way they always did at the farm. She doesn't mind that as much as she expected. It's been nice to have privacy, or at least what passes for privacy in Beulah.

On her way out the door to make what she has come to call her "P&P run"—the nearly daily trip to the post office and pharmacy—she grabs two packages of heat-and-serve dinner rolls from the top of the fridge. They're for the party tonight. Jodie likes to have everything on hand several hours ahead of time. The trip out to the farm, also, is a daily event for Rita.

But her day goes south when she turns the ignition key. The engine whines but won't turn over—for the third time this week. She huffs at the little car and tries again. She tries six times and then quits for a minute, feeling warm from the sun that surrounds her in the driveway.

Amos from next door comes out and stands in his drive just a few yards away. He puts his hands on his hips, which always looks funny when Amos does it, although Rita can't figure out why.

"Givin' you trouble again," he says, nodding toward the front end of the car.

"Of course. On a day when I really need to go somewhere."

"You're always needing to go somewhere." Amos smiles a little. He's so old and wrinkled that it looks like a wince.

"But some days it's not that important. Mack'll be home this evening."

"Will he? Well, that's just wonderful. I'm sure you're all happy about that."

"Yes, we are." She turns the key again and listens to the engine strain but not start.

"How old's this car?"

"Nearly eleven years. Taylor bought it for me just a few months before he died."

Amos looks impressed. "That's a real long time for a car to run without a lot of trouble."

"I know. Shouldn't complain, I guess."

"Have Tom Longman look at it."

"I probably should." She tries one more time, and the Ford comes to life grumpily. She raises her eyebrows at Amos. "Now that it's started, I better do all the running around I need to."

Mack's coming home. This is the thought she woke up with, and she's come around to it again at least twenty times. When her son's name flickers across her mind, something tugs at Rita from inside. It's a sensation that has visited her often since the first time her first child moved in the womb. During pregnancy, from the core of Rita's body would come a soft stirring—an echo, really, of the actual move-ment—and her whole self would huddle around that feeling, because every nerve ending seemed to understand that Rita was destined forever to have a center to her life that wasn't even her life. She and Taylor Barnes made a little baby way back when, and Rita hasn't for a day or an hour since felt that she is the focus of her own life. Over the years, as her children have grown up and faced the world, that slight echo in her belly has become sharper and stronger, and thus Rita has continued to respond to the tug in ways only a mother can. Her two children, both sons, grew up, and now one is dead and the other is within a short walk of death. They had children of their own. But still, just the thought of either name—Mack or Alex—reaches into Rita's belly and hooks in, as if there are special sockets in her soul that only her children can fit. Rita notices the yellowing locust branches sigh and sway in May Downer's yard as she drives by, and she thinks of Mack, her firstborn, now forty-three, arriving home from the hospital, and her old womb fills up with echoes.

She leaves the engine running when she stops for the mail and then walks three doors down to the grocery store to pick up extra margarine, in such a rush she hardly says hi to Bud at the register. She parks again at the pharmacy, on the other side of the square, picks up one medication for herself and one for a neighbor who can no longer drive. Then she travels the three miles to the farm. The cornstalks that line the road like multiple layers of picket fence are fading from the deep green of August to a lighter and drier shade. The sun, out hot, is making September feel more like late spring.

"You in a hurry?" Her daughter-in-law, Jodie, looks over Rita's shoulder to the driveway and idling car as Rita walks in the kitchen door with the dinner rolls.

"Starter's acting up. I'm not sure it will start if I shut it off."

"Better have Tom look at it." There was a time when Mack took care of mechanical matters in the family. But at some point Rita's Ford Escort dropped from his list of responsibilities. Rita isn't sure if Mack's refusal to deal with her car comes from frustration with the car or his overall tiredness and inability to deal with things.

"All I need right now, car trouble."

"Time to get another car."

Rita makes a face, and Jodie knows she's making a face and doesn't even look up. "You can't drive that little heap forever."

"I don't know why they make cars to fall apart like that."

"So they can sell you more cars."

Rita breathes easily again only after she has made her pharmacy delivery and is back home. Another little victory. But she'll have to see Tom. Of course, Tom will shake his head like always and give her ten reasons she should just buy another car. She has run out of support when it comes to this particular loyalty.

Lunch consists of cantaloupe and leftover macaroni and cheese. It doesn't feel wrong anymore that she doesn't spend most of her day in the kitchen, keeping husband, kids, in-laws, grandkids, and farmhands fed. Her days and hours are no longer tied to the rhythms of crops and livestock. And when she cleans house, it actually stays dust-free for a couple of days. Out on the farm, she dusted only right before company came. Oh, she'd scrubbed things down regularly. But dirty and dusty were not the same when she lived in the middle of cultivated fields.

At three in the afternoon, she comes to a stopping point and goes to the bedroom to close her eyes for a while. She's never been a napper, but maybe the stress of getting prepared for Mack's arrival has taken her energy today. She lies down, then suddenly she's opening her eyes and the angle of sunlight in the room tells her that nearly two hours have passed.

She tosses off the afghan and lies on her back, studying the tiny cobwebs that have collected around the ceiling light. She has been alone in this bed for years now, and her sleep has come to fill its entire breadth and length. It took several weeks after Taylor's passing for her to so much as venture a foot across the middle to rest in his space. She lay on her half and looked across to that emptiness as though it were another country.

That was back when this bed was still in the farmhouse. It was bad enough that everything outside—the buildings and machinery, the footpaths worn between places—spoke her husband's name like a chant. The whole place bore his signature and was so full of his presence that she couldn't bear to walk outdoors long enough to carry out garbage or feed the dogs. Indoors was almost as bad. Her sons insisted on helping her clean out closets and dressers and medicine cabinets. While she hated to lay eyes on the backyard fence Taylor had built, removing more intimate things such as his razor and socks did her a worse violence. Her sons forgot the closet on the back porch, and Rita didn't remind them. It was filled with boots and gloves, shirts and hats—parts of Taylor's uniform for his long hours in the fields and sheds. Later, she padlocked the closet, knowing every item in it, and took comfort in knowing that whenever she needed to she could open it and clutch the fabrics and breathe in once again her husband's scent.

The farm, as it was then, is long since gone. Thank God, the family managed to hang on to the house and the five acres right around it. And they'd kept the five down along the creek, where the original homestead had been and where the stone house still sets. With Mack's family in the farmhouse now, it is still part of home for Rita, even though she lives in town, in a small house holding fewer things. But in some ways her life has expanded. Now she sleeps across her marriage bed diagonally, taking up the whole space with no guilt at all and only twinges of sadness from time to time. A part of her is always in touch with Taylor—knowing how old he would be or what he would think of a particular piece of news or how much he would enjoy hearing his granddaughter sing. A very deep part of Rita will track with Taylor Barnes through eternity itself. But Rita has continued to exist and even learned how to live alone—not an easy lesson.

And she wears Taylor's shirts and hats when she gardens. She always took care to buy the best work shirts for him, and they've lasted well and fit her fine.

She puts on nice clothes now for Mack's party, then sits in the breakfast nook and sips iced tea. Her Bible and a little notebook lie on the windowsill. This morning her prayers included several people.

Jimmy Benson is scheduled for surgery Wednesday morning; Barb Hoffman is due for more tests sometime this week; Reverend Maynor is filling in for the pastor in Sigourney all this week; and the Walleys are traveling to Seattle to see the newest grandbaby. All of these names are written down in her small wire-bound notebook. They look as matter-of-fact as a shopping list. The name that is always there, in the way milk or bread starts off every list of groceries, is Mack's name. Her eldest boy. There are no words in the whole universe that she hasn't prayed for him at one time or another.

Now she looks out the window at her little bit of yard, here in town where all things are smaller and easier to deal with. She says a prayer that the car will start, get her to the party and back. She also says her son's name, softly. Her insides move, and she closes her eyes against memories both horrible and sweet.

Kenzie

If Kenzie Barnes stares at Jesus long enough, his eyes will shift slightly and rest on her. Although he stands at a garden door, hand raised to knock, his body is sideways just enough that his glance can take her in.

Kenzie has continued this spiritual practice for nearly two weeks. It began by accident; she got tired one afternoon, and her mind wandered while her stare fixed absently on the picture that hangs on the north wall of the church sanctuary. The moving eyes suddenly brought her around. She was alone in the church, and the afternoon light was moving like some special effect over the white walls. To have Jesus in the picture suddenly look at her wasn't frightening at all. There isn't a safer place in the world she could be than here at the prayer rail of First Baptist. So if Jesus moved his eyes, then it was a good thing. It had made her cry to receive such a special affirmation from the Lord. But what she hadn't expected was that it would happen more than once. Staring at Jesus as he stands at the garden door has become part of her devotion. He doesn't look at her every time, but the devotion itself is enough to shore up Kenzie's soul for another evening at home.

She's also discovered that when she closes her eyes and concentrates really hard and asks the Holy Spirit's presence, she will seem to float. Sometimes it feels as if she is leaving her own body. This was scary at first, but she knew that Jesus would not allow anything freaky to happen. So she does the two things now, the gazing upon Jesus's picture and the concentrating with her eyes closed.

She has floated in the Spirit for about five minutes today. During that time she praised God and asked to be made worthy of Jesus's name. She has stared at Jesus a long time, but his eyes haven't moved this afternoon. It is five-thirty, close to suppertime, so Kenzie stands up from the railing and tells Jesus good-bye. After making sure the door locks behind her, she descends the several cement steps and hops onto her bicycle, feeling the need to hurry home. The sun was out bright today, but thin clouds have spread across the sky during the past hour, making the light vague and distant.

The bicycle squeaks in the cool air of September. Quiet fills the countryside except for the constant breath of wind through the cornstalks that rise on either side of the road. This time of year, not far from harvest, the breezes stir up a musty, almost smoky smell. The stalks tower over Kenzie from either side of the road, but their leaves droop, and there's enough space between the rows to allow the pale western light to flicker through as she pedals by.

She pumps up the speed, feeling pursued. She knows that there's nothing behind her on the road and nothing in the surrounding fields other than mice and moles about their business. But she senses something in the air that means her harm—not only her, but her brother and mother and father and grandma. This feeling has plagued her for weeks, disturbing her so much that she's started the daily habit of praying at the church in the couple of hours after school and before she's expected home for supper.

The three people she knows who know much about spiritual things have said that prayer is the way to keep evil away. There aren't elaborate formulas for it, just the Bible's instructions to pray always and for everything you can think of. Reverend Darnelle told her this. So did Grandma and Mike Williamson, the youth pastor at First Baptist. But nobody in the family besides Grandma prays anymore, so Kenzie has taken up the task. She's nearly fifteen and supposes that this is part of what it means to be older and to carry more burdens. She knows that when she was small, her parents and grandparents prayed for her. Now it's her turn.

Though the church sanctuary in late afternoon has become a second home, the evening remains heavy with some unnamed threat, and Kenzie pedals over the graveled surface, the occasional bug hitting her face or jacket. Familiar fields grow arms and scowling faces as she races past breathing hard, the old bike sounding scared as it clatters up and down the hills. The exertion makes it impossible to sing, so mentally she goes through verses of "Jesus, Keep Me Near the Cross."

From a mile away she can see home. The two-story house, lined up with its barns and sheds and silos, looks smudgy against the early evening. Except for six large shade trees in the yard, the buildings sit alone on the horizon. Behind and above the farm, the clouds have separated into purple-gray streaks.

She doesn't notice until she is at the neighbor's mailbox that a man is standing there at the end of the driveway. He looks ready to walk right in front of her. She lets out a little shriek, slams on the brake, skids in the gravel, and nearly goes down several yards from the man. She catches herself with one leg, rights the bike, and stands in the middle of the road, feeling wobbly.

"Hey—you okay?" The man hurries up to her, one hand out. She sees now who it is: Mitchell Jaylee, who lives in the house that goes with the mailbox.

"Yeah, I just didn't see you."

"Sorry—didn't mean to scare you. You were coming along at quite a clip." He looks her over. "You come all the way from town?"

Not really, because the church is just outside the city limits. Kenzie looks at Mitchell's features, wondering how much to tell. His face is shadowy in the overcast sky of early evening, but his features are soft with concern.

"I ride to town all the time. But I started back too late today."

"Sure you're okay?"

"Yeah."

"You look sort of pale."

"I'm okay. I should probably get on home."

He backs away and smiles. "Take care now."

She ignores how much her legs are shaking and rides away from Mitchell. She can feel him watching her as she slides down the road away from him. That's kind of nice, someone watching over her. She almost turns to see if he's still standing there. She pictures his kind face, those eyes that seemed to connect with her in a split second. It was as if God arranged for her to find protection on her way.

She stops the bike about a quarter-mile from the house and stares hard to see which cars are in the drive: Grandma's and the family pickup. The Dodge, which her brother has been driving, is not there. Ed and Lacy's car is not there, which means that Dad isn't home yet. *Jesus, make tonight go all right. Help me say the right things to Dad.*

Tonight they will be a family again. Kenzie hopes in two directions at once. She wants Dad here with them. She wants Mom to not be so stressed. She isn't sure she can have both things at the same time, in the same house.

During the past two weeks, home has been calmer in some ways than it was when Dad was here. A lot of tension has left Mom's face, but that doesn't mean she's happy. Not having to worry so much about Dad has been good for her. She hasn't seemed as angry. She's repainted the downstairs bathroom and rearranged the outdoor potted plants in the spare bedroom, where they will catch the best light during the winter.

When Kenzie opens the kitchen door, heat and the aromas of ham and pecan pie surround her. Mom is coming in from the dining room. "Hey, can you finish setting the table?" She looks happy and scared.

She's wearing brown corduroys that match her hair and eyes, and a fluffy sort of tan turtleneck. Now that her hair is growing longer, nearly to her shoulders, she's begun to pull it back with combs. Kenzie's happy to see Mom looking dressed up, ready for something special. "I took the plates in already. Get the silverware and glasses." Mom turns to the sink and picks up the vegetable peeler.

"Okay." Kenzie brushes by and pats her on the shoulder. Mom doesn't know this, but each time Kenzie pats her like this, she says a prayer for her. It's usually short, like, *Jesus, bless Mom*, but she tries to do it a few times every day.

"Where's your brother?"

"Don't know."

Mom rips the skin off a carrot and says in a low voice, "Well, he'll be here or he won't, I guess."

"He'll be here. He just likes to make everybody wonder. It's part of being dramatic or something." Kenzie finishes with the silverware and glasses and goes upstairs to change. There's a little time left, so she writes in her journal for a few minutes. Thinking about Young Taylor has brought on the urge to do that.

Dear Jesus,

Last night was so awful. I tried to say the right things, but it fell apart anyway. Mom and Young Taylor and I were eating supper together, and Mom said that Dad would get to come home tonight, and she and Grandma were going to cook a nice meal to welcome him, and she wanted us to both be home early. She'd talked to Dad that afternoon, and he couldn't wait to see us.

Then Young Taylor has to ask if Dad would be taking medicine, and Mom says yes, for a while. And all I say is, that's normal for somebody who's been depressed. And Young Taylor gets snotty about it, asking how would I know, and I told him that Denise Lowell's mom went to the hospital for depression, and she was on medicine afterwards. Young Taylor's sitting there with his head down, so we can't see his eyes behind his bangs.

He's dyed his hair this really dark black, which looks lame, but Mom doesn't say anything about it. Young Taylor acts like he knows everything and the rest of us are stupid, and I shouldn't let it get to me but it does.

Then Mom says that the doctors think Dad's well enough to come home, but we can't expect everything to just go back to normal right away. She's not looking at me or Young Taylor—it's like she doesn't want us to argue with her.

And then Young Taylor says, "I hope we're not going back to normal." Does he say things like that just to hurt Mom? I wished Mom would get after him for talking like that, but she doesn't say anything. Young Taylor just sits there, not looking at us. He's wearing black boots with silver studs all over them. And tight black jeans and a black shirt with a black velvet vest. Who's he trying to impress? Does he know how ridiculous he looks hanging out at school by the bus barn with Lydia and Kyle, their little Goth trio trying to look too cool for the universe? Kids are saying that Lydia does it with every old divorced guy in town, and Kyle is so weird that even the teachers laugh at him behind his back. But Dale and Eric graduated last year, so maybe Young Taylor figures that Lydia and Kyle are better than nothing now that his real friends aren't in school anymore.

He's my brother, and in a way I feel sorry for him, and I pray for him every day, Lord, even though he's so irritating and tries to upset me. He seems lonely, but he'd never admit that. And he's become too good for normal people, and he acts like he knows he's handsome, which he is when he's not made up to look like a vampire or something. But it's the dark and dangerous kind of handsome that junior and senior girls go crazy for, at least when they're not around school, where talking to Young Taylor would kill their popularity.

I don't know why I'm writing all of this, Jesus, but who else can I tell it to? My friends are tired of me complaining about my brother, and they think he's kind of cute and I should just chill. But I'm afraid for his soul. The kind of music he listens to, and the way he talks—it's so far from what you want for him.

Anyway, help me act like a Christian toward him. And somehow make him behave when Dad gets home tonight.
Love and praise,
Kenzie

Before leaving her room, Kenzie studies her butt in the mirror. It seems to be getting wider, but she can't be sure. She returns downstairs to get Mom's input. Tonight needs to be perfect. She wants to be beautiful and happy for Dad. For everybody, Jesus included.

Mack

He never noticed before how many people around here drive Toyotas. While waiting for Ed to pick him up, he counts four Toyotas in twenty minutes. All several years old, bought used, no doubt. Tercels and Corollas from the late eighties appear at the rise in the road and slide down the hill and past the large, uneventful yard, making meek small-engine noises, tickety-tickety sounds that can barely be heard above the insects screeching in the tall grasses across the road.

It has seemed odd to Mack that a mental hospital would have a front porch. This facility, somehow connected to the mental health services out of Ottumwa, has moved into a large, refurbished farmhouse inn, and the porch bothers Mack for how peaceful it appears. As if aunts and uncles and grandparents and children would waddle out there after Sunday dinner and find their favorite spots and let the feast digest at leisure as they share gossip. People don't sit in this place in congenial chatter and silences. They don't daydream or lap up the breeze while gathering energy for the next task. If they sit quietly, they are usually drugged and empty-faced. They wander to remote posts within the confines of the sprawling house and pass the time either absently or desperately.

Mack now sits on the outdoor furniture, unconfined, waiting for his ride. He decides that the porch remains for just such an occasion.

His time is up, his small light blue Samsonite latched and at his knee. The porch is his entryway back to home. He dares to rock a bit in the large wicker chair, and he allows himself to breathe in the balm of the bright, harvesttime winds and to feel just a little bit hopeful.

He reaches down to feel the handle of the suitcase—from the luggage set he and Jodie received from his parents as a wedding present. They've used the complete set only once in nineteen years. When the kids were little, they visited Jodie's mom down in Galveston. That was a year after Jodie's dad passed and her mom sold the house in Oskaloosa and went to live close to her son. Jodie's brother has a small place near the ocean, and for weeks prior to the trip the kids jabbered like blue jays about everything they would do there. Young Taylor was ten then, and he packed his own suitcase—this very suitcase—and left out underwear. That was a decent year, Mack and Jodie together long enough that the new had worn off as well as their harsh edges. The children were so eager to dive into happiness as well as the salty sea.

Ed is suddenly in the drive. Mack wonders if he has blanked for a few minutes. They have him on all kinds of pills, and he often feels that his head is floating, just slightly detached from the rest of him. It annoys the hell out of him.

"Hey." Ed strides up and onto the porch. They shake hands.

"Thanks for doing this," says Mack.

"We'll pick up Lacy on our way to your place. This all you got?"

"Yeah. Thanks for doing this."

"No problem."

Mack puts his suitcase in the backseat and climbs into the front. Ed shifts quickly into reverse, and the car slips back onto the road. It is smooth, dark asphalt, just redone. From his bare window on the second floor, Mack watched the county crew do the finishing touches. Now he rolls down the car window and welcomes the cool wind that whips at his face as they pick up speed.

The ride feels light, easy, something people do every day.

Ed glances at Mack, looking happy. "Good to be takin' you home, buddy."

"Glad to be going."

"I think Jodie and your mom have been cooking all day."

Mack smiles. Food is love. "Oh, can we stop by the pharmacy?"

"Sure. The one here or home?"

"Home. They called it in already. They still want me on some of this stuff."

"Well, better follow your orders."

"Yeah."

It is a fairly long drive, across another county, to get back home. Mack notices with new clarity how the soft hills roll into one another, folding between them gatherings of trees and small streams that glitter shyly through the canary grass. The two men punctuate the time with comments about how the corn and beans look. Mack doesn't deal with his own crops anymore, but conversations like this one spin out of some automatic track inside him. He and Ed grew up a mile from each other and have maintained a running commentary about their surroundings for thirty-some years.

There's a line at the pharmacy window. Mack finally gets to the front, only to learn that the prescriptions aren't ready yet. It will be a wait, and he considers coming back later to pick them up, but Ed is patiently trying on reading glasses from a nearby rack.

Mack stares down the aisle. The back of his mind seems to stir from sleep, and he remembers all the things Jodie might have him pick up if she knew he was here. He wonders if the store still has that florist stand near the camera section. He should take Jodie flowers. His mother too. Pick up gifts for the kids. He walks around the corner and finds the flowers. He picks up three small bouquets. He's halfway back to the pharmacy window when he remembers that he has no cash. He has no idea how much money is in the account; he hasn't accessed it in about three weeks. Suddenly his head gets crowded. He returns the flowers quickly, hoping Ed hasn't seen him. Then he sits down on one of the chairs in the waiting area, his heart racing, and stares at a display of multivitamins guaranteed to restore prostate health.

In fifteen minutes, they are in the car and headed for Ed's place. A mile from the house, Mack begins formulating how to get through the conversation that will start once Ed's wife is in the car. Lacy is a sweetheart, probably unable to cause real harm to anybody. It should be easy to talk, to pass the few minutes it will take to arrive at the farmhouse. Still, there is something pulling at Mack's breath. He tries to think. To calm himself, he opens the white paper bag and looks over the medications, pretending to check the names and dosages. Four squat, plastic pill bottles tumble into his lap. They rattle, and Mack senses Ed gazing at the road with effort.

"They've got a pill for everything these days." Mack gives a sniff meant to sound like a chuckle.

"Good thing." Ed blinks behind his sunglasses. "Think of all the folks who used to just do without, just kept feelin' bad."

"Yeah, you've got a point." Mack turns the labels toward him, one by one: lithium, clonazepam, effexor. "It's not a permanent thing. After a while, they wean you off of it."

"Sure."

Ed's farm is coming into view. Mack thinks of his own house, and how full it is this moment with the people who have been without him for days, who have endured seeing him admitted and then at times have been kept from him. He thinks of all the conversations he will need to have in the days to come, all the forms of making up to people, of getting better and doing well. The pull on his breath tightens and reaches clear down to his heart. Then the bottles in his hands blur and his chest fills with weakness. The hold on his throat loosens for a second, and he hears the air rushing into him.

The wind on his neck gets calm suddenly. Ed is slowing the car. "You all right, Mack?"

Mack wipes his eyes. "If I'd ever thought I'd have to get my peace of mind from—" He can't finish. He holds up the medications.

Ed is saying something that Mack can't quite hear. The car is stopped, rumbling in place beneath them. Finally, Ed's sounds separate into words. "It's just what you need for now. It's like taking something for an infection, you know? When the infection's over, you don't have to take the medicine anymore." He clamps a hand on Mack's knee. Mack looks at it and remembers a younger hand throwing him a football, the glare of lights and the chatter of the high school crowd surrounding them. He remembers Ed's hands maneuvering wrenches around stubborn tractor parts and steadying the cows on their way up the chute. He thinks of Ed's grin the day he stood up in the church as best man, of Ed cradling one baby after another, as both of them brought children into the world. Mack had a brother, who is dead now. But in a lot of ways, Ed is closer than a brother. If Mack can't trust the kindness in this hand, he can't trust anything at all.

"I know. I'll be okay." Mack sniffs and breathes deeply, in and out, trying to turn the action into some form of comfort. Ed puts the car back into drive and his hand back on the steering wheel. They say no more, and then they pick up Lacy, and she carries the conversation over the remaining distance to Mack's home.

Jodie

For all of her life, evening has brought Jodie a few short moments of pure relief. She has always lived in the country, and many days there is a point at which the sun leaves, its pale train of light remaining in a perfectly still sky. A person has to stop at such a time and be quiet and realize that most of what was going to get done today has either gotten done or will wait for tomorrow. There are always tasks to do at night, in the house or under lights in an outbuilding. But the true energy of the day has subsided, and anyone who lives day after day with crops and creatures learns to sleep when nature sleeps and to get rest as regularly as possible, because once the sun is up the work comes back, and will always come back.

This evening she feels the need to wait for that still time, to go out in the yard and allow the smooth horizon to calm her. She knows that the sun will disappear around the time they are having dessert. She hardly ever puts on a big dinner, and when she does it's usually the noon meal after church or a weekend birthday dinner. But today isn't Sunday and it's nobody's birthday. Mack is due home any time now, and dinner is a half-hour from being on the table. Mom isn't here yet—could that mean that her car didn't start after all? But Rita would have called if that were the case. She was over here earlier in the day, to drop off heat-and-serve dinner rolls. Jodie has checked to be sure they are fresh. Rita would give the clothes off her back, but she's a scavenger when it comes to groceries. That's how she manages to feed half the town on a fixed income. But Jodie wants fresh rolls for this meal, nothing even day-old.

The radio is on and tuned to a local station that provides, in equal doses, the weather report, the farm report, local news, and gospel music. This evening there's the rebroadcast of some church service featuring music by a husband-and-wife team, Mavis and Danny Trotter. As Jodie arranges raw vegetables on a tray, Mavis and Danny fill the room with a hymn, and Jodie sings automatically.

"By and by, when the morning comes . . ." She has sung hymns all her life, and for most of her life she has believed them. They are written on her memory and can't be erased, even though she'd like to do that today and has wanted to for some time.

"We'll tell the story how we've overcome, for we'll understand it better by and by." What, exactly, must she overcome? Financial stress? Her husband's depression? Both are chronic and apparently beyond her ability to help. She listens to Mavis and Danny, and the old words sound like a foreign language.

Kenzie appeared ten minutes ago, helped set the table, and is upstairs now. But Young Taylor is missing. Jodie doesn't know when it's appropriate to worry about her seventeen-year-old disappearing, but he knows better than to be a no-show tonight. At times such as this, she wishes she had relented and let him buy a cell phone; at least she could have tracked him better. She will call the two or three homes where he often lands, but beyond that she can only hope that he shows up.

This evening needs to be special. Both the children must be here. And she, Jodie, must be glad for her husband to be home again. All of this feels so big to manage, so impossible to bring to fruition. So Mack will arrive home after being away from them—the first time he has ever been away from them—and she'll say that she's made his favorite dessert but that, by the way, Young Taylor isn't here.

"Mom, does this skirt ride up my butt?" Kenzie stands in the doorway looking marvelous in the way only a fourteen-year-old can. With hardly any makeup, her face is full of natural blushes. She wears a silky, fitted brown shirt that reminds Jodie of the living room curtains she loved a decade ago. Kenzie twists at the waist of her cream-colored straight skirt, which hits the lower part of her thighs, to show Jodie her behind. The child is beginning to develop slight, young curves, but she is essentially slender and straight up and down. Her arms and legs just keep going.

"Uh, no. No riding. Looks just right."

"Bekka's skirts climb up all the time, and I tell her it looks strange, but she won't listen to me."

Jodie bends to turn on the oven light so she can check on the pies. "Maybe she wants her skirts to ride up."

"I don't *think* so—not around the boys in *our* class."

"Well, your skirt is fine. I love that blouse—it's the exact same color as your hair."

"I want to put a rinse on my hair—make it darker now that summer's over."

"Not too dark—it'll wash out your complexion."

Jodie feels a hand on her shoulder, and a little pat. Ever since Mack was admitted, Kenzie has done this often—small, connecting touches throughout the day. A child's offering of comfort. Young Taylor's teen years have been a war, but their little girl stepped into puberty and Jesus's arms on practically the same day. She is always busy and trying to take care of people, a trait she has inherited from Rita evidently. This child is the unexpected blessing, a daily grace.

Jodie flips off the oven light but stays bent at the little window, no longer looking inside at the pies but at the glass itself and her reflection in it.

"Mom, you look fine." Another little pat.

They hear the Dodge then, and Young Taylor comes in the door without acknowledging them and makes a beeline for the stairs, even as Jodie reminds him that supper will be ready soon. Jodie is suddenly overwhelmed with anger at her son. This happens more all the time, anger flushing her veins without warning, like a flood through gulleys. Sometimes it's anger at people and sometimes at inanimate objects, the time, or a situation. But it roars from deep down, and it makes her feel out of control, which is the last thing she needs to be. She marches up the stairs and down to the end of the hall and Young Taylor's bedroom door, which is, of course, closed.

She raps hard. "Taylor!" She hears movements and a throat clearing. The door opens, and the lanky, black-haired kid stands there like a rock star, in a fog of sweet smoke. She keeps telling herself that she should be glad the boy doesn't chew tobacco, but she can't bring herself to appreciate his clove cigarettes.

She tries not to notice the silver bone earring dangling at the bottom of an ear rimmed by a series of smaller studs. Maybe she'll say something if he jams some decorative item through both cheeks, but anything smaller can't take up space in her mind right now.

"It's almost time for dinner—Dad'll be here soon."

"I won't eat ham."

"There's plenty else. Why don't you wear the shirt Grandma got you for your birthday."

The shoulders slump, but he rubs an eye and says, "Okay."

When Jodie hits the ground floor, Rita is in the kitchen. The oven door is open, and she is placing the second pie on the cabinet, making pleased sounds.

"They didn't burn, did they?"

"Oh, no. Perfect as usual."

"Kenzie—ice in the glasses, please."

"Hey, look at that feast."

Mack's quiet comment trips across all other sounds in the kitchen and brings Jodie to attention. He stands in the doorway, Ed and Lacy

Timmons just behind him. They have come in the front door, as if they are guests.

Her husband's smile warms his thin face. Gray highlights in the straight brown hair make his features look older than they really are. It occurs to Jodie that he's had that haircut since high school, semi-long but clipped away from his ears and neck. He stands in the center of the arched doorway, fists in the pockets of his denim jacket. Jodie watches the hands come out as Mack raises his arms and Kenzie nestles into him. Rita comes up close enough for Mack to kiss her cheek.

This is too fast. I'm not ready. Nothing's ready. Jodie watches Mack, and she is stuck to the floor. Mack looks at her, the gleam in his eyes deepening.

She sees, or her memory sees, a cake pan flying past Mack's head. Did she really throw it at him? Did he anger or frustrate her that much? Was it some private comedy that they couldn't fully appreciate at the time? Or did the family put the wrong person in the hospital? Jodie feels a wave of shame at the person she has become during these hurtful times. She should have been better at understanding Mack's struggles. She shouldn't have grown angry, sarcastic, vindictive. Shouldn't have thrown things.

"Hey, Dad." Jodie hears Young Taylor's soft voice behind her. She moves to the side and watches him, dressed in the birthday shirt, go over and hug his father.

Rita addresses the Timmonses. "Good to see you two."

Jodie is finally able to speak. "Thanks for picking him up, Ed. Glad you could come over tonight." She raises her face to accept Ed's customary peck on the cheek. Lacy has already pulled Kenzie into a hug. The presence of these friends allows Jodie to feel more safety in her own home. Rita starts directing everyone to the dining room.

The others move toward the table, and Jodie sees Mack's eyes fix upon her as he crosses the room to where she stands. The distance falls away and she knows that in a short moment her husband's arms will wrap around her. Never mind her former words and flying objects; Mack will always be a gentle soul who doesn't know the meaning of a grudge. She hugged him not long ago, on her last visit to the hospital, but this is different, with him back in the house. She tries to think of how it should feel to be embraced by him, but there is no time to think or prepare.

"Hi, sweet." His voice in her ear is like a tide lapping into a cavern.

She brings her arms up to feel the jacket as his hair presses into her cheek and against her neck. For a moment she is nearly overcome by the textures of his skin and clothing. It is impossible to do this— to be wrapped into Mack when around them everything is so public and calm. Jodie feels a dark habit take over: something within her turns hard and passive. She eases out of Mack's embrace and holds his hand as they walk to the table.

Dinner is pleasant. Ed and Lacy's latest news has to do with their daughter Alison being away at college for the first year. Lacy's telling of any story is filled with drama and hyperbole. It's good to laugh and not talk too much.

Jodie watches the evening's scenes slip by and keeps trying to hold some thought about them. What she really wants is for everything to stop long enough for her to think, to recognize something, to form a plan. But all of it keeps coming and coming and leaving her wordless.

Eventually the meal winds down; they clear the table and have pie and coffee in the living room. Then Ed and Lacy stretch and say their good-byes. Jodie and Mack walk them out to their car.

"He's looking good," Lacy says, close to Jodie's ear. She gives Jodie's hand a squeeze before getting into the car.

Jodie nods. "Thanks for everything." Mack comes up beside her as they watch the Timmonses leave.

The air is just crisp enough that their breath appears faintly in the glow of the yard light. Jodie turns to face her husband in their first moments alone.

"Hi, babe." She touches his cheek, and he kisses the palm of her hand.

"Hi." His eyes peer right into her. "Thanks for the party."

"I didn't know if it would be too much for the first night."

"It was just right." He leans toward her, and they kiss. Jodie allows that toughness within her to soften a little. She hasn't allowed herself to miss the kisses and hugs. She's been so afraid of losing it all forever. But now their lips meet gently, like old friends. Jodie and Mack wrap arms around one another, ignoring the night chill. They hug and sway in a small, quiet dance and pull away only when Rita's voice hovers near the kitchen window behind them.

"Kenzie, does your mom still have those big freezer bags?"

Mack's mouth twitches. "Better make sure Mom gets her leftovers." He guides Jodie up the steps, a hand resting on the small of her back.

Once they load the front seat of Rita's Ford with a little mountain of clear bags full of food, the car won't start. Rita tries, and then Mack does, but the engine won't turn over.

"I'll drive you home, Mom. I can take the car in tomorrow."

"Don't you work tomorrow?"

"I'll call Tom and have him tow it in."

"Don't let him haul it to the junkyard."

They transfer Rita and her leftovers to the cab of the pickup. Jodie watches Mack climb into the driver's seat. His movements are slower than she remembers.

When Mack returns, Jodie and the kids are in the family room, the TV on.

"That was a good dinner," says Mack.

"Sure was." Kenzie looks up at her father brightly. He takes a seat next to her on the sofa and brings his arm around her.

Jodie sits on the footstool in front of Young Taylor, who is in the easy chair nearest the TV. He appears to be watching it.

Jodie taps her son on the foot. "Your dad needs the car back, you know."

"Sure." Young Taylor has taken command of the second vehicle. It's given him the freedom to get away from home, which Jodie sees as good for all of them these days. When her son isn't around looking like Count Dracula, she can imagine that he's off doing normal things with other kids his age.

"Sorry I have to take away your wheels." Mack makes half a grin. Young Taylor doesn't look in his direction.

"It's your car. No big deal."

The room becomes silent, and familiar tensions begin to creep back in. Young Taylor gets up abruptly. "G'night."

"Good night, son." Mack looks as if he wants to do something, but he holds on to Kenzie and follows Young Taylor's exit with sorrowful eyes.

"Good night." The two words slam upon Jodie's mind with more finality than they really mean. She shifts to let Young Taylor walk around her and to the hall and stairway. She despises her lack of faith even as the thought forms: *Our happy evening is over.*

Half an hour later, both kids are in their rooms and Jodie lies beside Mack under the midnight blue comforter. The warmth that glowed between them out under the yard light is gone now. They are in old, difficult territory. They are not merely in this bed in this moment but also reliving all the moments before this: the relentless whispered arguments in the dark as they lay stiffly side by side; the awful silences that took up residence as their lovemaking wore thin and finally wore out; the timid hoping they managed during calmer moments. Jodie wonders what Mack expects now, in this bed, with her. She wonders what he thinks she expects. She doesn't know what she expects. Hope for anything tangible just hurts too much.

After a few moments, Jodie turns to Mack, resting a hand on his chest. He wears a fresh T-shirt and boxers.

"I bet you're tired."

He doesn't answer. She can't quite read his features. The clouds have swallowed the moon, and their room is dark except for a streak on the far wall cast by the yard light.

She leans closer and kisses his cheek. "I'm glad you're home, babe."

He sighs. "You sure about that?"

"Yes."

"I want everything to get better, sweet."

"I know. I'm just glad you're home. Let's take our time."

He leans closer, shyly, and kisses her. She kisses in return, but it is a good-night kiss rather than a pre-love one. They hold each other, and she is surprised at how comforting that is. Mack has been the source of so much anxiety and hurt that it is strange to feel any ease in his closeness. Maybe Mack is a different man now. He looks much the same. He feels the same. She imagines that something in his eyes is calmer, but she can't be sure. She will have to wait through the coming days and see who emerges from her husband's body. She will have to wait and see what person emerges from her own. She looks in the mirror now and doesn't recognize anything she loves.

When Mack turns his back to her, his usual posture for sleep, she rubs his neck until his muscles relax. The last thing she remembers is his hand coming across his shoulder to touch her fingers.

2

TAKING CARE

Savior, like a shepherd lead us,
   much we need thy tender care;
In thy pleasant pastures feed us,
   for our use thy folds prepare:
Blessed Jesus, blessed Jesus,
   thou hast bought us, thine we are;
Blessed Jesus, blessed Jesus,
   thou hast bought us, thine we are.
                    — *"Savior, Like a Shepherd Lead Us"*

Mack

Mack comes home from the hospital on a Thursday evening. Friday at midmorning he goes to Hendrikson's Tractor & Implement Company, where he has worked as a mechanic for two years or so. Harold Hendrikson is happy to see him, and by noon Mack is elbow deep in work and chatting with Cheryl, Harold's daughter, who comes in once a week to do the books. Mack continues to feel as if he's moving in slow motion, but he is surprised at how this day seems like any other, as if he's not been off somewhere else and fighting for his life. Engines work the same as they always have, thank God. He's grateful that his tasks are physical and for the most part uncomplicated. He tastes the autumn air that sweeps across the oily garage floor. And on his way home he drives slowly, startled by how the corn tassels in the Merkles' seed plot form a cream-colored fringe that rides atop the rows of drying stalks. He's watched the progress of corn for years, but today is the first time it's made him think like this.

He's home by six, and Jodie has set out leftovers from last night's dinner. Kenzie eats supper with them, but Young Taylor is at his friend Dale's. This too is normal, and a comfort. Evidently his nearly grown son considers Mack well enough that it's not necessary to stay close to home. Mack imagines that his wife and daughter watch him closely, but there's no fear in their attention. He remembers their fear. Even when they didn't speak it, their motions and tone of voice made it clear that they were uneasy around him. Well, that doesn't seem to be the case now. Maybe this will work out after all. He will go to work every day, family life will carry on, and the past few weeks will have just been a glitch in his life.

On Sunday they attend church as a family. Mack is self-conscious as he takes Jodie's elbow and follows her to their usual pew. She wears a sage green jacket over tan pants and turtleneck. Mack has always liked the way she can look comfortable no matter what she wears. Nothing fancy, no starched lace or tough-looking suits. Even her colors are soothing to be near. She wears no perfume, but the heat of her body pulses out jasmine scent from the soap she used early this morning. Mack knows that while the rest of them slept Jodie rose and showered and dressed in the quiet. She put herself together with care, just so she could stand beside him now steady and sweet.

Folks greet them, smiling pleasantly at Mack. They welcome him back but make their greetings short, as if they understand how much he does not want to be put on the spot. It is the same way they greet someone who has lost a loved one or begun chemotherapy. The suffering is clear enough to everybody; what is necessary is saying hello, giving a bit of acknowledgment, that nod or handshake that lets a person know he is still one of them. He will always receive a handshake as long as he walks in the door. At the same time, his battles are his own, and no one pretends that they can do the fighting for him. They are here, just the same, and they won't forget his name or his pain.

Kenzie tucks herself into the pew on Mack's other side, and he enjoys the curl of his daughter's arm around the crook in his own and the brush of her cheek against his shoulder. Young Taylor has come today, which is uncharacteristic. He looks almost normal in jeans and a regular shirt rather than the all-black stuff. Jodie says that Young Taylor has begun wearing makeup, white face and black lips, but Mack has yet to see this. He's disappointed that, in his absence, Young Taylor didn't settle down and give his mother nothing else to worry about. The boy walks in behind his grandma Rita, who turns to talk with him several times, as if he always accompanies her. Young Taylor sits on the back pew, while Rita slides in beside Kenzie and pats her leg.

As normal as it seems for them to be seated in a row with people filling the spaces around them, Mack is lightheaded for most of the service. A few weeks ago he couldn't hold in his mind for the shortest second a picture like this one, and it still seems as though the simplest, most ordinary things have run away from him. During the opening hymn he's aware of his body taking breaths and joining in, and he listens with some wonder to the sound coming out of his mouth.

In a moment that hangs there for his pleasure, he feels the weight of the hymnbook and the sensation of his daughter clearing her throat beside him. He breathes in the calming atmosphere of his wife. He watches Bernice Warner's hands move over the piano keys and the shadows of small clouds travel across the sanctuary. There is still a deep tiredness in Mack's soul, left over from days of fighting himself and searching for death, of tedious sessions with doctors and tiny paper cups of colorful pills, of dull hallways and echoing sounds of despair. But he sits down after the invocation and recognizes the creaks of everyone sitting at once on the eighty-year-old pews. The tears pool in his eyes, and he knows precisely what it feels like to come home.

It seems like months ago that he was last with his family on Sunday, although not that much time has passed. They went to church, just like today, and invited the pastor to eat with them. They came home, and Rita and Jodie put on dinner. They ate at one o'clock, as always. They sat around and passed the casseroles and salads and sliced roast beef. The weather carried the weight of August humidity, and while they were eating, a late summer thunderstorm rolled through, causing Rita to hurry to the window nearest the dining room table and pull it down against the wind.

Then they moved into the living room for banana cream pie. And while Mack was digging into the crust and whipped cream, the pastor, Reverend Alice Maynor, began to talk.

"Mack, several of us have been concerned about you lately. We can see that you're not feeling well."

Before Mack realized what was happening, his wife and mother were in tears, and the children sat motionless and wide-eyed, while the pastor's voice became urgent, even though she spoke in low tones.

"It's time to see a doctor."

"You've not been yourself for a long time."

"We've set up an appointment tomorrow morning."

Suddenly the pie was melting on his tongue without flavor. Suddenly he was one person against a multitude. They kept assuring him that they weren't angry. But it felt like anger just the same—the scheming they had done to gang up on him like this, the precision of their planning. The way they were in such agreement that they were nodding and finishing one another's sentences. He'd been left out of all of it—they'd taken the chalk and made the mark just short of where he sat. He set down his dessert bowl and felt the blood rush at his temples and his mouth go dry. He couldn't bring himself to agree with them at that moment—it would have been like transferring every last bit of power from himself to them. He was no longer safe in their midst. He remembers feeling exposed and hounded, shut out and smothered all at once.

But underneath those immediate reactions there flowed a deep, black fear that had swelled about him for days and weeks on end. A panic that never left, a jittery sense that kept him off balance. He'd

taken all his guns out to the barn and cleaned them and loaded them
and held them toward himself in ghostly practice runs. He'd watched
himself deliberate and arrange and rehearse. Of course, he would
never admit that here, in this room. It took him three days to confess
to a doctor, and that under medication. The darkness had ridden so
low in his soul that he couldn't put words to it all at once, and when
he did, he couldn't connect to what the words really meant.

"Have you planned how you will do it?"

"Yes."

"Have you made arrangements?"

"Most of them."

As if they were discussing tractor repairs.

It was one of many tedious and devastating conversations between Mack and strangers, in rooms that were too clean and bare,
where everything smelled like old medicine and laundered sheets.
They wouldn't leave him alone. Eventually there would be exchanges
of words. And even that wasn't enough. Words began to mean less
and less, and emotions began to be the goal. *Lord God, get me out of
here, away from all my words. Please, please take away every thought I've
ever had. Maybe if the thoughts get taken away, I can finally sleep in
peace. Just to sleep on my own, no drugs. Just to sleep and wake up and
be better. Lord God, I'm begging you. Take every bad thought out of my
head.*

All of it started that Sunday afternoon, in the room where Mack
sits now, in his place at the head of the table. His mother is at the
other end, his wife and children in between. They pass baked
chicken, sweet potatoes, applesauce, fried onions and peppers. The
furnace kicks on, the windows are all shut tight. Jodie has put in a
tape of religious instrumental music. The room is warm and full of
good aromas. It cannot be the same room in which the hospital seg-
ment of his life began, and these cannot be the same people. Yet he
knows that the hospital has saved his life; he still feels somewhat be-
grudging about that. He has no choice but to call it a good thing—
even so, good can be beneficial in one sense and horrifying in another.

He doesn't feel any relief or safety when he remembers the hospital.
He feels only that it is over, and that it is good to be back here, in his
house.

Jodie

This morning, in church, for the first time in months, Jodie said a
prayer. She sang it, really, but she's certain that this counts as prayer.
Haley Jones, who leads the music at Grace Methodist, ended the service with "Savior, Like a Shepherd Lead Us," an old, old song, and
Jodie sang without looking at the hymnal. By the third verse, when
they got to the chorus, "Blessed Jesus, blessed Jesus, thou has loved
us, love us still," Jodie's voice had kicked into a different gear. She was
aware of her words and spirit merging, and she sang each phrase from
a deep place, understanding that she was begging Jesus, just then, to
not give up on her. It was a startling experience of maybe ten seconds,
but its importance registers with her hours later.

She has never been a vocal person in the congregation. She's more
of a doer, someone who helps collect clothing and other items for the
Community Closet, someone who can always be counted on to cook
a huge pan of lasagna for a funeral dinner. Once in a great while she
sings in the choir, usually when Haley calls her because she's missing
two of her three altos. Grace Methodist is a fifteen-minute drive because it is in Oskaloosa, not Beulah. Jodie's family does not have the
history in the Oskaloosa congregation that they do in the one closest
to home. At Grace, no one remembers their struggles, the sale of the
farm, or the death of Alex, because no one was witness to those
events. After Alex died, and when weeks had passed and Jodie and
Rita were desperate to go to church somewhere, they visited Grace
Methodist and decided to call it home.

Jodie is still unwilling to say that the people of Beulah First
Methodist failed her family. She looks back at the worst days and
must admit to herself that people did care, they did say how sorry
they were, did bring casseroles to the door. But those people are

woven into the bad memories. And that is enough to make it impossible to be with them.

Mack's eyes lit up this morning when he walked into the kitchen before church and saw her. She didn't really dress up, but Sunday attire is always a notch or two up from everyday clothes. She bothers to put on some makeup for church, doubting that anyone else notices but knowing that she feels a little better for it. Well, Mack noticed. He truly looked at her. He hugged her and gave her a kiss and seemed so grateful.

She tried to be grateful too and returned the kiss, but something in her system seized up and stayed that way even while she kissed Mack. She doesn't think he noticed the tension, but she worries about what it means that she feels this way around him. Now she's in the bathroom, changing into her everyday clothes while Sunday dinner is simmering. She tries to pinpoint why she's holding back from Mack, her lifelong love, the man she knew before he was a man, when they were in school together and making love eyes in study hall.

She takes off her bra and replaces it with a jersey tank that serves as underwear beneath her flannel shirt. Although she has nursed two children, her breasts don't look worn out yet. They sag some, but when Jodie complained about it once, Mack stretched out on the bed and smiled. "Aw, they just look lived-in and happy." Having entered her forties, Jodie has at last become grateful for small boobs; she can go braless and get away with it. Her hair is growing out, its natural curl beginning to go flat. At least there's not much gray visible yet, maybe because her hair is light brown to begin with. It still streaks a little in the summer.

She turns from the mirror and finishes dressing, aware that she thinks a lot about her looks these days, and not because of Mack. Over the past several weeks, another audience has entered her consciousness. This is embarrassing to admit, and she has stayed extra busy in order to distract herself. But she buttons her shirt and thinks of Terry Jenkins and how his smile lights up when he comes through the cafeteria line at school.

He's the social studies teacher for the junior high, and his class schedule now has him in the last lunch shift. When Jodie stands behind the counter dipping up food, she is encased in an apron, plastic gloves, and a hairnet. So she was startled to look up the other day to see his brilliant green eyes watching her. She says hello to all the teachers, but she was compelled to say hello and then return his gaze. He was smiling.

"What do you recommend from today's menu?"

She laughed a little. "The tater tots are nice and crispy."

"Can't go wrong with tater tots." He took his tray, nodded, and was on his way. That was all that happened. But his look—and she realizes this just now, as she pulls on blue jeans—was the same look Mack used to give her. The same twinkle, just on the edge of laughter. The same acute interest. Yes, interest.

She is too young to be without sex, yet she has been without it for some time. The depression stole what passion Mack had left, and the meds that now keep depression at bay mute other feelings as well. At least that's what Jodie assumes. Mack has said little about it, only referred to the several medicines he has to take and told her they have side effects. They have not ventured to talk about anything more specific. When Mack looks at her, as he did this morning, she knows that some light remains in his gaze, but it is shadowed by so many other things.

She finishes dressing and goes down to the kitchen. Kenzie and Rita are setting the table, and Mack is in the family room with Young Taylor, surfing between sporting events. This is a positive sign, given Young Taylor's general absence from family activity. Jodie would give anything to see her son put away his black wardrobe and vegetate in front of a ball game for an afternoon.

As they move through an uneventful Sunday dinner, Jodie finds herself studying Mack and thinking of Terry. She tries to see in her husband the fire that used to be there for her. She attempts to interpret Mack's every glance as meaning something, but he looks merely tired, and now he doesn't meet her gaze at all. He's still fighting battles that have little to do with her.

Terry Jenkins has become a presence, very much alive in her mind, whether she wants him there or not. She catches herself going through the day and imagining Terry as her silent audience. In her own house she is posturing for someone who really has no right to her life. And in fact, he probably has no real interest in her; it is her own desperation that manufactured the glint in his eye. She's become so pathetic.

Kenzie

She has been watching Mom and Dad closely the past four days. They aren't fighting at least. Dad's staying busy, and that's good. She saw them take a walk together down to the pond and back, and that's especially good. Part of the time they were holding hands.

They all went to church Sunday. It was the Methodist church in Oskaloosa, the one Kenzie went to until a few months ago, when she started going to the Baptist church just outside of Beulah. The Methodists don't teach from the Bible enough, and the Baptists have a youth group that actually does things. They have movie nights at the church and invite non-Christian friends; they pass out evangelical tracts at the county fair; they have their own Bible study and prayer time. This is what a person needs. But it has been so long since her whole family has gone to church that Kenzie is more than happy to return to the Methodist service for a Sunday or two.

She wants to talk with Dad about his soul, but it's still too scary to talk with him alone. She doesn't want to say anything that would make him feel sad or rejected or afraid. She still doesn't know what exactly made him want to die. Satan would love to trick her into saying the very thing that might send her father back into despair. So she hasn't said much of anything. She did mention, on his second day home, that she prays for him every day, in the morning and the evening, and if there's anything special he wants her to pray about to let her know. He gave her a strange look at first, but then he smiled and said that he would. But that led to no more talk of any importance. In fact, Dad found something he needed to do then, and their conversation ended altogether.

Spiritual warfare is a very tricky thing. Most of the time Kenzie doesn't feel that she's up to it at all. She's talked to Pastor Williamson about it—he's a really good youth director, and he makes you feel as if you can ask him anything. He keeps encouraging her to pray and to spend time with her parents; the best thing she can do for them, he says, is to take care of her own spiritual life so that they won't feel the need to worry about her. She does that, but there are big holes in her day when she's not praying or meditating or spending time with family, when she's doing homework or hanging out with a couple of friends from school. And at those times she feels that she should be close by Mom and Dad, just in case. She needs to be there to pray if they start to argue or if Dad begins staying off to himself too much, the way he did before they took him to the hospital. There are so many bad things that can happen at home, and they can happen quickly, and their lives could change, and so how can she just hang out with Bekka at the mall?

She has begun to write down her prayers; they feel more solid that way. She's not so nervous when she's busy documenting her relationship with God. She can look back and see what she's prayed about, and she can see what God said to her or which specific Bible verses gave her wisdom or comfort. It is all right there, in her journal. She carries it everywhere, along with her Bible. Her small cloth backpack has become part of her body, as if she is storing her spiritual life where she can get to it easily.

Today is Monday, the second day Dad has gone to his job at Hendrikson's. Two sort of normal days: Mom going to the school cafeteria earlier than the rest of them, to start her day; Dad dropping Kenzie and Young Taylor at school on his way to work. So there is now a several-hour block of time when everyone is busy. This too is a good thing.

And today she waves at Mitchell Jaylee. He is in his old green van, stopped at the corner, when she bikes up from his left, on her way to the church. He must be going into town for something. He recognizes her right away and smiles, lifts his forefinger from the top of the steering wheel in that country wave that is a sign of courtesy regardless of how well people know each other. Mitchell waits for Kenzie to turn the corner and stop at his window.

"Hey, you get a lot of exercise," he says.

She laughs a little, not knowing what else to say.

"How are you?" He seems to really want to know.

"Fine. You?"

"No complaints. Just going to get the oil changed." He allows the engine to idle a few more seconds, then eases off the brake and smiles at her. "You drive careful." And before she can say anything, he crosses the road and heads for town.

Rita

With her son home, the borders of Rita's life pull in and resume their old shape. She made several trips to see Mack while he was in the hospital. Even though he wasn't away long, Rita's schedule molded itself around the crisis. She'd sit in the room with Mack or walk the grounds with him, make as much conversation as either of them dared, and then come home before nightfall. Her night vision anymore is nearly worthless. Although the country roads are completely familiar, in the dark they play tricks on her. So she made only afternoon visits, sometimes with Jodie, sometimes alone, a couple of times with the pastor. She would have made those visits to the end of her life had they been necessary. (She can recall a period in Alex's life when she considered the possibility of having to visit him in prison for the next twenty years.) But she's mighty glad now that her day's edges don't extend much beyond Beulah's city limits.

She knows that they wouldn't have kept Mack hospitalized more than a few days except that Dr. Wenders, the doctor who treated him, knew that Rita's husband and other son were dead. She still remembers how his eyes focused on the chart while he made the word *Barnes* silently with his mouth. Taylor died in an accident with the tractor, and Alex passed out drunk in below-zero weather. Dr. Wenders, who works at the clinic in town, knew their stories and Mack's too. Taylor and Alex and Mack had all had farming and despair in common. So in a time when health insurance sends people home in a day or two, Wenders ordered tests and wrote down who-knows-what to justify Mack's confinement.

Rita sees the fates of her three men as fairly unrelated, but she would lie under oath to save any member of her family. While Mack waited in a nearby examining room, Rita sat in the doctor's office with Jodie and listed symptoms she wasn't even sure her son had. Jodie, nearly mute with fear, didn't blink; she'd found the loaded shotgun and recognized its significance. Since the kids had been older, they'd kept a hunting rifle loaded and in the storage space under the stairwell, for security. It had been long-standing family policy to keep all other firearms empty. When Jodie told her about the loaded shotgun, it occurred to Rita in a horrifying flash that a person really can't miss with a shotgun; one shot would take off most of your head—none of this nonsense about surviving in a vegetative state thanks to a shaky hand.

But Mack is home now and taking medicine to calm his nerves and help him sleep. No one in Rita's family is particularly high-strung, but Mack has always been the most likely to be anxious, probably because he's the oldest and feels responsible. Rita called at Hendrikson's this morning, just to be sure Mack made it to work. He talked with her a minute, not sounding too irritated at her checking up on him. He will be all right—Rita feels this more than knows it. After so much grief, a family has to land at a resting place. Sooner or later things get better—that's the way it's always worked. After you suffer a little while, the Lord lifts you up and restores you. She can't remember the chapter and verse that makes this claim, but she knows it's there.

Against what Tom the mechanic claims is his better judgment, he's installed a new starter in the Ford, and now the car sits in Rita's driveway. She notices that it could stand a good washing. This thought brings Amos Mosley to mind. Rita developed a relationship with Amos merely by watering her car on the same Saturday afternoon that he watered his. They wandered around their tires and fenders, tepid water splashing out of green hoses, and exchanged some pointless remarks about weather before eventually talking of how the kids were doing and who was living where now and what the latest count of grandchildren was. Amos offered to wash Rita's car whenever he washed his. She said it wasn't necessary, but she wouldn't stand in the way if he decided to give the Ford a squirt or two while he was at it. Two weeks later Amos was hosing down his car, and Rita wandered out to chat and offer him a glass of iced tea. It was June and hot enough to dry a person out even as he hoisted a garden hose. Amos washed his car, then wandered across the strip of grass between their properties and washed Rita's car. She protested, but mildly. It isn't a romantic relationship, but a friendly one, a small, regular contact with another person.

Amos has a bad autumn cold this week—allergies probably—and both cars look neglected. But it's shopping time. Rita snaps on her seatbelt and heads for the grocery store.

When Rita walks in the door, Bud says, "Got stuff here for you," meaning a bag of vegetables and day-old baked goods behind the magazine rack. Bud is the only person manning the store. It is definitely a one-person grocery, a small storefront that at one time was part of a larger store. Some days, especially bright autumn ones when kids go back to school, Rita walks along Main Street and is caught up in old visions. She sees Beulah as its old self, full of folks, noisy but not too much, with posses of children stopping at this very grocery (it was Bruener's Grocery back then) on their way home from school, sorting pennies, nickels, and dimes out of sweaty palms for just the right selection of bubble gum and jawbreakers, Tootsie Rolls, Fireballs, the sweet wax fangs and mustaches around Halloween, and wintergreen candy cigarettes. Years ago a wall went up where the bread and bakery aisle used to be, and now the area churches use the other side as a thrift store, collecting odd pillowcases, pans, and clothing donations to distribute to the poorest of the poor. The grocery is a small, depressed version of its older self; Bud hires help from time to time but mostly handles every bit of stocking, pricing, and checking by himself.

He expects Rita every Monday afternoon. She shops for herself and half a dozen other old folks, and she scavenges the produce that is beyond selling at regular price—the too soft or too ripe or too spotted. In larger groceries such items would get shrink-wrapped together and sold at a deep discount. But Rita is on a mission, and Bud goes ahead of her, setting aside the not-so-prime goods and having them ready Monday afternoon, because most of his shipments come in on Monday morning. This way he deprives no one and puts the lesser products in able hands.

Rita comes by for meat scraps later in the week. Bud still cuts meat to order; this is a necessity in a town with so many older citizens. Some of them are too shaky to handle a butcher knife anymore. And most live alone and buy tiny bits at a time. For a few extra cents, Bud slices and chops, trims fat, divides chickens. The remains—bones, gristle, fat, innards—go into plastic ice cream containers in the back freezer. Rita picks them up, takes them home, and boils the life out of them. Boils them with bits of nearly too far gone onion and pepper, with the herbs from her little garden. She lets the pots of cast-off goods simmer all day on the back burner while she goes about her business. When she has steeped the last rumor of flavor from marrow and cartilage, she strains the broth twice and stores it in bags in the freezer. On Saturdays she makes soup—from the stock she's boiled and from the leftover vegetables from Bud. Week in and week out, in all kinds of weather, Rita gathers questionable goods and makes soup. She has done this for five years.

This practice started because of Bernie Hallsted. Eighty-four years old and too feeble and absentminded to cook for himself, he lives two doors north of Rita. Bernie developed the habit of making one can of tuna and one can of pork-and-beans last a week. Just left them sitting there in the fridge. That, and crackers. Rita happened to look in Bernie's fridge one day when she dropped off a prescription and asked if he had some cold water to drink. She found the chipped plastic container with ice water in it, a dried-up bottle of Tabasco in the door, and the two cans, forks sticking out of them, on the second shelf.

That day Rita went home and wept for the first time in years. The next day she concocted soup from whatever was in reach and took it over to Bernie. He lapped it up, his face shining with happy surprise.

"I'll bring you bean soup next week."

"Oh—navy bean?"

"If that's what you like."

"Oh, sure. Love navy bean soup."

The next week it was navy bean with bits of ham left over after a church potluck.

She started looking carefully then at other seniors who lived around her. She realized that nearly everyone in her neighborhood was old, retired, without a spouse, and barely making it on Social Security. It was especially hard for those with medical bills, which included nearly everyone. Several people had stopped taking medicine, since they couldn't afford prescriptions and the light bill in the same month. Groceries were often one of the first expenses to eliminate, after the telephone.

One gray day in late August—a close, irritating day when dust and sour smells clung to everything—Rita nearly passed out from the heat in her kitchen. She'd gone to Bud's and bought up all the vegetables she could afford, along with beans and stew meat. It was ninety in the shade, but never mind, soup was the best way to get nearly every food group accounted for: rice and kidney beans, onions, peppers, zucchini, corn, tomatoes. Faded celery leaves, sprigs of thyme from her patch outside, lots of salt and pepper—old folks couldn't taste too well. For good measure she'd added a glob of peanut butter, which thickened the broth and added flavor. The pot was filled to the brim before she began dipping its brew into mason jars. At four in the afternoon, she hauled a cardboard box full of sixteen jars, all gleaming and warm. Real food floating in there. Nothing starched up or full of additives. It didn't taste bad.

She offered the same transparent story at every doorstep. *I made way too much soup—all those years of feeding a family, can't get out of the habit of making enough for an army. It's not much, just old vegetable soup. Hope you like it.* The next week she couldn't think of a story that was plausible. *Edie, d'you like the soup last week? I'm trying a new recipe this time around. Tell me what you think.* After that, she didn't explain, and the acceptance was settled. She'd take soup on Saturdays. Along about Thursday, the squeaky clean jars would show up on her back step, little thank-you notes or no notes at all. Sometimes there'd be a can of beans or something: *Had extra. Maybe you can use this.*

But Rita was on a fixed income too, and soon after she began making soup for her neighbors she was picking up those Saran-wrapped odds and ends on the less-than-glorious table of the produce section. After a while Bud caught on (hard not to do when a dozen senior citizens tell you within the same few days that Rita makes the best darn soup—and have that happen three weeks in a row), and he made sure Rita found everything there was to find. He saw her eyeing the stew meat and walking on by, and the thought struck him about the meat scraps. And then the day-old bakery items.

Now it is custom and sacred, Rita's soup. No more dried-out, stinky cans of tuna stretched beyond possibility. In the winter she bakes bread sometimes to go with the soup. But most weeks there is bread enough from the day-old supply.

Rita has always been a decent cook, although, on a farm, you cooked what was in season, and there were never a lot of extras to spice things up. You could be creative within limits. Jodie bought her starts of herbs one Christmas, and between the two of them they kept most of the plants alive through a nearly sunless winter. Now Rita's herb garden takes over a new square yard of ground with each summer. So maybe her cooking is better, even if it's mostly soups and casseroles.

It was never her intent to become the neighborhood cook. She's not terribly fond of cooking. But sometimes a thing just clearly needs to be done, and no one else is doing it. Maybe no one else is left to do it—the kids are all grown and moved away; the husband or wife is gone. Rita thinks that a lot of holy callings must happen just this way. Some little congregation without a pastor can't afford one of those seminary graduates from the city. Bill Winney's son is a good boy with a strong voice; he loves talking about God and has a soft spot for people. Hard to say which happens first—the call into a preaching ministry or a need that leads to a solution. If soup every Saturday is a divine solution, then it is the only such divinity Rita has touched in her lifetime. It isn't much, but, at her age, it will have to be enough.

She finishes her shopping at Bud's, stops at the pharmacy—the only other real business left on Main Street—picks up prescriptions for Flo Dansen and Eloise Waul, then gets mail for half a dozen people and makes her deliveries. The car behaves itself, although the first few times she switches it off a little panic grabs her. Here in town, she could walk to about anyplace she needs to go, but she is used to having a car with a seat and plenty of room to stash things. She'll lock herself up in her own house the day she has to wander the streets with a grocery cart like some city bag lady.

At Eloise's place, she visits for twenty minutes because Eloise has no family left and is too feeble to go to church regularly anymore.

"Eloise, I got your prescriptions here. You need anything from the store?" Rita's voice booms in the small living room where Eloise spends most of her time. She has retired in the same sizable house where she raised her children, but she lives in essentially two rooms of it now.

"Oh, no. No need to bother any." Eloise has the round, smiley face of a woman who once looked like a perfect china doll. She reaches out with cool, paper-thin fingers to grasp Rita's hand. Her eyes are light blue and watery, looking as if they see when mostly they remember. "Thank you, Rita. Don't know what I'd do without you."

"Well, you know my number if you need anything."

"I do. But I'm just fine. Could you bring me a glass of water? I'll take these pills right now before I forget."

Rita gets the water, remembering Eloise as a girl, vivacious as could be and simply lost without an audience. It's a cruel thing to see her alone now. Rita didn't like Eloise much back when they were young women with families and living on their respective farms. Eloise was older, had more money, more children, and went to cities often. She imagined herself in another class, no doubt. But her husband Gerald came back from Korea an invalid, and Eloise's life has shrunk up ever since.

"I'll check on you in a couple of days, all right?" Rita makes sure the trash hasn't piled up too much. She checks the refrigerator. There are a few single-serving things lined up on the second shelf. Rita opens each one, using a can opener or a flip top, and leaves the lids setting in place. She unseals the half-gallon of milk she just bought and punches holes in the top of the apple juice can. She tosses several things that no longer look edible. On her way down the back steps, she notes the three or four potted plants that are miraculously carrying on. No hard frost yet.

As talkative as Eloise is around town, evidently she never got along well with most of her kids. They are all elsewhere now, off in those cities Eloise used to visit. A couple of the older ones have offered to have her come live with them, but there is always a reason she can't abide that particular home or that particular child. Now here she is, doomed to a quiet house in a town where nothing much happens. To Rita it is a classic lesson in "the first shall be last and the last first."

She passes the Methodist parsonage. The Sipeses used to live there, but they have moved on. Still, the sight of the yard awakens bad memories in Rita.

"But, reverend, you've got two deacons who've plumb taken advantage of every farmer in this county."

"Rita, they're not breaking any laws. And besides, I don't know the particulars of all these situations. The man's a banker, and he has to answer to people too."

"He makes his own decisions about foreclosures—you know that."

"It's not my business."

"If a family losing its livelihood isn't your business, then I don't know what is."

After that, Rita stopped volunteering at the church or attending anything but Sunday morning worship. Helen Sipes tried to visit after Taylor died, but for the first time in her life Rita put good manners behind her. She turned away the covered dishes and refused to answer the phone. She stood at the front door of the farmhouse and told Helen that she was wasting her time.

"The time you and your husband could have helped is long past."

Well, a lot has happened since then, and Rita does church in the next town. But she looks at the weedy little patches that Helen used to coax into blankets of chrysanthemums, and she feels a certain loss.

Mack

Mack drives out of his own county and well into the next one before entering a town he doesn't know that well and then finding the address they gave him at the clinic. It goes with a double-wide mobile home, but the sign on the door identifies it as the Family Support Service. It is subsidized by three or four denominations and is therefore free to Mack, at least for now. Who knows how long an outfit like this can keep going, but Mack has picked it for its relative distance from his home and neighbors. Until the hospital business, he'd never gone to any doctor who traded in people's minds and emotions. His guts are in a knot when he opens the door, but the girl at the desk acts like it's completely normal for people to walk in and talk for a while. She gives him a form to fill out and then points to a plastic chair among several that are lined up where probably the living room used to be, when this was a home and not an office. He writes down his information and returns the form. Ten more minutes go by, and the girl directs him to the door at the far end of the trailer.

George Dooley looks like a guy who has blown one career and then become a counselor by default. He appears as Irish as his name, ruddy cheeks and reddish-brown hair and a burly physique that makes his friendly manner all the more a relief. George's office is chaos, and for this first session they go to someone else's office while a woman mutters and frantically sorts through the papers on George's desk. "I've lost something important," says George. "Fortunately, Maryanne has a knack for getting the rest of us organized." Then he chuckles softly, a coffee-stained front tooth catching the light.

Mack sighs and waits for George to get on with his questions.

George allows the smile to fade, then settles back and looks at Mack intently. He says not a word.

Mack shifts in the chair. It is too soft and full of stuffing. He tries to find a point of balance, where he can be comfortable without listing to one side. George is still looking at him. Mack makes a little motion with his hands.

"I guess I filled out all the papers they needed."

"If you didn't, I wouldn't know anyway. We can proceed as if all the paperwork's in order." George is not smiling but looks pleasant.

"I don't know what you want," Mack says.

"This isn't about what I want, is it?"

"It's not about what I want either." Mack can feel sweat breaking out on his palms. "When they released me, I agreed to come here once a week."

"A parole situation, is it?" Mack expects George to chuckle again, but he doesn't.

"That's what it feels like."

"Well, since you have to be here, maybe you could come up with something you might get out of it. Then at least we can make it worth your while."

The room is uncomfortably warm. Mack tries to get a good breath.

"It's a nerve-wracking thing, having to talk to a total stranger about what's going on in your guts." George crosses his legs and appears to get comfortable in the straight-backed chair.

"I don't really see the point. I'm all right now. Just got too tired, I think. There for several weeks I didn't sleep. Put everything out of whack. But they've got me on this stuff for the sleep."

"Sleep deprivation is a serious matter. I suppose that's what led to your depression."

"Yeah, I think that was it." This is easy enough. George talks like he's the pragmatic type, not one to get so concerned about what Mack might be feeling this particular second. Not likely to put great stock in dreams or in coaxing out tears or angry outbursts. This might turn out okay.

"But there's a reason you weren't sleeping. And we want to be certain you've dealt with that original cause. Otherwise, sooner or later, it'll all start again."

A long silence follows these remarks. Mack finds it difficult to look directly at George. He searches desperately for something to say. "I guess you've got the records from the hospital."

"Yes." George's eyes stay fixed on Mack. Mack knows this even though he is looking at the window opposite.

"So if you've read all that, there's a lot of ground you and I shouldn't have to cover."

"Oh, I've read it all. But why don't we leave the hospital stuff off to itself for now? What do you want to tell me today?"

"I don't want to tell you anything."

The words echo in the small room. Mack's eyes are glued to the oak branches framing the small view out the window. He knows that George looks at him and waits for him to break and talk anyway. He's gone through this same thing with other people who were out to help him.

Mack spreads his hands, feeling helpless and irritated and suddenly very tired. "The thing is, things are all right for us. My wife and I both have jobs. Our kids are doing okay. I had a bad spell, but I'm over it, and I've got nothing to complain about, especially compared to other people."

"Which other people?"

Mack's mouth is dry. "Lots of other people. Just look around."

"But I think you have specific people in mind when you say that. At least, that's what it sounded like."

Mack grasps the pillowy arm of the chair. "Like I said, we're doing all right. Mom's been in town for a while, and she's okay, close by, where I can help out when I need to."

"She was out at the farm before?"

"It's actually her farm. Hers and Dad's. But after he died, she moved to town. I inherit the place anyway, so we moved on out there."

"That was fine with everybody?"

"Yeah. We were all agreed on it."

"You and your mother."

"My brother too."

"How did he figure in?"

Mack levels a look at George. "I thought you read my history."

George doesn't reply, but he doesn't take his eyes away either.

"And if you read the history, you know that my brother's dead. He lost his farm and he died."

George closes his eyes and nods. "And when you say that you're better off than other people, maybe it's your brother you're talking about."

Mack glares out the window.

"And since you've got a home and a family and a job, and you're not dead, then you'd better not have any complaints."

"I've got no complaints."

"But in spite of all your good fortune, you became so severely depressed that your family intervened, and you just spent two weeks in the hospital."

Mack looks at the therapist, but he sees no rebuke. The look on George's face does not match how harsh these words sound. He cocks his head a bit, and says, in a much gentler tone, "Mack, there's something going on here. You'd like to think there's not, but you're an intelligent man, and you've got to find the thing that's making all this mess. So why don't you just open your mouth and let's see what comes out."

"I'm tired to death of talking."

"I know you are. I can see it in your face. I could see it in the way you walked into this room."

"I'm plumb out of words." Mack shakes his head slowly. "I've said all I know about everything I know. I just want to get settled in now, go to work, look after my family."

"I want to help you do that."

"So what do I do?"

"Let's start with something simple. Give me a short history of your family. You've mentioned your mother and brother, your wife and kids. I don't know much about any of them. Have you always lived around here? You've always been farmers?"

A short history turns out not to be simple. Mack can't talk about his family without backing up a century at least. His history is wrapped up in the property, or the property he used to own. So he re-lates the family tree: his mother's ancestor homesteaded back in the 1850s. That spot by the creek where the stone house now stands, that was the original home. Over five generations the 40 acres grew to 380. It passed from old Hiram Decker to his son Andrew, who left it to his daughter, who married another farmer and bore children, one of whom was Sarah, Rita's mother. Due to tragic loss of her siblings, Sarah and her husband John inherited the farm, then passed it on to Rita, their eldest, and signed over a portion to their other daughter, Delores. Delores set up her household three miles east of her sister Rita and the original farm. Rita married Taylor Barnes, and they had two sons, Mack and Alex. Mack was the eldest, and the original farm would go to him. A good portion of it was given to Alex when Alex turned twenty-one.

"Was that ever a problem for Alex, that the original farm would go to you?"

"No. It's the way property has always been passed down. To the el-dest son, and if there wasn't a son, to the eldest daughter. No one ever questioned it. And Alex ended up having a bigger spread than I did anyway. Dad also gave him an equal portion of the best land. He was as fair a man as they come. I never knew Alex to feel slighted."

George's eyebrows scoot up. "I feel as if there's a 'but' there some-where."

"Alex never cared for farming. Not like Dad and I did. It's that way with some people. Even if I'd kept farming, I wouldn't have expected my boy Young Taylor to carry it on. Partly, the times have changed and it's just too hard to make it. But partly I've always known he wasn't a farmer by heart. Taylor's a lot like Alex."

"How does a man who doesn't like to farm make a go of it?"

"When you live in these parts, there aren't a lot of options. Alex's wife had farming in her blood. She's helping her folks work their place in Nebraska now. Her boy's right in there with them. I think Alex thought that it was better to just stay with it."

"It didn't work out for him?"

Mack's words have become troublesome in his mouth. "You know what happened."

"Yes, but I don't know why."

Mack shrugs. "He let things slip. Didn't keep up even when he could have. He'd always liked the liquor—drank heavy back in high school. It caught up with him. Marty and the kids finally left, went to stay with her folks. Alex made a few bad choices. And sometimes one bad choice, if it's big enough, can put you under."

The room rings with quiet. George is fingering the pen in his hand.

"The bank was about to foreclose. So Alex sold the whole kit and caboodle. Auctioned it off. He barely broke even."

"That happens a lot."

"To good farmers and bad ones. Sometimes it doesn't matter what you do."

"According to what I've read in your files, your mother found Alex dead in the house he was renting."

"He finally drank more than he could take."

"I lost a brother in Vietnam. It's a hard thing, no matter what the circumstances."

"I think we did all we could. But you always wonder if maybe you'd kicked butt one more time . . ."

"That's a hard question to ask yourself."

The room isn't so warm anymore, but Mack's heart is pounding. "We need to stop for today."

Relieved, Mack makes his way out of the chair. He feels too weak to meet George's gaze, but he's been brought up to look people in the eye, especially if business is involved. George has just rendered a service. Mack looks at the blue eyes long enough to make contact. He says thank you.

"Next week, same time, Mack?"

"I guess so."

And so the first appointment has gone its own direction, as therapy sessions tend to do. Mack thinks he's figured out these people by now, thinks he knows what they want to hear. By the time he finished at the hospital, it seemed to him that he'd filled in the right blanks and that this had been the goal all along—to have the right answers to the questions that counted. He was never quite sure which questions those were. He figured out that some questions got thrown in just to get him comfortable or something, and once his guard was down the critical questions were slipped in.

On the drive home his attention is captured by odd details. He has not farmed in four years, and lately he comes to the scenery as if it's new or he's a stranger passing through. He is startled now by the lushness of the goldenrod, Indian grass, and other gold and lavender flowers (Jodie can name them all) along the roadside. Clumps of purple aster look like bright bouquets that have tumbled out of crop rows to rest in the ditches. His route home takes him through Oskaloosa, but he stops a ways before town, pulling onto a side road at Maskunky Marsh. A new shade of white catches his eye. He gazes over the water and its reflection of the steel-blue sky and strains to identify the two or three dozen large birds that have landed there. He knows well the shapes of herons and egrets, but these birds are something else. Mack gets out of the car and walks to the edge of the shore, then laughs spontaneously at the unmistakable beaks. Pelicans. He's heard about this but has never seen it. The birds nest in western states and Canada and migrate south this time of year. Mack watches them flap around each other and mingle with the other waterfowl. They present an exotic little picture, and Mack is visited by a sudden moment of happiness.

Jodie

They still have a little patch of purple prairie clover west of the house. Jodie has seeded it with other wildflowers and forbidden anyone to mow this part of the yard. When they sold the acreage in '96, sharp corners formed around the acres on which the house and other buildings still stand; that acre on the west side of the house bumps up against the new boundary line. Last year Samuels planted those fields in beans. He'll likely never put up a fence; they're neighbors, after all. But he plowed right along the boundary, and so now there is a clear division between the soybeans, which are drying into a brown, brittle expanse, and the clover in its last flush before frost. Today a few butterflies linger among its remaining blooms.

She wanders outside a lot these days. The air of the house is too heavy, and too familiar. This morning she and Mack had another little spat, over who would drive which vehicle. Not a big deal—they've always traded off according to errands. Jodie likes the pickup more than the Dodge because it's heavier and can hold its place better when she's on gravel roads. But when Mack needs to move things or haul a part out to some farmer, he takes the truck. There is no his and hers; they're just vehicles. And Mack should have just said this morning that he needed the truck. But Jodie had already loaded several bags of old clothes and blankets to drop off at the bin in the Methodist church parking lot before shopping for groceries after school. The church is having its annual drive for winter items to be sorted out and given to people who need them, and Jodie has been going through closets for three or four days. Mack might have noticed that and not come undone when he walked out to the truck to find it full of her stuff.

He could have just said something. But he got that look of panic, the one that says life is not going to be okay today. Jodie is so desperately tired of that look. She's tired of him not just saying what he means instead of sighing and shooting dark eyes at her and expecting her to figure out his dilemma.

It's starting all over again, the lack of functioning. Then her anger at him because he doesn't function. Then his hurt and anger that she's angry. And then the silences and stomping around. When she saw him standing with hands jammed into pockets, staring into the truck bed, she was the one who had to go out and ask if anything was wrong. And she can't simply ask. She has to sigh and glare back at him.

She didn't try to mask her irritation. "You might have told me last night that you'd need the truck today, since I leave an hour before you. Good thing you got up early, or I'd be gone already." This point is moot; he always gets up when she does.

"I can borrow the company truck, then drive it back to the shop and get the car." The words were reasonable, but the tone wasn't.

She was already pulling the bags out of the truck bed. "I can drop these off anytime. I'll do it tomorrow."

"Here. I'll get that." He reached for a bag, but she'd grabbed it already.

"I've got it." She didn't look at him.

"You don't have to sound so pissed."

"I'm not. I'm just in a hurry, okay?"

They've had that sort of exchange many times before. But each time it feels bigger, more dangerous for some reason. So she fumed all the way to work, made a point to enjoy Terry's lunchtime smile, and came home to her house, which makes her feel exhausted the minute she walks in the door. She microwaves some leftover coffee from this morning and brings it outside, to stand near the clover. As she sips it she tries to conjure the memory of butterflies in July. They do pretty much the same two or three things day after day. But they look so happy, just flit-flitting like that. She must learn to flit, to dance across her hours of work. Float across her life. Sweep and dart around Mack's moods, as if they don't have much to do with her. They really don't. That's what the doctors say—that Mack's struggles are not her fault.

Still, she doesn't need to sound so pissed. Mack is right about that.

Mack

As is his custom, Mack stops by his mother's on the way home. After Pop died, it seemed better for Mack and Jodie and the kids to move into the farmhouse and for Rita to move to town. She was too melancholy out there by herself. And Mack's family spent most of their time there anyway. The rent they were paying on the house down the road got rerouted to payments on the house Rita moved to in Beulah. They miss her presence in the rooms of the farmhouse, and Mack comes to see his mother nearly every day. He fixes a faucet or moves furniture or hammers a nail if she needs it. Often he picks up a delivery from Mom to Jodie—a start of some plant or an extra package of macaroni or can of tomatoes. Mainly, he walks in the door after a call through the screen, and they chat for a while.

There was a time when the chats were about Alex. What would they do about him? Had Mack talked to him lately? Yes, but did he listen? Had he been in touch with Marty and David and Sharon? Had he even started getting his fields ready for planting, or whatever it was time to do? Was he keeping up his payments? Around and around they'd talk, much of it meaningless since all they knew was what Alex told them, and often he didn't give out any information. When he got in trouble with his payments, eventually a number of people knew, because that kind of news seemed to get out. That was how Mack had learned of the impending foreclosure—through Pete Jasper, who'd heard about it at the co-op from Dan Thomason, who'd heard it from his wife, who worked at the bank and knew everybody's business.

Now, though, when Mack stops by, he and his mother speak of mundane things, which are easy to manage but in the end don't mean anything at all. They don't miss the stress they suffered when worrying over Alex's life, but they miss the topic more than they would dare put into words. Mack never mentions it. Rita often does, as if saying her son's name will allow her to remember him better.

Today Mom is yakking at Amos Mosley across the fence. They are discussing tomato hybrids and peering at one another's garden patches. They continue chattering even as Rita acknowledges Mack and the two of them turn and walk toward the house.

"G'bye, Amos." Rita pulls the door shut behind them and looks at Mack. "How's Jodie's thyme doing? Mine's gone crazy. I can send a start if she wants it."

"Mom, you know I don't know about that. She screeches if I come within ten yards of her spice bed."

"It's an herb garden."

"Same thing."

"Well, ask about her thyme."

"Your phone not working?"

Rita purses her lips and glances at him over the top of her glasses. "If you actually ask her about it, you'll be more likely to remember to make the delivery. The last time I sent something, I found it dried up in the truck bed a week later."

"All the more reason for you to deliver it yourself."

"Honestly."

"How you doing, Mom?"

"I'm fine. How'd your appointment go?"

The woman doesn't miss a thing. He didn't mention his appointment to a soul. But of course Jodie knew. And if Jodie knew, then Mom knew.

"About as well as could be expected."

"Is it one of the doctors from the hospital?"

"No. This is through some deal with the Lutherans and Methodists and whoever else. Some program that brings in therapists."

"The Faith and Family something or other."

"I guess that's it."

"He any good?"

"Hard to say, the first appointment. Is your dryer still on the blink?" Any new subject would do at this point.

"I did two loads so far this week, and it seems to be all right. I never had a washer or dryer that I didn't have to coddle along one way or the other."

"Let me know if you need me to look at it." The one useful thing he can still do is fix things. He's taken apart and put back together all manner of moving parts since he was seven years old. He worked for the school district before the machine parts job opened up. All he did was make sure the buses were running. Basic engine work, basic hours. He still kind of misses that job.

"How's Jodie?"

Mack can't think of an answer. He's been home only a few days, and the two of them are still giving each other lots of space, both of them too afraid to move fast or expect much.

"Pretty good, I think. Doesn't say much, but she looks more relaxed than I've seen her in a while."

"I wish that Young Taylor would straighten up."

Mack's stomach tightens. "Things are pretty calm on that front too," he says.

Rita angles a look at him. "They are today maybe. People are worried that he's on drugs—or in some cult."

"Have these *people* actually sat down and talked with Young Taylor?"

"That I don't know."

"He's a kid. Kids get weird."

"This is the first one I've seen that wears black every moment of every day. He's even dyed his hair that awful, unnatural black."

"It's just some dye."

"But why in the world?"

"Who knows? As long as he's still in school and isn't in jail, I'm grateful."

"Those are pretty low expectations."

"They'll have to do for now. I'll keep an eye on him."

"If you can find him. He just disappears for hours at a time. I'm pretty sure he's skipping school."

"I'll look into it."

"He was always a sweet-natured boy. Hate to see him get like this."

"He'll be all right, Mom."

"Here." Rita swings her hips around the corner cabinet and heads out the back door. "Help me with this. My knee's giving me fits." He follows her out and obediently takes the trowel. She points out a plant —thyme, he guesses—and Mack digs it up and puts it into a box. He leaves through the back gate.

"I'll see you tomorrow," he says back across his shoulder.

"Bye, son."

The sun is riding low in the sky, pulling evening after it. All Mack can think of is how good it will feel to go to bed. He could almost skip supper and go straight there. He never imagined that he'd miss the deadly routine of the hospital, but the different routine of being home and going to work and being with family makes him feel as if he were getting over the flu.

Today's appointment with George has him arriving home close to sunset. The kitchen light is on. When Mack gets out of the car, a dozen or more sparrows fly from the oak near the porch, scattering like ashes into the soft sky.

He puts the thyme on the cabinet, near where Jodie is working, putting dishes away. A clean bowl and spoon wait on the table for him. He smells chili that's simmering on the stove.

"She still trying to get rid of this stuff?" Jodie nods toward the plant, which looks bedraggled at the moment, alone in its little plastic box next to the flour canister.

"She forced me. I had no choice." He leans close enough to plant a kiss on Jodie's temple. Her skin is damp and smells sweet.

She laughs a little and just shakes her head. Mack marvels at how smooth and young her face looks, there in the pinkish light coming in from the west. Her hair is gathered into a wispy knot in back, held in place by one of those hinged combs. She looks like a girl, not the mother of two teenagers, not the wife of a damaged man.

"The kids home?"

"Kenzie's at church, something with the youth group. I think Young Taylor's in his room. But you have to open the door to get his attention. His earphones are always on."

Mack heads for the stairwell. Maybe he's missed something. Rita is a true grandma, always concerned about something that might go wrong. But she isn't stupid. And she understood Alex's troubles long before the rest of them did. What if she is seeing some destructiveness in Young Taylor now?

The door to Young Taylor's room is cracked a couple of inches. Mack peers in and sees the kid lying on the bed, on his back. The earphones are wrapped around his face, and his eyes are closed.

"Hey." Mack knocks on the doorjamb. The boy doesn't budge. Mack walks over and gently taps him on the knee. Young Taylor's eyes fly open.

"Yeah?"

"What's up?" Mack sits on the edge of the bed, not far from where Young Taylor's legs hang over it.

Young Taylor takes off the phones and rises up as far as his elbows. "Huh?"

"What's up?"

"Nothing." His hair is indeed too black for such a fair-skinned kid. It is a strange cut, close to his head yet poking out in a few places, as if he's just gotten out of bed.

"School all right?"

"I guess." Are his eyes glassy? It's hard to tell. He is staring intently at Mack, and Mack is suddenly ill at ease. He can remember days when the two of them talked easily about this and that. This is as hard to do as therapy. He thinks he would prefer dealing with George's gaze.

"I'm trying to get caught up on what you and Kenzie have been doing."

"You haven't missed much."

"You talked to your grandma lately?"

"I was there three days ago. Took a bunch of bricks over for her flower bed."

"You visit with her?"

Young Taylor closes his eyes. Mack can't tell what that means.

"You know how she likes to keep up with you kids."

"She doesn't like my hair."

"Well . . ."

The dark eyes dart at him and away. "You and Mom don't either. So what else is new?"

"She still likes to visit with you."

"Nothing to talk about."

"If you give her five seconds, she'll think of something."

"So are you sending me over there on assignment?"

"Not this minute. But she worries about you, and if you go by and visit, she won't worry so much."

Young Taylor just closes his eyes. Mack taps his knee again and stands up. "See you later." The boy offers no response.

On the landing between floors, Mack pauses and looks out the narrow window that faces the north fields. Samuels has them in good shape. It is a little bit comforting that even though the land no longer belongs to Mack, at least it is in good hands. Samuels is a sensible farmer and a decent guy. Still, the picture framed in this single window flickers in Mack's memory, bringing up earlier renditions of the scene, years before, decades before. For generations his family has gazed across the hills and planned their beauty and purpose, season by season. He can glance out his little window and know at once the sensation of earth under his feet, and how the texture changes from one area to the next, can smell its degrees of growth and decay, can feel in his now-empty hands the silky and scratchy tones of corn in its successive phases.

Memory has always figured into his every day of getting up and judging the air and earth and doing what is best. A good farmer remembers the meanings of smells and tastes and temperatures. He remembers them from one year to the next. He can't necessarily separate them and explain his thoughts to anyone, but all the information comes to rest on his mind and heart, and it remains stored there, and that remembered knowledge enables him to make the next step today or this week.

Mack didn't think about memory, back when it served him on a daily basis. He didn't give a thought to how he knew what he knew or why he lived out his work in any particular way. But now that it is no longer his work, he is plagued constantly by memories. A scent on the breeze pulls him to a particular day from five years ago. The sun filters through the cottonwoods near the barn, and he relives entire days of the life he has lost.

He pulls his gaze from the outdoors and concentrates on the aroma of Jodie's chili. He hopes that the sight of her innocent stance at the counter will not stab him as other familiar things do.

"How's your mother?" Jodie doesn't look at Mack as she sits at the table with her own bowl of chili; evidently the kids ate earlier, but she has waited for him.

"All right, I guess. Was drilling me about Young Taylor."

Jodie frowns. "Like you would know anything."

The comment hurts. He knows she doesn't intend hurt, and she doesn't seem to realize that she has harmed him. *Like you'd be any help at all with a troubled kid.* No, she wouldn't mean something like that. Or would she? Mack stares at her and forces a little laugh.

"I told Young Taylor to go visit her, so she wouldn't worry so much."

"That could work."

"He been skipping school?" Mack has served himself from the pot on the stove and sits at the table near her.

"Could be."

"You don't know?"

"He learned to forge my name on absentee excuses about three years ago. If he really wanted to skip out, he could. I've not spent a lot of time snooping after him."

Has she always been this sarcastic?

Already the bright glow from the west has gone out, leaving a flat gray horizon, and the kitchen is dim except for the ceiling fan-lamp that hangs over them. In their quiet together, he looks at Jodie, and she sends a beam of smile over to him. He knows that it costs her a lot to smile at him and welcome him to be here. It is no easy thing after what he's put her through.

3

SAYING PRAYERS

I come to the garden alone,
   while the dew is still on the roses,
And the voice I hear falling on my ear
   the Son of God discloses.
And he walks with me and he talks with me,
   and he tells me I am his own.
And the joy we share as we tarry there,
   none other has ever known.
                    — *"In the Garden"*

Jodie

She stands near her dead coneflowers. In July they were glorious and
filled with lavender lights. Their life slipped away weeks ago, and a
few of them are still standing, their brown petals stuck out from used-
up centers, thin and dry as wasp wings. She remembers how depressed she was about her coneflowers when Mack went away. That's
how it has felt to her, that he simply went away. She knew he was in
the hospital, but it was too difficult to think about that. Even when
she went to visit him, she was going to the place that he had gone
away to. Maybe he was doing well, or maybe hospital existence was
miserable. All she could register was that he was away, that he had

gone of his own will. She had insisted that he see a doctor, that's all. She never asked him to go away. Never even suggested it.

Jodie's mother, who now lives far away and can see the ocean from her living room, grew up in Iowa, barely a hundred miles from Mack's mother. Jodie's parents were schoolteachers, both reared in the country, and they would have taught until retirement—she language arts and he biology and physics—but her father died in his fifties of something viral and sudden, when Young Taylor was nine and Kenzie seven. Jodie's brother Paul had settled in Galveston of all places, to manage a small packaging company, and within two years of Dad's death Mom moved to be near her son and new daughter-in-law and saltwater. The farmland that had nurtured her seemed hostile without her one love in it, and she still talks to Jodie about the sensation of looking out over the water and watching it change colors and breathing something invigorating but not quite nameable. Jodie guesses that manure and wet fields and dusty winds are invigorating but not in a healthful way. She and Mom talk every couple of weeks, and Jodie hears in her mother's voice a triumph of some sort. She is making it without her Ben, and she has befriended a different sort of environment, one that allows her dreams to fly farther.

It was Mom who sang so many hymns when Jodie and Paul were growing up. Her favorite was "In the Garden." Jodie wonders if she still sings it, there near the seashore where she keeps not a garden but a low-maintenance lawn decorated in carefully chosen stones and shells. Mom has never indicated that she didn't like Iowa or that she longed for anything else. But Jodie often wonders these days if her mother ever loved her garden or if she sang her hymns in the same way Jodie sings them now—out of distraction, the pressed need to make sound but not release the heart's little secrets. Poetry, hymns, and prayers give a person stability by way of pattern and repetition. Do the meanings of the words even matter?

Patterns and repetition became more important to Jodie the day Mack went to see the doctor and didn't come home. Even when they fought, their union was solid and reliable. The fights were part of how they remained so resilient. Over the years they had said all the cruel things they had feared to say when they were young and starting out. They had said those things and survived. But when depression descended on Mack, their resiliency cracked. They tried to restore it through more fights and tugs-of-war, but none of that worked anymore. So Jodie left Mack in a doctor's care, took Rita back to her house in town, and all the way home counted fence posts. She counted cows. She made her fingers work the same movements over and over on the steering wheel while she traced the ripples of cloud with her eyes five times, ten times. Her counting games held her together as she drove through the county, afternoon light slanting through the car. She came home to an empty house. Young Taylor had gone to the bluegrass festival in Oskaloosa, even though he'd never shown an interest in bluegrass music. Kenzie was attending a youth retreat with the Baptists, at a camp in the next county. Jodie stood in the wistful air that day, out beside the wildflower patch, and she noticed the lifeless coneflowers. The sadness was overwhelming. She didn't know what to think—about Mack or herself, or anything.

But he was gone, and she was so relieved. She couldn't allow herself to think the word *relief.* The house was quiet, the day was getting over, and she thought she might draw a tub of hot water and use bubble bath. She thought that possibly she was relaxed enough to consider something luxurious. She hated herself for thinking that way, as if she were glad to be rid of her suffering husband. She drew the bath anyway, after the light had weakened and disappeared and all colors had been rinsed from the outdoors beyond the bathroom window. She lit a candle—a half-burnt one left deep in the closet from last Christmas—and opened the window above the bathtub in order to hear the slight evening air rattle in the cottonwood. She soaked for an hour, but her eyes remained strangely dry. And she sang "In the Garden" over and over again. She forced herself to remember Dad in his blue jeans and flannel shirts, throwing a softball for little Paul to hit. She pictured Mom bent among the tomato and sweet pea vines, singing her hymns. Jodie joined her in the chorus.

She has been singing ever since. She tries pop tunes that were on the radio when she was in high school, but she has trouble remembering the words. Always, her voice stumbles back to those gray verses and their antique King James phrases. She sings as if the words are comforting, but they don't feel personal at all. Their repetition helps her get up in the morning, get through her day, and face bedtime at the end of it.

Now Mack is back, and what is she to do? They are all right so far, mainly because they don't try to do anything. A holding pattern, a loss for words, a flagless truce. They are polite to each other. They pass out affections throughout the day, the movements that have become second nature and that need no emotion behind them. The quick rub along the back of the neck, the stroking of hair that seems an afterthought. These are safe movements that offer no new ideas and open no old hurts.

She turns from the scratchy flower garden to go into the house and is startled by Young Taylor, who stands just a few feet from her. The look on his face is even more unsettling than his black clothes and hair. He is gazing hard at her, and when her eyes meet his, he doesn't flinch in that adolescent habit of keeping distance. He keeps looking, right into her eyes. She can't determine his mood—is he sullen or merely curious about his mother standing in a dead garden? His eyes seem to have grown blacker and blacker over the past years. The very color of his corneas has deepened with the rest of him.

"You startled me," she says.

"Sorry. What are you doing?"

"Oh." She looks away, at the drying soybeans. She didn't expect a question from him. "Just taking a break, checking out the wildflowers."

"I thought you were mad."

"Mad?" Now she is confused. "No. Don't know what gave you that idea."

"Just a mistake." He shrugs and turns toward the house. They walk together, loosely, a few yards between them.

"How was school today?" She can't believe that this is the most inventive thing she can say to her eldest child.

"Fine."

"You had a test in social studies, didn't you?"

"That was last week. I got a C."

"Oh."

Young Taylor glances in her direction and seems to decide to be easy on her and answer the question before she asks. "I didn't study."

"Meaning, if you did, a B or A wouldn't be that hard to get?"

"No. But if I got all the answers right according to the textbook we're using, I'd be wrong. I think the book was printed when I was in first grade."

"Not much money for textbooks, I guess."

"Or teachers who know anything."

"I thought Art Samson was pretty good."

Young Taylor makes a dry sound, not quite a snort. Jodie never knows how to respond to that sound.

"I'm going to Iowa City this weekend."

"Who are you going with?"

"Some friends."

"Which friends?"

The look on Young Taylor's face tells her she's gone too far. "Can I take Dad's car?"

"Ask him."

He rolls his eyes.

"What? Just ask him."

"He'll tell me yes even if he needs the car. All he wants to do is make us like him or something."

Jodie stops to stare at Young Taylor. "You'd rather he want us not to like him?"

"Never mind," he mumbles, walking away.

"What? Don't mumble. If you have something to say, say it."

"I said, never mind!" The mean-spirited son is back, walking right into the body of the son she gave birth to, who just seconds ago carried on a civil conversation with her.

"Look," she says, coming closer, "your dad's trying to get back into the swing of things. He wants you kids to keep doing the things you like to do. You don't have to make it sound like he's—what did you say just then?—'trying to get us to like him.' Jesus! What's that about?"

She says "Jesus" a lot these days, in ways that she was taught always to avoid. A confounded person in her mind's attic asks, "Why Jesus?" but she shuts that door.

"I'm not talking to you now." Young Taylor turns sharply and walks toward the stand of oaks that separates the yard from the soybeans beyond. She knows that it's hopeless to call after him.

Half an hour later, Jodie watches her other child leave the driveway on her bike. Headed for the Baptist church, no doubt. Kenzie has found a haven there, with other kids who are hot on religion. Oh, well, it's a phase. Jodie's own churchgoing helps mainly to keep her in place; it offers a different manner of repetition, something like the hymn singing. The words and motions of a church service feel distant to her now. For a long time she tried to pretend, to turn nonsense and tragedy into some form of devotion, a spiritual lesson maybe. But with three deaths in the family, a sister-in-law and sweet niece and nephew lost to them now, Mack always on some brink, and the children twirling off on their own tangents, no spirituality Jodie has learned or even recited can justify, make sense, redeem, or offer wisdom.

Yet United Methodist is where her life joins other lives, and with family members cut adrift, any lifeline is important. Now that she is not a struggling farmer's wife but a woman with a regular job who is no longer begging help, however mutely, in the back row of pews, she can walk in, sit down, and not feel that her presence is troubling to anyone else. Her life is not an indictment to families that are doing well.

Mack

He told Ed he would help him get the combine ready for the corn. Ever since Mack stopped farming on his own, he's continued to lend a hand to whatever Ed has going on. There is always machinery to condition or repair, vehicles to move from place to place, buildings to clean out or fix up, and animals to tend. Ed still has a few head of cattle and his hogs. And he is growing corn and beans. If the weather catches them just so, a harvest might need to be turned around in a handful of days. Mack, Ed, and other neighbors have been in and out of one another's fields and lives as they are called for. They trade information, assistance, and storage space. Although Mack has slipped out of the farming life, even at his worst he can't leave Ed stranded with 120 acres of corn to get in. Lacy can run the rest of the farm during harvest, but she steps back and lets the men run the combine, a large, complicated beast that has to be listened to and watched every minute, a powerful contraption that needs to be guided and turned with care. Jodie has driven their combine, but it makes her nervous. A person has to be accustomed to the machine, know it well enough to recognize when a sound has changed even slightly. The men take their machines apart regularly, to ready them for different crops, to service and repair them. So they are more intimate with the sounds and bumps.

When Mack pulls up at the gate nearest Ed's tractor barn, two other pickups are already in the drive. Hal Winters and Coke Muller stand in the shadow of the high barn entrance, each settled back on a hip, posed for conversation. Ed is between them, having a smoke. The three of them nod when Mack walks up.

"You farmers can't find any work to do?" Mack says.

"Hell, there's too much work. We're makin' our to-do lists." Hal's voice has the gravel of a man who has swallowed decades of dust. He spits tobacco off to the side.

"Ed, I see you brought in the expert." Hal points to Mack with his chin.

"Damn straight."

"If Mack can't fix it, just send the sumabitch back to the factory," Coke says.

Mack smiles. "I've seen you wrestling with hardware a time or two, Coke."

Coke's only response is an expletive, as if the memory is enough to make his bones ache.

Mack gazes into the rafters, feeling strained but not as much as he expected. He doesn't know what these men have said about him lately, but he can guess. *Shame about Mack. I hate to see times get to a guy like that. Good man, hard worker. Damn shame.* Farmers in general aren't judgmental about a man who falls on hard times. They talk about him if he's lazy or a cheat or if he leaves his machinery out in the weather. If he loses his shirt, maybe they question some of his business decisions. But all of them are too close to disaster on a seasonal basis to be very uppity about another man's misfortunes.

"How's it goin', Mack?" Hal decides to be direct, and the others turn as if relieved that someone has asked. "I hear Hendrikson's real glad to have you back."

"It's fine. We've got plenty of work."

"Good machine man'll always have plenty around here. I'm on the lookout for a round baler, by the way."

"We moved a used one three days ago. Harold's going to an auction up near What Cheer next week. I'll see if he's got a list on it yet."

They spend another fifteen minutes discussing equipment. The only thing Mack's sure of anymore is that he knows machinery. There really isn't much he can't fix, and everyone in the county knows it. Farmers twice his age call him up or stop at the house. Most of the time now they stop at Hendrikson's. It hasn't occurred to him until just now that in spite of everything that's happened, the men around here respect him. When Hal and Coke take off, he feels warm and stirred up in a good way.

"Okay, buddy," he says, as Ed grinds out his second cigarette, "let's get you ready to pick corn."

They spend the afternoon in the barn, lubing the combine, checking the hydraulics, testing both the corn and bean heads. The air is
crisp, and the wind gusts through the barn occasionally, smelling of
ripe fields. Lacy invites Mack to stay for supper, and they eat ham and
beans with cornbread on the large porch. It is closed in with windows, and most of the storm windows are shut now, with just two
open screens. They warm their hands on coffee cups while the fields
to the east reflect the bronze of the opposite sky.

As he raises dust along the chat road toward home, Mack notices
how the green is draining from the corn rows like blood leaving a face.
And the stalks are growing pale and papery, turning the fields golden.
When the sun strikes the hills a certain way, Mack is reminded of
pictures he's seen in *National Geographic* of deserts in Africa or the
Middle East.

When he gets home, Kenzie is washing the supper dishes.

"Hi, Dad. Heard you were helping Uncle Ed."

"Yep, we're ready for the corn now."

Jodie comes in, a pile of mail in her hands. She spreads it out on
the kitchen table. "Is it ready to go?"

"In a couple weeks probably." He looks at the envelopes, most of
them recognizable by their shades of gray and blue: bills to pay.
"Want some help with that?"

"No. I got it."

Mack chews his lip. She's been handling the money for a long
time. "Maybe you'd like a break from it."

"Wouldn't we all." She is tossing envelopes into three different
piles. He sits down at the table and tries to figure out her system.
"I may as well do some of this. If you show me what's what."

"It's easier to just do it. I've got it." Her face is closed to him. It
often gets this way when money is part of the conversation. There was
a time when he had to leave it to her. Partly he did it because it upset
him too much to see his financial failures spread out and articulated in
cold numbers. Partly he left the money to her because his concentration was shot. He couldn't do simple math anymore. He'd sit at the

table, checkbook and envelopes around him, and forget what he was doing. He bounced some checks, and that was the end of that. Once your credit is shot, you have no place to go. Everybody who does business with you finds out about it. So Mack gave it all to his wife, who could still juggle all the numbers and stretch the grocery money.

There is no sense sitting at the table, because he can't talk with Jodie while she is paying bills. So he goes to the living room and turns on the television. He flips through the channels, finds a movie, and calls into the kitchen, "Where's Young Taylor?"

"Went to the cineplex."

"On a school night? They don't give homework anymore?"

"They give it," answers Kenzie, coming in to sit on the couch. "He just doesn't do it."

"He'd better do it."

Jodie stays out of the conversation.

"What about you? You have homework?" Mack looks at his daughter.

"A little. I can get it done before bed."

"How are your classes?"

She shrugs.

"You still doing the drama stuff? You in a play again this year?"

"I'm working backstage for the fall play. Maybe I'll try out for the spring."

"Stagehand, huh?"

"Prop girl. I've got to find stuff that looks like it's from the 1940s."

"Talk to your grandma."

She looks up. "Oh, yeah, she'd have stuff."

"Kenzie, there's a whole museum right on Main Street," Jodie calls from the kitchen table. "We can go there this weekend if you want. Naomi can help you find whatever you need."

"They'd let me use antiques?"

"They've got piles of stuff they'll never find a place for."

"I'll bring Tamara along. She's in charge of costumes. They'd have old clothes, right?"

"For every shape and size."

"Thanks, Mom." She pops off the couch. "I'm going upstairs." She breezes past Mack. He puts out a hand, and she gives it a little slap as she goes by.

The movie is from the eighties, and it depresses Mack to see how young the movie stars look. He's seen Gene Hackman in something more recent and knows that what he is looking at now is a past version of the man. He shuts off the set and scavenges in the kitchen for something sweet, settling on cold cereal and milk. Jodie is putting her bookkeeping items away, in the old desk near the door to the back porch.

"What can I help you with?" He tries to sound casual as he takes a spoon of cereal. She is in the pantry, pulling clothes out of the dryer.

"You can carry up some of this, once I fold it."

"Okay. I'll do that." He can hear the dry sounds of fabric being shaken and folded, stacked on the small table just around the corner. "Ed's fields are lookin' good."

"How about Ed? Lacy said he's got another bladder infection or something like that."

"Didn't say anything about it. Looked all right." He doesn't know why the women around him are so intense about everybody's ailments. He does remember Ed stopping a few times to go take a leak. Mack finishes the cereal as Jodie brings stacks of towels and clothing to the table and sets them down. He finds himself in a canyon, surrounded by soft, worn colors. They smell clean, almost acidic. When he carries them upstairs, the strong, artificial sweetness fills his lungs. These are the smells that make up his life now. They are safe and sterile, like those in the hospital. When he goes to the bedroom to undress for the night, he raises the window and lets the chilly air pour in.

Kenzie

"I'm not sure I can be friends with someone who listens to so many Jesus songs."

Kenzie looks at Bekka over a raised taco that is losing globs of meat and lettuce and tiny curls of orange cheese. The Saturday afternoon mall mob undulates around them.

"What about Jesus songs?"

Bekka sits in that angled way that makes her appear on the verge of saying something sarcastic. "It's just that you know a *lot* of Jesus songs—how healthy can that be?"

"More healthy than being plugged into Christina and Justin twenty-four hours a day."

"I listen to other stuff too."

"At least Jesus songs are about stuff that means something."

Bekka sucks down more cola and rolls her eyes toward the closest corner of the food court, near the cineplex entrance. "Let's see a movie."

Kenzie makes a face, unwilling to admit that she's out of money. They have landed here because Bekka's brother has better things to do than haul them around. Ottumwa is no Des Moines, but at least there's a shopping center, and Regan has friends here. He dumped Kenzie and Bekka at the mall at eleven. They have tried on clothes in three different shops, bought some bracelets, and listened to the demos at Music Century, and now they're having lunch. Kenzie's tired of the usual topics. She feels as if she and Bekka are near their limit of tolerating each other.

Regan picks them up at four, as they agreed, not because he keeps promises to his sister but because his job in Oskaloosa starts at five-thirty and his girlfriend's shift ends at four-thirty, leaving them a small window for finding food and pawing each other. Kenzie watches the countryside and feels quiet pain and longing while Bekka and her brother argue about nothing in particular the whole way. Regan dumps them at the Wal-Mart in Oskaloosa, from which they'll need to find their own way home. The girls stand inside the store for a few minutes, long enough for Bekka to buy a giant bag of popcorn. They stay in the entryway munching, near the pay phones.

"Call Young Taylor and ask him to come get us." Bekka, always full of ideas about how to kill time, actually looks tired.

"I don't even know if he's home."

"Try, okay? Use my cell. Ask him please, please to come get us."

Kenzie does reach Young Taylor, who, miraculously, agrees to come get them. When he pulls up a few minutes later, Bekka bounces into the front seat. "Tay-lor, what's up?" She offers him popcorn, and he waves it away.

"Thanks, Tay." Kenzie tries to sound in charge from the backseat. She doesn't make eye contact with her brother.

Young Taylor doesn't seem irritated, but he says nothing to them. His agenda these days is to be mysterious.

"We're so sorry, but Regan was being a jerk, as usual. Forgive us? Pleeze?" Bekka tugs on a strand of Taylor's hair near his ear. "Your hair is really good this black. What shade is it?"

"Black."

"What shade of black? What name?"

Taylor puts a CD in the player and ignores them. In a few minutes they are at Bekka's house. She says good-bye, and Kenzie moves to the front seat. They listen to the music.

"What exactly does that mean?" she asks after a rather rapid and convoluted sentence goes past them. It's hard to understand the words of someone who's moaning and screaming.

Taylor just looks at the road.

"Really, I want to know. What's it about?"

Her brother turns his head slowly to look at her. He switches down the volume and says, appearing solemn, "It means that Jesus is coming back soon."

Kenzie looks away from him. "You're so not funny."

"Leave me alone."

"It was an honest question."

Young Taylor turns up the volume.

Lately Bekka brings up topics she knows we disagree on. And she seems to show off what she knows will bother me. Today we had to go outside twice so she could smoke. She has this pink cigarette case and a book of matches some senior boy gave her. The matches are from Camp's bar, where all the seniors and dropouts go. Like she "needs" to smoke, because it helps her "focus." Give me a break. And she talks about how she thinks all the light beers don't have any taste, and how her favorite drink right now is a chocolate martini, but once the weather gets warm again she'll go back to margaritas, and she knows the best brand of tequila, like she's a bartender or something.

It wasn't that long ago when Bekka went to church and youth camp along with the rest of us. But now she's trying to look wild and rebellious. I feel like I have to choose between hanging out with Bekka, who's been my best friend since fourth grade, or hanging out with other people who are interested in the same things I'm interested in. I don't feel so close to anyone in the youth group at church—well, except for Jenna, who's a couple years older than me but treats me like we're equals.

Sometimes it seems like I know Jesus better than I know people who are here around me on earth. It's such a comfort to know he understands me when other people don't, even though they love me a lot. Like the Scripture says, "Jesus is the same yesterday, today, and forever." What else can you say that about? Nothing. Nothing in this life lasts forever. But Jesus has no beginning or end, and he's holding me close to his heart. Knowing how much he loves me makes it possible to get through the darkest days. No matter what happens in this sinful world or what people in my life say and do, Jesus will make sure my life pleases God, and he won't let me fall into sin.

Mack

By his tenth day back home, Mack finds that he can't move in any direction without being stopped by his senses. Each day has become an obstacle course as all the familiar places deepen, darken, and become wild to him. He has tried to explain this to George.

"My cousin Will—he was over in Nam—said that sometimes every sense was turned way up. Every smell was sharper, every sound louder, everything you touched full of more information. He thought it had to do with being so close to death. You knew that you could be walking through a field on a nice day and in the next few seconds see parts of your own body flying away from you."

George remained silent, his concentration total.

"It seems like that right now. The super-tuned-in part." Mack shook his head. "Maybe I'm too drugged up."

"Have you told the doctor?"

"Not yet. I see him next week."

They sat in silence then. Silences weren't getting much easier, just more familiar.

Mack heard George take a breath. "I get the feeling you don't really think it's the medications."

Mack didn't reply to that. He allowed the words and thoughts to dissipate in the therapist's room. The session ended, and he walked out to the car, feeling that he'd held his ground in some way.

But now, driving home, he feels cut loose and unsure. The landscape, with its vivid details, dogs him, demanding his attention. Finally, he pulls over, several miles from home, and shuts off the engine. He gets out of the Dodge and walks around it.

He is alone on the road. A few hundred yards to the east is the old Jefferson place. The abandoned house, gray from weather and years, has crumbled in upon itself, its one remaining wall rising up from the ruins like a single playing card. On the other side of the road, large round hay bales are lined up, snug against a fence, a cornfield just yards on the other side.

Mack leans against the front of the car and watches a few dirty-looking cumulus clouds drift overhead. In front of him, the road just keeps going. Where he stands it seems wide as a room, but as he watches it fall away from him its two edges draw closer together. Sunlight angles over the place, and each small stone of the gravel surface throws a shadow, making the road seem deeper than it is and oddly important.

"What's happening?" he murmurs just over the breeze. He folds his arms and looks in every direction. Although he feels sure that something is about to move or speak, the afternoon remains steadfast and uneventful.

He gets back in the car and turns on the radio the rest of the way. He notices, for possibly the first time in his life, how many small cemeteries there are around here. Midwestern rose-yellow light descends on the landscape like curtains ending a scene. The country roads look old as they ribbon over hills and divide the fields.

Chat and dust fly at the house when he brakes and parks. He didn't realize how fast he was driving. He shuts off the engine and sees the kitchen curtains part as Jodie checks out the racket.

He sits there while the engine whirs down to silence. Listens to himself breathe, coaches himself for walking into the house. *Calm down. The day's over. You're home now.* He and George talked about this, about how to talk to himself when his emotions are running riot. So far he's not been very successful at it.

He sees Young Taylor walking up from the edge of the alfalfa, to the south. Behind the field, where the land drops toward the creek, is a stand of poplars and box elders. What did Mom say, something about Young Taylor disappearing for hours at a time? The boy's long legs carry him past the old chicken coop and the low apple trees just east of it. He wears a black turtleneck and blue jeans and nothing else in the cold wind. When he stalks up the back steps, he doesn't appear to notice Mack sitting in the car yards away.

Mack takes one more long breath and gets out of the car. He will forget the day and enter his home and talk with his kids and wife.

Jodie's look asks the question: *You all right?* When Mack doesn't answer, she asks, "What's with the skidding stop clear up to my windowsill?" There is no humor in her tone.

"Didn't mean to. I saw Young Taylor walk in." He looks into the family room, which is empty, the TV blaring. "Kenzie home? It's getting dark."

"She's at the church."

"What's going on there?"

"Youth group or something." She sees his confusion and adds, "At the Baptist church."

"She joined the Baptists now?"

She turns to him, and he can detect her stifled frustration. "She's been going to their youth group for a few months now. She was attending before you went to the hospital."

Everything in their family life is now marked by Before Hospital and After Hospital. "I forgot," he says quietly.

Jodie turns back to the lettuce she's tearing up. "Anyway, sometimes she stays for a while to pray or whatever."

"By herself in the church?"

"Yeah. Says she likes to pray in the quiet."

Mack sits at the kitchen table, leaking a sigh. "Is that where she is every day after school? Is that why she's never home until right at suppertime?"

"I don't know. Part of the time she's there. I don't pry—you know how kids are at this age."

"I don't remember any kids that age spending half their life alone in a church."

"You didn't run around with those kids."

"I didn't know she did."

She's chopping cucumber. "There are worse people she could be hanging out with."

"The pastor knows she's there? They just leave it unlocked, or what?"

"I think she has a key. She's there early to open up the nights they have youth group and choir practice. Of course the pastor knows." She sets the salad bowl on the table in front of him, reaches into the fridge for the small carafe of homemade dressing. "Mack, it's a thing she's going through."

Kenzie

Once, Kenzie and Grandma Rita figured out that Kenzie bikes about eight miles every evening. There are a couple of places where the land is particularly hilly and slashed through by little streams and patches of trees, and the road goes off the grid for a bit. But Grandma Rita and Kenzie drove one day, along Kenzie's usual route, and the odometer registered eight miles. When weather is bearable, this bike ride is her daily workout.

She became more interested in staying in shape after youth camp, summer before last. The speaker every night was Jackie Cleveland, an evangelist who had traveled a lot in China and other places where Christians are being persecuted. Jackie personally knew people who had spent years in labor camps. Always stay strong, he said, because if you live for Christ you might have to suffer for him someday. And if America doesn't mend its ways and repent and purify itself morally, then God will continue to judge America by allowing it to be taken over by the atheists or the Muslims. There may come a time in your lifetime, Jackie said, when, because you are a Christian, you won't get a decent job and you'll have to work with your hands. Or if things get really bad, you might spend years in a labor camp. So stay in shape. Be soldiers and athletes for the Lord.

So Kenzie bikes every evening she can, imagining the answers she will give in the event that she gets interrogated one day. She formulates how she will defend the truth—by quoting Scripture—and how her interrogators will be left with nothing to say because God's Word will stand on its own. So she bikes and thinks and memorizes critical Bible verses. She has memorized all of the second chapter of Galatians and the fourth chapter of Philippians. Plus about fifteen Psalms, to comfort her and other prisoners while they face torture or death. She has found, too, that setting verses to her own melodies helps her remember them.

A few times lately Kenzie has been interrogated in her dreams, and the person questioning her has sat in shadow the whole time, until the very end. And when the face finally comes into view, it is Young Taylor's. Young Taylor with his black hair and dark made-up circles around his eyes. Kenzie knows that it's a sign to pray for her brother.

She can feel in every part of her spirit that God is calling her to intercede for her family. She doesn't have to go to China; there are plenty of people here to minister to.

The pink clouds have faded, and now long, flat stretches of pigeon-feather gray levitate just above the horizon. Kenzie realizes that her arms are shaking. The air has gotten cold. At the next intersection she turns back toward home.

As she approaches Mitchell Jaylee's place, she considers what she knows about him. Since nearly running him over that one day, she has prayed for him at least once a day. He is about thirty and is unemployed most of the time. He grew up in the very house he lives in now, went away to some place on the West Coast for several years, then came back to claim the little two-bedroom house, all that is left of his great-uncle's farm. The great-uncle died years ago, and since he never had any kids of his own, his property went to Mitchell, whose parents died when they drove into a freight train late one night when Mitchell was only twenty.

At least this is the information that Kenzie has heard, piece by piece, in various conversations. People talk about Mitchell as if he's been in prison or has a drug habit, but no one can prove anything like that. Young Taylor says it isn't drugs, just mental problems he was probably born with. Mitchell doesn't work regularly, just takes a job here and there. He builds things—sheds, fences, chicken houses, gazebos. He isn't very fast but does decent work. And then he won't work for a long time. He doesn't talk to people, and then he'll be having conversations with everyone. This kind of inconsistency scares people, and they usually leave him alone, although they joke about him. Kenzie overheard Janelle's dad, at the Citgo station, say one day, "Oh, Mitch is in a babbling phase this week."

Kenzie is almost past Mitchell's driveway when she sees him, bent over beside the fence near the mailbox. Is he throwing up? She turns and looks back at him, then stops, reverses direction, and comes up to him slowly.

"Mr. Jaylee, you all right?"

He straightens up, slowly, and when he turns she can see a white gauze patch over his right eye. With his other eye, he stares at her. "I'm okay. Got dizzy. Sinus headache. And my eye." He wears no jacket, and his shirt gapes partway up, revealing dark hair on his chest.

"Does it hurt?" Kenzie looks at the patch.

"Some. Splashed it with paint thinner."

Kenzie makes a sympathetic face.

"I dropped some of the mail, then got dizzy when I bent over to pick it up." He raises a handful of envelopes.

"Can I help with anything?"

Warmth comes to his face. "That's really kind. No, I'm fine, but thanks for asking. What's your name? Kendra?"

"Kenzie. For Mackenzie."

"Your dad's name."

She nods. He keeps staring at her, and she comes up with another sentence, quick. "So you're painting something?"

"No. Stripping off paint, for my newest creation." He smiles.

"What creation?"

"Come on. I'll show you." He doesn't wait for her to agree, just turns and walks up the drive. She walks the bike slowly a few steps after him. He turns and says over his shoulder, "It's in the barn. I've been working on it for nearly two months."

"What is it?" She stays a yard or two behind him but continues to walk the bike.

"I guess you'd call it a sculpture." He's in the large doorway of the barn. He leans against the side of it and watches Kenzie as she covers the last few yards. Then he reaches behind him and flips a switch and points toward the center of the space.

Kenzie follows his gesture and says automatically, "Wow." She is looking at a structure that is probably twelve feet high and several feet across. It is made of every sort of metal imaginable: old bedsprings, various implements, strips of aluminum, buckets and cans, chicken wire, the chrome fender of some lost vehicle. "You did this?"

"Yep. Just a little hobby." He walks over to it and touches a blade that juts out from a sphere made of screen mesh. "I call it 'War of the Worlds.'"

"It looks like a war—but it's really beautiful too." Kenzie walks up to the sculpture and runs her hand along a piece of it.

"Careful. Some jagged edges there."

"Is it finished?"

"I don't know yet. I just come out here and work on it, then I can't work on it anymore, then I think it's finished, then I walk out here one morning and decide it isn't yet." He smiles at her. "You like it?"

She smiles back. "A lot. I've never seen anything like it."

"I could tell you had an artistic soul." He pauses. "I remember when you were a little thing." He hasn't taken his eye off her. "You're almost a lady now."

"I've seen you at the church, haven't I?" It seems the right thing to say, to bring up something Christian and fill the gap she feels when guys talk to her in a personal way. How else do you answer when a guy says you're almost a lady? It's a perfect opportunity to invite him to church.

"Yeah, I like to sit in God's house sometimes."

Something in her spirit perks up. "I know what you mean."

"Really?" He steps closer, and she sees that he doesn't look loony, just shy. Like someone who doesn't exist in the midst of people much. "Yeah, you look like the type of person who thinks about spiritual things. You have soul, I bet."

She smiles, embarrassed. "I hope so."

"I know so. Some people just have it."

"Have what?"

"That spiritual connection. I bet you get misunderstood a lot."

Now Kenzie takes a step to close the remaining yard between them. "I do. But I don't mind."

"No, a spiritual person doesn't mind. It goes with the territory, people not seeing the world in the same way."

"You sound like you're interested in the spirit too."

He shrugs, and looks almost as young as Young Taylor. But the muscles under his shirt belong to an older man, one who's worked a long time.

"Do you like Bible study, stuff like that?" It's such a natural ques- tion, Kenzie feels confidence bubbling far below. This meeting has some divine intention behind it, she just knows it.

"Depends. Lot of preachers don't get it, you know?"

It is her turn to nod. He's hit on the very reason she switched from the Methodist church to the Baptist.

"Well, there's a study Thursday night at the Baptist church, led by the youth pastor. I think he gets it."

"Really. I'm not much for groups. I do like talking about the Bible sometimes, though."

Kenzie smiles. Somehow it is easier to meet Mitchell's gaze since he has only one eye visible. "I need to get home."

"Yeah. Don't want to be out on these roads in the dark."

"Nice talking to you."

"Same here. You take care. Stay in the spirit now."

Her legs have extra energy in the remaining half-mile. What a con- versation! She doesn't know any adults, except for pastors and the youth leader, who will jump right in talking about the spiritual life like that.

But her mood shifts once she is in the house. Dad is in his chair in the family room, staring at the television. Mom is in the kitchen. They both say hi but clearly have other things on their minds. She wonders if they've had an argument. Worse, maybe they haven't talked at all.

The next day after school, she stops at the church and prays for nearly an hour. She feels so full of . . . something . . . like longing—for people to find peace with God. Full of wonder at the fields glittering just beyond the soft windows. Full of a sharp hope that has arisen fresh from her conversation with Mitchell. She replays it again and again, regretting the things she could have said. She isn't very good at witnessing to people, at bringing the Good News into conversation at any point, finding connection with whatever a person says. Mitchell planted almost every sentence with a spiritual question, even though he didn't ask the question itself. But to someone more experienced at evangelism, it would have been easy to bring the conversation around to something more pointed and effective.

Mike Williamson walks in when Kenzie is finishing her prayer at the altar rail. Sensing his step behind her, she turns around. "Hi. I'm almost finished."

"You're fine. I'm on my way to the storage room."

She watches him go by and suddenly calls after him, "I had a really strange conversation yesterday."

He turns and strolls back toward her. She sits on the raised floor in front of the railing, looking up at him.

"You did? In what way?"

"This guy, a neighbor. He was really hungry to talk about spiritual things. I've never had that happen before."

"Yeah, it doesn't happen often, but it's really cool when it does."

"I'm not very good at witnessing when I don't have time to prepare."

"That's why we have to be prepared all the time." His smile makes it clear that this statement isn't a rebuke. "You're more prepared than you know. But it's hard to speak up when you get surprised like that. With practice, it gets easier."

"He doesn't come to church, at least not here, hardly ever anywhere. I invited him to your Thursday study, because he's interested in the Bible."

"Now, see, you did just fine."

"Maybe I'll talk to him again."

"You know this guy?"

She senses that mentioning Mitchell's name isn't a good idea. "Oh, yeah, for a long time. We've never talked much, though."

He is turning back toward the storage room. "Keep it up, Kenzie. You need a ride home?"

"I've got my bike."

"Shouldn't be out after dark."

Mitchell has straight black hair, sort of long, that swings around his face when he walks. Although he isn't that old, he moves with an old-man sort of shuffle, as if he isn't sure of himself. He's a bit bigger than Dad, with pretty wide shoulders but a thinner face, dark eyes close together and a black mustache. There are little bags under his eyes. He looks sort of like a tormented soul, and several times a year when Reverend Darnelle asks for prayer requests, Mitchell's name comes up.

Of course I should pray for him. God has caused our paths to cross, and I feel like Mitchell and I have an understanding. It's almost like a spiritual link. I'm not sure what he believes about God and Jesus. But I bet he would talk about it if I brought it up sometime.

When I passed Mitchell's place, there was one little light behind the sheer curtain of his back window. The rest of the place—the garage that sort of leans, the three sheds and old barn—just look like long shadows. Sort of like Mitchell's life, all mysterious. Maybe a person's house represents that person.

Like our house. It's bigger and busier than Mitchell's. But some days it feels sad, like Mom, or dark and depressed like Dad. And the upstairs especially can feel angry like Young Taylor.

Then I think about me. If I had my own house, what would it be like?

Quiet, I think. And full of prayer. At least that's what I hope I am. I think God wants me to be quiet and strong and praying every moment.

Jodie

Her afternoon plays out like a bad movie. She leaves the school and heads to Oskaloosa to do grocery shopping. This takes well over an hour, stretched by an extra half-hour when she pushes her full cart out to the parking lot and realizes that she doesn't have her ATM card. She hurries back into the store and asks at the register where she checked out and at the two registers on either side. No one has seen the card. She retraces her steps, walking frantically up and down aisles, trying to remember where she stopped to pick up more than one item at a time or to examine the produce a little closer. Then she makes her way out to the car, her gaze scouring the ground. From there she looks up to the gray sky, wishing she could just cry or scream. Life does not allow her to vent so freely; she has too much else to do. Finally she rummages through each bulging plastic bag before putting it in the truck cab. Sometimes she throws change into a bag rather than wrestle it into the zippered compartment of her billfold. Maybe she threw the ATM card in along with that and the receipt. But all she finds are two quarters and a penny. She stands there by the truck, swearing profusely, and goes through her jacket pockets one more time. Then, in a flash of memory, she checks her jeans pockets and finds it in the back right one, where she never puts anything. She is standing there putting the card into her billfold when Terry Jenkins comes up from the next row of cars.

There goes that smile. Damn it. Here she is wearing the face of a wild woman, having just played through her mind all the hassle of getting a new bank card, after spending the past ten minutes fuming and sweating. Of course it's him. And he is lit up with that look that says she's wonderful anyway.

No, of course not. There must be another reason for all that hope in his eyes, something that has nothing to do with her. He must have come straight from the school, which probably let out a few minutes ago. He's just glad that the day's over.

"Hey, Jodie, how are you?"

"Oh, same as always—trying to get shopping out of the way."

He is four years younger than Mack, two years younger than she is. Full, blond head of hair, tawny, long-fingered hands. He places one of them on the truck fender, the other in the pocket of his jacket, a tan suede that gathers at his slim waist. "I usually get here right at suppertime," he says, "when everybody else discovers that there's nothing at home to eat."

"I try to avoid that time of day—too dangerous." She laughs.

"Can I help you with anything?"

"No. Everything's loaded."

His eyes linger on her for just a moment longer. "Do you ever get a break?"

She is startled by such a frank question and decides to treat it lightly. "A break—what's that?" She laughs a little and hopes he'll stop looking at her so intently. He smiles and finally shifts his gaze to the fender and his hand on it.

Jodie tries to bring the conversation to conclusion. "I'm fine—just a busy day—you know, shopping day."

"Good. I hope you stay fine." He reaches for the empty cart and pulls it away from her. "I'll just grab this."

"Go ahead."

"Nice to see you, Jodie."

"You too." She watches him turn and wheel the cart toward the store entrance. He's still smiling. She calls after him, "Watch out for those moms with toddlers."

He laughs into the wind and waves back at her.

In the silence of the truck cab, she allows herself to sigh. Her heart stays revved up as she drives across the parking lot. The afternoon is as dark and chill as evening, thanks to a cold front that blows in atop a dense bank of clouds. Jodie takes the east entrance so that she can cut over to the filling station on the next street. After that stop, she drives the few miles back to Beulah and takes the street that cuts straight through the town, then turns off of it to drive past Rita's, sees the car gone, and so doesn't stop. Her mother-in-law is likely at some neighbor's administering medicine or a meal. Much of the time she's not home, but Jodie and Mack both drive by anyway, a habit so entrenched that their vehicles would take that route even with no one at the wheel.

The only stop after that is the post office, and when she finds their box empty she remembers that Mack has resumed this duty; the post office lies on his route home from Hendrikson's. "Well, gee, I guess I can finally go home now." She talks to herself a lot, certain that it helps her maintain a sense of humor. By now she is over the adrenaline rush from both the lost ATM card and the Terry en-

counter. She is ready to go home and arrange the groceries in her cup-
boards, an action that involves order and thus some comfort.

She is almost past the old town square when a patrol car slowly
turns the corner and passes her. Stan the deputy is looking toward
the band gazebo that stands near the center of the little park. Jodie
follows the direction of his gaze and sees several kids around the
gazebo. In the same moment she categorizes them as high school students, she sees Young Taylor sitting on the gazebo steps. She has to
look twice to be sure, because he and two other kids are in black garb
and dyed hair. But her son's stance is unmistakable. The kid standing
closest to him is a girl in black fishnet hose, leather boots, tattooed
arms that are bare to the weather, and enough eye makeup for the entire senior class. She and Young Taylor are smoking while the third
member of their party exchanges words with several boys who stand
near the sidewalk, a pickup parked at the curb behind them.

Jodie rolls down the window to hear what the kids are saying. It's
too windy to hear words, but it's clear that the conversation is hostile.
Jodie watches the patrol car pull a U-turn and head toward the truck.
She pulls into a parking spot in front of the pharmacy, which puts her
on the side of the square that's to the left of Young Taylor and his
friends. She turns in the seat to watch. The boy in black takes a few
steps toward the ones by the vehicle. By now Jodie has recognized all
but one of the kids. They're just students, not known for trouble. She
trains her gaze upon Young Taylor, hoping that he stays seated. Stan
gets out of the patrol car and walks up to the group on the sidewalk.

There are raised voices, still unintelligible, and arms pointing back
and forth between the kids at the curb and the boy in black. Stan
walks closer to him, and Young Taylor rises from his place on the
gazebo steps.

"No, just stay there." Jodie's words whisper out the open window
and are absorbed into the wind. Above the little park, ancient oak
branches sway in slow motion. Jodie is ready to jump out of the truck
and prevent Young Taylor from tangling with Stan. But he and the officer never get closer than ten yards or so. Young Taylor is talking but

in that offhand way of his, not making direct eye contact, hunching his shoulders and drawing on the cigarette. The boys on the sidewalk have moved closer, but Stan turns and walks back toward them, and they slowly back up and get in the truck.

Then Stan turns and shouts something at Young Taylor, the girl, and the other boy. He shouts not in anger but to be heard over the weather. Still, Jodie can detect the sternness in his voice. He takes a few steps toward the three and motions them out of the park. Then Young Taylor begins to argue, raising his arms in protest and finally looking at the officer.

"Taylor, just keep your mouth shut." Jodie's hands grasp the handle of the truck door. Just as she's ready to go intervene, Young Taylor and his crew stride quickly across the bare lawn and away from Stan. Stan watches them for a moment, and Jodie is sure that he sees the finger that Young Taylor flips in his direction. She holds her breath. "Just let it go, Stan, please." Stan gets in the patrol car and backs into the street. He drives in the opposite direction the kids are walking, but he watches a few more moments before continuing his rounds.

Her heart is racing again. The events of her afternoon clash, and she can't make sense of their sequence. She wishes right then that Terry would walk up to the truck and sit in the cab with her. They could talk about these troublesome kids. He's a teacher, and she's a mother. She knows that she won't go home to Mack and tell him what she has just seen. She won't tell him about Terry in the parking lot. She won't even mention the missing ATM card. All of these things that make her catch her breath must remain in her heart and roam only in her thoughts.

She wants to drive to the other side of the square and catch up with Young Taylor, order him to get his butt in the cab and explain himself to her. She wants to look more closely at this trashy girl he's hanging out with—she thinks it's Lydia Streeter, a sophomore. And the other kid is Kyle something or other. But right now she's afraid to come upon the three of them together. She's never been afraid of her own kid before. He's never looked so sinister before either. Maybe Rita's fears about drugs and so forth are well founded. Maybe it's time to do something more forceful with Young Taylor, like forbid him to wear freaky clothing or to spend time with these friends. How do you do that with a seventeen-year-old who is taller than you are?

It is four o'clock by the time she's on the last mile to home. Her radio is on, and she sings some forgotten song about devotion, about the blood of Jesus and the rescue of those who are perishing. She's forgotten the verses, but she joins in on every chorus.

Mack

He feels worse all through dinner. He is sure that the kids and Jodie are talking over and around him. Everything that comes up in the conversation is a topic of which he is nearly ignorant. He has to keep asking questions. They answer and then just go on talking.

"Mom, I'm skipping supper tomorrow," Kenzie says when she gets up from the table.

"You'll be somewhere?"

"Not really."

"She's fasting," Young Taylor says, tapping his fork against the knife that crosses his plate. "Aren't you, Kenzie?"

"None of your business."

"Are you?" Jodie asks. Kenzie glares at Young Taylor.

"It's all right if you are, I just want to know where you're going to be."

"With friends probably, at the church."

"But, you know, fasting doesn't count if people know about it. You're supposed to do that stuff in secret." Young Taylor pretends concern, raising eyebrows at his sister.

"Just cool it." Jodie takes the fork from his hand and gathers his plate and other silverware.

"You're not trying to lose weight, are you, Kenz?" Mack tries to catch his daughter's eyes. She seems distressed at all this attention. "No, Dad, we just fast so we can pray together. Christians have been doing it for centuries. Jesus talked about it. It's not so weird, there just aren't many people who do it anymore."

When they get ready for bed a few hours later, Mack sits on the chair and takes off his boots. He sighs loudly, as a signal, then says, "I'm going to talk with Kenzie about all this church business. Or maybe I should talk with that youth pastor or whoever he is."

Jodie twists from the open closet door and frowns at him. "Why would you do that?"

"She spends all her time at the church! That's not normal, even for a religious kid. She's going overboard with this stuff—like kids that end up in cults, led by maniacs who convince them to wait for flying saucers or to poison themselves."

"Mack, there is nothing bad going on here. I can remember going through a real religious spell when I was about Kenzie's age, and she went through some sort of experience a few months ago, when she went to the revival over at the Baptist church with some of her friends. She really went through something, and we have to respect that. She'll be fine."

"Religion is okay in regular doses, but when a kid that age is so wrapped up in it, it's some sort of escape." He turns to point a finger at Jodie. "And a church leader who encourages kids to spend all their time praying or fasting or whatever is taking advantage in some way. I want to get to the bottom of this."

"No. You can't do that. This is Kenzie's thing, and you just stay out of it. I've talked with the pastor over there and met the youth pastor. They're fine. They're just trying to give the kids healthy ways to spend their time. They organize cheap trips to Des Moines to go to rallies or sometimes just take the kids together to a movie or something. They sponsor lock-ins where the kids all spend the night together, usually on prom night or some other time when they're under pressure to go out drinking or sleeping around. You just leave it alone."

"All I want to know is what they're teaching about fasting."

"She goes without food for a day every month or something. That is not extreme. It's for prayer time."

"All I hear from her is Jesus, Jesus. She's got to learn to keep her mind on what's going on here and now."

She stands near him then, full of exasperation. "If her grades aren't suffering and she's not getting in with the wrong kids, I see no reason to interfere." She pauses and then averts her eyes from him, turning back toward the closet. "Little wonder she obsesses over Jesus. All the men in this family have checked out."

"Oh, well, there we have it." Mack brings a hand down to slap his thigh. "One more thing that's my fault. My kids are off doing things I don't even know about—because nobody bothers to tell me any-thing—and it's automatically traced back to me. I can see where this is going."

She takes a breath and begins to answer, but he cuts her off.

"I spend my days building arguments to defend myself, giving my-self reasons to explain things that happen *that have nothing to do with me!*"

"I'm not saying it's all your fault. But you have to understand that the child's lost an uncle and aunt and her cousins, and in some ways she's lost you too. She's just fourteen. She can't just suck it in and go on."

"She hasn't lost me. She never lost me."

"Yes, she did. When you wanted to die, you turned your back on her. No one blames you—you were ill and couldn't help it. But to a kid it feels like rejection when a parent doesn't want to stick around anymore."

He looks at her a long moment. "I'm back now. I'm right here. Does that even count to anybody here?"

Her lower lip sucks on the upper one, to keep words in, but it doesn't work. He can see that he is about to regret his insistence.

"Nothing counts right now," she says, a shirt in one hand, hanger in the other. "I can't afford to hope, Mack. I can't bring myself to rely on you. Sometime I will, but not now."

"Then why am I here?" He is louder than he means to be, and he glances toward the hallway and the kids' rooms.

She is calm, as she always is. Calm and unmoved. "You're here be-cause this is your home."

"But why? Why do you even want me back?"

"Mack, how am I supposed to answer that? What am I supposed to say? This is hard for everybody, you know that?"

"But especially for you, that's what you mean, isn't it?"

"Don't start this. Don't start this." Her hand is up like a shield. "Don't make this my fault."

"I wouldn't think of it. Because we all know it's my fault, right?" He jams a finger into his chest. "*I'm* the problem here."

"You're saying that—no one else is."

"No one else is saying *anything*, not to me anyway. I'm just the crazy guy come home to live. But no one's talking to me about any-thing."

She waves her arms. "What are we not talking to you about? Are we having secret discussions behind your back?"

"My guess is that you are."

"Oh!" She claps both hands to her head and walks to the window. "Please, please don't get paranoid on me. Please don't do that." She swings to look at him. "Are you taking your meds?"

"Yes, I'm on my meds. I'm doing everything the friggin' doctors tell me to do. I'm doing everything Mom tells me and everything you tell me. I'm being good!"

"Stop this!"

"You stop it!"

"Stop *what?*"

"Stop . . ." he wanders to the opposite corner, searching wildly for the thought he needs. "Stop treating me like I don't count anymore. Like you can't count on me—you said that yourself." He leans against the wall, bone-tired.

She puts down her flailing arms, walks back to the bed, and sits down. She doesn't look at him but stares out at the beanfield. Her voice softens. "There's a difference between not counting on you at all and not being willing to give you major responsibilities. I'm not going to ask you to jump in three weeks after getting home and take over finances, medical stuff, the kids' troubles, and all the rest. For one thing, I'd like to give you more time to get settled. For another, all those things are so critical that you can't let up the least little bit and keep up. I spend hours and hours a week dealing with all this. I've kept up with it for about three years now, and it's hard to just give it up and trust it to somebody else. I have my systems worked out."

"So what is it you can't count on me for, if you're not expecting me to do any of that?"

"I'm not sure. Just never mind."

"I can't 'never mind' when you say something like that. Look, I know you're mad as hell about all this—all of it. I know you've had to carry everything for a long time, and I think it *is* time that I take over something. I'm not the invalid everybody seems to think I am."

"It hasn't been that long, babe, since we were sitting up with you and hiding the guns."

The silence that follows expands between them. His words come out short, bitten: "So every time you need to win an argument now you'll be throwing that in my face?"

Color rises in her cheeks. She gets up from the bed and walks past him to the door. "If that's what you think I'm doing, then we've got no more to say to each other." He listens to her angry steps descending the stairs. There was a time when he would have heard sniffles too, but as far as he knows, she hasn't cried in a very long time. This in itself is reason enough to believe that she has withdrawn from him completely. His pain does not hurt her anymore. And she no longer responds with pain, but with anger—refined and practiced and filled with words so articulate they are sharp.

He looks at the bed, the dresser and closet, the chair, finally the window that faces the fields and fading sky.

This is not his home anymore. He finds no comfort here.

PART TWO

DISORIENTATION

4

BREAKING GROUND

I am a poor, wayfaring stranger, while journeying through
    this world of woe,
Yet, there's no sickness, toil nor danger, in that bright
    world to which I go.
I'm going there to see my Father, I'm going there no more
    to roam;
I'm only going over Jordan; I'm only going over home.
                 — *"Wayfaring Stranger"*

Rita

She can't believe that the world is well into October, until she steps
out the door and is chilled instantly. Wood smoke streams from two
or three nearby chimneys and lingers in a faint haze above backyards.
Whereas recent weeks were filled with the near-ominous presence of
fields brimming over and extending to every horizon, these days offer
a sort of emptiness. The harvested cornfields are dark expanses of
stubble, while the land looks shaved where soybeans stood just days
ago.

Rita gets in the car and drives in darkness past empty fields;
whether corn or beans, the bounty has been cut and cleared, stored or
sold, depending on market prices. The place always feels different the

first few days after combines have shuttled over the last acres. Once the ever-present crop dust has cleared, the country is less dense, the land swept by steady gusts that arrive from colder, distant places. People and livestock gulp at the atmosphere, enjoying the lower humidity and a slight spiciness in their nostrils.

Every autumn Rita finds a certain relief: the high-labor seasons are over for now, and all that's left are the shortening days and hardening land. Remaining plant matter sours and disintegrates into the topsoil. The cold and quiet are on their way, and nearly everything will soon have opportunity for rest.

There is no real rest for the weary, however, and Rita has been in overdrive all day, having begun her fall cleaning at six this morning. She has sorted through her kitchen, leaving just one cupboard for tomorrow. After a tuna-sandwich supper, she listened to the news on television while sorting through her coupon drawer, and in doing so she discovered about twenty coupons that were but a day or two from expiration. Well, Jodie goes shopping in Oskaloosa tomorrow. Between her cart and Rita's, hardly a bargain will be lost.

Maybe she's restless from a day of sifting through things. Really, though, she just wants to see the kids. No one dropped by today, which is unusual but not unheard of. Whenever Mack goes more than a day without showing up, she goes to him. She tells herself that it's because of his recent rough spell. But mainly she needs to see her boy. It's just natural. He lives but a few miles away, and cold or not, Rita starts up her poor car and heads for the farm. It's late, but no one goes to bed early anymore now that the kids are teenagers.

When she turns down the long driveway, it is nearly ten at night, and every light in the house is on—like an old factory with the late shift in full swing. In windows on both floors she can see their silhouettes: Kenzie in her bedroom, Jodie in the kitchen, and Mack in their bedroom upstairs. It should make Rita happy, seeing her family home at day's end. But even the unoccupied rooms are fully lit, and the house looks strangely alert, as if someone were very ill and other family members were trying to find medicine or extra blankets and calling a doctor or the pastor. The outdoors has turned quite brisk since nightfall, and it's time for people to be snug under covers, not wandering around in confusion.

"Oh, Lord, Lord, what's going on?" The air bites at her joints when she gets out of the car. She sees Jodie look out the window in her direction, then move toward the back door. It opens before Rita reaches the steps.

"Mom, what are you doing out this time of night?"

"Oh, I found some coupons. You said you'd be going to town early tomorrow."

Jodie doesn't respond to that. She could say, *And you're going with me—why drive out here now?* But that would miss the point entirely. The warm kitchen smells of garlic and apples—and maybe muffins of some kind. Rita has started coughing, and Jodie guides her to a chair at the table.

"That sounds awful. You're really congested."

"Oh—" Rita stops to take a better breath. She can hear the slight sound of her own chest whistling. "It's worse at night, you know."

"Have you taken anything?"

"This afternoon I took one of those fizzy cold tablets. I think the date on them is old."

"I've got some high-powered stuff." Jodie has a glass in hand. She opens the narrow cupboard next to the window over the sink and picks through medicine bottles and small pieces of bubbled cardboard with colored pills encased in the plastic. "Here. This will help you sleep too."

"Where are the kids?"

"Upstairs. Kenzie's got her nose in a book probably." Jodie doesn't venture any ideas about Young Taylor. About all the boy does these days is listen to music and read magazines with names like *Industrial Nation*.

"What's Mack up to?"

Jodie seems preoccupied and doesn't answer.

"If he's up, I'll go say hello before I go."

"How's the car doing? I'm surprised you'd bring it out this time of night."

"It's just fine. That new starter did the trick." Rita gets up from her chair and reaches around Jodie to put her glass in the dishwater. "I'll say hi to Mack."

"He might be in bed."

After all these years, Rita can sense when Jodie is withholding information, something she rarely does with Rita, even though she's pretty tight-lipped around people outside the family. The shape of her shoulders just now, when she is turned away from Rita, gives the impression of something gone wrong. Rita does her best not to grunt as her sore knees move her up the stairs. She walks past Kenzie's room; its door is shut, as is Young Taylor's. Rita can see the slit of light under the door to Mack and Jodie's bedroom. She steps up to it and taps lightly.

The door opens and Mack, fully dressed, looks at her in surprise. "Mom? Everything okay? Kind of late to be out."

There are white dots at his cheekbones, the signal Rita feared. Those dots appear when he's upset. And his eyes hold the same desperation and great fatigue that glowered in them during the weeks prior to the hospital business.

"I'm fine, Mack. How about you?"

He doesn't answer. Just looks at her, his lips in a straight line.

"Are you feeling all right?" She stands ready to hear the worst. Lord knows, she tries to be an optimist, but so many times the worst has been exactly what she's had to hear.

"Oh, I've decided to take a little break."

Rita can't make sense of that. "From what?"

He opens the door then, sighing a bit, and lets her in. There is his suitcase on the bed, open and half filled with clothes. It makes her think of those scenes in the movies when a couple has had a fight and one of them reaches up into the closet and pulls down a suitcase. Which is funny, because most suitcases are pushed back out of reach and covered with blankets or old clothes. And then when they're opened, they've likely got other stuff inside them—wrapping paper, wool sweaters, or receipts and records a person is afraid to throw away. It's never as simple as one-two-three.

But here is Mack's suitcase, which he unpacked barely a month ago, when he got home from the hospital.

Rita tries to read his face for more information. "What's going on?"

He looks down the hall, toward the kids' rooms, and then closes the door and walks over to the bed. He sits on one side of the suitcase, Rita on the other. She looks at the rolled-up socks, the shirts neatly folded.

"I'm going out to the stone house for a while."

"Why on earth?"

He shrugs, trying to make this a small thing. He's had that shrug since he was a toddler. "Just need some time to myself. Jodie and me—we're both feeling a lot of pressure right now."

She doesn't know what to say. Time to himself? Two weeks in the hospital wasn't enough?

"Well, you can't stay out there. It's nearly winter."

"The stove still works. We used to stay out there all the time, fall and winter both."

"But it's not set up for someone to stay more than a few days. There's no refrigerator, no real furniture that I can remember."

"I'll pull together some things. I won't be there long."

"If you need to get away, come to my place. I've got that extra bed-room. I'll just cook for two—would be a nice change."

"No, I appreciate that, but I need this other thing right now."

Rita picks up a pair of socks, unrolls them, and then rolls them back again. "Mack, you and Jodie can't split up so soon after this spell you've had. You've got to give it time. What does she think about this?"

"She's not real happy about it." Mack looks at his hands. "But she wants me to do . . . what I need to do."

"Did you have a bad argument or something?"

"We're working on things." Despite his worry dots, Mack appears to be quite calm. He makes a point to meet Rita's gaze. "We're okay."

Rita looks back down at the suitcase. She sighs, but it turns into another fit of coughing.

"What are you doing out in this cold, coughing like that?" The shrugging toddler is her grown son again, trying to sound authoritative with her.

"I forgot to bring some things to Jodie today. I wasn't sleeping anyway."

"Want me to drive you home?"

"No! The car is just fine. I drove here, and I'll drive back." She gets up and goes to the door. "I don't like this, Mack. It can't be good for you to be out there by yourself." She turns suddenly. "Does that counselor know about this?"

"Not yet."

"Well, why don't you wait until you talk with him?"

Her son doesn't answer but ushers her out to the hallway. He walks her as far as the stairwell. They stop on the landing, surrounded by a history of the kids' school years, static smiles hung in patterns against the wallpaper.

"I'll come out there and bring you something to eat at least. I'll find some furniture for you too. Lord knows I've got too much for that little house of mine."

"No need for that, Mom. I'll be fine." His words echo down the stairwell, sounding confident.

Jodie is seated at the kitchen table, doing nothing. Rita sits down across from her. "What happened?"

"I don't know."

"Did you have a fight?"

Jodie's glance tells her that this is a silly question. She and Mack have had fights for years. They fight, they make up. "Not lately, but I've known for a few weeks that he's unsettled."

"Oh, Lord—"

"Not like before. He swears he's not depressed, and he doesn't act like he is."

"I don't think it's good for him to move out."

"He's not going far. We'll still see him every day. I don't think we need to look at this as some major thing."

"Well, I do."

"He'll be fine, Mom."

"Maybe you should go to counseling together."

"I'm ready to go anytime he and the therapist think it's time."

"Mack knows that?"

"Of course he does. Let me walk you out. Do you want Young Taylor to follow you into town?"

"No." Rita can hear the anger in her own voice. It disturbs her to sound like this. She's upset more than angry, but she knows that she sounds angry and that Jodie will think she's decided this mess is all Jodie's fault.

The thought of Mack out there in that old house keeps Rita awake, although the cold medicine makes her groggy. She fixes herself some tea and decides to go ahead and write this new prayer in her little book, a prayer requesting that the Lord shake some sense into her son. And she wanders all through the house, even out to the garage, finding things to take out to the stone house tomorrow.

Mack

The next morning the kids are ready for school earlier than usual. On a typical day, Mack hears them sniping at each other in hoarse, waking-up voices while he sits downstairs and watches the early news out of Des Moines. But today they are nearly finished with breakfast when Mack sits at the table. Before leaving for the school cafeteria, Jodie fixed the coffee and put out the cereal and milk, as she always does. But when Mack sits down, he knows that the quiet at the table is unnatural, the sign of his kids waiting for another shoe to drop.

"Young Taylor, I'll need your help later today," he says after a moment.

"Okay."

Mack pours milk over the cereal. Young Taylor takes a bite of his, then says, "When?"

"After school. It won't take long. I need to move some things to the stone house."

"What's going out there?" Young Taylor stares at the glass he's just emptied of milk, turning it in his hand as though to assess its value.

"The old sofa. The refrigerator from the garage."

Kenzie looks at him for the first time, and he can see that she feels betrayed. Surely they know. Jodie probably told them last night after he went to bed. He decides to make it clear, just in case.

"I'll be staying out there for a while."

They don't ask if he is going hunting. They don't ask him anything, just finish their breakfast and gather their things for school.

Well, no time would have been right for this. He made the decision weeks ago, after his blowout with Jodie over Kenzie's church business. But things kept happening—extra busy at Hendrikson's, then he was in Ed's fields, helping get the corn in. And Young Taylor's attitude was particularly nasty for a few days. But last night Mack sat across from his wife after supper was cleared, and they looked at each other, and he could not form any sentences for her, or them. The pressure moved in on him from all sides, and he took a last gulp of coffee and didn't look at her when he spoke.

"Jo, I've gotta find some space somewhere. I'm no good to you here."

Her face told him nothing; maybe there was a flicker of fear, or hurt, but he couldn't linger with it.

"Where do you want to be, Mack?"

"Close by, but just not here all the time."

The stone house stands on the original Decker homestead. In 1854 Mack's forebears built a cabin there, on the higher bank of the stream, one of many little branches off the North Skunk River. The wife, Elda, insisted that they build near the water and in the woods. They'd moved over from Indiana, and she needed the feel of trees about her.

This five acres has never been cleared of hackberry, silver maples, and cottonwoods. The Deckers' son built the larger farmhouse a generation after them. The sturdier parts of that original house form the center of the house Mack's family lives in. Over the years and generations, rooms were added to every side of the house, and outbuildings were built, torn down, or left to sag gradually back to earth.

Elda and Hiram's son, Andrew, married once and lost his wife when she bore their first child, a daughter. The girl loved the land and found for herself a young farmer who was more than happy to find not only a wife but one with land. Together they added six children to the family, four of whom lived past the age of ten. Two of the remaining four were sons, and both died in the war, so the homestead went to the eldest daughter, Mack's grandmother. During that generation of births and losses, the family added acres to the farm. By the time Mack was born, it was a sizeable spread.

Sixty years ago, Mack's grandfather and Taylor Senior replaced the original cabin ruins by the stream with a two-room lodge of native limestone, equipping it with a wood-burning stove and running water. It stands near the corner of two county roads, which over time have gathered other farmhouses. The horse barn that stood not far from the cabin was torn down years ago to its lower stone level and replaced with a simpler structure where hay and feed could be stored and cattle sheltered in cold weather.

Now Tom Adams rents the barn and its surrounding small pasture. Today the wind whistles through the cracks, and a dozen or so head of Holsteins congregate there when Mack and Young Taylor pull up the gravel drive.

The drive leads to the barn and gives no indication that a few hundred yards to the east, in the middle of old, tall trees, there sits a small stone house. It has become a place for the kids to play in warm weather, for extra relatives to sleep when necessary, and for the men to occupy when fishing and hunting. It can comfortably sleep six or seven full-grown men in sleeping bags, and no women fret when they track in mud or blood, rise up and clatter coffee cups and thermoses at ungodly hours, or stay up late smoking and having more beer than usual.

The old Frigidaire played out several years ago; its corpse lies on its side, the door removed, on the west side of the barn. The last several years have been so full of fatigue and panic that Mack and Alex didn't need the stone house for hunting or fishing. After Mack gave up his part of the farm, his time with Alex was strained.

So the place has gathered dust and the droppings of small animals. The daybed against the wall squeaks but seems sturdy enough. Young Taylor and Mack scoot the refrigerator into the place of the old one. This one needs to be defrosted often and is marred and rusty, the place where they've been keeping extra ice and soft drinks and frozen items. Jodie wordlessly cleared out what she wanted last night. She even dug out a blanket for covering the sofa, the one on the back porch piled with boxes and work jackets. It is the type of furniture that would have been moved to the stone house long ago if the house had been in use, if that part of family life had continued—the summer fun, the men's time together, the little getaways.

When he and Young Taylor finish with the moving, Mack takes his son back to the farmhouse. "Thanks, son. I'll see you all in the morning." Young Taylor says good-bye, lightly. Mack doesn't know what the lightness means, and his own emotions stop him from pondering that.

This first evening, Mack spends an hour cleaning out the stove, gathering wood, and starting a decent fire. By then the sky has gone dark, and he doesn't catch the sun sliding down and the colors changing. He planned on those moments, feeling the need for that kind of transition to mark this retreat he's made for himself. But by the time he deals with the stove and fire, he is tired and sore and hungry and thirsty. Most of all, he feels so alone that he wants to march back up the road and into his home. He wants to snap out of this and just settle down and make life work. But the small room is gritty and cold around him, and the night outside is too quiet. From time to time he hears a vehicle over on the road, just barely. If he strains, he can hear some burbling from the stream, but the night and cold dampen every-thing. He wishes he'd brought a radio or a book, something to help pass the time.

Kenzie

Prayer time today is painful and tiring. Kenzie's heart just isn't in it. Something dark and uncomfortable keeps welling up there. Instead of praising God and thanking him for all his goodness, she keeps hearing questions pop out of her mouth.

"Why are you letting Dad do this?"

"I thought you were healing him. How am I supposed to pray when I can't tell if you've really answered the prayers I prayed be-fore?"

"If you'd just tell me what to do, I'd do it. Why don't you have something to tell me about Mom and Dad? Don't you think I'd be faithful?"

She leaves the sanctuary totally frustrated. The gray evening clouds spread over her as she pedals down the road. So it is with a sudden, overwhelming relief that she sees Mitchell Jaylee standing at his mailbox, one elbow resting on top of it. She stops in front of him and says hi.

"How are you this evening? About to freeze?" His face looks full of conversation he is waiting to have. The injury to his right eye is healed, and the patch is gone. Even in the twilight his eyes have warm light in them.

"Yes."

"Want some cocoa?"

"I need to get home." The word *home* makes her realize how much she dreads being there. "But I can take time for cocoa."

She follows him inside the house. It is dim but seems clean enough, with magazines and tools lying around. She sits in the tiny breakfast nook and watches him put water on to boil and get out cups and packets of hot chocolate.

"How's your sculpture coming?" It is so cool to be in on Mitchell's artistic life. Because she's never heard anyone talk about it, Kenzie fig-ures that she is the only person who has seen his work.

"Oh, great! I added three pieces to it since you were here last time."

"Wow. What are they?"

"Let's see, the seat of an old lawn mower . . . a scythe . . . and one of those old baking tins that has indentions shaped like corncobs."

"Awesome."

"I'll show you while the water's heating." He leads the way through the back door and into the barn. When he turns on the lights, the cold, dusty space is flooded with orange-yellow. Kenzie walks closer to the sculpture.

"I see the mower seat . . . and there's the pan." She looks and looks but can't find the scythe.

"Give up?"

"No!" She points a warning finger, and he laughs. "I'll find it." As her eyes search through the scramble of metal for the round blade, she feels Mitchell watching her. It makes it hard for her to get a good breath. It also makes her feel safe. He comes closer while she searches. Finally, she sees the scythe, worked into the chicken wire so that the blade itself hardly shows, but the handle forms a sudden angle. "There it is."

"Good. I think you should try sculpting for yourself."

"I don't think I really get it."

"You don't get it before you do it. It gets *you*."

"Huh." This is a different concept, but she sees the sense of it right away—the idea that something determines your destiny rather than you determining anything. After all, Jesus said, "You did not choose me, but I chose you." He said it to the disciples. Kenzie thinks about how every person is probably chosen for something.

Mitchell laughs again, softly. "You're shivering. Let's go back in-side." He waits until she is outside before reaching back and shutting off the lights. Then he rests a hand, just barely, on her waist. "Watch it—I've got some old boards here to your left."

"Thanks." She walks slowly enough to keep that contact between them, all the way to the house. It makes her feel so cared for, this hand on her back. Suddenly her throat hurts and hot tears form in her eyes. She blinks frantically so that Mitchell won't see once they are in the house again.

But he is noticing everything. She isn't used to being studied like this. "You got a cold?" he asks.

"Uh, yeah, a little." She sits at the table and won't look at him. He finds a paper napkin and hands it to her.

"Guess it's time I put you on *my* prayer list," he says, smiling.

She stares at him. Could he know this—that his name is written on her list?

"I know you pray for me, Kenzie." He empties the chocolate pack-ets into the cups of hot water.

"How would you know who I pray for?"

"Oh, I can just tell. You've got that kind of a soul. I bet you pray for a lot of people. And I bet that anybody you meet goes on that list in your head."

"Are you mad that somebody would pray for you?"

"Oh, no! It really touches me that you would do that. Are you cry-ing?"

This moment has slipped out of her control. Something inside her collapses, and the tears spill out of her eyes and down her face. She tries to catch them with the napkin. She feels Mitchell close beside her, pressing a fresh one into her hand.

"I didn't mean to upset you, Kenzie." His voice is gentler than any voice of any person who has ever talked to her.

"You didn't upset me. I was already upset. Everything's so awful."

"What's awful?" He is stroking her sleeve. It's just a matter of Kenzie leaning a little bit for her to be against his chest and for his arms to be around her shoulders. She lets go then, and her crying shakes both of them.

After that part is over and she's blown her nose and Mitchell has set their cups of cocoa on the table, Kenzie talks a long time. About

Dad and Mom. About her discipline of prayer and the times when Jesus's eyes move and when she floats. About how Young Taylor is into things he shouldn't be. About how nobody else in her family seems to have faith anymore, and now they need it more than ever. She talks, and Mitchell just listens.

After she's finished talking and the cocoa is gone and after Mitchell has given her a strong hug good-bye, Kenzie rides home feeling changed. Jesus knew that she needed a spiritual friend. This has been the plan all along. He is watching over her after all. God has heard her prayers and answered them better than she would have answered them herself.

She gets home late, and Mom and Young Taylor have already eaten. Mom doesn't ask questions about where Kenzie has been. She is distracted, cleaning out one of the closets upstairs. Mom sorts things when she is upset. She throws things away too. Kenzie decides to look through the spare room first thing tomorrow to make sure there's nothing in there she still wants. It's the room where all the odd clothes go—the jacket that needs the lining fixed or the jeans with a stuck zipper. But other items land there too, when Mom picks them up and doesn't know where they go or who they belong to. So Kenzie will look out for her personal property, because, with Dad gone again, Mom will likely clean and sort and throw things away all week.

Jodie

It is the worst of all times to get a call from her former sister-in-law. Jodie isn't in the mood to talk with anybody. But Marty's voice is friendly, and it sounds as close as next door rather than all the way to Omaha.

Marty just wants to hear how everybody is. Even though she hasn't lived in the area for nearly three years, she has a couple of friends who keep her updated. For instance, she knew about Mack's hospital stay. She called Jodie that very week. Marty has never stopped caring about her husband's family. But some ties are just too tender to put much weight on. Jodie and Marty have kept a polite distance, especially since Alex's death. It's as if both of them know that any conversation will have to lead to that event and to other events that are over with and that nobody can fix.

"So how are you, Jo?"

"Oh, doing all right. You?"

"We're fine. I'm thinking we'll come down sometime around Christmas."

"Good. We'll put you up here."

Jodie becomes sad all over again, about Marty and the kids not living around here anymore. They don't live that far away even now. And Marty has been dating someone pretty seriously. Well, good for her. Jodie wonders if the guy is someone her niece and nephew like, or if this shift is one more variation of hell for them to survive. But she sincerely hopes Marty will get back on her feet.

"I heard that Mack's back from the hospital."

"Yeah, he's back." Jodie can't think of a single word to follow that.

"God, Jo, is it that bad?"

Jodie sighs into the receiver. "To be honest with you, I feel like I'm always one dinnertime away from complete annihilation."

"I know, I know. I'm sorry it's so hard."

Jodie remembers the day her sister-in-law stopped by and sat at this kitchen table and said, "I can't do this anymore." She could no longer bear to walk into the bank to ask for more money. Alex's lack of coping skills left everything up to Marty. All the juggling of bills to pay and no money to pay them with. All the times picking up the phone and having to hear from creditor after creditor. All the trips to this business and that to explain, once more, why the balance couldn't be paid off yet. Her life, like every farmer's wife's, was filled with record keeping and calculations, endless forms and appeals. Marty sat up later and later, strategizing with pencil and calculator, and Alex disappeared frequently to drink, more than once bringing the pickup back late at night, dented and scratched up from forays into ditches and fence posts. So that bright afternoon in March, Marty spoke the unthinkable to Jodie in a deathly quiet kitchen. She said that maybe if she just quit taking care of everything, something in Alex would come to life again. She didn't know, but this was where she had to stop.

Of course, Alex did not rise and heal, did not sober up. Everything fell deeper into the hole. And he and Marty fought so horribly that the whole family thought one of them might kill the other.

"It's not as bad as I'm making it sound," Jodie says. She realizes how quiet the house is. She has no idea where her kids have gone. "He's trying so hard to be useful, and I wish he'd just relax. And then he gets defensive because he doesn't think I trust him to do any-thing."

"It's that idiot guy stuff. Got to be competent, in control."

"I think that's what brought him down the first time."

"It'll work out, Jo. You and Mack have a real strength between you."

Jodie does not say that Mack has moved out of the house. Instead, she remembers vividly when Marty packed up the kids and headed for Omaha to stay with her parents. They stopped long enough to say good-bye to Rita, Mack, Jodie, and the kids. But she'd left the family before that day. They'd all felt her twisting against the tight-lipped resignation they had all grown to wear so well. She left, and Alex died, and God only knows what suffering that has dealt her. Jodie wonders if Marty lies awake still, all this time later, and replays her last words to Alex, replays herself walking out the door, and condemns herself for his death. Some things Jodie will not allow herself to think about for more than a second or two, the pain of those seconds being so swift and complete.

After she hangs up the phone, Jodie walks into the front room of the house. Its picture window overlooks a harvested beanfield, its au-tumn presence lumpy and gray. During the warm months Jodie gazed over the endless rows, their young leaves twittering and green, inch-ing up and filling out, day by day. She has stood here and watched the motion of breezes through the rows, has breathed in the smell of seedlings growing earthy and luxurious.

When she was a child, living with her parents on the edge of another farm town, she imagined that angels played in the fields, that the wind sounds were really angel whispers, and that when the greenness rippled from one end of the field to the other, the angels were playing. She remembers how intent she used to be on seeing the angels. She would wander out in early mornings, through her parents' back gate, and venture into the neighbors' fields. Somewhere she'd gotten the idea that angels become visible in the half-light exactly between night and day. So she would shiver in her pajamas and jacket and tiptoe into a row of corn and look hard at the spaces between the stalks. The angels never became visible to her, but she never doubted they were there.

She stares now, through the large window Mack and Alex installed when their families were young, and the view before her appears infinite. The sense of distance cuts her to the core. So many people she loves are far away now. Her mother and brother Paul, Marty and the kids. Wayfarers, they are off to other regions, following their individual roads. And then there are the dead, who are farthest away of all. She wonders if Daddy, Taylor Senior, and Alex wander the fields as she once imagined the angels did, playing in the breezes and watching over the ongoing family story.

Maybe Jodie is the true wayfarer. Mom and Paul, Marty and Sharon and David are at least headed somewhere. And the deceased have arrived to wherever they were going. It is Jodie who wanders now, from room to room and memory to memory. Even as she stands fast in her living room, she is lost. When she scans the field beyond her window, it is for some sign. She remembers vividly the day she lost five-year-old Kenzie. One moment Kenzie was playing in the sandbox Mack had built for the kids to the east of the vegetable garden; the next moment she was simply gone. Jodie was alone—Mack and Alex were in fields several acres away—and her frightened calls for little Kenzie turned quickly into screams. Then, as she looked out at the soybeans for maybe the twentieth time, there was the rapid bobbing of a sun-streaked head of hair, nearly a hundred yards out. Jodie ran toward the movement in the field, and mother and daughter met and locked under the glare of midday.

The old hymn about the wayfarer puts reunion in each verse: "I'm going there to see my father ... savior ... companions." Jodie no longer knows who exactly she longs to meet in that awful space between now and forever, who she hopes will appear between the crop rows. All she knows is how much it hurts to stand alone at her window now, and how much she wants to believe in angels again.

She leaves the front room and studies the calendar on the kitchen wall. Before long, her niece and nephew will be here. Marty will once again sit at the table and sip coffee and wax gently sarcastic about any and all matters. Christmas. Jodie can't bring herself to think about that. It is just two months away, and nothing is ready. Worse, she doesn't have any inclination to work at a celebration of any kind. She flirts with the idea of going by herself down to Galveston right on the holiday, let the rest of them fend for themselves. But no, that would be too simple. It would be too much of a comfort for her, to be with her own mom, near the ocean, not having to lift a finger.

5

BUYING TIME

Beneath the cross of Jesus I fain would take my stand,
The shadow of a mighty rock within a weary land;
A home within the wilderness, a rest upon the way,
From the burning of the noontide heat, and the burden of
    the day.

—*"Beneath the Cross of Jesus"*

Rita

In the space of a morning, Rita has pulled together three boxes of items to take out to the stone house. Pots and pans, linens, soap, cereal and all manner of canned goods, blankets—she even bought a new one at the pharmacy. If Mack is going to soul-search out by himself in the woods, then he needs to at least be comfortable. This is still within Rita's power.

Amos helps her load the stuff. He doesn't ask where it is going, just assumes that she is taking it to somebody's house or to the local food pantry or something. And Rita doesn't enlighten him. He is half-deaf and not that connected to community gossip anymore, so chances are Mack will do his little retreat and get himself back home without Amos—or her other neighbors—hearing anything about it.

Mack isn't at the stone house when she pulls up. It occurs to her then that this is a weekday and of course he'd be at Hendrikson's. He is still holding down his job, after all.

Well, she can't carry the boxes in by herself. She sits in the concealed drive, a chilly wind whipping against the car. The minute she gets out in that wind, she knows the coughing will start again. And she'll have to make trip after trip to the house, unloading the boxes a handful at a time.

She looks at her watch. Young Taylor should be out of school by now. She shifts into reverse and heads for the farmhouse.

When she gets there, she stays in the car and honks. Jodie appears at the back door. She reaches for a corduroy jacket and wraps it around herself as she skips out to the car. Rita rolls down the window just enough to talk.

"Young Taylor here?"

"No."

"I need him to help me."

"Can I do it?"

"Can you leave now?"

"Sure." Jodie hops in.

"I'm just taking some things out to Mack."

Jodie looks into the boxes on the backseat and says nothing.

"Got extra—it's just taking up space."

"He told me he didn't need anything."

"He does—just doesn't know it yet."

Jodie laughs.

"What's so funny?"

"Oh. That's quite a statement: he needs something but doesn't know it yet."

Rita thinks about that and chuckles. "I suppose that applies to just about everybody, doesn't it?"

Jodie insists that Rita stay in the car while she carries the boxes in. It takes her all of ten minutes. Her cheeks are pink by the time she gets back in the car.

"He'll think it's Christmas."

"Have you seen him today?"

"No, he's at work."

"He doesn't even stop by in the morning?"

"Just to pick up the kids and take them to school. Speaking of Christmas, Marty called and said that she and the kids were planning to come down for the holidays."

Rita's heart makes an extra powerful thump. She'll finally get to see David and Sharon. They are both teenagers now. Immediately, a new list forms in her brain, all that she has to get accomplished before they come. When they get back to the farm, she is so distracted by the sudden new plans that she barely hears Jodie say good-bye.

My Lord, Christmas is around the corner, isn't it? She has lots of cooking to do in the next few weeks. And shopping. And helping all her old folks with their shopping and their Christmas cards. And extra church events.

As she enters Beulah's city limits she sees Young Taylor on foot, apparently heading home. She slams on the brakes and honks. He looks up and doesn't appear happy. But he comes to her side of the car.

"Let me give you a ride."

"I'm fine, Grandma."

"It's miles to walk!"

"I'm not going straight home. Eric's meeting me at the video store."

"It's too cold out here! And why aren't you getting a lift from your dad? He should be getting off work in just a little while."

"Dad needs his space."

She stares at her grandson, trying to read something in those shadowy eyes of his. "What in the world does that mean?"

"I don't think he wants any company right now. Eric will drive me home later."

He turns from her suddenly and continues down the street. Rita slowly pushes on the gas and moves toward home. What makes teenagers so sullen? Were they always that way? What a thing for Young Taylor to say about his dad. She needs to talk to Mack about this. Maybe she should stop at Hendrikson's before he gets off work. Maybe she should drive back out to the stone house and be waiting for him there. She could cook something and have it ready for him.

But she hasn't yet delivered medicine to Mrs. Garvey. Since her stroke, Mrs. Garvey depends on Rita—and others—a lot. It is that or the nursing home. Rita has long suspected that the day Elaine Garvey figures out they are planning to ship her to the nursing home, she'll eat rat poison or something.

So here is an old woman who'll die before leaving her house. And then here is this son who is compelled to not be in his home at all. In a perfect world, Rita would own a mansion and just put everybody in his or her own room. At least then she could stay out of the weather.

Mack

The first Sunday after his move, Mack wakes up at five because he's cold. He digs out one of the blankets his mother brought. But he can't sleep, so decides to get up. The dawn has slipped behind lately, brightening the woods later and later. For a few moments, while Mack stokes the fire and revels in the heat and makes his coffee, his mind fills with plans for the day, even the week. This is a new start. He will figure things out here. But the enthusiasm fades when he stands up and looks around the place, looks outside at the dark sodden ground. His ideas always require much more energy than he actually has. For all of his planning, he comes to consciousness at about nine o'clock and realizes that he is still hunched beside the stove, clutching a cold and empty coffee cup.

He goes to church and is glad to see Jodie there. Religion used to be a simple thing. Life was arranged around regular times of worship, prayer meetings sometimes, holiday programs, and the church dinners that felt as familiar as noonday meals at the Lunch Hour. The same people were always at church. The same women prepared the same dishes for potlucks. The same folks became disgruntled over every little thing or helped the rest of them keep a sense of humor. Belief about God wove in and out of conversations with people in the next pew and then in the discussion of pork prices over doughnuts and coffee after the prayers were finished.

Now there is some hitch in all of this. Mack sits next to Jodie this morning and tries to feel calm and normal. He tries to be comforted by the words he has always known by heart: the story of the woman at the well, the prayer requests that nearly always include someone entering chemotherapy or facing surgery. The announcements of church events that remain essentially the same year in and year out. There is the pancake breakfast to raise money for the senior ministry, a request from the local food pantry for extra donations with the holidays coming up. But Mack can't listen to them in the same way. He feels twitchy and tired at once. When the prayer requests roll around in their predictability, he silently questions their usefulness. *Will this make any difference? Will the cancer disappear now that we've mentioned it?* He has the sudden urge to add to the list. *I can't bring myself to live in my own house with my wife and kids—how would you announce that, pastor? The Barrys aren't here this week; I heard at work that she's filed for divorce. Where does that fit? An announcement or a prayer request?*

To stop these thoughts, he blinks several times and shifts position. Why should he suddenly be so bothered? Why can't he just sit here and let the words come and go, same as always? They sing the closing hymn, and he turns to Jodie. Seeing the blankness in her face, he wonders if she ever has the sort of mental arguments he's just waged in his own head.

"Sweet, do you want to go over to the steak place for lunch?"

Her expression is pleasant enough. "Well, I was just going to make spaghetti anyway. Sure." She turns to Rita and then informs Kenzie. Young Taylor didn't come to church. They leave in their three vehicles, Mack taking the lead, and travel a couple of miles down the highway and pull into the parking lot that is just beginning to fill; it's a popular after-church place. The steaks are cheap and come with baked potato and salad bar. Rita mentions another restaurant that has added a hot food bar as well, but she's not complaining. This is merely her ongoing assessment of local food establishments.

As they sit at the table together, Mack watches his mother, wife, and daughter. He misses his son but knows that Young Taylor's presence would add more tension than pleasure. It seems to be Young Taylor's job in life to add tension and see what the rest of them do with it. This thought occurs to Mack just as swiftly as the other thoughts intruded during church. He piles sour cream on his baked potato and asks his mother if she still goes to the nursing home every Sunday afternoon. He knows that she does and that she will now give them the rundown on the residents they know, and on some they don't. He is able to relax as the space fills with her words; he doesn't have to respond to them, only to let them be. This is what he wants more than anything in life—to let things be, and to be left alone.

They say good-bye in the parking lot. Mack takes his time driving back to the stone house, going by a different route to lengthen the trip. He is not yet comfortable with being alone for hours. Maybe he should have accepted Jodie's invitation to come hang out with her and Kenzie at the farmhouse. But he needs to dive into solitude and suffer through it and come out on the other side. He's not sure there is another side, but he may as well find out sooner rather than later.

Most of the trees have faded lately under harvest dust, but the burr oaks and maples around the stone house have turned, filling the atmosphere with their own lights. This time of year the air is faintly sour with early decay. Already the cottonwoods have shaken leaves from their highest branches, layering the ground in dull brown.

He spends the afternoon gathering wood. He does nothing but walk slowly in one direction and then another, gazing along the ground for twigs and limbs. After a while he begins to separate the wood according to size. He finds a box that once contained a microwave and fills it with kindling. He fills a leaky bucket with the driest twigs. He piles larger sticks to themselves, breaking them across his knee to make them kindling size. Fallen limbs are another pile; these he'll have to saw into manageable pieces.

There is a lot to be gathered right around the house. The clearing has filled up over the years with underbrush and small trees. But a bit farther out the woods are older, and the trees there have been shedding dead branches for decades. A broken limb, a tree split by lightning. Through an afternoon of searching the ground for firewood, Mack is aware of just how cluttered the ground can be without looking cluttered. When he sleeps that night, he dreams of tree parts in all their shapes and thicknesses. He keeps picking up branches through the night.

The next afternoon, when he gets home from work, he repairs the firewood rack his dad made years ago, and he fills it with the larger logs. By then, it's too dark to work. So the next day he searches out a few larger limbs and saws them into firewood, using an old bow saw. There was a time when Mack would have tossed that aside and gone back to the farm for the chainsaw. But now he has lots of empty time, and it's satisfying to do the cutting by hand. The following afternoon he is back at it again. It is a sunny day, and cold enough for a jacket. After a while Mack has slowed to an easy rhythm with the saw. He finds himself watching with interest the teeth biting into the wood and the orange dust building up around the blade.

He spends hours and hours with wood. With trees and twigs, breathing in the scent of fresh shavings and rotted stumps. By midweek he can close his eyes and identify five or six types of trees just by feeling their bark. He wakes up each morning, and his gaze wanders out to treetops. Wherever he goes he walks over roots. Trees become his habit.

He moved to the stone house on Friday, and by Monday he knew that he'd not moved far enough. Rita showed up with a backseat full of canned goods and blankets and old dinnerware. She soon ascertained that there was no place to store most of it, so she hauled him back to town to help her load a dresser and utility shelf. Of course, she insisted on staying to cook dinner. Mack decided to stand back from all of this and not get upset. The old leopard would not change her spots, and she seemed less panicky about the situation as long as she was doing something. So let her bring out a dozen bran-banana muffins. That was less cooking he had to do.

But by now, Wednesday, when the old car rumbles up to his door, something inside Mack reaches its limit. Mom has worn a whole new set of ruts in the ground around the house. He looks out and sees her trying to wrestle a footstool out of the trunk—the one covered with curtain fabric that has been filled for years with old hunting maga- zines—and he strides out the door, both hands in the air.

"Mom, I don't need that. No. Leave it—just take it to the thrift store."

"But you've always used a footstool."

"Well, I don't now." He grabs the edge of the stool and maneuvers it back into the trunk. She glares at him when he shuts the lid. "I don't need anything else."

She changes gears in record time, turning toward the house. "You've not had any supper I'll bet."

"I've got everything I need. You just go home. It's getting too cold for you to be driving around this late in the day."

She stops and does her pressed-lips look, pulling her jacket tighter. "You act like you're trying to get rid of me."

"I'm out here by myself for a reason."

"What do you think about out here?" Her directness takes him by surprise. She has shifted her weight to one leg, her arms crossed and making her look more formidable than ever. "Out here all by your- self—what do you think about, son? That's what worries me. When people stay to themselves too much, they start having thoughts that aren't good for them."

"Not always."

"Sometimes they go a little crazy."

"Well, I've already been crazy, so the prospect doesn't scare me so much now." He sees her immediate disapproval and laughs to indicate that he's joking. "Mom, I'm doing all right."

"You're sleeping well?" There's that mother tone that is so hard to resist. "You still have an appetite?"

"I'm sleeping and eating just fine."

Her eyes mist over then, and she reaches up and pecks him on the cheek. Then she pulls away fast and goes back to her car. Mack wishes he'd taken that moment to give her a hug, something she probably needs more than she would admit. But she flashes that strong smile and a little wave, and drives off without looking back.

Mack goes back to the house and sits on one of the two chairs left from an old dinette set, his feet up on the daybed. He's arranged it so that he can sit like this and look out the window and into the woods. He does this often, and many minutes might go by before he notices or changes position.

Jodie

"This is a bad idea. A really bad idea."

In the privacy of the truck cab, Jodie tries to entertain common sense. She's had so many discussions with herself in this junky space that she may as well just tape the set of speeches and replay them when appropriate. There's the speech reminding herself that even ob-noxious teenagers grow up and into nice people eventually. And the one about the home repairs that would be nice but are not urgent. It is three in the afternoon, and the sun is hitting her right in the eyes and turning the dust on the windshield into a bright murkiness that cuts visibility to nearly nothing. Pop cans roll in the floorboards among the fast-food trash. The dash and passenger seat are cluttered by stiff work gloves, some loose and dusty books on tape, four weeks of church bulletins, and a plastic grocery bag full of canned diced tomatoes she was supposed to have delivered to Rita.

During the past couple of years she has reentered the adolescent stage of imagining elaborate scenarios in which she will somehow, in the course of her regular and grueling life, happen on to one of her fa-vorite actors. Perhaps John Cusack will have a flat tire while wheeling

across the state of Iowa on his way to some offbeat film festival. Or
Harvey Keitel will stop at the house, wanting directions to the
colonies of Amana or the bridges of Madison County. Jodie has allowed herself rampant fantasies; she doesn't even feel embarrassed
about them anymore.

Back when this started, Mack was keeping her up nights with his
pacing. His agitation put them all on edge. That, and the anger that
would flash out of him when he made the slightest error or couldn't
put his thoughts together fast enough. The worst times, though, were
when he wandered between the house and outbuildings, or just stood
in the alfalfa, looking frightened. When he did manage to lie down
and try to sleep, and when Jodie lay beside him, her heart clattering
almost audibly, it had been such a relief, such a break from her mind's
real work, to fantasize about romances that would never happen.

Foolish fantasies work better than allowing panic to fill the bedroom. They work better than praying to the God she no longer trusts
to protect her family. And while pastors and Sunday School teachers
always warned about the sinfulness of such daydreams, this season of
Jodie's life has revealed to her how little she concerns herself with
right and wrong anymore. Her remaining virtue seems to be the will
to survive. If imaginary diversions can help her get through another
few hours, then God will simply have to cut her some slack.

But at moments like this, driving along in a filthy pickup littered
with the family's trash and chaos, if Jodie were to see John and Harvey
in the same car, stalled right in front of her, she would step on the gas.
She has stopped checking the rearview mirror to see if, in the past
week, the tiredness has emptied from her face, to glance at the little
lines forming around her mouth, the diminished eyes and lifeless hair.
She wears jeans stained with either paint or spaghetti sauce, she can't
remember which. Twenty years ago her oversized flannel shirt would
have made her look cute, but now it just adds weight to her natural
baggage. She doesn't even want friends and neighbors to see her anymore, let alone some handsome guy looking for an afternoon ro-
mance.

The truck makes its automatic way into town. She watches her hands, her dry-looking, forty-something hands, grip the steering wheel and look as if they were expert at something. She glances a second time at the wedding band. Dull with time, but sturdy as ever.

She has agreed to meet Terry Jenkins for coffee at the Lunch Hour, that's all. He will walk over from the school, after gathering materials from his classroom. It isn't unusual for Terry to be at the school on a Saturday. He heads up one or two faculty committees and is involved in some extracurricular activities with students. He asked Jodie to help him organize a local history tour for his social studies classes. Jodie is friends with Naomi Muller, who is one of the several senior citizen curators of Beulah's small but growing museum. That's what Jodie and Terry will talk about over coffee at the town's only café. They will meet in the daylight where everyone can see them, and they will make plans for a series of tours during the dreary winter months. Within several counties are nearly as many museums, most of them housed in old buildings or otherwise vacant storefronts along near-deserted main streets. Most are piled high with items that testify to the way people lived in every era of the past 150 years. These museums have no official guardians or professional curators, just old folks who want to preserve the history of their communities and have little else to do. It will be a good way to spark the interest of a few bored kids in the middle of February.

Jodie is aware of other sparks that might ignite as well over this innocent coffee. She has been out of circulation for years where flirtation is concerned, but right now her gut apparently knows more than she is willing to admit. She remembers Terry's longer-than-normal gaze in the parking lot weeks ago. And the chemistry between them has become palpable enough that she makes an effort to avoid seeing him or talking to him directly at school—or, depending on the day and her mood, she does make the effort to do so. While she tells herself with perfect logic that this is just coffee, her palms get sweaty.

She pulls up to the café beside three other vehicles she recognizes. Terry's isn't one of them. He rents a small house three blocks away.

Since moving back to Beulah eighteen months ago, he has adopted the town's shrinking core as his home space. His parents still farm a few miles north of here. Terry went to college right after he graduated, about the time Mack and Jodie were getting married. Jodie is two years older than Terry and can remember him vaguely from school years. When people are under the age of twenty, two or three years' differ-ence in age separates entire worlds. So when Terry returned, after years of teaching in other places and a short, childless marriage, Jodie noticed his presence on the faculty but didn't give it a second thought.

There he is, at a table in the window, coffee in hand, a pile of pa-pers in front of him. When she steps onto the sidewalk, he looks up and smiles. That same smile—innocuous enough, but shining at her almost daily for the past several months.

"Hey," she says lightly. Settling on the other side of the booth, she is acutely aware of her sloppy jeans and shirt, her drab face. At least he can never accuse her of trying to encourage anything.

"Hey, yourself. You look tired. Sure you're up to this?"

"Oh, yeah. Once the weekend gets here, I feel obligated to try to catch up on everything at home. You'd think I'd learn." She offers a smile.

"I hate to see you so tired all the time. I feel guilty for asking your help on this."

"Oh, this'll be fun. Something different."

He looks at her a bit too long, just as he's been doing for weeks, al-lowing his eyes to remain on hers just a second past what would be normal for acquaintances. She knows he is waiting for her to decide one day to not disconnect their gaze. She shifts hers now to the pa-pers. "Grading, I see."

"I never finish."

"Like my housework."

"Mine too, if I gave a rip about housework." He laughs. Those eyes. Marble green.

"What plan do you have so far, about the tours?"

"Nothing official. First we need to set them up with each museum, get a tentative schedule, then get that approved. Shouldn't be hard."

"I know they've cut way back on school trips."

"We've got no budget. But Pepperdell will scrounge up the gas money if he sees the value of the trip."

"What do you need me to do? These are just field trips."

"I'd like another adult along, especially with the eighth-graders. I'm convinced that half of them will be incarcerated within five years."

She laughs and sees immediately how much that pleases him.

"Anyway, a parent volunteer is always welcome on field trips."

"But I don't have an eighth-grader,"

"You have connections to the museums."

"One museum, the one six blocks away, that you can all walk to."

He slumps over his coffee and leans closer, speaking softly. "Maybe I just want the company."

She does it finally, looks right at him and keeps looking. He doesn't blink but warms to her gaze, and somewhere an invisible door swings open.

"If you want company, you should talk to someone who's eligible," she says.

"You're not eligible for friendship?"

She closes her eyes, then turns and opens them to Main Street.

"I think you need a friend too, Jodie." His voice is still low, although the three other customers are at the snack bar, yards away.

"Well, I need a lot of things, but it's not so simple."

"I'm just offering a day or two away, chaperoning some kids and nosing around some history."

"I don't think it's a good idea."

"Then why are you here?"

She trains her gaze on the tip of the grain elevator two streets over. She wants to do this, and they both know it. She makes a little shrug. "Sounded like an interesting idea."

"How's Mack?"

This startles her enough to look at him. His gaze doesn't flicker. "He's okay."

"I heard he's moved out."

She tries to hide the surprise at his bluntness. "He's home, just not at the house. We see him every day."

"And you're still exhausted." He shifts, and she can tell he wants to reach across and grasp her hand. She's never been sure of that, during other incidental discussions between them. But now he appears to clutch the coffee cup with both hands to keep from reaching for her. "I just hate to see you hang on to something that can't work."

She leans toward him, pretending to sip her coffee. "You shouldn't be saying these things to me."

"Okay." He seems alarmed at the tone she's taken. "I'm sorry. Didn't mean to insult you."

"I know."

They both lean back, for a deeper breath.

"I care about you, Jodie."

These are the words her imaginary lovers have said over and over again. It is the one thing she has hungered to hear. And now someone has said it aloud, and it is the wrong person at the worst time.

Terry goes on, not realizing what he's just accomplished. Now he sounds almost nonchalant. "Why don't you forget this field trip stuff. It's a bad idea."

She feels the backs of her eyes heating up. The prospect of letting go entirely of this small possibility makes her throat hurt. She blinks so that he won't see her tears. "No. I want to help. If you really want this to work, then I should go to each museum and work out with them a real schedule, you know, make sure they pull out the stuff that's interesting to junior high kids instead of parading them past twenty quilt patterns."

His face fills with relief. For now at least, they have some days ahead, during the long winter, to help each other through its loneliness.

She feels much better, driving home. For one thing, the sun isn't in her eyes, and she's run a couple of errands between her talk with

Terry and the drive back to the farm. But mainly, she feels so much at home with herself after just an hour of conversation with this man. Chatting with him for a minute or two when he goes by in the lunch-room line makes her feel that she is indeed her former, okay self. He brings her health. She knows this. She struggles with this fact. This is wrong, even this comfort without sex, without a handhold or a kiss. But she senses that each small exchange of words, no matter how inane, brings them closer to a real embrace.

"I'm a grown woman. I know how these things happen." She listens to herself argue as the truck bounces through potholes in the orange-tinted evening. "But the minute we're in the same room, I am so comforted. Lord, it's the only comfort I know."

It is something like a prayer, but not really. For a long time now her only prayers have been asides to herself, in closed-up places like a locked bathroom or a pickup truck. She will throw in "Lord" just in case God is happening through her world at that moment.

Which is about as likely as Harvey Keitel ringing her doorbell.

Mack

When Mack told George about his move out to the stone house, the man displayed no surprise or worry, but merely asked Mack what he did with his hours out there. Mack tried to explain about sitting and doing nothing, about the methodical work of clearing branches, and George's eyes gleamed a little, but he simply said, "You may be right. Sometimes a person needs stillness that can't be found in a house with other people. Are you deeply sad out there?"

"No. A little lonely is all. Mostly I feel like I'm just soaking in everything—the trees and the creek. Time slows down, but it doesn't feel bad."

"We'll just wait and see then." That was that. No dire instructions about checking in with his family, or reminders about the warning signs of depression. George is becoming a person, in Mack's mind at least, with whom a man can be honest. George trusts him more than his family does, a sad commentary but reassuring anyway. During the workday, Mack takes refuge at Hendrikson's, another place where people have faith in him.

But talk of any kind stirs up a person's mind and heart. Mack has been dreaming a lot since moving to the stone house. His dreams have become more real than his real life. They steal him in the quiet hours and take him to places full of color and promise. Upon waking, he wonders how, in the midst of his life falling apart, his dreams have taken a beautiful turn.

He is ten years old on a day in early May. His morning chores are done, and he has a few hours all his, enough time to walk to the pond and swim and feel the sun. He is on that path through the pasture that leads to the pond on the western end of the farm.

The air is filled with sun, but because it is early in the day, the dust under his bare feet is cool as velvet. At one point, the path breaks through a clump of chokecherry trees and lilacs; the giant bushes drip deep lavender blossoms by the score, their sweetness heavy as a grandma's bosom.

Lilacs remind Mack of Grandma, but she died when he was four, and his memory of her is a vapor in which floats a happy face behind spec-tacles and the smell of lavender blooms near a back door. When Mack's parents added on the family room decades ago, the bushes had to go. But in this dream he is at the house of Aunt Delores, the place just down the road where she lived until her death in '84. There were lilacs there too, and they bloomed every spring. They called her Aunt Lorie. Her husband had died of a brain aneurysm before they could have ba-bies together. She was young when it happened, and everyone thought she'd marry again, but she liked to say, "Don was the only guy ornery enough to put up with me. I'll see him soon enough, I suppose; it makes me not so afraid to die." She raised vegetables and planted peach, apple, cherry, and plum trees, making a bit of money off the fruit and the jams she made from it. She was tall and angular and had a lopsided face that seemed always to be grinning at you and measuring your worth all at once. Nothing like her sister Rita, Lorie liked to stir up trouble and ask preachers all the wrong questions and make home brew and cook anything the men brought back from the hunt. When other women in the family turned up their noses at mangled squirrels, too many doves, or yet another mess of fish, Lorie plunged in with a laugh and informed everyone else that the meal would be ready by seven, and they'd better come early because she was flat-out hungry herself.

Mack awakes, and though it is October and the cabin is cold and full of tired light, his memory catches a whiff of lilac, and he smells Aunt Lorie's fried perch. He cries for the lane that went to the pond. The pasture and pond belong to other people now, and even though that family has children, Mack has never seen them naked and muddy and happy the way he was, so many years ago. His heart catches with a special pain when he recalls the bulldozer taking down Aunt Lorie's small frame house. She died of lung cancer when not that old, and she left her little place to a nephew of her husband's, a young business-man in Cedar Rapids. He had no use for a few acres and a decrepit house. He sold it all to one of Mack's neighbors, who cleared off the house, fruit trees, and lilac bushes, turned all of it under with the grass, and by the next planting season had driven it through with even rows of corn. Not a trace was left of what used to be.

Late Saturday morning, Mack is sitting on one of the chairs outside the stone house when Ed comes by, just to chew the fat. Mack pulls the other chair out, and they sit in little patches of light while the cold seeps through their jackets. In a pause of conversation, several rifle shots report from the west.

"Lord, they're all over the place," says Ed. "Saw a license plate this morning from Delaware."

"They don't have pheasants up there anymore?"

Ed shrugs. "I guess there's more here. Heard that pesticides have thinned 'em out other places."

"You gonna hunt this year?"

"My brother-in-law'll be here next weekend. Come along if you want."

"Maybe." Mack has seen the pickups parked here and there, just off the roadsides, empty dog crates in the back. The Lunch Hour fills up these days with neighbors and visitors alike, orange caps resting beside coffee cups. "Couple years ago I took Young Taylor. He's not much interested now."

Ed clears his throat. "Maybe I'm just getting older and dumber, but the birds sure as hell seem smarter every year."

Mack laughs and tips his can of cola. In a bit, Ed puts out his third cigarette, stretches, groans a little, and climbs into his truck. "Holler if you need somethin', okay?"

Mack waves his reply. He walks around the stone house, zipping up his jacket. He has begun to enjoy moving slowly. During all those years of farming, life was a practice of waiting and then hurrying. When the time was right, the planting had to be done. When the moisture and temperature met where they must, the corn or the beans had to be harvested, now. If something wasn't happening now, then waiting put everything else on hold. And in the waiting there were always bits and pieces of the place to be repaired or replaced. The only way to get ahead was to work always, even while waiting.

He tries to pinpoint the day, or the time of year, when he finally saw the truth, when he understood that working harder for more hours didn't make any difference. By then he was working full-time for the school district, maintaining and driving buses, then farming at night and through the weekend. Even so, the money coming in fell far short of the money needing to go out. In spite of knowing how the numbers added up, Dad and Alex and Mack had, for a long time, done all they knew to do: worked more hours and got busier still. The constant motion of mind and body broke each of them eventually. Dad lost his concentration. Alex drank himself into a cold death. And Mack went crazy and had to be put away.

All of that feels long ago as Mack sits in the stone house or gathers wood from the quiet spaces around it. Now time feels different. Mack goes to his job during the day, working regular hours, although for not much pay. He finishes at five and stops at Mom's, stops at the grocery if he needs to, stops to say hi to Jodie and the kids. Twice he has eaten dinner with them before going on to the stone house, to silence and more stopping. It seems that all he does now is come to a halt many times a day. And in the stone house time itself waits. Mack sits and observes time, and it observes him. He can't help but think that it is time that waits to reveal its final fate for him. One of these days time will sweep over him with an awareness of some crucial task he has left undone. That one neglected work will spell the final destruction of his family. Mack is certain that this fear has tangible foundations; he just can't get them to come clear yet.

In the woods life has a different demeanor. Mack can't tell if it's hostile or not. For all he knows, the final destruction will happen out here in the midst of trees. But he isn't so scared anymore. A deep patience has taken him over, and he can sit on the step of the cabin and gaze into the web of branches and vines and dead grasses and stay that way a long time. The panic about what might be next drifts low in his gut and doesn't seem to interfere with anything else. Finally, no racing heart, no desperate thoughts.

Mack hopes that this is some form of getting well. He feels different, but none of the facts of his life have changed. Maybe he has simply stopped caring too much. The more you care about things, the more power they have to hurt you and make you crazy.

Kenzie

She has been working all morning, on a dreary Saturday, while Mom is running errands and Young Taylor is hogging the sound system in the living room. Her bedroom door is shut, but still all the screeching and gory verse filters into her atmosphere. She has two Bibles open on the bed before her, one the Living Bible and the other the New International Version. Pastor Williamson uses the NIV for study purposes, but the Living Bible says things in more down-to-earth language.

There are index cards in three different colors scattered around her. And on several she has written favorite verses in her best possible handwriting. On her dresser are several small bunches of silk flowers, the best she can do in October. Little daisies and pansies mainly. She found thin purple ribbon in Mom's wrapping paper drawer, and she has gathered the silk flowers and tied them up as artistically as she can. She's taken a hole punch to the corner of each index card and tied two or three cards together into as many bunches as she has flowers. There are five sets of cards and flowers, one for each day of the coming week.

If Dad is going to stay to himself in the stone house, Kenzie will leave encouragement in little gifts. One bunch of flowers and set of Scripture verse cards every day. He drops her at school in the mornings, and she will leave the gifts on the seat when she gets out. She won't make a big production of it, just give him a good-bye kiss and leave flowers and verses.

The difficult part is choosing from so many wonderful Bible passages. So far she's used about an equal number from Psalms, the Gospels, and other New Testament books—all very encouraging stuff. Much of the Old Testament beyond the Psalms is rather harsh, and she doesn't think that Dad needs to hear so much about judgment just now. She holds one of her favorite cards up so the weak light from the window shines on it:

> Now you don't need to be afraid of the dark any more, nor fear the
> dangers of the day; nor dread the plagues of darkness, nor
> disasters in the morning.
> Though a thousand fall at my side, though ten thousand are dying
> around me, the evil will not touch me.
>   —Psalm 91:5–7

She has thought about leaving the encouragement gifts out at the stone house, but it feels creepy out there, and she doesn't want to bother Dad, who obviously wants to be away from all of them. She couldn't bear it if he were to catch her leaving him Bible verses and if the look on his face were anger. She just couldn't handle that. She's gotten used to Mom's anger, which is mainly irritation about everyday hassles. But Dad has never been an angry person at all, and on the rare occasions when he has been, it has hurt so much to be around him.

Dear Jesus,

It's really hard, helping a person who doesn't want you around. I wish Dad could see how much I do to support him during these dark days. I want to tell him how many times I fasted and prayed while he was in the hospital. Or that I gave up television, and stayed up nights praying through whole chapters of the Scriptures, just to keep him safe. I want him to know so he'll be encouraged, but if I told him this stuff he might just feel guilty for causing concern. Grandma Rita said that he didn't want to be a burden and that's why he wanted to die. So I can't say or do anything that might make him feel that way again.

So little bunches of flowers and Bible verses should be okay, shouldn't they? Flowers are kind of lighthearted and happy. And sharing Your Word is always the right thing to do.

Please help Dad find some comfort in these little gifts.

Love and praise,

Kenzie

6

SEEING GHOSTS

I ask no dream, no prophet ecstasies,
No sudden rending of the veil of clay,
No angel visitant, no opening skies;
But take the dimness of my soul away.
— *"Spirit of God, Descend upon My
Heart"*

Mack

Sunday evening, Mack hears Jodie's truck pull up outside the stone
house. The engine stops, and the headlights go out. Jodie emerges,
then gets something off the passenger seat. She walks up, her breath a
little fog.

"Is it against the rules to bring you food?"

He can't tell if she is joking or not. She holds out a small cooler,
looking apprehensive.

"No rules." He takes the cooler. "Thank you. Want to eat with
me?"

Her fine eyebrows come up a notch, and she shrugs. "Only if you
want me to."

"I do."

"You do?"

He can see a measure of hurt in her eyes, the evidence of the rejection she feels in spite of anything he says.

"Yes, I'd like you to stay." He leads the way into the house. He can feel her a step or two behind, looking the place over.

"You warm enough?" she asks, standing near the woodstove. She extends her hands toward the heat.

"Yeah. Drafty when the wind kicks up, but there's not much space to heat."

He sets the cooler on the table.

"It's beef stew," she says.

"Great! It's still warm." He holds the container in both hands and smiles at her.

"Biscuits too. But you'll need to heat them."

He places the foil-wrapped biscuits on the stove and puts out bowls and plates and spoons while she takes quiet steps around the room. They sit at the small table in silence.

"This is good, sweet."

"Thank you."

They blow on spoonfuls of stew and take several bites.

"How are the kids?" he asks.

"All right." They keep eating as fire pops inside the iron stove. Wind whispers down the vent. "Kenzie's with the youth group. Young Taylor's out somewhere. I didn't go to church today." She glances at him, and he takes the cue.

"I didn't either. I hoped nobody would look for me."

"People ask about you. But I only make it there once or twice a month myself."

"It doesn't feel the same, does it?"

"What?" She looks at him, and he catches a hint of fear in her eyes.

"Being in church." He takes the biscuits off the stove and hands her one.

"Oh." She looks back at her food. "Well, it hasn't been exactly a haven, has it? At least not for me."

"No. Me either." He reaches toward his mother's cast-off utility shelf that serves as storage space for everything, grabs two napkins, and hands her one. "I don't know if it would help to go back, you know, on a regular basis."

"You don't have to decide today."

"Right."

"Are you out here because you need to be away from me?" The emotion behind those words does not show in her eyes or sound in her voice.

"This isn't because of you. I just need to be here." He looks at her over his raised spoon. "I can't explain why I need it."

"Maybe I put too much pressure on you."

"Right now everything feels like pressure, even things that should just feel normal. Standing in the garage feels like pressure. Picking up the morning paper."

"But what can you do for yourself isolated out here?"

"I'm all right."

"But if you weren't all right, no one would know it."

"I'm at work every day. You and the kids see me all the time."

"It's not the same."

Mack sits back in his chair and gazes at his wife. Her face is all shadows and angles. A light in her has gone out. He can't confess that seeing her like this is in fact part of the reason he's in the woods now. She would think it was her fault. But Mack knows that she isn't responsible for snuffing out her own light. He has done that. But he snuffed out her light because he was groping after his own light, which had gone out. And he didn't put out his own light. Something else started all this, broke into their lives and stole their lights.

"Sweet, I promise, if I have a rough time I won't stay out here. I'm keeping my appointments. I'm on my meds."

She looks as if she might cry, that trickling tearfulness that is usually her emotions' way of conserving energy. But at the moment her eyes are simply tired.

"You didn't stop by the house last night," she says.

"I worked late. And didn't want to barge in past suppertime."

"It's not barging in when it's your own family."

"All right, I'll stop by every night, if you think that's best."

Then he launches into what he hopes is a humorous diatribe about his mother's latest efforts to make him better.

"Brought all these damn bottles of herbal remedies. Saint-John's-wort and who knows what else. Don't know where she got them or how long she's had 'em."

"Oh, probably leftovers from one of the people she buys medicine for. She's a traveling pharmacy."

"Probably cleaned out the medicine cabinet of whoever's kicked the bucket lately."

She's just taken a bite and puts a hand to her mouth to avoid spitting when she laughs. He enjoys seeing this. It is still possible to reach past all those other things to whatever it is that releases her specific kind of chuckle, deep in the throat, almost a man's chuckle only with more melody to it.

Before she leaves, they stand in the center of the small room and hold each other. She is as familiar to him as he is to himself, but he doesn't feel her as he did in the old days. Every sensation between them is pleasant but muted, as if they touch through some middle space or substance.

He sees her glance at the narrow bed before walking out into the cold air. Someone in the back of his heart wants to keep her there, to lie with her in those good, well-remembered ways. But that possibility seems furthest away of all.

Jodie

She has just wandered through the drugstore section of Wal-Mart for twenty minutes. She awoke this morning full of longing, and although the economic situation of recent years has prevented her from using shopping as an emotional outlet, the longing has brought her here, to rows of shampoo and conditioner, skin care products, and hair fasteners. She now stands at the head of the aisle for bath products—shower gels, bath crystals, loofahs, and the like—and marvels at how much merchandise there is. This is her experience more and more when she comes to Wal-Mart: amazement at the sheer abundance of stuff. It makes her anxious. How can all this bounty appear regularly in a place where so many people cannot stretch paychecks from one month to the next? What law of nature is being upended? *Who is paying for all of this?*

Putting her apprehensions aside for now, she stares hungrily at the milky-toned containers of bath oils. All she knows is that she *wants*, she's not sure what. Two neighbors walk past, on their way to cleaning supplies, and Jodie feels like diving for cover. She is an alien in this section. A teenager brushes past to study facial products the next aisle over. Beauty products are for young women, girls who still hope for love and take some pleasure in their own reflection. Kenzie should be standing here, deciding between lipstick shades, looking for lotions and shampoos that smell like peaches. The panic rises as Jodie stands fixed between the shelves on the right and the left. What is she doing here? What could she possibly squeeze out of a bottle that would make things better?

Well, she needs makeup at least. She's run out, and her skin is more rough and red all the time. She maneuvers the cart to the far aisle, where she is faced by a thousand options. The first choice, however, eliminates most of them: she skips the brand names that have their own TV commercials. Her price range eliminates all but two brands, so she stands before those sections, down at the end, and ponders what to put on her face.

Choosing the right color of foundation doesn't take long, because there are only four. She picks the best and throws it into the cart, then grasps the handle of the shopping cart as if to get on with her real business, which is to pick up some household necessities. But she can't move. Her sight rests upon the racks of ascending colors—blushes, eye shadows, eyeliners, mascaras, lipsticks, lip brushes . . .

She settles on a powder blush that is somewhat bronzy. Next comes the lipstick. She contemplates all the warm colors—the cinnamons, the coffees and berries—and chooses one that is dark but muted, well suited to autumn. Black eyeliner is more dramatic, so she picks it, along with matching mascara, the "thick and luscious" kind. To go with that she finds a smoky brown eye shadow. Finally, a translucent loose powder and a separate, long-handled brush for applying it—not that she knows how to use the brush. Jodie looks in her cart at forty dollars' worth of items to use on nothing but her face. The blood rushes up her neck, and she looks around to see if anyone has witnessed her extravagance.

She stares at the cosmetics but doesn't put back a single thing. She rolls the cart to Housewares and buys the laundry soap, skips the bleach, picks up toilet paper but no tissues, loads an economy-sized generic disinfectant cleaner, and ignores the remaining three items on her list.

She makes tuna sandwiches for supper, opening a can of pork-and-beans and putting out a half-empty bag of potato chips. The kids don't expect her to really cook. Mack comes by and enjoys the food, mainly because he is where he has promised he will be, and she and the kids talk with him easily enough. When Mack leaves for the stone house, Young Taylor and Kenzie both go out—Jodie realizes only then that it's Halloween. Her insides shake as she clears the table and washes dishes. She takes half an hour to straighten the rest of the house and put in a load of laundry. Then she goes upstairs.

The Wal-Mart sack is stuffed into her bottom dresser drawer, along with the heating pad and extra set of sheets. She takes the bag into the bathroom and shuts the door, then places each new item on the vanity. She doesn't dare look in the mirror; if she sees herself, she might lose courage. Her hands tremble as she tears off the packaging and lines up the products, in order of their use.

She really should take a bath first, soak in the tub and get relaxed. But that would take too long. So she scrubs and moisturizes her face instead, pulls her hair back and out of the way, and begins with the foundation.

Thirty minutes later, Jodie stands in the still air of the closed bathroom and studies her face. The colors seem to work. For a moment or two, she imagines that her eyes look brighter and her skin more taut. Yes, she does look better. She smiles at the reflection, trying to help the makeup's effect. No, she merely looks like someone else. She turns away from the mirror and cries. Then she washes it all off, brushes her teeth, and goes to bed.

Her body is numb. It wants nothing and gives nothing. There was a time when an hour to herself late in the evening might have led to her own pleasure. Especially after Mack got sick, she learned, tentatively and with a little guilt, to please herself. No big deal. But it was nice sometimes, even liberating, to know that she did not depend on Mack for her sexual life. And he seemed relieved that she no longer brought it up.

But tonight she might as well be dead. She is free and alone and has lost all desire.

"Why bother?" she asks the late evening sky. "Who am I primping for? Why do I think it matters?" The makeup is packed away, back in the bottom dresser drawer. No point in throwing it out. She'll use some of it anyway. To attend someone's wedding or graduation. Or something.

Kenzie

"Thanks for letting me spend the evening here." Kenzie is tucked into Mitchell's couch, cocoa in hand. He walks in with a bowl of popcorn. A video is in the player. Mitchell sits on the couch, a few inches from Kenzie, and hits the remote.

"No problem."

"Everybody makes like Halloween is just a party or something. But its meaning goes a lot deeper." Kenzie takes a handful of popcorn. "I don't even want to think about what my brother's doing."

"Well, we can pray for him, if you want."

The video begins. A slender man with thick, smooth gray hair and wearing a dark green suit stands at a lectern.

The man begins by raising both hands and launching into a fervent prayer to the Holy Spirit, his eyes closed tightly and a beam upon his face. This is tape two of the five Mitchell owns. He's gotten them through the mail, from the Francis Dowell Ministries. Mitchell says he is headquartered in Lawrence, Kansas, but comes from Tennessee or somewhere in that region. In a clear, striking voice, with a hint of southern accent, the Reverend Francis (as he prefers to be called) expounds upon the Book of Revelation.

"Brothers and sisters, let me proclaim to you the prophecy found in Revelation six, verses nine through eleven:

"And when he had opened the fifth seal, I saw under the altar the souls of them that were slain for the word of God, and for the testimony which they held: And they cried with a loud voice, saying, How long, O Lord, holy and true, doest thou not judge and avenge our blood on them that dwell on the earth? And white robes were given unto every one of them; and it was said unto them, that they should rest yet for a little season, until their fellow servants also and their brethren, that should be killed as they were, should be fulfilled."

Reverend Francis straightens his green and gold tie, which shimmers against a gold shirt. He brushes one wave of hair while turning first to one side and then the other. The camera scans the audience, rows of people in a darkened theater, all looking at a single point behind the camera. In the first row several Bibles are held open on laps.

"God did not say that there would not be death and suffering. God has clearly told us that many servants will die for the sake of the gospel. But what we must understand is that death is sometimes not *physical* death." He bends at the waist for emphasis. "We die a lot of deaths in this life. Your loved one, who loves the Lord and has never drunk a drop of liquor, is killed or maimed by a drunk driver. Or

the bank—which, you must remember, is controlled by big government—forecloses on your property, even though you have been
faithful as is humanly possible, even though you have honored God
your whole life. You suffer at work because you pray to the Lord
Jesus on your lunch break—and you notice that those promotions
just pass you by. Or some bunch of secular humanist judges miles
away from here makes it so your little girls and boys can no longer
pray at school. People, there's a lot of death in this world, and it's the
death of people who are God-fearing, who pray faithfully and who
fast, and who know the word of the Lord!"

The camera pans again, as people nod and say amen. Then back to
Reverend Francis, who has stepped from behind the pulpit and taken a
stance at the very front of the platform. It reminds Kenzie of when
Coach Arbuch stands before the gym bleachers to explain something
that he wants to explain only once. In contrast, Reverend Francis's face
looks full of concern about eternal things, not just rules or warnings.

"When these good people are killed off, then it's clear as day that
Revelation has come to pass. This *is* the Tribulation, brothers and sisters. The Anti-Christ is *here*, and he's already got the government in
his pocket, the educational system in his pocket, even most of the
stores you shop at are in his pocket."

Kenzie takes notes and glances at Mitchell, who is entranced.

She thinks about earlier in the week, when she worked up the
nerve to knock on Mitchell's back door. He welcomed her with a
huge smile and soon put water on to boil. He brought out cinnamon
rolls, the kind you buy in packages.

"Hey, I want you to watch something," he said. Then he put a cas-
sette in the VCR.

"What is it?"

"Somebody I think you'll like." And then the teaching began. After
a few minutes, Kenzie pulled her own Bible from her backpack, just
to keep up. This guy went through more Scriptures faster than anyone she'd ever heard, even the special speakers who came to the youth
group retreats.

It was hard for Kenzie to concentrate on the lesson because she was so thoroughly enjoying herself. Here she was in Mitchell's cozy kitchen, having cocoa and cinnamon rolls, with Mitchell smiling at her the way a real friend smiles, and on top of all that listening to really good Bible teaching. It just didn't get any better than this. When God answered a prayer, he wasn't stingy. When the tape was over, Kenzie hurried home, but they agreed to watch the other tapes together too.

She brings her attention back to the present, as Reverend Francis describes the world they live in—full of people turning from the faith and turning to the occult, controlled by a government that has become atheistic, even anti-Christ. He describes it with such vivid phrases that Kenzie and Mitchell just stare at each other. Then Reverend Francis states that "what I've just read is not from some newspaper, not from some talk show, not from some opinion poll. These prophetic words were given to us thousands of years ago by the Apostle John, and they are right in the Bible you hold in your hand. God *knew* we would need this comfort. He looked ahead at the America we have today, and he told the apostle, 'John, your brothers and sisters of the future are gonna need these visions. You see before you a vision of what those poor folks will be living in the middle of. So write it down. Write it down. Write it down.'"

Here it is, Halloween night, a night that generally belongs to Satan. But she is safe in Mitchell's house, enveloped in God's Word. After the tape is over, they take turns praying for Young Taylor and all the other kids who are deceived and heading for trouble.

At the end of each tape, Reverend Francis talks of a place where suffering Christians can "rest for a little season." It's a retreat center his ministry has built, thanks to the generous donations of listeners. "You come to the Haven of Life and Truth, and we will let you rest. We'll feed you on God's Word—we'll even give you a white robe! And we'll prepare you for the battle to come."

Mitchell's eyes appear to gaze into the future itself. "Sometimes I think that what I need most is to rest a while at Reverend Francis's Haven."

"It sounds like a wonderful place."

"Yeah, I'll check it out one of these days." He smiles at Kenzie. "We can both check it out."

Kenzie knows that even as she pedals hard and stares straight ahead, her new friend is watching until she disappears down the rise. It is reassuring to know this, because now her night vision has become home to dragons and white horses and demons, foretold by the prophets and winging their way to Beulah even now. Kenzie feels waves of fear from deep in her soul. But more than that she senses a new strength and determination that will give energy and power to her prayers.

Mack

Mack runs past the barn, down beyond the pond. His heart thumps violently, and his legs feel too heavy but labor forward anyway. Behind him he can hear his brother breathing hard, trying to follow him.

"Mack! Wait! You've gotta wait for me!"

But Mack runs anyway. If Alex catches up with him, something horrible will happen to them both. So Mack ignores his brother's cries. Why are they always in trouble? Why are they running? Mack can't understand the sharp pain in his heart, or why he can't bring himself to look at Alex. The sight and sound of his brother cause Mack to hurt all over. And the fear makes his feet keep going.

He wakes up cold, looks at the alarm clock, and sees that it's one in the morning. Alex's voice woke him. But of course not. His brother's voice leaked out of a dream and into this dark, chilly room in the middle of the woods. Maybe Mack's own voice woke him up. He watches his breath drift toward the ceiling. He can still feel his feet pounding over the pasture, can sense Alex just behind him. Mack used to tease Alex when they were small, used to take off when he got tired of Alex tailing him. Mack would just run somewhere, and Alex would yell and try to keep up, but Mack was not only older but faster. It was all in fun anyway.

But in the dream it felt utterly wrong and dark and full of sadness. His brother's voice still echoes around him, clear and desperate. A shudder goes through Mack, and for a few moments he feels that Alex is right beside him, a sensation he's never experienced.

Then again, it's never felt this cold in the stone house. It can't be below freezing. But he's never been alone here in late October—what is it, Halloween? But before, Alex was here with him, or Dad or Young Taylor, or all three. A couple of times he and Jodie stole a night or two, but that was summertime. Another body in the room makes a difference, whatever time of year. He gets out of bed and wrestles with the woodpile, hops around a bit while the fire gets going.

He does all of this without turning on a light. The moon is overflowing the cold sky, and the room seems in the middle of dawn or twilight. As the fire starts and snaps Mack stands at the north window and peers into the woods. There is nothing so still as trees on a frigid night. They appear to be waiting patiently for something—for snow or sunrise or deer.

Mack puts on his coat and boots. The woods look like a dream, a place that holds secrets. Since talking with George, Mack thinks more about dreams and secrets. He still doesn't put much stock in all the talking or in what his tired brain invents when he's not conscious. But most things feel like dreams these days, like locations that are more than they actually are. He walks across the clearing, toward the creek. The twigs and crusty leaves that crackle under his steps send echoes into the web of branches above him. He winces for the noise. A night like this shouldn't be disturbed. He looks for softer places and ends up on the side of the bank. The creek itself lies just over a small ridge. He finds the damp layers of fallen leaves, glued together with mud. His feet make no noise at all.

He comes up over the ridge and notices a tree he hasn't seen before, short and gnarly. How could that be? He knows this place by heart. But the tree moves, and he recognizes the large trunk as a long, dark garment. And what had seemed a broken end, a top without a top, is a face. What he first perceived to be light sky at the end of the trunk is a face whiter than the moon. Mack sucks in air and feels his eyes grow large to understand what image they are registering.

He is seeing a profile. A man with a colorless face and dark hollows for eyes. The coat falls about the bank where he sits. Midway rest white hands, slender hands. One comes up to touch the nose briefly. This movement jars Mack to his center. His eyes and mind finally come together. He is looking at Alex. Alex, his dead brother. The dream was more than a dream after all. The angles of the face, the ges-ture of the hand. It is all perfectly familiar. The only things that don't match are the ghostly skin and absent eyes.

From where Mack stands, he knows that a person sitting where Alex sits cannot see him. Behind Mack is the house and trees, not the middle-of-night pale sky. He's come halfway down the bank and blended into the muddy absence of color or shape. He stands, his legs grown straight into the bedrock, and his thoughts gasp and leap. It is Alex. Mack has never believed in ghosts. Such things are not part of his religion or his family's stories. Yet the moon shines clearly on this person only yards away. Foggy breaths whisper from Alex's mouth. Ghosts aren't physical, are they? They wouldn't breathe real air, don't have hearts and lungs. None of this makes sense.

Mack extends his arms behind him and forces his knees to bend enough so that he gradually seats himself against the slope of the bank. This is a hallucination. It's the drugs or the stress or just his crazed mind and heart bursting out of bounds, going places they shouldn't be going. He is not right in his mind. Until now he has believed that things really weren't that bad, that it was mainly fatigue and grief that made his thoughts spin in his head with no place to land. That made him fear his own family, even himself. But this is a critical thing hap-pening to him now. He is seeing, sensing a presence that cannot be. He almost shouts his brother's name, sure that the image will evaporate instantly, but then he realizes that if he has so little control over his mind that this thing could appear, what else might it do?

He should want to see his brother again, to talk with him, to seize the chance to say how much they've all missed him. But he imagines

Alex standing up, facing him, and speaking truth that the living cannot bear. *If only I could have talked to you. If only you had been stronger.
If only you had helped me more to manage things.*

Mack has to get out of here. He's shivering too violently to move
with ease, so he inches backwards up the bank, the sounds of his
movement covered by the gurgling of water in the stream. He crawls
on all fours over the ridge but stays just the other side of it, where the
ground is soft and soundless. He crawls along the bank at least fifty
yards, then cuts across and back to the house from the other side. For
a moment he considers getting in the car and driving somewhere,
driving the roads until dawn, but he needs to get warm first. He all
but sits on the stove until the trembling stops. He turns on the lamp
by the sofa. He wishes like anything he had strong drink nearby,
something to muffle his mind and take his fear away.

An hour goes by. For every minute of it he tries to imagine what
Alex is doing. Still sitting beside the water? Walking through the
woods? Walking toward him? Standing just outside the door? At three
o'clock, he grabs the flashlight and heads for the stream. It has to be
someone else. The moon was playing tricks on him. He marches nois-
ily to the place he was before. The bank is empty except for its usual
rocks and trunks. No sign of anyone. Mack walks up and down the
bank, then cuts through the woods on a return to the house. He walks
beyond it to the drive and the old barn. He disturbs the cows, who shift
and grunt at him. Pigeons glare down at him from their beds upon the
rafters. Mack goes back to the house, suddenly exhausted. He turns the
radio on for company, but sleeps almost as soon as he lies down.

Rita

Rita watches Amos hand out Tootsie Rolls to the three youngsters on
her doorstep. They are Disney characters, she thinks. She has already
given each a handful of assorted wrapped candies and chocolates from
the bulk bins at Wal-Mart. Amos brought his coffee can full of Tootsie Rolls and stationed himself in her living room, where he can watch

through the front window for trick-or-treaters and also see through the doorway to the television that's on in Rita's combination family room/dining room. Rita feels like telling him that kids hardly know what Tootsie Rolls are anymore, but she saves her breath. He thinks he's helping. He thinks she wants company. In a way she does, but Amos is clumsy and forgetful, and she feels inclined to look after him. "Company" for her would be someone who needs no looking after. She considers briefly—very briefly—that maybe there's good reason that some women become lesbians as they get older. They just get tired of taking care of men. They'd rather somebody take care of *them*. They find companions who can cook and deal with the house if necessary, somebody who understands the difference between bath salts and Epsom salts.

This afternoon she talked with Jodie, who doesn't bother with treats anymore. The few farm families nearby no longer have small children. Plus, Halloween's not much fun if your own children are too big to dress up and take around. Still, Rita feels abandoned. She and Jodie used to haul Young Taylor and Kenzie all over town and through the countryside too. The kids haven't done that for years, but it couldn't hurt to at least stay in the spirit of the thing. Jodie could have come over and sat here with Rita. They could pass out treats together and just visit in between knocks on the door.

She's got two teenagers and a husband who's not well, plus a job at the school. She doesn't have the time or energy to hang around with anybody, much less her mother-in-law. Rita worries sometimes that she's turning into one of those old people who feel that everybody ought to love and serve them and who grow resentful at every hint of neglect, such as not getting called on the phone daily or not getting invited to every gathering. She delivers soup to a couple of people like that, and she tells herself at nearly every visit, *Just a little slip in your attitude, and that'll be you.*

"Look at that little dollie—I think she's supposed to be Heidi. You know, the little girl who grew up in the Swiss Alps with her grandpa? I just loved that story." Amos is grinning at six-year-old Stacy Enders, pigtails bouncing, whose nine-year-old brother, Spiderman, is guiding her up the walk. Their mom, Jennifer, who used to babysit Young Taylor, waits in the idling car.

"I think she's supposed to be Dorothy from *The Wizard of Oz*— but you're right, she could be Heidi." Rita opens the door and the children cry, "Trick or treat!" A lump rises in Rita's throat. She could be standing in the middle of 1963, when Mack was Superman, or in 1991, when Young Taylor was a midget with an ax buried in his head. "And are you Dorothy?" She puts a handful of candy into each of their plastic pumpkins.

"No, I'm Buttercup!" She sees Rita's blank look and adds, "You know the Power Puff Girls."

"Well, so you are." Amos bends down to drop in Tootsie Rolls. Spiderman lingers just long enough to say thank you (after all, Mom is watching from the car), and Heidi-Dorothy-Buttercup runs back down the walk.

Maybe twenty kids come by in the course of the evening. Rita recognizes some of them as being connected to neighbors or people at church, the children of children she used to know, but many of them she doesn't know by name. Genevieve, six doors down, knows them all.

"If you'd get your hair done regularly like I do, you'd keep up better," she'd said recently. "Everybody gets their hair done at Marybeth's, and that's where you find out things." Marybeth Ross operates a small beauty salon out of her home; she started a few years ago using what had once been a large storage shed, but business was so good that her husband, Dave, converted their two-car garage into a nice space for her. Their various vehicles (which number between four and six—the Rosses have two teenage sons) have taken shelter under a carport and in the old barn that serves no other purpose now.

"I can wash my own hair," Rita had answered. "No reason on earth to pay someone else to do it."

"But Marybeth can keep it trimmed. And she'll style it and spray it so you don't have to touch it for the rest of the week."

Genevieve does in fact go week to week without running a comb through her own head of hair. This makes no sense to Rita.

"Besides, half the reason to go to Marybeth's is to get caught up with everybody. I know about every baby shower, wedding, and hospital stay even before it hits the church bulletin."

"Well, Genevieve, I don't need Marybeth's because I've got you, don't I?"

Genevieve just laughed at that.

Genevieve helped her deliver Halloween to her old folks earlier this afternoon. They packaged up little boxes of dietetic hard candies and those single-serve puddings. Rita knows that single-serve puddings were invented for children, but they are perfect for the elderly who don't eat a lot at one sitting and who can usually peel off the tops for themselves, even if their hands are messed up by arthritis.

For Bernie Hallsted she bought some packaged cotton candy. Kenzie was the one who noticed it at the convenience store right here in Beulah. It was balled up in small striped-paper packages, hanging there on clips just like packs of potato chips. Kenzie brought some to Rita, and they decided that it wasn't as good as the freshly spun cotton candy you get at the county fair. But it was pretty close. Bernie now talks in cycles, telling Rita the same stories several times in the course of a half-hour visit. And at least once a week he travels back a good fifty years to the time his daughter Amy won a blue ribbon at the fair for her calf. To celebrate, they ate barbecue. And Bernie bought Amy and her mom each a huge cloud of pink cotton candy. They stood and watched as the sugar blew into strands inside the glass case and the vendor caught them on the white paper tube. The stuff was still warm and felt sparkly as it melted on their tongues.

"I'd give anything for some cotton candy," Bernie says at the end of that story every time he tells it. So Rita makes sure he gets a pack every week or two. She doesn't think that so much sugar would be good for him on a daily basis. In another hour he would probably forget that he'd eaten it anyway.

Jodie

Jodie hears the back door squeak. Moon floods the double bed and her solitary self. She gets up out of duty more than any sense that confronting Young Taylor will make any difference. She meets him in the family room. He's turned on a light and is reaching for the remote. Jodie gasps in spite of herself. Her son is in his full Goth makeup. Long black trench coat, white makeup on his hands and face, what looks like black greasepaint around his eyes and mouth. She remembers then that it's Halloween and checks her reaction as best she can.

"Where are you trick-or-treating at three in the morning?"

"I don't trick-or-treat."

"Then where have you been in that getup?"

"Out."

"That is not an answer. You tell me where you have been." She aims words at him, one by one.

"Out walking."

"But I heard the car."

"Well, I wasn't walking around here."

"Where?"

He fingers the remote and seems to be thinking hard. He speaks without turning back to her. "Out at the stone house."

"You've been with Dad?"

"No. I didn't want to wake him."

"You were in the house watching him sleep?"

He sighs, disgusted and impatient. "No. Just in the woods."

Jodie sits on the couch and looks at him. "Please help me understand why I shouldn't be worried right now."

"I don't like him being by himself."

The words take the wind out of her. Her children do this to her constantly, acting as if they are clueless and careless, only to prove through a single statement that they not only are full of understanding but have agendas of their own. "I don't either. But he feels like this is what he needs to do."

"Or maybe he feels like you don't want him here."

She forces herself to ignore the pain her son's words have just inflicted. "I really don't think that's what he thinks. And as his wife, I probably know more about what he thinks than you do." She can use words too. She feels slightly guilty, although she has aimed not to hurt but to stun. This child is old enough to do war with her; he is old enough to be put in his place. Some days she marvels at how heartless she has become.

"Whatever." Young Taylor heads for the stairs.

"Don't 'whatever' me. It's not okay for you to run around the country in the middle of the night, especially in that getup. What if Jerry or the state patrol had stopped you? You expect them to see you and not think you're on dope or something?"

He starts up the stairs, not defiantly but deliberately. Jodie fights to keep words in, and for once she doesn't spin into a maniacal bitch who threatens all but hell itself at her firstborn. She is tired of yelling and threatening. Tired of this kid who is set against them all.

PART THREE

DESOLATION

7

LOSING FAITH

Come, ye weary, heavy laden, lost and ruined by the fall;
If you tarry till you're better, you will never come at all.
I will arise and go to Jesus, he will embrace me in his
    arms;
In the arms of my dear Savior, o there are ten thousand
    charms.
    — *"Come, Ye Sinners, Poor and Needy"*

Mack

He noticed the camera three weeks ago when reaching into the linen closet at the farmhouse. While he was searching for old blankets, his fingers found the cool lens and drew back in confusion. Pulled-back linens revealed the Vivitar, its shoulder strap still attached. Young Taylor had dabbled with photography back in eighth grade. Rita found the camera in a garage sale and bought the strap in the old Woolworth's in Beulah, the one recently replaced by two smaller businesses, an insurance office and a salon for doing fingernails. The photography phase lasted nearly a year, and then the camera became family property. Jodie played around with shots of her flower garden two or three springs ago. It hasn't been dragged out at a church or family function for a long time.

For no particular reason, Mack has brought the camera to the stone house. Now it is November, and there isn't a lot to do in the woods that is functional, other than gather firewood. Maybe he should roam around and see what he can find through this lens. Maybe not. These days he can't tell when a sudden idea will lead to something or fizzle. Thoughts can be thin and unreliable. On a good day he might, on his drive to or from work, have an idea about what to do that evening or that year. There might even be a momentary feeling of purpose or enthusiasm. The plan could be as mundane as systematically checking his own remaining machinery—the garden tiller, the mower, the small John Deere that escaped the auction because it had barely any of its original parts left and just about every farmer in the county has a similar machine gathering cobwebs in a dark shed. Or he could sort through the junk in the back of the barn. He can be a little bit happy, imagining this useful thing he might do. It might take him as long as a day or two, and at the end of it he could see what he's accomplished. But something as minor as a song on the radio or a bug hitting the windshield can loosen that idea and weaken any impulse he has toward carrying it out. This is how worthless his mind is now.

In spite of all that, he buys the cheapest film he can find at Wal-Mart, two color rolls of twenty-four exposures.

The camera sits on the passenger side of the car, tucked between his thermos and the seat back. He looks at it briefly, suspiciously, knowing that he is probably setting himself up for failure.

But this evening, as he exits town on the county road leading home, the early winter heaven releases amazing colors, smudges of gunmetal and peace rose. He pulls onto the shoulder and aims the camera at the expanse. He's frustrated immediately at how little of it fits into the small square of the viewfinder, but snaps the shot anyway. A mile farther, the colors go miraculous. Just in front of great sweeps of mad ruby, with the light shining through, is Jameson's old barn, a piece of tiller jutting out from one side, boards missing like lost puzzle pieces. This gives the picture something more specific and manageable than the entire horizon. When he looks through the lens, the shape of the barn seems to sharpen, and he is stabbed by a feeling of loss. He remembers when it wasn't abandoned, when cattle gathered around it at the end of the day, and when machinery that wasn't broken or rusted was parked by seasons, according to which task was called for. He can see it clearly, and when he snaps the picture, he feels that he has snatched the last glimmer of memory. Like the fast-leaving western light, the images are slipping and disintegrating.

After that evening, he can't take his eyes off abandoned barns. He can't stop noticing how many there are. He is compelled to gather their memories against the final winds and rains that will toss aside their remaining walls.

Sometimes abandoned barns sit beside newer generations of buildings. There are several working farms within a few miles on which Mack counts three or even four different versions of the barn, with the oldest a mere foundation or a ramshackle shadow of building that leans toward its successors as if bowing out and into retirement. Those that don't stand empty appear to be held up by the machinery or the hay they store. It isn't unusual for the oldest barn to house all the bits and pieces that no one has bothered hauling off to a junkyard. In this way families store their histories, the refuse along with the memories. Maybe it has to do with the long habit of never wasting anything. Garbage goes to the hogs or the compost; old curtains become rags; used pantyhose becomes twine for tying up tomato plants; used clothing goes to the church or community pantry. Leftover plant life gets tilled back into the earthy bed from which it sprouted. What can't go back directly travels somewhere else in the form of smoke from harvest bonfires. A man keeps whatever part might work again, even if in another machine entirely. All these pieces of life find their succession of homes, all of them within a hundred yards of each other. Nothing is lost permanently. The totally unusable items rest at last beyond all the usable things, stored in a heap at the far end of the barnyard or in a gully that can serve no other purpose but to hide broken appliances and other various items removed from living space during someone's fit of sorting and pitching.

Mack begins to take note of these patterns of objects that until now have been—he supposes—too everyday to notice. His vision begins to hook onto ordinary sights and turn them into new information. He counts old barns, takes pictures of a family's history as represented by its unique configuration of outbuildings. He tries to capture all the straight lines: roofs of buildings, seams in the asphalt, power lines, thin shelves of clouds, planes of light, boards in old bridges, wires in fences. In fact, the earth itself is a dark and silent horizon, straight as a yard-stick, sprouting electrical poles into a nearly colorless sky.

The pictures come back from Wal-Mart and are nothing like what he saw. The images are smaller and less sharp, the colors just not there in the same way. The emotions are gone. Mack tacks them up on one wall of the stone house. He arranges them several times but then takes them all down—except for a couple—and throws them away. For the life of him he can't understand why any of this is sud-denly important. But he is at the mercy of some hunger that has risen up out of his days of solitude. He needs to see the second level of things. He wants to search the outward signs of others' lives and see how much those lives match his own.

But of course their lives will never match his. *They* are not roaming the roads, slowing down to look at buildings, stopping to take ama-teurish pictures of the county's life. They are too busy living that life, unlike Mack, who in some bizarre way has stepped outside it. That's it, he decides. He isn't trying to document anything or make artistic portraits of the countryside. He is searching for an entrance some-where, a way back into his life, their life, the life of the place, which is all he's ever learned but for some reason is unable to learn again.

He does not mention the photography to George. He knows that family and neighbors will see him with the camera and that word will get around, but to introduce the topic to George would open up a part of Mack's soul that is still being formed somehow. He cannot talk about something that he has not yet identified. And contrary to what therapists and preachers seem to think, talking is not always the way to learn things. For now, looking at things is his main conversation.

Rita

She wouldn't swear to it, but she thinks that Tom the mechanic shakes his head when he sees her pull in. Most mechanics are happy to see business roll into the driveway. Work is work, isn't it? But what for years was the periodic tune-up and tire rotation has turned into practically a monthly visit to fix some new ailment. "This car is going to nickel-and-dime you to death, Mrs. Barnes," he said to Rita, and that was two years ago. But Tom Longman is the son of Beth and Bill Longman, and he was brought up to have manners. When Rita stops the car and lowers the window, he smiles and walks right up to her and leans down politely.

"How can I help you, young lady?"

"You can find out what's making this bumping sound when I hit the brakes."

"What kind of bumping sound?"

"Don't know how to describe it, kind of a *chug-chug.*"

"Only when you brake?"

"Yes, and I don't like brakes that make noise."

"Well, noisy brakes are not something you want to get used to."

"Wouldn't want them to just give out on me."

"Especially the way you drive, tearing around town like a maniac."

She allows herself to chuckle. Tom is always trying to make her laugh, maybe because every time they meet she is anxious over some problem with her vehicle.

"Scoot over and let me see what's happening." He gets behind the wheel, and they drive around for about ten minutes. The car doesn't act up at first, but then, suddenly, there is a strange jolting underneath them, and that bumping. Tom doesn't say anything but turns the opposite direction of the garage. Rita figures out that he's taking her home, not a good sign.

"Well, we've got some kind of brake problem," he says as he turns onto her street.

"That sounds serious."

"You sure can't drive it this way. I can't really get under there until tomorrow morning. But I'll call you just as soon as I know what the problem is." He slides into her little driveway, hops out, and comes around to open her door.

"Thank you, Tom. Just call when you know." She doesn't even ask about the cost. Anything will be too much; she'll have to work numbers on this, just as she has to work numbers on everything else.

"Work numbers." That was Taylor Barnes's phrase. Over their years together, as problems of one sort or another came up, Taylor would bring them to moments of rest by stating, "Time to work numbers. We'll figure it out, Rita Mae." And they generally did. But the relief for Rita had always begun at that moment when Taylor told her it was time to work numbers. When he said that, she knew that he expected the numbers to work out eventually. He was stating that he had a plan and that they'd get through whatever it was they were in the middle of.

They had survived all the usual ups and downs, had kept on after failed crops and deaths of loved ones, long illnesses and bad bank sheets. But Rita had never become truly discouraged until Taylor stopped saying he would work numbers. And he stopped saying it at age sixty-two, two years before that damned tractor turned over on top of him. She's always suspected that the tractor would have stayed upright if Taylor had just kept working numbers. But it just wasn't in him anymore. He kept working as hard as always, but something important had left him.

For about ten years now, she has worked her own cussed numbers. She's worked numbers for both sons too. Lucky for her, she's got a daughter-in-law who can work numbers with the best of them. This is how they have all kept going, with Jodie and Rita working numbers, even after Alex died and Mack went silent and became unable to work numbers for himself.

She fixes herself instant hot chocolate, adding some powdered milk and cinnamon to give it more body. She drinks it sitting in her living room, which looks out at the street. She doesn't bother calling Mack at work or Jodie, who would be home about now. She'll wait until Tom knows what the verdict is, and then she'll do whatever she needs to do.

Tom calls by ten the next morning. The news is not good: she needs a new something-or-other, and it's a part he's got to order from somewhere else. She'll be without wheels for at least two more days.

She gets off the phone to Tom and punches in the number at the farmhouse. No one is home, but she'll leave a message. This is something she has finally become comfortable with. Jodie got their first answering machine about three years ago. She said it was just easier with all of them coming and going so much. She put a nice little message on there about how you'd reached the home of Mack, Jodie, Taylor, and Kenzie Barnes, and that no one was home to take your message but they'd be happy to get back to you as soon as they could. You were supposed to leave your name, number, and message after the beep. Then an uncomfortable few seconds passed before the beep came. And then once the beep happened, silence—and you realized that now it was your turn. And suddenly you were all flustered and couldn't even remember why you'd called. This whole process felt insulting at first, and Rita had refused to leave messages for the first two months they had the machine. That was one of the few times she'd ever seen Jodie truly irritated with her.

"Mom, if you don't leave a message, then I don't even know that you tried to call. Just talk as if one of us is at the other end."

"But what if I mess it up?"

"How can you mess it up?"

"By saying something that doesn't come out right. It's not like I can rewind the thing and then try again."

"If you mess up, just hang up and call back."

"Then I have to go through the whole process all over again. I may as well get in the car and drive out there and write a note on the door, all the time it takes to deal with the machine."

"Okay." Jodie has a way of saying that to indicate that she's had enough but is going to be polite about it. The next week, Rita used the machine. She wrote down what she wanted to say in case she panicked once the beep came and went. It worked out all right, but she'd ended her message and was about to hang up when she realized she hadn't even introduced herself. So she quickly tacked on, "This is Mom," and then hung up fast.

Now she doesn't even expect a real person to answer the phone. And she leaves messages two or three times on some days. It's part of how the family functions, and she's actually glad the machine is there, because that saves her a lot of time when she would otherwise have to call back again and again, hoping to get someone.

Thanks to her hacky cough, today she has to hang up the first time she tries to leave a message. On the second try she talks fast and keeps it short: "This is Mom. The car's at the shop again, some problem with the brakes. I probably won't have it back until Thursday. Jodie, could you pick me up if you grocery-shop sometime today? Talk to you later."

Amos has offered several times to drive her around. So far she hasn't taken him up on it. Some days she thinks that Amos could depend on her too much if she let him. He doesn't like living by himself. Rita doesn't either, but casual visiting over the fence is as much as she wants for now. Another person in her life, even just for regular conversation, feels like a little too much.

The day wears on, and she doesn't hear from Jodie, even after three, when Jodie usually gets home from the school cafeteria. It's not like her to leave a message hanging. Rita walks over to the pharmacy and to the grocery and to the post office. The weather is mild for mid-November, and she tells herself that she needs to walk more anyway. Julia at the pharmacy tries to sell her a little cart, one of those that old people push around town to carry their groceries in. She's just trying to be helpful. "My mother has worn out one already. It's real easy to push, and it holds two full sacks of groceries, plus her purse on the top. I can have Gary pull one down for you—see them there, on top of the shelves at aisle two?"

"Oh, I'm not getting that much today. I'm fine." Rita hurries to pay and get out of there. She doesn't need an old-lady cart. She'll have her car back in a couple of days. She wishes she'd thought to call Mack at work; he would have dropped by before going home and helped her run her errands. In fact, most days he does drop by, just to say hi. But maybe today he's busy or has his own errands to run. It feels odd and not very good to be out of touch with both Mack and Jodie for most of a day.

She's eating her microwaved dinner in front of the evening news when Jodie calls.

"Hi, Mom, sorry I didn't get back sooner."

"Everything okay over there?"

"Yeah, but I ran over to Ottumwa after work, just decided at the last minute. It was just a quick trip, but I should have given you a call. Have you had your supper? You want Young Taylor to come get you and you can eat with us?"

"No. I'm having supper. I walked over to the store—weather was nice."

"You get everything? The store's closed, but we can go over to Oskaloosa if you need to."

"No. Nothing urgent. Mack there?"

"No. He stopped by on his way to the stone house."

"He doesn't even eat dinner with you?"

"Most nights, but not tonight."

Jodie tells her that she'll come by tomorrow right after work, and they can run errands together. When Rita hangs up, she feels awful. The day will be going by like a regular day, and then she'll be forced to think about Mack out in that cabin by himself. And now that she doesn't have a car, she can't follow the urge to just go out there and try to talk sense into him. It's hard to take charge of anything when you're on foot.

Jodie

It takes some doing to go to Ottumwa without another family member. It isn't a particularly long trip, but it generally means shopping, and that is something a person does with someone else, probably family. And most of the time that family is Rita. What could she possibly be doing over there that Rita wouldn't be invited to?

In the end, she simply goes and decides to tell Rita later that it was a spur-of-the-moment thing. She might hint that Christmas shopping was involved and that she was shopping for gifts that needed to be kept secret. But for years now she has taken Rita shopping for most gifts, getting Rita to try on pantsuits or whatever and then buying her the one she wanted. Spur of the moment will have to be explanation enough.

This time of year hardly any cars roam into the parks. Red Haw State Park is about forty-five miles due west of Ottumwa, off the beaten path for anyone down Beulah way. She tries to hold in her mind how the world looks this afternoon as she travels toward what will likely become the place of an astounding sin. She drives with dread and sheer excitement. She has showered and used the blow dryer, has dared to apply the new makeup, and wears the jeans and shirt that help a person imagine that, under certain circumstances, she could look slender.

She hasn't thought of sex much during her nineteen years with Mack. They've gotten along just fine in that area, and even with two kids underfoot and extended family forever at the door, they've managed to have enough of each other. Enough, at least, until Mack changed, until everything got bleak. Since then, Jodie has discovered what a powerful thing it is that she'd taken for granted through the years. Suddenly it isn't there anymore, and they don't know what to do or how to talk about it. A whole part of their life has just dropped out of existence.

Before that point she never thought of herself as interested in sex more than the next person. But with it missing now, she is hungry as she's never been hungry before. Suddenly the hunger is defining her and presenting to her a whole new image of herself. Now she is a woman unloved, a woman without sex. She doesn't know which is the harder trial, to do without the sex or to see herself as someone without it. This new, unwelcome self-image seems to determine the direction of both her thoughts and her emotions most days.

And now here's Terry, and she can't look at him anymore without seeing all of him. She looks at his face but gathers from the corners of her vision his legs and arms, his chest and groin, his whole male self. She can't avoid this. Terry has become more than Terry a coworker. He is Terry a male, in close proximity to her. The proximity often fills with quick breaths and alarming little throbs. When Terry stands in the same room, Jodie imagines that she can feel him in her own pulse.

By the time she arrives at the park entrance, she is chilled to the bone. Her legs shake. Suddenly, she wants to cry.

What are you doing? What are you doing?

His car is at the far end of the main parking lot. She parks at the opposite end, walks across the pavement to the grass and trees, and wanders in the direction of his car. From the parking lot, the land inclines toward the lake. She sees Terry sitting on a picnic table halfway down the slope.

"Hi." She does her best not to sound panicked. She is startled by the look on his face, a weird mixture of relief and panic.

"I wasn't sure you'd come," he says as she gets closer.

"I wasn't sure either." Her nerves come through with a little burst of laughter.

"I'm so glad you're here." He reaches out to her then, and she reaches out to him with no effort at all. The feel of his bones and muscles through all their clothing makes her suddenly desire everything in life. It has been years since she has gripped anyone with such intent.

"I'm a little scared," she murmurs against his jacket. She feels a tear slip out.

He doesn't mind the tears. He comforts her with a kiss. And then another.

Her body goes its own way, as if it is a self-contained entity, defined by its own desire. With Terry, back in his car, parked in a little nook away from the lot and main walkways, her body takes the predictable course, and she sits back and watches herself undress and embrace and be embraced and do all the deeply personal things that have remained for most of her life in a particular house with one other person. She watches her body find its way with someone else. She doesn't quite know what to think of it.

She thought that this act would bring intense emotion—relief or happiness or guilt. She has dreaded the moment when all of these feelings would collide inside her.

But after they have made love, she leans against the backseat of Terry's car and watches him put on his shirt, and the action looks entirely ordinary. She studies his face, gazes with detachment at the lips that kissed her with such power, at the body, now clothed, that pressed urgently. Although Jodie's head still buzzes, the memories are already dissipating into the chilly air.

She sees him looking at her.

"I know," he says quietly, "that there are all sorts of reasons I should regret what just happened, but I honestly can't bring myself to regret it at all."

She doesn't reply. She notices just then that Terry uses a lot of words to say not very much. Already a hazy discomfort has begun to slip in. She guesses that this is an early symptom of regret.

"You okay?" For the first time he looks worried.

"Sure. Just don't know what to say."

He grins but takes a shaky breath. Jodie realizes then the danger of what they have just done. The lovemaking itself is the least of it. Her real concern is what the lovemaking has started between them. In that moment, when Terry breathes in and out, Jodie understands that she can't just stop at this. She can never hear him breathe again or watch him walk across a room again. She will have to be held by him again. Something bigger than her will determines this. She wonders if it has hit Terry yet, or if, in the way stereotypical of males, he is even

now wracking his brain for a way out, to let her down without seeming heartless.

But what kind of a letdown could it be? What could be damaged in
her life or her marriage that isn't already near death? Mack is the one
who went to the hospital. He is the official victim. And there can't be
a victim without an offender. Of course that would be her. All of
them have considered, silently, that if she had been a better wife, her
husband would not have wanted to die. Such a thing is common
knowledge. Wives are for supporting and loving and helping. Never
mind if they don't get any of that themselves.

With these few thoughts, she attempts self-justification, some
cushioning by way of memories of all the love she has lost. But over
these thoughts rests a mist of discontent. Even this longed-for, forbidden act has turned out to be one more motion she has forced herself through, yet another strategy for saving herself. Just Jodie taking
charge of Jodie's life and dragging it across another bumpy threshold
into nothing.

"So what happens now?" Terry's voice is deep, covered in late sun
sparkles through the back glass of the car. They parked at the end of a
little road that peters out near the water.

"What do you want to happen?" she asks. She pauses and studies
him. His face appears so much younger than Mack's.

He shrugs, his eyebrows arching. "I want to see you again."

She nods but slides her look away from him. "Me too."

"It's hard to plan very far ahead ..." He stares into trees bereft of
their leaves.

"That's for sure. I can't plan anything right now."

"I'm with you there."

She touches his face, then withdraws her hand when she realizes
that it is the very same way she has touched Mack's face hundreds of
times. "I guess that for now I just want to try out how it might be."

Terry appears profoundly relieved. "That's the way I look at it.
This isn't some fling for me—I don't want you to think that. I think
it could really turn into something. But it's complicated."

They plan their next meeting. There is a tiny motel in a neighboring town. As far as they know, nobody in Beulah has relatives there. And no one would drive through there for any other reason; there is no industry or shop that a farmer couldn't find closer to home. Terry's last class of the day is a study hall, and he can get out early, claiming a need for personal time to go to the doctor or something. Jodie is finished in the cafeteria by two-thirty. There is some dead time between then and when she tries to corral the kids for dinner. She'll leave them a note, claiming that she's running errands and they can throw something in the microwave. With Mack not in the house, it should be easy enough to get away, taking a back road or two rather than going directly to the main highway within ten miles of town.

She stops at a fabric store at the mall in Ottumwa. Rita knows that she shops there a couple times a year, because they have good sales and a wide selection. As she throws the bag into the front seat of the truck and turns the key, she sees Terry beside her clear as day. She even hears him breathing. Moments from the past hour flicker through her memory. But nothing inside her jars or even sways. What she expected to be relief is only a form of sadness. A thought floats up: *Well, you did what you set out to do.* She doesn't really feel guilt either, but a deep disappointment in herself, for committing an act so unoriginal and yet quite apt to damage them all.

Kenzie

She is nervous almost from the start of the Tuesday night youth group Bible study. Everyone is way too chatty. Here they are, trying to understand God's mysteries and determine what Jesus would do in real-life situations, and Carol is whispering gossip to Jenna, and Bobby keeps trying to hit the wastebasket with tiny pieces of chalk from the blackboard tray. Pastor Williamson, as always, is patient. He and Trent are doing most of the talking; Trent usually takes the Scripture seriously, but that's because he's a geek and doesn't really have friends. He likes to talk to Pastor Williamson as though they are friends, and Pastor Williamson lets him do that because he's a compassionate guy, but even he doesn't seem inclined to like Trent very much. This evening they are discussing First Thessalonians, chapter five, about being alert now that it is the last days.

"If we stay sharp, we can see the signs. That's what Paul is saying." Trent acts as though he has just delivered wisdom never heard before.

"That's right. And if we're out partying all the time, using drugs and getting drunk and hanging out with people who aren't awake, our chances of seeing the truth are not that great." Pastor Williamson has mentioned drugs and alcohol more lately. Kenzie thinks this is because a couple of families in the church have heard about kids at the high school partaking at a recent party. They called the pastor, and the pastor of course handed responsibility to the man in charge of the youth. Kenzie is certain that Pastor Williamson has been instructed to step up preaching against substance abuse. So he inserts it now, in a place where it sort of belongs, but Kenzie has little patience for it today.

"Excuse me," she says suddenly, "but we're already not awake enough. After all, the Tribulation has started."

Everyone gets quiet then and looks at her. Pastor Williamson bends his neck to the side, a habit that apparently keeps him loose but that he does mainly when he senses conflict. He repeats what she's just said.

"The Tribulation has already started. What makes you say that, Kenzie?"

She raises both hands, feeling frustrated at their blank stares. "Satan's in control of most of the churches right now. They've stopped preaching against sin, and they go against God's laws."

"Could you be more specific?"

"Well, it's illegal to pray in school, and there's a movement to take 'under God' out of the Pledge of Allegiance. And you can't even put Christmas decorations in the town square anymore—because anything Christian gets persecuted."

Jenna wags her head a little. "We still have a nativity in our square."

"Only because nobody's challenged it. If an atheist or a person of some false religion took the matter to court, we'd have no nativity. The government already belongs to Satan."

"That's right," Carol says suddenly. "It allows homosexuality and abortion."

"But the Rapture has to come before the Tribulation," Trent says. He has read every book in the Left Behind series and will sometimes quote from them as well as from Scripture. "Everybody knows that the Tribulation can't happen until we're taken into heaven."

"I don't think so. I'm watching these teaching tapes on Revelation, and Reverend Francis says that the Tribulation's already begun, that Christians have to band together right now to fight evil. He even has a retreat center in Lawrence, Kansas, where people can go. Because the enemy will become more and more powerful."

"Well, we know that 'greater is he that is in us than he that is in the world,'" Pastor Williamson breaks in. He is smiling but looks as if he'd rather be somewhere else.

"But who is in the church—the one who is greater or the one who is in the world?" Kenzie's voice has become strong, and it trembles some.

Jenna laughs nervously. "Jesus is in the church," she says. "You think he'd just leave without telling us?" The rest of them laugh then, not in a harsh way, but Kenzie's heart sinks when she sees Pastor Williamson smiling. Of course he doesn't get it. They're all blind.

"Kenzie, there are a lot of ways to interpret the Book of Revelation, and I'm sure this teacher you're listening to has some good points, but we have to beware of people who try to scare us. Christians shouldn't live in fear."

"I'd like you to listen to these tapes, because I think Reverend Francis is telling the truth. I'm sure we're in the Tribulation." She says this with finality, unwilling to argue anymore.

"I'd be happy to listen to those tapes. Just drop them by the office this week, and you and I can talk about it later."

And that is that. They go on talking about staying awake and sober, and whatever. Kenzie can't wait to leave. She does want to press Pastor Williamson further after the meeting's over, but of course Trent has him in some deep discussion and no one else can get near. And Jenna gave her a ride tonight and won't stay a minute longer than she has to. Jenna's mom has been working a lot of over-time lately, and Jenna has to put her little brother to bed. She's dis-tracted while she drives Kenzie home, and Kenzie's too discouraged to attempt conversation.

Jodie

She marvels at how her bright moments with Terry are followed by immediate catastrophe. There was the day in the parking lot when he appeared like a fantasy—and then the business in the park with Young Taylor and his weird friends. This evening, when she gets home, she is still energized by sex accomplished and decides to calm down by surfing the Net for a while. She and Mack finally bought a computer last year and hooked it up in the family room. The kids use it mainly, but Jodie has logged on about once a week to look for news or recipes and open her e-mail from two or three acquaintances who routinely send items of interest to neighbors and former class-mates.

The computer software rings to be connected, loud against the evening. Once online, Jodie mistakenly opens a window showing her the sites most recently visited. The first one reads simply "suicide by gunshot." Fear moves through her veins in a sick rush. She clicks on the site and is confronted by a black-and-white photo of a man on a couch, his head and face a knob of bloody pulp. She clicks on NEXT, and there is a close-up of another man's head, misshapen and with the top blown off completely. The caption explains that the quickly ex-panding gases created by the shotgun blast at close range caused the extreme bloat of the lower face and head.

She closes the site and gets off the Web. She finds neither of the kids upstairs. Empty microwave dinner trays were in the trash when she came in; apparently they've been home long enough to eat.

She hurries out to the truck and heads for the stone house. It's nearly dark, and when she pulls into the driveway, she sees that there's a light on in the main room. She taps on the door and calls, "Mack?"

She hears him shuffle abruptly. The door opens, and his surprised face is inches from hers. "Hi, sweet. What's up?"

Jodie hesitates, and Mack brings her inside. "Something wrong? The kids okay? I stopped by a couple hours ago, and Kenzie was leaving for youth group and Young Taylor was gone."

"Sorry I wasn't there. I had some stuff to do and just left frozen dinners to nuke. Did you use the computer?"

He stares at her, confused. "Not for a couple of weeks. Why?"

She shakes her head. "Oh, I just had some trouble with it—locked up on me—and I wondered if anyone else had the same problem." She makes a smile. "And ... I wondered if you'd eaten yet. I could make spaghetti or something." She notices the tan of his throat, near the collarbone. He has the outdoorsy look that used to be normal for him. She sees Terry's throat, paler, a freckle here and there. Then she sees that awful head from the Internet with its top missing. She has to work at listening to Mack's reply.

"No, thanks. I grabbed a bite after work."

"You doing okay? Warm enough?"

"Yeah."

She notices for the first time a few snapshots that are thumbtacked into the paneling. "Doing some photography, I see."

"Trying to invent a hobby. I'm pretty crappy at it."

She notes the lightness of his voice, the absence of storms in his eyes. This is not a man with violence on his mind. "Well, I'd better get back."

"You okay?"

She is walking out the door and to the truck, and nods without looking back at him.

When Kenzie gets home from youth group about twenty minutes later, Jodie decides to be direct. "Have you been online today?"

"Early this morning, before school."

She offers no more information, so Jodie moves the discussion along. "Did you have any problem with it locking up on you?"

"No. Did it with you?"

"Yes, a while ago."

"Was it the mouse or the whole computer?"

"The screen just sort of froze."

Kenzie asks a few more diagnostic questions. She appears steady and focused as ever. Jodie thinks of how upset her daughter gets when any hint of violence or cruelty pops up in a movie or television show. There's no way she is examining pictures of splattered brains, but Jodie presses on.

"Any particular sites you go to—like the news or weather?"

Kenzie hesitates. Her eyes are wandering over a page of her history book. "There are a couple of websites I check a few times a week. I check out the news, stuff about movies. And there's this preacher I listen to sometimes on TV. He does Bible studies online."

Jodie nods, at a loss. "What about Young Taylor? He uses it quite a bit, doesn't he?"

"Usually after we're all in bed." Young Taylor has always resented that the computer is in the family room, which affords him no privacy. "He goes to Goth sites mainly, far as I know."

"Well, I'll see if it will behave for me now." Jodie descends the stairs, feeling as if her soul is floating about, dissected. Was it barely two hours ago that she and Terry were going at it in his backseat? Is Young Taylor really troubled, as Rita has insisted for weeks? Should Jodie search his room now, something she swore she would never do to her kids? No, she will just ask him, because she can still see into his eyes and tell when he's lying. He's fooled Mack a time or two, but never her.

She sits in the living room, which is quiet and fairly undisturbed; most of their communal living happens in the adjacent family room. In this northernmost room of the downstairs, the one directly under her and Mack's bedroom, there is no television or radio, just chairs and a sofa and tables with her nicer lamps. She considers it her room, because the kids have no interest in its quiet; Kenzie prefers her own bedroom when she reads, and Mack has always avoided it for fear of bringing dirt in on his clothes and shoes. When they used to be more sociable, company gathered here. Jodie sits on the sofa, which faces the north window. Darkness is on the other side of the sheer green curtains. She doesn't turn on a lamp but sits there until she can see the room's lines. She sat here right after she found Mack's loaded shotgun. She sat on this side of the sofa and whispered bits of thought to herself, which is what she does now.

"I can't save the life of one more person. I can't pull my son away from the edge, or help my husband come home. I can't do another thing."

She longs for a voice to collude with hers. She reaches into twilight for some comforting turn of phrase. Months ago, or even just weeks ago, she might have prayed or turned to a favorite song. But the words that stir deep down, about vulnerable little lambs and safety in darkness, stop just this side of consciousness. After the lawless pleasure of the afternoon, any movement toward God is brought up short.

8

GOING BROKE

But none of the ransomed ever knew how deep were the
    waters crossed;
Nor how dark was the night the Lord passed through
Ere he found his sheep that was lost.
Out in the desert he heard its cry, sick and helpless and
    ready to die;
Sick and helpless and ready to die.
                      —*"The Ninety and Nine"*

Mack

He is going home from work the first time he hears it. It sounds so
much like a voice that he looks at the radio and determines that it's
turned off. He drives another mile and hears it again.

"Everything is working out."

He stops the car. "What the hell?" He sits still as his heart picks
up its rhythm, waiting for the voice. Just a regular voice, not creepy or
anything. But there's no one in the car with him.

He sits for two minutes, kills the engine. No more voice.

Ever since Halloween night and what seemed to be the ghost of
Alex showing up in the woods, Mack's imagination has become as active as a six-year-old's. He falls asleep with some difficulty, out in the

lonely stone house. He hates waking up in the middle of the night, when silence is at its thickest, when it seems that anything could appear. And now this, a voice from nowhere. He tries to figure out how to ask George about it without admitting that it's happening to him. *Ask about side effects of the meds maybe. That's got to be it.*

Two days later he is picking up groceries for Jodie in Oskaloosa, fixings for Thanksgiving dinner. They will gather at the farmhouse in a few days. Jodie and Mom will begin cooking before that. Mack's contribution is to haul the turkey home, go hunt the supermarket shelves, list in hand, then stand in line and hand over the money. This standard participation is somewhat comforting.

He is loading the last of the grocery sacks into the truck. As he gets into the cab someone says, "Love is always the last thing standing." He can't recognize who it is, or who would say such an off-the-wall thing, so he turns toward the voice—and sees nothing but parking lot. The nearest people are several spaces over, two teenage girls getting into a Honda.

His skin tingles. There is no question that he heard something. This has got to stop. He is finally going around the bend.

He cranks the radio up full blast, windows shut, on the drive to the farmhouse. Yet he has an uncanny sense that the scenery—the iron-colored fields and naked gray trees—is pressed to the glass, looking in at him. Every house, cemetery stone, and cluster of cattle watches him with great care. Though it's late autumn, the surrounding world is more present than a lush day in spring.

The world expects something of him. The landscape waits for him to make his move. He doesn't know how to move or what to do. He wishes his senses would just go to sleep and stay that way for a long time.

He drops the groceries at the house and visits with Jodie for a while. They sit in the family room, not at the kitchen table, which is their habit. Jodie is distant, though friendly enough. How can he expect her to be anything else with him living off to himself?

Then he survives the looming countryside enough to get to the stone house and shut himself inside. He turns on the radio and eats leftover stew. Spread across the south wall are his pitiful photographs, dangling cockeyed. All dead buildings, forsaken homes, empty places. Once more he takes them down and sorts through them, throws away a few, and puts the remaining ones back on the wall.

It's a puzzle, that's all. Some puzzle with pieces but no theme. Just like his life. It's only pieces now. And yet he thinks that being out here all alone will help him find the theme.

Mack presses fingers into his forehead. He tries to think of how it would be that love is always the last thing standing.

Kenzie

The one event, next to prayer time, that now holds her life together is her nearly daily visit with Mitchell. She never dreamed that God would meet her needs so perfectly, so on time and truly matched to her deepest desires. But why should she doubt God Almighty? He is the God who parted the Red Sea, who made the sun stand still, who brought husbands and wives together, even through strange circumstances. God listened to every heartfelt prayer of David the shepherd, songwriter, and king. God sent an angel to bring Peter out of prison, made the oil in the widow's bottle last and last beyond what it should have. God made Saul blind and then turned him into Paul, a new man. God raised Lazarus from the dead and fed a whole crowd with a few loaves and fishes. God has been working miracles in the lives of his people since before people started writing down the stories. Well, now God is writing Kenzie Barnes's story, and why should it be less glorious than the others? What is to prevent her from becoming a Sarah or a Mary, or even a Deborah, who was a warrior and judge back before women did stuff like that?

Finally, in view of what is happening in her life lately, all those Bible stories make perfect sense. Miracles don't always make sense, but the life of God's child is miraculous even when it's just normal. She should have figured that out by now. It has taken Mitchell Jaylee's spiritual companionship to help her understand what she's always known and believe what she's always hoped for.

At the same time, it makes perfect sense that, now that she and Mitchell have found each other, the Enemy is bringing out all the worst ammunition. Dad is still out at the stone house. He's still taking all those medications, which, according to Reverend Francis, are crutches that people use when they have no faith in the healing work of Christ crucified. As long as Dad is doped up, his spirit won't have a chance to find its way free.

Young Taylor is spookier all the time. Kenzie heard his argument with Mom that night through the heat register—an advantage of having a bedroom directly over the family room. Mom found this suicide website and figured out that Young Taylor was the only person who could have been looking at it. He didn't even deny it, and he spoke so calmly that it made Kenzie feel cold. He called it simple curiosity, and wasn't Mom even curious about things that scared her? What a question to ask. Mom went at him for a long time, one question after another, and he answered every one in that dead voice, which seemed to make Mom more worried than ever. She told him it was cruel to even have something like that in the house, considering what the family had been through. He said that was reason enough to look closer. At that point, Mom gave up and slammed kitchen cabinets and cleaned things unnecessarily for an hour or more.

So Kenzie prays for the blood of Jesus to cover Young Taylor and protect him from the Evil One.

Bekka and other friends understand Kenzie less all the time. It seems that since she's been seeing Mitchell, everybody else has been demanding time with her. They want to go to the mall or a movie or hang out at somebody's house, gossiping and messing with makeup or clothes or hairstyles or any number of things that have no eternal value whatsoever. She tries to talk to them about spiritual things, but they just sigh as if she were stupid but there is nothing to be done about it.

She has the sense that Mitchell is the one thing in her life that must be kept from Bekka and the others. Deep in her spirit she knows that they would not get it. They would make gagging sounds if she were to admit that she finds Mitchell Jaylee the least bit attractive or that she has any kind of friendly relationship with him. Mitchell Jaylee is so off their radar that they don't even mention him when they are naming the people they don't like or the ones they think are really bad or weird in some way. She knows that if she ever mentions his name, something bad will happen. Bekka and Janelle and the others will pass judgment and then cause trouble if Kenzie doesn't admit on the spot that she's just being silly. They will never, ever understand. Just as they have never understood her praying at the altar every day. She hasn't risked telling them about Jesus's eyes or about floating as she prays.

All of these things—the holiest parts of her life—seem to be hers alone. She shares them endlessly with Jesus, and that will have to be enough for now. That, and her visits with Mitchell.

There are days when Mitchell's features are so animated that she imagines him to be part angel. He talks with such passion—about anything and everything—and he sketches out all sorts of plans for their lives. When that spiritual brightness is about him, sometimes he stays up all night, working on his art out in the barn. She'll come by that afternoon and find him asleep on the couch or the back porch. His energy is so immense and single-minded.

"There are times, Kenzie, when I see God in everything," he whispered to her a few days ago. "I believe that I'm put on this earth to create works that will help other people see God too. But it's so hard." His eyes glistened. "It's so hard when they look at what I've done and they don't see anything."

"That's their fault, not yours. You know what the Bible says about how to the pure all things are pure. People who love God can see God, but people who hate God don't see anything. You have to let God take control of how your art affects people. That's the Holy Spirit's job, isn't it?"

He had smiled so beautifully, and hugged her. "I can count on you to keep my head straight. I love you so much, Kenzie."

He's looking at her now, and she wonders if he can read her mind, can see it replaying these conversations they've had. He's not glowing so brightly today. "I think demons are after me," he stated quietly when he let her in a few minutes ago. He tells her that she's never really seen him when he's under satanic attack, and he hopes she never has to. This frightens her, but she sees his honesty and his heart for God, and she knows that God calls her only to what she is able to bear or carry out. She will stand by Mitchell no matter what attacks him or for how long.

When she gets home, there are two messages on the answering machine for her, one from Bekka and the other from Janelle. Both sound irritated.

From Bekka: "Kenzie, didn't you say you'd study with us tonight? We've got that biology exam tomorrow—remember? Do you remember that we have school tomorrow and that, like, this is a really crucial test? We're at Janelle's—just come over."

From Janelle: "Hey, Kenz. Are you feeling okay? Today you looked like you were out of it. Even if you don't want to study, come over, okay? We can hang out, you know, not study the whole time. If you can't come over, please call, so we'll know, okay?"

She listens to both messages, with Mom nearby fixing supper. Mom doesn't react; she's intent on the onion she's chopping. Mom is pretty good about staying out of Kenzie's business unless it's important or Kenzie asks for input. Bekka's mom is much pushier, which is why Bekka is a brat so much of the time. But Mom is okay, just distracted and busy now, with Dad living at the stone house. She's busy but doesn't appear to consider that anything she does is that important. She pushes the knife through the onion in an intense way, but Kenzie knows that she will forget all about the onion a minute from now—throw it into the meatloaf or whatever and never think about it again. Sometimes Kenzie thinks that Mom has learned to get through her troubles by deciding that nothing is that important. She wonders if Mom ever prays. She goes to church, but concentrates on the singing and the praying and the sermon as though they were onions that need to be chopped and thrown into a skillet. They are things she needs to do for just a moment or two.

Jesus, don't let me ever be like that about you. Don't let me ever think that spiritual things aren't important, or forget that the thing I do right this moment could change the rest of my life.

She picks up the phone in the family room, out of Mom's hearing. Her friendship with Bekka has been closest, so she calls Janelle.

"Hi, Janelle. Sorry I didn't call earlier. I can't come over—some stuff I need to do here at home."

"You aren't going to study for biology? Why don't you come over for just an hour?" Janelle sounds more upset than she should be. Kenzie hears Bekka's voice in the background. "What's the problem? Does she need a ride?"

"I studied earlier—I know I said I'd study with you, but I really can't leave the house right now."

"Is everything okay?"

No, Kenzie thinks, *nothing is okay. If you were any kind of friend you wouldn't ask such a shallow question.*

"Yeah, I'm okay. But I can't come over tonight. See you tomorrow." She hangs up before Bekka can grab the phone at the other end.

The pressure she feels now, when she's at school among her friends, is ominous, like the pressure she has felt many times lately as she finished praying at the church and rode home quickly through the evening. Only lately has it occurred to her that Satan would of course use her closest friends to harm her.

Her only safe place is with Mitchell. And because of that, she must keep him safe from even her best friends.

When she puts down the phone, she wants to cry. She feels something ending inside her. She thinks that maybe the friendships that have been part of her life for years are now fading into something else. Not only will she not study with Bekka and Janelle tonight, but she probably will never study with them again. They are in one place, and her life has shifted to someplace else. It's not just Mitchell, it's her whole existence. Her prayers have called her away from the former life. She and Mitchell have talked about this, how they feel that they are being called to special service. They are scared, but also excited, so amazed that God would give them duties beyond what ordinary life has given them so far.

She goes upstairs and lies on her bed and looks out the window. She can see the dark mass that is the outline of the trees at the edge of the alfalfa. The land is so bare and quiet. There's a little sigh around the window, telling her that the wind is picking up a bit. Usually it's not as windy at night, but the weather itself seems to know that her life has changed today, that she has made an important choice.

She wants to record every bit of this journey. Life has become so complex that she is afraid she won't remember the details later. She needs to be able to look back at this time and see for herself how God's hand was guiding every step. Satan will try to confuse her later, when she and Mitchell are in the midst of their work for God's kingdom.

Dear Jesus,

Mitchell kisses me sometimes, when I first come to see him, or right before I leave. He's careful not to kiss too long or too hard, though. And today he made a confession to me. He said that sometimes he sins against me in his mind.

He was so embarrassed—I'd never seen him like that before. He said, "It's hard to be close to you sometimes, and not think about what it could be like to, you know . . ." And then he acted shy all of a sudden—it was really sweet.

So I said that I understood how he felt—sometimes I feel that way too. And he said that he didn't know how two people can really care about each other and not think about it sometimes.

I was really glad we could talk about it, you know, be so honest. It's what I always imagined a man would act like who really loves you, Lord, and wants to do what's best.

Things are happening so fast, Jesus. You wonder for years and years if you'll ever find true love. And then when it comes, you can hardly believe it. Thank you, thank you!

Love and praise,

Kenzie

Mack

He can tell by her face that Jodie is scared when she hops out of the truck and heads for the doorway of the stone house, where he's standing.

"Young Taylor's in jail."

"No, what happened?" He puts down his coffee.

"Oh, he went to school in all that makeup, with his black trench coat on. The principal called him in and told him to go home and clean up, that it wasn't appropriate dress for school. And Young Taylor got belligerent, said, 'Show me where it's written down I can't wear a coat or makeup.' And it just got worse. The principal called Jerry over to escort him out and—" Finally her voice breaks, just barely. "And he started a fight. Wouldn't go with Jerry, took a swing or something."

Mack is already reaching inside to grab his jacket. He swears softly and guides Jodie back toward the truck. "Go on home. I'll go to town."

"I should go with you."

"No, you've been through enough. I'll deal with this."

"I don't know what he was thinking, wearing a black trench coat to school." She gets into the truck and rolls down the window to hear what Mack is saying.

"He's trying to raise hell. Has he been fighting with you at home?"

"No more than the usual sassing and moping."

He jumps into the car and follows her to the farmhouse, where she turns in, and then he steps on the gas.

He would let the boy stay the night in jail—he can remember his own father doing that once when he and Alex got into a brawl and tore up a bar two counties over, back when they were just out of school. But he and Alex had had each other. It hadn't been such a bad night, hardly anybody else there, and the guards were bored and talkative. But Young Taylor is still a minor and would be shipped to juvenile detention, which could turn this event into something more complicated than it needs to be.

When Mack gets to the sheriff's office and sees his son, the kid looks ready to implode, burning with an inward intensity that glows through the white-and-black face. Mack sees the look and is reminded of his own periods of destruction, and he convinces Jerry Hawles to let Young Taylor come home with him. Jerry, still ticked off at having to manhandle a nearly grown kid, is nevertheless not eager to turn this into an official incident. Mack thanks Jerry for being understanding.

"This kid owes you some time. Just tell me when you need him."

"I could use about twenty hours of community service, especially after things thaw and we clean out the park buildings."

Young Taylor gets in the car and slams the door. Then he slams a foot into the dash. On this car, that doesn't make any difference at all, and they both know it. Mack tries to take a big breath without sounding as scared as he is. He is used to anger in this kid, but he can't keep up anymore. For a while he managed to stay a step ahead, to see things coming. But it is way beyond him now. He is out of psychology, out of intelligence or intuition. The only thing he seems to have—miraculously—is patience. He looks at the white-and-black face, the tattooed hand (when did that happen?), the foot jammed against the fiberglass, and decides to start at a point of total ignorance.

He turns to face Taylor's profile. "Just how mad are you trying to make me?"

He sees a flicker in the cheekbone, but Young Taylor doesn't answer.

"You enjoy looking like a freak, bringing all sorts of extra attention to yourself?"

"I'm not trying to do anything."

"From where I sit, you look to be begging for something."

Young Taylor blows out a hard breath but says nothing.

"Why don't you just tell me what you want? You know that if it's reasonable, Mom and I will always try to get you what you want."

"I don't want anything from you."

"But you're doing your best to push every button I've got."

"I'm not trying to do anything to you. I don't even think about you. You're not the center of my universe, all right?"

"Well, son," Mack swallows, his mouth dry, "you're still the center of mine. You and Mom and Kenzie."

"You're too screwed up to even know which universe you're in."

"You think this is news to me?"

Young Taylor lowers his eyes.

"We're all doing the best we can. I think you are too. But this crap has got to stop. All it does is scare people. Maybe you think you're making some kind of point, but nobody around here gets it."

"They don't get much of anything."

"So you have to make some allowances." They are talking in normal tones now. "You wear whatever you want at home. Watch whatever movies you want, listen to your music. Don't talk to us for days at a time if that's what you need to do. But wearing this getup to school is just mean, because it makes people think of Columbine. I've never known you to be a mean person, Taylor."

Something moves in the boy's face. When Mack or Jodie call him simply "Taylor," he knows that they are trying to treat him like an adult.

Their quiet has the sense of retreat in it. Young Taylor has lost some of his steam, and Mack has become more earnest than angry. He puts the car into gear and speaks as they pull out of the parking lot.

"In the next two days, you go back to Jerry and apologize and sign up for cleaning out gutters or whatever."

"He was acting like a big shot."

"He is a big shot. He's the sheriff."

"More like Barney Fife."

"Well, we love Barney around here."

They are halfway to the farmhouse when Young Taylor speaks again. "So am I grounded or what?"

"Ten P.M. curfew for the next two weeks."

"My day doesn't even begin until nine."

"You'll have to adjust, I guess."

"I was going to Iowa City this weekend with Dale and Eric."

"Not now you aren't."

"We already made plans."

"Change your plans." He glances at Young Taylor and sees him begin to speak but think better of it. "What do you *do* after ten at night?"

"Sacrifice virgins in Dale's back forty."

"What else?"

"Nothing important. Just hang out. Make it midnight, okay?"

Mack relaxes slightly, seeing that he's won this round. "Your grandma's sure that you're on dope."

"She needs to chill. You all need to chill."

"You know," Mack ventures, "you can just make me the bad guy."

"You *are* the bad guy."

"Just tell Dale and Eric that your old man's a mental case."

The boy looks out his window, at the gray evening all around them. "I don't talk like that about you."

"Well, maybe you should. It's a convenient excuse. 'Sorry, guys, ol' loony tunes has to have everyone in the house by ten o'clock.'"

He grins at Taylor, but Taylor returns a flat, unreadable look.

"'Mom needs me to help restrain him sometimes.'" Mack widens his eyes to make a crazy expression.

"Stop it! God, how can you make jokes?"

"You'd be surprised at what I can laugh at these days."

"Can we stop talking about this now?"

"What do we tell your mother?"

"Tell her whatever you want."

"She'll want to hear that this won't happen again."

"Tell her that then."

They ride the strip of county road in silence, surrounded by fields that are bare, stubbly, and hard with two or three frosts by now. For a moment Mack senses the horizon of the entire world close at hand. Just another rise and fall, and there they will be, going over the edge, hearts in their throats.

Jodie

She awakens to a sick feeling. At first she thinks it is connected with Young Taylor's trouble yesterday. But Mack and Young Taylor were both pretty calm when they arrived home. Her son actually apologized to her later when she told him good-night. He's a good kid, just weird, and he has some reason to be. She looks forward to knowing him ten years from now, when he's grown past all of this.

But it is not Young Taylor's image that hangs in front of her constantly. Terry is with her no matter what she's doing or what other crises may be happening. They've spent little real time together, but her feelings register another reality entirely. She is worn out from thinking of him—of them—but can't drag her mind anywhere else.

"I've got to stop this," she whispers to her clock at five A.M. "Maybe I had to start it, for some sick reason. But I've got to stop it now."

She wishes Mack were here beside her. Even with all the problems, Mack is safe in a way Terry is not. Terry is completely new territory, a whole other set of personality quirks and frailties to learn and understand and, ultimately, put up with. But now she gets out of bed, goes to the bathroom, washes her face, looks in the mirror, and the bigger reality is once more apparent: life with Mack became too difficult and painful to manage. And there is no guarantee it will get better, no matter how hard they work at it. Terry is a bird in hand. Terry's problems are at least new and, at this point, unknown. She will have— who knows?—maybe several months of bliss before the faults begin to show. She needs the bliss, really needs it. A few months of bliss are worth it. She showers, and the stream of water over her skin makes her want Terry on her skin and inside her skin. She wants him right now, trapping her against the shower stall, pounding into her. After so long a time of desiring nothing, it is such a welcome change to want anything that the wanting itself is worth the cost.

Saturday mornings are now tedious because her schedule is open but her options are not. The kids sleep in, are in the house until past noon usually, and Jodie doesn't feel free to get away. She does house-work, then goes over to Rita's by ten, and they grocery-shop. They avoid Wal-Mart because it's a zoo on the weekend, but they drive to two or three other small towns in the vicinity and browse the tiny groceries, looking for the best seasonal produce, particular bakery items, and the sales advertised in the newspaper. Because Jodie and Rita have always visited easily with each other, they manage to turn this chore into a pleasant experience. There's a little ice cream and sandwich shop near the county line where they stop for old-fashioned cheeseburgers and root beer floats. It's family-owned and no-frills—the vinyl booths and chairs repaired with tape to the extent that Rita has them memorized and always heads for the booth with the least obtrusive patch job. But the lack of remodeling means that the food is cheap. It's also good, and Babe, the owner, runs her kitchen like an Old World grandma; this is one place where a person doesn't have to worry about what may be in the food or who may not have washed his hands before handling the cheese slices.

Jodie faces this weekend routine with dread today. She fears that Rita will sense her inner upheaval and prod her about it. Rita always asks about Mack, and that is annoying now that he's at the stone house—as if Jodie knows every detail of his day anyway. In Rita's world, Mack is Jodie's responsibility, as are her children. Their wrongs become her wrongs. It is her job to keep up. If Rita didn't work so hard herself to keep up with all of them, Jodie would resent her more than she does. Rita will die helping someone get straight-ened out or taken care of; she is not going to change such a deep and enduring habit. And she could be a lot more pushy and verbal with Jodie than she is. Underneath all the work is real compassion, and Jodie has always known that Rita understands the specific pains and anxieties in Jodie's life. Rita lost a husband and son to the same forces that now batter Jodie and Mack and their kids. So she and Jodie are joined at the soul, whether either of them wants it or not. Jodie senses, at the root of her anger and fear, that if Rita goes, they all will.

So she will call Rita in a few minutes, and they will shop together. And while they drive from one place to another, they will talk about family. They will discuss how Mack is looking and whatever Rita has heard other townspeople say about his work (and that's always positive). Unless Rita has heard through the grapevine about Young Taylor, Jodie will not bring him up at all. They will share their pleasure in Kenzie's good grades. Then they will come around to Mack again. Both of them are very protective of family, so whatever anxiety gets aroused while they are in the car will be left there while they do the shopping. In public, they discuss prices and clothing sizes. Back in the car, maybe they will revisit family topics, or maybe not. Often, one will say, "Well, I'm sure things will straighten out," and the other will agree. Through this discussion they have performed an important function, so important that Jodie feels both relief and satisfaction when they return home and unload the car.

Rita calls before Jodie has a chance to pick up the phone. This happens a lot. They agree that Jodie will pick up Rita in about half an hour. When Jodie puts down the phone, Kenzie is standing at the kitchen sink, looking at her.

"Hi, sweetie—you find something to eat?"

"Yeah." Kenzie looks worried, or expectant.

"Everything okay?" Jodie moves close enough to brush Kenzie's hair back from her face. The child is perfect, absolutely blooming. Jodie can feel the energy sparking off of her. What she would give to feel that new and full of promise.

"Mom, have you heard about the women's retreat in January?"

"At the Baptist church?"

"Uh-huh. I hear it's really a good retreat. Jenna's mom went last year and is going again. Their speaker for the day is this woman who's written a book—" Kenzie holds up a pink brochure. On the first fold is the barely intelligible photocopy of a book cover. The title is in loopy script above a picture of a calendar page: "Being God's Woman in a World of Change."

"I see." Jodie takes the brochure and tries to read it as she searches for reasons not to go. "January?"

"Yes, and they're taking registrations now. It looks really helpful." Kenzie's eyes are full of more than energy or enthusiasm. Jodie sees longing there too, not unlike what she has seen in her own reflection lately.

"Is it a mother-daughter thing?" Jodie hands back the brochure. "Are you planning to go?"

"It's not mother-daughter, but I'll go with you if you want."

"Well, I'll think about it, okay?"

"Okay. You want Jenna's mom to call you and tell you about last year's retreat?"

"Sure, if she wants." Jodie feels the need to change the subject. "What about you? Is the youth group planning a fall or winter re-treat?"

"Sure, but I don't think I'll go."

"Why not?" Jodie gets her purse from the desk near the pantry. Time to go get Rita.

"I'd rather go to the adult retreat. The youth group is kind of lame these days."

"Really? I thought you liked it. You're spending a lot of time there."

Kenzie looks away. "But they're not very mature." When Jodie smiles, Kenzie adds, "I mean, as far as Scripture goes, they're not very understanding. I just feel like God is showing me so much, and the others don't get it."

"Well, give them time. Maybe you're just a few steps ahead of them. You always were very smart." Jodie grabs the truck keys from the hook beside the back door. She looks back at her daughter, who seems a bit sad. "You want to come shopping with Grandma and me?"

"No, that's all right. I've got stuff to do," she says as Jodie goes out the door.

9

LETTING GO

Come, ye thankful people, come, raise the song of harvest
  home;
All is safely gathered in, ere the winter storms begin.
God our Maker doth provide for our wants to be supplied;
Come to God's own temple, come, raise the song of
  harvest home.

— "Come, Ye Thankful People, Come"

Jodie

She can vaguely remember when it was a joy to cook a holiday dinner. She and Rita (and in the old days, Marty) set up stations all over the kitchen and dining room, cutting up vegetables, mixing up pies, getting out the good china, decorating more than usual. The preparation was actually more enjoyable than the eating. Talk was easy when they were all working with their hands. They would trade advice and be one another's taste testers. And they had made most of the dishes many times before; there was little stress about how anything would turn out. They started early in the day and knew that everything would get done.

The aromas would hang first in the kitchen and then seep into other rooms of the house as the hours went by. A cloud of food smells would drug the men and kids when they came in the door, bringing with them crisp air from outdoors.

It was a lot of hard work, but it never felt hard. But today, with Rita and her awful cough and no one else around, there is little talk and no satisfaction to speak of. The two of them must do it all, even though they call on Kenzie several times to help and she does so happily enough.

Rita is obviously not well, but the woman is unable to admit physical failures of any kind. She treats every ailment with Alka-Seltzer, cough drops, Vick's Vaporub, and Epsom salts. She drinks coffee with extra milk sometimes, or she makes hot lemonade with honey and a bit of whiskey or rum. She believes that antibiotics weaken a person's immune system, so does not go to the doctor because the first thing a doctor does for infection is prescribe antibiotics. Rita gathers her information from a variety of sources, everything from *Reader's Digest* to Paul Harvey and talk radio, but regardless of what information is actually given, she comes down on the side of not trusting medical doctors. First of all, they charge too much. Second, they don't treat old people with much respect. They act like they don't hear questions, or they don't think older folks can understand a reasonable explanation anyway.

Rita has no personal history of mistreatment by doctors. She distrusts them out of general principle. She doesn't want the doctor bills. She hates taking medicine, even though she delivers pills to half a dozen of her neighbors and helps them count out what they'll need for each day so they don't get confused and overdose or forget to take them. She reads the labels and directions carefully, and if the directions aren't clear, she calls the pharmacist and batters him with questions. If one of her "patients" is taking several medications at once, she calls the pharmacist to make sure they're not going to form some deadly reaction. Mom should have been a nurse, Jodie thinks, because she likes taking command of situations, and she manages to get people to do what's good for them, even if they don't want to. But she could never have been a nurse, despising medicine as she does.

Today she has already had a hot rum toddy, and it's only ten in the morning. The cough is horribly congested, and at times Mom wheezes after a coughing spell. Twice Jodie considers hauling her to the emergency room. But she knows the scene that will cause. So she works intently on dough for dinner rolls and the extra pan of dressing and the honeyed carrots and the gelatin salad and the other dishes that are under her charge. Maybe working in the school cafeteria has soured her on cooking. Or maybe she's just not thankful on this Thanksgiving. Maybe what she really dreads is the moment when they all sit down together and have little to say to each other; she has come to dread dinnertime on any day, even if it's only Mack and Kenzie with her. She hears them talking to each other, and she can tell how hard they're trying to make everybody happy. Mack is trying to prove that his life is worth something, and Kenzie is trying to bring them all back to God. Neither of them can speak in a way that other people understand. Mack will list all that he's done today; he'll voice opinions that aren't even important to him anymore, then sit back and look haunted when silence falls. And in Kenzie there now seems to be a constant, quiet panic. She talks more and more about Jesus and prayer and Satan. They do their best to tolerate it without participating in her fervor. They had a small portion of such fervor themselves, years ago, back when faith was a manageable, reasonable thing. But it has ceased to be either for a long time now.

After lunch, Rita lies down in the living room for a nap. She's taken cold medicine and is groggy. Mack is halfway to Iowa City by now, to pick up Aunt Linda, who is eighty-four and resides in an assisted living community. It's hard for her to travel much anymore, but she wanted to be here on the farm for Thanksgiving, and they've not been to see her in a while.

The kids are somewhere, maybe upstairs or roaming the countryside. She doesn't try to keep track.

The house is quiet. Jodie's feet and legs hurt; she's been up and working on food since five this morning. She'll take a break while Rita naps.

She eyes the kitchen phone and considers risks. Rita is three rooms away, and no one else is close enough to overhear a word she says.

He said that he would be home until early evening, when he'd go out to his parents' for Thanksgiving dinner. She said that she wouldn't have opportunity to call him, with family around all day.

It is understood between the two of them that he must never call her at home. But she can call him when it's safe to do so. It's also understood that talking every day isn't appropriate. They've been together four times now, and they're enjoying it a lot, but they are both still afraid to be too close too soon.

She punches in the number. He picks up on the first ring.

"Hey," she says, knowing that he'll know even from one word that it's her. "Happy Thanksgiving."

"Happy Thanksgiving. I'm glad you called."

"Are you just sitting at home by yourself?"

"Been watching parades and football, doing stuff around the house. I'm just chilling out, channel surfing, drinking some beer."

"Oh, that's nice."

"Thinking of you."

The words bring instant happiness. "That's nice too."

"How are you?"

"Oh, you know. It's Thanksgiving. I'm cooking all day."

"You having a bunch of people over?"

"Just Mack and the kids and his mom and great-aunt. But it's still a major dinner. I'm not in the mood to do it really, but it's what we do."

"What are you in the mood for?"

"I think you know." She hides her face behind the receiver, even though nobody's around to see her grin like an idiot.

"Just run over here for a quickie."

"Right. I'll do that between the pumpkin pie and cranberry salad."

"I know. Can't blame me for asking."

They talk for ten minutes, about nothing in particular. It's just good to hear his voice and to give him the sound of hers. It's good to know that he's out there thinking of her, that he can't wait to get his hands on her again. Suddenly her day is full of energy. Suddenly she's thankful.

When they hang up, she can't go back to work right away. Rita is still asleep on the sofa. Jodie wanders the house, looking out of windows, smoothing tablecloths, and rearranging throws on chairs and sofas. She is restless, happy, sad, anxious. All she really wants is to be in a bed in some other county with Terry all over her. To find a special place full of liveliness and hope.

Rita

Rita has never felt particularly close to Aunt Linda. She's actually Taylor Senior's aunt, although she is young enough to be his older sister. Has a lot of Dutch in her, which may be the problem. The Dutch people Rita has known tend to be tight-lipped and judgmental, as if they're sure you haven't cleaned your house well enough. Actually, she's not known that many Dutch people, but it only takes a couple to make a strong impression. Taylor's parents were good people but sort of stiff. They died in the early years of Rita and Taylor's marriage, and she never felt very close to them either.

Aunt Linda walks in the house ahead of Mack wearing a dark green plush coat. Her silver hair is shaped against her head in careful curls; the woman has had her hair done once a week for decades, one thing that makes her indiscernible to Rita. Aunt Linda always looks good for her age, but today she walks much more slowly than before. She has survived hip surgery this past year, and a person her age doesn't recover from such things quickly. Her face is made up just enough to be appropriate, and she wears nice jewelry but not a lot of it. She wraps herself and her green coat around one person after another, including Rita. Aunt Linda is much older than Rita. She towers over Rita by a foot and is slender in the way well-to-do people stay slender; they have the luxury of eating just the right foods, and they go to the doctor for every little ailment. For years Aunt Linda has walked every day—for no reason except to walk. Her joints haven't been ruined by labor on a farm; her husband owned a clothing store and made a good living for them. Rita doesn't consider that envy has anything to do with her lack of connection to Aunt Linda; she decided long ago that envy is a waste of time. The woman has simply never interested her much. Rita greets her with the usual warmth and respect.

Rita wishes Jodie could be a little brighter today. Usually she's more energetic and talkative at holiday time. She chatters about the recipes or recounts family stories while they work. Jodie has always been a fine person to be with during celebrations; she can make any dinner into a feast. But Jodie has been quiet today, and she acts irritated every time Rita has a coughing fit, as if it were purposeful.

They eat at five, the world outside already growing dark and chilly, while the room inside glows with silverware and steamy bowls. The conversation is fairly slow until Kenzie asks Aunt Linda about her grandfather, and the old woman lights up and pats her curls and begins to tell stories of former generations. Her grandfather was a circuit rider, a preacher who traveled through the countryside tending to small, scattered Methodist congregations. Aunt Linda quickly moves to the story of her brother, who fought in World War II, was wounded in France, and befriended the Belgian soldier in the next bed, who later came to the States to visit and ended up marrying Aunt Linda. Young Taylor perks up and asks more questions about the war, and Rita finds herself in a strange but friendly dialogue with Aunt Linda. Their memories merge in some places, but because of their age difference they have quite different recollections of the times and events. It's as if they are filling in gaps for each other. An hour later everyone has finished Thanksgiving dinner, and Jodie is clearing the table. She's hardly said a word.

It is the scene in the kitchen a while later that startles Rita. Jodie is making coffee to go with the pumpkin and pecan pies. Kenzie is washing dishes. Aunt Linda and Mack both stand at the counter near the doorway to the dining room. They are bending over something intently. Rita comes closer to see what is going on.

"I take two of these a day, three of these. On some days, when I feel the need, I take one of those in the morning. This one I take at night only." Aunt Linda is speaking over a pill container, the kind with sections labeled for days of the week and morning, afternoon, or evening. Her well-kept hands are pointing out various pills in pinks and yellows. She's explaining her regimen to Mack.

"Well, I may have you beat. Look at this." Mack has taken small prescription bottles out of the pocket of his jacket, which hangs on the back of the door. He lays them out and recites:

"Both of these morning and evening. This three times a day. This in the morning only. This one at night."

"How do you keep them straight?"

"I line them up on the shelf. So far it hasn't been a problem."

"You need a little box like mine. I load it up at the beginning of the week, then just obey the little lids." She chuckles. They both raise pills and glasses of water. "Bon appetit," says Aunt Linda. Mack nods and clinks his glass against hers.

Rita walks away, shaking her head. As if this medicine business were a laughing matter. Although she wishes for stronger medicine of her own about now. The coughing has persisted all evening, making the rest of them look at her with concern on their faces, which is irritating. She left her cough syrup at home, and the kind Jodie gave her isn't as potent.

Kenzie

Being around Aunt Linda always makes Kenzie feel better. The woman is old and gentle and sophisticated, and the calm about her makes Kenzie think that this must be what nuns are like. She's hardly ever been around nuns, but she can't imagine such serenity existing without some direct connection to Jesus. She knows that Aunt Linda has gone to the same church for years and years. She wants to ask her some question that will draw the conversation to that. She tried to do that when she asked, during dinner, about Grandfather Loughlin, who had been a pastor on the frontier. But Aunt Linda slipped past that to war stories. Evidently, to her, conviction by the Holy Spirit was just normal life and conviction worth talking about was the kind that would sneak behind enemy lines. Kenzie wants to ask Aunt Linda about her prayer life, but she senses that prayer is a very private thing to her. This Kenzie can understand. But she likes to imagine Aunt Linda praying at an altar, maybe one different from the altar at the Baptist church, but similar in a lot of ways. She walks and talks like someone who has practiced true devotion for many years.

This impression doesn't add up when Aunt Linda gets out all her pill bottles. Kenzie has to remind herself that it wasn't until recently, not until she discovered the teachings of Reverend Francis, that she herself realized the spiritual compromise in the taking of medicines. Kenzie decides to give Aunt Linda some slack in this area, since she is obviously godly and not the type to lean on crutches. In some scheme of need and answer, medicine for blood pressure is probably not in the same category with medicine for despair. She listens closely to Aunt Linda and Dad comparing their medicines. She wishes Aunt Linda would ask more questions about exactly why Dad is taking this or that. She's not sure how much Aunt Linda knows about Dad's stay at the hospital, but she looks like the type who could get to the bottom of something fast.

After dessert and helping Mom clean up, Kenzie hides out in her room. Young Taylor is in his as well, burning incense, from the smell of it. Kenzie trips past the door and shuts her own, turning on her desk lamp, the one in the shape of a cream-colored stallion, a lightbulb and fringed shade sprouting up from the wild mane. She has had this lamp since she was nine. The horse's name is Pallie, for Palomino. Pallie lights her darkness when she awakens in the middle of the night afraid of demons and the coming apocalypse. Pallie has glowed over her for the duration of the mumps and the flu, has made it possible for Mom to read a thermometer while half-asleep. Right now Pallie looks like a toy that a grown-up girl would have given away by now. Kenzie pushes him to the side and gets out her journal.

Dear Jesus,

My heart is full of so many things. I just want my whole family to know the peace I've found. I want to put my hands on each and every person and claim Jesus' healing over that life. I want to cast out demons and pronounce the truth about everything that's hurting Mom, Dad, Grandma Rita, and Young Taylor. I want, want, want! This desire is about to kill me, Jesus. Something's got to happen soon. Something has to be made right.

When I see how Mom and Dad still don't talk much, it makes me want to scream. When I see the darkness in Young Taylor's life, I just want to shake all the bad things right out of him. And I see Grandma worry and I want to hold her and calm her down. I want to know Aunt Linda a lot better than I do—I need some help in this never-ending war.

I'm tired of the war. I'm tired of wondering if they'll be okay, and hoping that I'm doing everything I can. Jesus, you have to help me see the truth. I can't wander in darkness. I have to be sure of your presence and your promise. I'm not as strong as I should be, so you have to help me be strong and wise. You have to show me what to do. I feel like there's hardly any time left. I know it's not your will that I be afraid or full of panic.

She writes in Pallie's light for more than an hour. She stops a couple of times to read from Revelation and then from Psalms. She says the verses as her prayers. She inserts the name of her loved ones where the Psalmist wrote "I" or "we." She kneels by the bed and reads Revelation 21:5–8 about six times, memorizing as much as she can. When the end comes, all she will have are the words here, the ones she has stored in her heart.

Her meditation is interrupted by sounds downstairs. It's Grandma Rita coughing. It sounds worse than usual. Then she hears murmurings from her parents and finally hears Dad say, "That's it, Mom. I'm taking you to the hospital." Kenzie rushes downstairs to see Mom and Aunt Linda helping Grandma into her coat. Grandma's face is pale, and she looks so weary that Kenzie is afraid she's dying.

"Mom? What do you want me to do?"

"You stay here with Aunt Linda. Dad and I will take Grandma to the hospital." Mom looks at Kenzie then and says quickly, "She'll be fine, but I'm sure she needs some antibiotics."

They bundle Grandma Rita into the car. She is too overcome by the coughing and shortness of breath to argue. Kenzie turns on the yard light that's closest to the sidewalk. She watches the car go toward town, then turns to see Aunt Linda standing there, concern on her face. She looks tired.

"I think she has pneumonia," says Aunt Linda. "All that congestion—it must be in her lungs."

"I don't think she's ever had it before."

"They'll fix her up just fine. Do you have hot chocolate?"

The mention of hot chocolate makes Kenzie long for Mitchell. That's where she needs to be right now. But she can't leave Aunt Linda.

"Yes. I'll fix some for us."

Young Taylor appears then, in the doorway.

"Mom and Dad taking Grandma home?"

"No, to the hospital. Her coughing got really bad."

Young Taylor looks as if he's about to swear, but maybe because Aunt Linda is standing there, he turns away and sits on the couch.

"You want hot chocolate? Aunt Linda and I are having some."

"Sure. Any pie left?"

"I don't know. Look for yourself."

The three of them sit in front of *Miracle on 34th Street* and sip hot chocolate. During the climactic scene, Mom comes in the back door. They can hear the car leaving the drive again.

"How's Grandma?" Kenzie hops off the couch.

"She has pneumonia. She'll be there a couple of days."

"Where's Dad?"

"He's staying there tonight."

"She's really bad?"

"Mainly she's upset because they won't let her go home. Dad will stay there until she gets to sleep and then stay at her house. Then he can go check on her in the morning."

Kenzie's glad that Dad won't be at the stone house tonight. She had dreaded the moment when he would leave them all and go out into the cold and aloneness.

At nine-thirty, Mom is in the dining room, putting away the good dishes. Aunt Linda is tucked away in the guest room. She will stay until Sunday, when Dad will take her back to Iowa City. There's a knock on the door, and Dale is standing there. He follows Young Taylor upstairs, and they disappear into his bedroom. This is how Young Taylor gets around being grounded: his friends just camp out upstairs for hours at a time.

Kenzie sits in the family room and tries to figure out how to get to Mitchell's house without anyone knowing. At ten o'clock she stands in the doorway to the dining room.

"Mom, I'm going to bed. You need me to do anything?"

"No." Mom turns to her briefly. She is at the dining room table, putting the good silver back into its velvet case that will in turn go to its place in the dining room cupboard. "Night, honey."

"Night." She goes upstairs and does what she always does before bed, taking her normal time in the bathroom. Then she goes to her bedroom and fluffs up the blankets and pillows. She puts on her sweats and her jacket. Then she closes the bedroom door and slips downstairs, skipping the three steps that squeak. She ducks around the corner into the front room of the house. With the television still on, Mom won't hear the sucking sound of the front door opening. Kenzie leaves the house, hops off the front porch, and goes to the road the long way around, behind the garage and away from the yard light.

The sky is swollen with clouds and filled with a heavy darkness, the air so chilly that Kenzie coughs once or twice, getting used to it. She smells wood smoke from somewhere, probably the Timmonses' place over south. As she comes up the rise, within a quarter-mile of Mitchell's place, her gaze reaches and reaches for that speck of light that means he's awake. Finally she sees a dim point of yellow, the light above the kitchen sink. It is then that she runs, feeling that something evil is right at her heels.

Mitchell looks startled when he opens the door to her wild knock-ing. "Kenzie." His voice is flat. Kenzie goes inside. She hugs him, and only after a moment does he return the hug.

"You shouldn't be out here now." His eyes are dull.

"You don't want me here?"

"Sure, I want you here. But what about your folks?"

She tells him the events of her day, working backwards from Grandma being at the hospital and Dad in town. She is ready to un-leash all the wants that she wrote about in her journal, but the look on Mitchell's face stops her.

"Are you okay?" she says.

He winces a little. "It's been a bad day, Kenzie."

"What happened?"

"Nothing happened."

She waits for an explanation. He slumps at the kitchen table and looks at her tiredly.

"Nothing?" she asks.

"Nothing." His expression tells her that he considers this answer significant. Then he leans toward her a little. "That's it. Nothing. Nothing happened today. Nothing came. I couldn't work on anything I couldn't think anything. It's like my system is shutting down."

She doesn't know what to say. She thinks that maybe the world will just end tonight. That would be convenient. It would spare her figuring out what to do about all the people in her life. She is totally disappointed at the reception she has received.

"I've got to get out of here, Kenzie."

"What do you mean?"

"I mean, I need to leave. The oppression is coming. Maybe it's here already. I can't live through another siege like this. I can't go through days and days of nothing."

It is quiet, and Kenzie notices how cold the house is. She wonders why he hasn't turned up the heat.

"I'm going to Reverend Francis's retreat center. I know I'll be better there. The demons can't get me there. I'm not strong enough here."

"When will you go?" It feels as if her life is just leaking away.

"Soon. Maybe tomorrow. Maybe next week."

"I want to come with you."

He looks at her, and his eyes clear for a moment. "Oh, no. I can't take you there."

"Why not?"

"You're fourteen." He says it as if he despises her suddenly.

"That's never mattered to you before. I thought you said we're meant to be together."

"We are, but I can't take you with me, not now."

She is too tired to fight the tears. Her hands on the table blur in front of her. She was expecting comfort, not this. She has come to this safe room, but it's as dark as the rooms she just left.

"Mitchell, I need you. You're my only real friend." She can barely talk for crying. To her surprise, she hears not sympathy but a frustrated sigh from across the table.

"Go home. This isn't good, you being here now. Just go." He gets up and lifts her out of the chair. She tries to hang on to him, but he twists her around to face the door. He pulls her jacket around her.

"Don't leave, Mitchell! I need you here. I can't fight the battle by myself!"

She is standing on his porch and listening to the door shut behind her.

She stumbles down the road to home in the pitch dark. She doesn't care, because her tears keep her from seeing anyway. She sobs and she shouts. "Jesus! What are you doing to me? Why are you taking my friend away from me?" She huddles behind the garage to finish crying. Then she sneaks around the house and sees that Mom's bedroom light is on. The front door has been locked; for some reason Mom locks that door but not the back one. Every night before bed she turns out the kitchen light, then locks the front door. Kenzie steps in the back and up to her room.

She undresses in the dark, and the tears start again. In the pale reflection of the yard light, she sees her journal on the desk, next to Pallie.

Her first impulse is to turn on the light and write this fresh, pain-filled prayer to Jesus. But it hits her that she is so tired she can barely stand. She puts on her nightgown and cries into her pillow for possibly five minutes before falling asleep.

Mack

He debates with himself the whole drive to see George. He trusts the man, but how much should he tell him? What's important to tell?

Well, hearing voices would probably be significant. But that really just happened a couple of times, and there could be lots of explanations—a radio from a passing car or something.

The other things are probably coincidences too. The memory of Pop coming through so clearly the other day, so clear it was like having Pop there in the truck with him. The day he happened to look up as he passed a sign on the highway that read: LIFE BEGINS TODAY. It was put there as some sort of pro-life message, but what's troublesome is that earlier that morning Mack had gotten out of bed feeling too weary and sad to go to work. And out of the blue he'd said those very words to himself, a little pep talk as he drank his coffee. Of course, he must have seen the sign sometime before but not thought of it consciously, and it came out of him that morning, and then he noticed the sign for the first time half an hour later. There's always an explanation for these things.

The sky has that hard, white look of snow waiting to fall. It will likely storm tonight. Maybe it isn't such a good idea to travel forty miles from home. He can go back now and call George and postpone at least until next week.

That would be a whole week for him to try to reason with himself about voices and coincidences. He ignores every feeling he has, ignores the sky, and grips the wheel.

"Well, I've finally gone round the bend." He sits in his spot and looks straight at George. May as well get right to it.

"Round the bend? As in going crazy?"

"Yep."

They look at each other, George's eyebrows at attention.

"I'm hearing voices."

George nods slowly, as if he understands, has been expecting this. But his face remains a blank.

"I didn't used to hear voices—even in the worst times, even when I was playing with guns out in the barn. There were never voices."

"But there are now. When did they start?"

"A few days ago."

"What was happening prior to your hearing these voices?"

"Nothing. I was driving home from work."

"And the voices came then? What did they say?"

Mack looks at him. "Does it matter? Seems to me that the main thing is that I'm hearing anything at all."

"Well, I'm interested to know the content, the message."

"'Everything is working out,' or something to that effect."

George looks at him, presses his lips together, and grunts, "Hmm."

"And another time I was in the parking lot loading up groceries, and somebody said, 'Love is always the last thing standing.' I'm sure somebody must have said it, but I couldn't see anybody close by."

"That's quite a statement. 'Love is always the last thing standing.' I like that." George pauses. "Anything else?"

Mack is trapped. He started this mess, and it doesn't make sense to hold back now. "I'm just ... noticing things. Coincidences ... but they feel like they have purpose behind them."

George waits.

"You know, remembering certain things at the very moment I need to—something my dad said twenty years ago in a whole other situation. Highway signs that all of a sudden have some kind of personal meaning. And two days ago, it was the strangest thing ..."

Mack plays with the unbuttoned cuff of his sleeve. "I hadn't walked into the Beulah museum in I don't know how long. But my daughter and I went there so she could return some props she'd used in the school play. And I'm wandering through all these piles of junk—old clothes and tools—and on this shelf at eye level is a pair of work boots. And they're exactly like a pair Pop had when I was a kid—same laces, soles, leather, fasteners—exactly the same boots, only I know we burned Pop's years ago when we cleaned out the shed."

Mack stops to take a breath. He feels George's attention, quiet and focused.

"And this memory just flashed across my mind, clear as anything. When I was about nine, I went hunting with Pop—for rabbits. There were several inches of snow on the ground, but no sign of more coming when we took out across the fields. We'd been out about an hour when the temperature dropped and a storm blew in. A blizzard—God, we couldn't see, and the wind was practically blowing me over. We were in the open—no place for shelter—so Pop said, 'We need to just walk. We'll either reach the road or the house. But we can't stay out here.' He had me grab the back of his jacket and walk right behind him, and he said, 'You step right into my tracks. That's all you need to do. Hang on and walk in my tracks.' And we got home that way. I'll never forget watching those big old boots one step ahead of me."

He realizes that he's close to tears. He stares up at George. "And I'd forgotten all about that—hadn't thought about it for years. But those boots on the shelf—it's like they opened me up. I just stood there in the aisle, couldn't talk or move." He shakes his head.

"Objects have a way of jarring memories loose. It's astounding what you can remember when you're triggered just right."

"I suppose that's normal enough, having something come back to me like that. But I took a different meaning from it this time—stepping in his tracks."

George nods slowly. "Following in his footsteps."

"That's right." He studies his sleeve again. "But this hearing voices stuff—I was afraid to even tell you about that. Good way to end up in the hospital again."

George lets out a sigh. "Gee, Mack, it sounds like a pretty sane voice to me."

"But where is it coming from?"

"What do you think?"

"I think it's me going crazy at last."

"No, no, no. That's too easy. Just think about it. Where might such helpful, positive thoughts come from?"

"Feels like it's from outside me, not like I'm talking to myself. If I were still religious at all . . ." He avoids looking at George. "There was a time when I would have interpreted all this in a more . . . religious way."

"Such as, maybe it's God's voice, interrupting your calm afternoons?"

Mack laughs nervously. "Something like that."

"But you don't look at it that way now."

"No. My daughter claims to talk to God all the time. But she's a kid and into this religious kick right now. I'm worried about her, frankly. But I don't . . ."

"You don't pray?" George gazes at Mack the way he often does, even when Mack isn't looking at him but knows he's being gazed at. "You've told me what a religious family you come from, how you've been churchgoing most of your life, even recently."

"I go for the family, mainly."

"Mack, what if God is talking to you?"

Mack meets The Gaze in spite of himself.

"Can you be absolutely sure that God would never talk to you in a voice so clear it seems audible? After all, is it telling you to do anything destructive? Is it telling you lies? Is it outside the realm of possibility?"

"God has nothing to do with me—hasn't in a long time."

"Since when?"

"I don't know . . . when I stopped believing everything I heard in church."

"What about outside of church? What did God have to do with you in everyday life, back when you believed?"

Mack thinks for nearly a minute. The words gather slowly, and the pain gathers with them.

"Well," he says, his voice hoarse, "out in the fields, I guess. Nature—you know. I used to feel like God was part of it—the way things worked, the seasons." He has to stop, but after a second forces a harsh laugh. "I actually thought of me and God as being partners." His voice breaks again, and tears began to trickle from his eyes. He wipes them away. "Way back when I believed stuff like that." A sob escapes him suddenly, and he puts a hand over his trembling mouth.

"And when did you stop believing stuff like that?"

"When Pop died. Whether it was an accident or intentional, it was too high a price."

He cries freely now. George passes him the box of tissue that has remained unused through all their previous sessions.

"What if you consider that God *may have been* out there, in the fields and the seasons?"

Mack looks at his hands. "If that was God out there all those years, then I'm mighty disappointed in him for letting us lose all that we have."

As Mack drives down the highway, he squints against the sun that has broken through the dense layer of clouds. It seems to him that the horizon might slant out of kilter or the truck might take its own path. Just as his life's landscape has run off somewhere or been broken into pieces and scattered. Just as the steadiness of God's provision has been auctioned off with the combine and the hay truck. Nothing can be counted on to stay in place. The plain is buckling into dangerous jags, the stream is flowing to other lands. God's geography has changed.

But the sunset begins sweetly, a soft pink-yellow that flows down the ledges of clouds and spills into a lavender pool above the fields. Fields he does not own or tend. Yet they shine as Mack has always believed Heaven would shine—golden with light even in the cold of death.

The layers of color glimmer upon the tears that fill and refill Mack's eyes. The voice is coming from inside him now, from a profound location that is his alone: *Everything is working out. It will keep working out. And love grows and fails and grows again.*

God's geography has changed. Now it is everywhere.

PART FOUR

DECLARATION

FACING TRUTH

Cease, ye pilgrims, cease to mourn, press onward to the
   prize;
Soon thy savior will return, to take thee to the skies:
Yet a season, and you know happy entrance will be given,
All our sorrows left below and earth exchanged for heaven.
                                    —"Rise, My Soul, and Stretch Thy
                                    Wings"

Jodie

Mack appears so determined as he gets out of the car and walks up to
the back door that Jodie's impulse is to run upstairs. Has he found
out about Terry? What else would make him look like that? But she
leaves her hands in dishwater and doesn't move a foot, even when he
comes in the door and stands near her.

"Jodie."

She turns to him and waits.

"I think I've done all the thinking I'm going to do out there at the
house."

"Oh? Is that good?"

"Yeah, I think so. If it's all right with you, I'd like to move back."

"Sure, babe." She knows that a hug or kiss would be appropriate, but she can't get herself to take the two steps toward him. She resumes washing a bowl in the sudsy water.

"That's all right?" He sounds so unsure. She wishes he'd just announce that he's going to do it, and not leave the approval up to her. But she makes a point to smile. "I wasn't crazy about you being out there in the first place."

He goes outside and gathers some things from the truck. She opens the storm door and calls, "You need help?"

"No, I've got it." She holds the door open for him, because both his hands are full. He comes into the kitchen, then turns to her. "I'll understand if you'd rather I take the spare room, at least for a while."

She doesn't know what to say. He looks nervous, standing there with his suitcase. Is he trying to take the pressure off both of them, or is he saying he's not ready yet to be intimate with her? "Do whatever makes you comfortable."

"Does it matter to you?"

Another loaded question. How is she supposed to answer that? But his eyes are steady, his posture questioning rather than defensive.

"It matters to me that you feel at home, babe. And I never asked you to leave, remember?"

He takes a step and kisses her cheek. "I'll move into our room then."

It is Saturday, and the kids are somewhere else. Jodie continues to work around the house while Mack moves in. He finds her in the laundry room a while later.

"I've got a job over at Danson's place today—probably be back by suppertime."

"Okay." It's good to see him busy. Since being at Hendrikson's, Mack gets a good deal of freelance work. She's glad he has something to do, that he doesn't have time to sit and think too much. Although he's had plenty of time to do that by himself in the woods. Maybe time to think was exactly what he needed. Time to think without other people interrupting. Maybe Jodie's main fault is that she interrupted too much, trying to help.

Young Taylor troops through the house an hour later. "I'll be gone tonight."

"As long as you're back by curfew."

He shrugs. "I won't be here for supper."

"Your dad just moved back."

"Really?" Young Taylor contemplates that. "So he seems all right?"

"Yes, he thinks it's time."

"Cool." Then he disappears upstairs.

She tells Kenzie the same thing when the two of them prepare supper. She wants to tell their daughter before Mack walks in the door. Kenzie barely makes it in time to set the table—youth group gets more demanding all the time.

Kenzie's response is more measured than her brother's. She's happy enough that her dad is moving back, but Jodie expected more enthusiasm.

"Is he still taking all those medications?"

"Yes, until the doctor thinks he doesn't need them."

"Do you think the doctor really wants him to stop?"

Jodie turns to look at her daughter. "Why would he not want that?"

Kenzie raises her shoulders high. "Most doctors depend on the drug companies, right? And the drug companies want to keep selling people drugs. So maybe the doctors look for reasons to keep people on medications."

Jodie gives an uneasy laugh. "Where did you get all that?"

"Just open your eyes, Mom. The first thing a doctor does when you go to him is push pills at you. They never ask about your whole life, like your relationships or your lifestyle. They don't ask about the important things, like what you're afraid of or what you believe in."

"Sweetie, fears and beliefs are not what doctors get degrees in. They study the body. They're scientists."

"And most scientists believe in evolution."

Jodie sits down. The conversation is unsteadying her. "Kenzie, what does believing in evolution have to do with a doctor's ability to care for your body?"

"Evolutionists don't believe in God, and without faith in God, you can't be sure that anything else in your life is right either. No matter how smart you are or how important or rich or whatever, if you don't have faith, none of it matters. And you can be totally misled. Doctors may be smart, but that's not the same as having God's wisdom." Kenzie sits down too, as though she were an attorney who has just finished her summation.

For a moment, Jodie is speechless. Part of her wants to laugh at this ridiculous line of reasoning, but the sheer earnestness in Kenzie's eyes prevents her.

"Sweetie, who's been teaching you this?"

Kenzie looks away. "You know, at church and youth group. And it's right in the Bible. You want to see the verses?"

"No, I'm familiar with the Bible. But I didn't know that you were hearing this kind of thing at the Baptist church."

"Why does it matter where I hear it, if it's true?"

"You're making some really big assumptions, and I don't think they're completely true."

Kenzie looks down at her arms, which rest on her lap. "I know you don't believe. Dad doesn't either. I don't know what happened to everyone's faith around here."

"Well, whatever faith we have—or had—never included some of the stuff you're talking about now. Do you think people should just not go to doctors?"

"Sure, but they should be doctors who have faith."

"Oh, I see." Jodie sees the agitation in Kenzie's expression and de-cides not to take the conversation any further.

"I was hoping Daddy wouldn't have to stay on all those pills." Still, the child won't look at her.

"I wish he didn't either, and he probably won't have to forever." Jodie makes her voice as gentle as she can. "But we remember what he was like before he had the pills, don't we?"

Kenzie nods and gets up abruptly. "I'm glad he's home anyway."

Mack walks in a few minutes later. He looks tired but in a good way, exhausted from hoisting machinery and solving machinery problems. He washes up and greets Kenzie when he sits at the table. She tells him that she's glad he's home.

"Young Taylor's with friends," Jodie says, putting the last dish on the table. Mack nods. He doesn't seem as worried about Young Taylor as he used to be, and Jodie hopes this is a good sign. Since the incident at school, Young Taylor has been calmer, less hostile. Mack is tight-lipped about it all, but Jodie suspects that it's just as well. Fathers and sons should be able to confide in each other without sending out bulletins to everyone else.

It's when she enters the bedroom a while later that she's stopped cold. All over the top of the dresser are little bunches of silk flowers. When she looks closer, she sees that each bunch is attached to a small card with Bible verses written on it. The handwriting is Kenzie's. Jodie is pondering over all the fake blossoms when Mack walks in quietly.

"She's something, isn't she?" His voice is right behind her.

"Did she put all of these here?"

"No, she left one for me in the car every day I took her to school. Never said anything about it."

Jodie picks up some little pansies with Psalm 23 dangling from them.

"We can put them someplace else, if you want," says Mack. "I couldn't throw them away."

"No. This is fine." She feels guilty, suddenly, that her daughter has worked harder to encourage Mack than she has.

"It's all she knows to do, I guess," he says. "Can't hurt anything."

"You never know what will help." She says this more to herself than to him.

Mack

Very recently, George confessed that he used to be a Presbyterian pastor.

"You lose your faith, or what?" Mack asked.

"When I realized how badly prepared I was to deal with people's troubles, I went back to school for a degree in counseling."

"What are you doing here?"

A little shrug. "Decided to get some experience before working with a church again. Believe me, it's much easier listening to folks like you than trying to sort out the very odd family dynamics that get going in a congregation."

"Folks like me?"

"You're here because you recognize the need for a little assistance. You've come to a point that you're willing to change some things if need be, if that's what it takes for life to get better. In so many church situations, nobody thinks they have problems. They simply have *convictions*, and they're trying to get everyone else to live up to them."

Today George is settled into his chair, looking rumpled. His chin rests on the hand he's brought up to scratch his cheek. Mack wonders what kind of pastor this guy was, but he can't linger on that thought. Instead, he dives right into the conversation, all business.

"I used to think that if I could just get over the hump, make the money, keep things together, I'd be okay. For a year I worked at the school bus barn during the day and farmed nights and weekends. Then we lost the farm." Mack is just a few minutes into today's session. It's easier to get started nowadays. He just starts talking without thinking too much. "Then I thought that I needed to find new work to do, more steady income. I've been at Hendrikson's for nearly two years, and the pay's all right, but that's not enough either."

George's eyes are steady. It occurs to Mack that those eyes are a lot like the eyes of his father, or Ed, or the other men he's spent his life with. No nonsense. A lot of things hidden there.

"And now . . . it feels like nothing's enough. Like I need other reasons to be here." Mack stops and takes a sip of coffee.

"You want to know why you're on this earth."

"Something like that."

"That's a big question. A lot of brilliant philosophers have failed to answer it."

"Well, I don't care about philosophers. I don't live with them or meet them on the street."

The bushy head of hair dips a little deeper, and George stares over his glasses at Mack. "So who do you care about?"

"My family, I guess. I don't know. Maybe I don't care one way or the other."

"Do you want to know just for yourself?"

"Maybe."

"What I mean is, what do *you* think? Why does it matter to you that you're here?"

Mack looks straight at the blue eyes. "I honest to God don't know. I'm not sure it's that important anymore. I used to think I needed to be around for the kids. But kids do whatever they want to do. Both of mine seem to be surviving, and they're not that interested in being in-volved with me."

"What makes you think that?"

"I try to talk to them, but they never say much. It's like they're being polite but they're keeping the important stuff close to the vest."

"Keep in mind that they're teenagers."

"I know that. That's my point. They're nearly grown, and if I'm here or not, they'll find their way."

"You think they don't care if you're around or not?"

Mack sniffs and shrugs, turning his gaze to the window he has come to know so well. At last George straightens up in his chair. He uncrosses his legs, then recrosses them at the ankles.

"In my professional opinion, I think it's safe to say that it does matter to your kids whether you're around or not. Children feel a need for their parents, in different capacities at different times. Does it matter to you that your own father's not around anymore?"

"Yeah, but we worked together. In a lot of ways we were partners. Young Taylor hasn't known me in the same way."

"So you're sayin' that not only did the farm define your work but it defined your relationship with your father."

Mack sighs. Here comes another little path to walk down. Another topic full of sneaky turns. He decides that George probably likes to play chess.

"See, what you're doing, Mack, is redefining your whole life. It's not enough to just get another job. Something fundamental has changed, and the old ways of dealing with life aren't going to match up anymore."

Mack rubs his eyes. "I don't have the energy to reinvent myself."

"I don't think that's what you have to do. More like finding your-self. There are other parts of yourself that've always been there but just didn't get much time or attention, because of the particular life you had. Now that life is over, and you've the opportunity to get to know more of Mack."

"I don't see that."

"Okay. I suppose I'm getting pushy."

"Not pushy, just too psychological."

"Oh no, not that."

Rita

She got to bed at midnight and has been up since five. At ten A.M. she is wrapping the last of the date breads and tying up little baggies of peanut brittle. The cookies have been done since yesterday about this time. She surveys her work and declares it good, but not before a coughing fit bends her double. She curses, but only in her mind. It took her strongest will to lie in that hospital bed and take what they gave her until she could go home. Now the cough is working its way back. When did she get to be so weak?

All the treats are divided into piles and labeled with the names of their recipients. Each pile she transfers to a clean paper grocery sack; she's been saving them for months. Everybody hands you plas-tic now; she's got enough plastic bags to wad up and use for insulation. Bud the grocer knows that she likes real grocery sacks. Now she loads up a sack for each person on her list, packing and repacking so as to avoid breaking fragile sugar cookies or mashing bread loaves. There are sixteen sacks, and it takes more than an hour to pack them to her satisfaction. She coughs and sips tea with lemon and honey, deciding to hold off on the brandy until she's finished driving for the day.

Finally, she folds over the tops of the sacks and is able to put four to a box (also from Bud's) by stacking them two deep. The boxes are labeled and sorted according to which sacks will go to houses in the same general vicinity and which sacks contain treats meeting special dietary requirements. Two boxes are for diabetics only; unfortunately, her diabetics are scattered all over town, but she packs them together anyway. It's only after the sacks are packed into the boxes that Rita remembers she was going to put holiday stickers on them. (She found two packs of them for a quarter at a flea market last March.) She puts stickers where she's able, without taking the sacks out of the boxes. She's too tired to be a perfectionist today.

For the second time this week, she calls Amos for help. She can't lift the boxes when they're full. She can't ask Mack or Jodie for help because they are insisting that she stay inside for a few days, while the wind is so sharp and until her cough is completely gone. That's easy for them to require, since they are not sick and do not have holiday deliveries to make. It may be a full two weeks before Christmas, but the point of *these* gifts is to provide good eating up until, and even after, Christmas Day. It's called the Christmas *season* for a reason: one day is not enough to pack everything in. So she will not call her son or daughter-in-law and listen to them harp about her health. Amos does not interrogate her about her health, and he's right next door. Two minutes after she calls, he comes over and loads up the boxes. He offers to drive her, and Rita almost turns him down without considering it. But then she thinks it will be easier to get in and out of the car if she's not behind the wheel. She decides that this is the perfect time to let Amos be her chauffeur.

Naturally, as if the Good Lord planned it to try her patience, the snow begins the minute they get in the car. It would be pretty were it not horizontal; the wind has come into town like a razor. For a moment the two of them sit and watch the flakes shoot past, neither one daring to suggest that the weather might keep them from their appointed rounds. Amos clears his throat and starts the car. It makes a sound not unlike Rita's hacking cough but turns over after a second or two. Amos pushes on the gas pedal ever so lightly. Rita stares at him.

"Something wrong with the gas?" she asks.

"No, no. I always like to get the feel of the gas and the brakes before I pick up speed." Amos is staring into the rearview mirror as if expecting to back off a precipice at any moment. He backs up another foot or so, while Rita holds back a sigh. Poor Amos. Either he can't see or he's got a cramp in his leg, but God forbid he just say that. Once they're out on the street, Rita pulls a sheet of notebook paper from her coat pocket and begins directing.

"Go left, down to the end of the block, then right." She watches, eagle-eyed, while Amos makes the requisite turns. "Now right for another block. There's a stop sign, Amos." Her voice sharpens, and he slams on the brake. "Not yet—at the corner. Okay, now go right . . . and right again. It's that second drive on the right. Now . . . pull in— watch out for the ditch. There you have it. Good." She gets out of the car, opens the back door, and very carefully pulls out a bag from the second box. She taps on the front door of the yellow frame house and walks in without waiting for a response.

Bertie Russell is in her recliner in the sitting room, the television on, a little artificial tree twinkling lights from a small table in the front window. She is surrounded by plates and cups, and her phone is off the hook again. Bertie's palsy makes everything haphazard these days, but she's chipper and ready to visit when Rita makes her entrance.

"Bertie, hon, I can't visit just now, but I'll come over this evening when I finish making my deliveries."

"That's all right, Rita. You just come over whenever you're ready. Oh my!" Bertie acts as if she's never seen food before. Rita takes out every item (she can reuse the sack) and places it on the coffee table just a foot away. "You'll have to come over and help me eat all this! Now, put that down." She motions Rita to leave the dirty dishes where they are. "Evelyn will be over in a while, and she'll take care of all that."

"I'll just put them in the sink." Rita clears the dishes, then hurries back in and replaces the phone on the hook. "Your phone was off again, Bertie. Have Evelyn rearrange things so it's closer to you. I'll see you later." She gives Bertie a peck on the cheek and is out the door, feeling bad that she didn't at least sit down. But Bertie's the cheerful understanding sort and won't read it as poor manners.

When she gets in the car, Amos is grinning.

"What's so funny?"

"Why, we're practically across the street from your place!"

"I know that." She tries not to sound irritated but doesn't appreciate his grin.

"You had me drive all the way around the block when you could've walked across the street. What sense does that make?"

"The sense it makes is that I don't *want* to walk across the street. That wind'll blow me over, and it's snowing, in case you didn't notice."

"Well, *I* could've walked it over, or just backed all the way across and into this driveway."

"Amos, the point of having a car is to drive where you'd otherwise have to walk. And we're not directly across—you could've backed into Bertie's ditch. Now don't argue with me, or I'll drive myself."

Amos backs onto the road with a bit more speed this time. "Just makes no sense. Waste of gasoline—but I'll not say any more. Just tell me where to go—so to speak." He chuckles at his own joke. Rita ignores it and begins with the next set of directions.

For most of the afternoon, Amos drives and Rita delivers. They stop at the Lunch Hour for a bowl of soup. Rita sucks down three cups of hot tea and pops in two throat lozenges at once. Because the coughing originates from her lungs and not her throat, the lozenges

do no good, but the menthol feels comforting roaming through her
nasal passages. They have six more deliveries to make, and Rita can't
wait to go home, fill the tub, and soak for a while. Amos has mentioned a Christmas classic movie that's on in a bit, but she doesn't accept his invitation to watch it with him. At that point, they are both
tired, and she knows that he will conk out on his couch and sleep
through the movie anyway. She knows this not because she is familiar
with his habits but because old men sleep in the afternoons as regularly as housecats. And even though all he's done is load some boxes
and drive her around, the afternoon is taking its toll. She feels a stab
of guilt at how little affection she feels for Amos. The older and more
tired he becomes, the less attached she becomes. It's a cold way to be,
but no sense dwelling on it.

When they pull back into her drive, there's an inch of fluffy snow
all around them but nothing in the air. The wind has let up some too.

"Amos, let's put the car in the garage. I'm not going anywhere else
today." She doesn't relish watching him maneuver the car into the
small space, but she's not sure she can get back to the house on
steady feet, let alone get in and out of the car another time. Yesterday
Mack cleared the little walk between the garage and back door, and it
will be easier to walk on than the uneven chat of the driveway, even
with the fresh snow. Amos goes all the way up the drive to the garage,
which sits near the alley. He parks the car, then helps Rita out. He
helps her carry the boxes and folded-up, empty sacks into the house.
One of the boxes has some loose items in it—last-minute changes
made when she remembered that John can't stand bread with nuts in
it and Louisa gets headaches from chocolate.

Rita offers to make Amos some coffee, but he declines and says
good-bye. Rita thanks him profusely, newly appreciative of what the
man has helped her accomplish today. She's not used to feeling miserable, and she's not at all sure she could have gotten all her Christmas
food delivered if Amos hadn't been along.

She sits at the kitchen table and reaches for the little notebook on
top of her Bible. On today's page of prayer requests is written: "help

me deliver Christmas food." She uncaps her pen, makes a thick check mark beside that line, recaps the pen, and closes the notebook. If a person were to ask her exactly how God had been involved today, she couldn't really answer. For all she knows—and this thought she swats away as if it were a hornet—the Lord wasn't involved at all. Was He behind the bad weather, or her bronchitis? If so, He wasn't much help. But if He was involved with Amos being there to carry and drive, and with the car behaving itself, then He was helpful indeed. Her check marks these days are more habit than faith, but she figures it can't hurt to give the Lord some credit, whatever the case.

Mack

When he stops at his mother's, a bad sense hits him. He parks the truck in the alley and goes up the back walk to the kitchen door. Rita is visible through the sheer curtains above the sink. She is coughing as if to rid herself of some creature at the bottom of her gut, leaning over the sink and grabbing its rim for support. Mack doesn't even knock, just opens the back door and hurries in.

"Mom, are you choking?"

She shakes her head vigorously, turns to motion at him, and manages to say, "No, just some phlegm I can't get up."

The coughing settles down, and she does too, in the closest kitchen chair.

"You're taking the antibiotics, right?"

She frowns. "Yes."

"Because you've got to take 'em until they're gone. You know that, right? If you start feeling better, you take the pills anyway."

She squeezes her eyes shut, as if Mack might be gone when she opens them again. "How many years have I lived on this planet, son?"

"More years than I have, but you manage to ignore the information you don't like." He sits in the chair next to her and puts a hand on her arm.

"I'm taking the antibiotics, so just hush up."

He notices then the cardboard boxes lined up on the cabinet. "What's this?" He gets up to see. The boxes are empty, except for a few items: zucchini bread wrapped in plastic, baggies full of assorted cookies, some fudge. He can tell by the red and green ribbons what he's looking at.

"Have you been out?" He looks at her sharply.

"Of course. I've got folks to deal with."

"You were out today, in this weather?"

"If I waited for sunshiny days, that stuff might sit till Easter."

"Mom! You're not supposed to be out—we could've delivered this stuff for you."

"All of you are busy, and it's just a few houses in town. And Amos drove me." She throws in this last bit of information as if that changes everything.

He looms over her, and she looks up at him, defiant as Young Taylor.

"Do you hear a word the doctor says?" he asks.

"That doctor is unrealistic. And he's overcautious. They're all just trying to keep from getting sued."

"No, he's trying to keep you from getting another infection. He said that your lungs are weak and you've got to be careful." Mack looks back at the food items. "You've been up all hours baking this stuff, and then you go out into the snow hauling these boxes around—"

"I am *not* going to just sit in my house! It's Christmas, and most of these old folks don't have much else to look forward to."

"They'd be just as happy if Jodie and I delivered the stuff and told them you'll visit when you're feeling better."

She looks away, and neither of them speaks for a long moment. Finally, she says, "It's not the same if somebody else delivers it. And I'll do whatever I see fit."

Mack sits again, an elbow on the table, fingers kneading his head. "What is it with this family?"

"What?" She glares at him.

"We're just not satisfied until we work ourselves to death. First Pop, and now you."

Her eyes appear suddenly to focus. "What about your dad?"

"You know what I'm talking about." They lock gazes, and Mack knows now why he had such an ominous feeling when he drove up. He stopped here to have the conversation that's about to happen. "Pop thought it was more important to take care of everybody than to keep living."

Rita's gaze is steely. "He was a hard worker."

"That's not what I'm talking about."

"Then what *are* you talking about?"

"I'm talking about an accident that shouldn't have happened." He can't believe what he's about to say next but listens to it come out of his mouth anyway. "I've wondered for a long time if it *was* an accident."

She draws up to perfect posture but doesn't reply for a long while. When she does speak, Mack is surprised at her composure.

"It was always in your father's character to sacrifice himself for others. It was his choice, his way. I'll not dishonor his memory by questioning his motives or his actions." Rita says these words with a steadiness and clarity that make it seem she has rehearsed them many times for years, day after day, to herself.

Mack tries to read the depths of his mother's eyes. Of course she will defend Pop's actions, even his final one. What did Mack expect? He realizes that the question hanging in the air is not whether or not his father's death was intentional.

"Is that what you're going to do too? Sacrifice your health without even consulting the rest of us? Will we find you dead in this house one of these days, and are we supposed to be happy about it when it happens?"

Rita's face trembles unnaturally. For a moment, Mack thinks she will slap him hard across the mouth. She did it once, long ago, when Mack was a kid and back-talking her. It was the only time she'd laid a hand on him, beyond the mere spankings when he was a small child—the swat that warned him away from the hog pen, the smack on the hand that kept him far from the stovetop when she was canning. But just that once, a real blow. It had shocked them both, but she never apologized, and he never expected it. He'd been mean-mouthed that day, a sassy kid about Young Taylor's age, too big to be speaking so ignorantly and so hatefully. He'd deserved that slap. Right now, he wonders if he deserves another. But Rita sits like a statue, trembling in her cheeks, her very eyelids.

Unable to maintain eye contact, Mack looks away. His sight lands on the Bible and little notebook that are stacked neatly against the windowsill. "You're not Jesus, Mom." The words leave him like a gentle wind. He doesn't want them to damage her in any way.

"I'm not trying to be."

"Yes, you are. You think it's all up to you, how everything turns out. It just doesn't work that way. No matter what we do, things slip away, Mom."

"Well—" Her voice is hoarse, from congestion or from tears. "I'm not willing to let you and the kids slip away."

"We're not going anywhere. You know I'm back home now."

"Yes."

"And we can help you do whatever you need to do."

"I'm just fine."

"Don't go out by yourself. We'll help you deliver the rest of your Christmas presents."

She won't answer. He can tell that the conversation is over and that he's probably not done any good whatsoever. Mom believes what she needs to believe. She gets up, not looking at him. "I'm taking a nap." And she walks back toward her bedroom. As Mack heads for the door she reappears abruptly, in the hallway.

"There was never a note, Mack. He would've left one."

Mack swallows. "You're right. He was probably too tired to watch what he was doing."

She turns and leaves him again. He doesn't know if the relief he feels is for this conclusion they have arrived at or for their conversation ending on a better note. "Bye, Mom." He shuts the back door behind him, but instead of walking all the way to his truck angles toward the garage and enters it by the side door. There his mother's car sits, still warm to the touch. He raises the hood, does what he has to do, and closes it up again. When he gets home, he'll call Tom and instruct him to pretend ignorance when Rita calls him to figure out why her car won't start. Tom's an honest mechanic but a good neighbor too.

He drives home through cold drizzle, repeating what he said to his mother, wondering if he really said it. "You're not Jesus." He feels old. He never thought he'd come to this, sabotaging his mother's car to keep her indoors. "I'm not Jesus either." He feels an urgency to get home to his family. It will be good to be in from this weather, to gather in warm rooms, speak to each child, and hug his wife. He realizes that those things will be enough to bring him happiness this evening. "We're not Jesus, but we'll have to do."

HOLDING STILL

Alone with thee, amid the mystic shadows,
The solemn hush of nature newly born;
Alone with thee in breathless adoration,
In the calm dew and freshness of the morn.
Still, still with thee, as to each newborn morning,
A fresh and solemn splendor still is given,
So does this blessed consciousness, awaking,
Breathe each day nearness unto thee and heaven.
— *"Still, Still with Thee"*

Mack

The sun is rising into a clear sky this morning, making the day appear warmer even though the thermometer outside the kitchen reads twenty degrees. Mack has the day off because Nancy Hendrikson's father passed away last night—massive heart attack. He was seventy-five and had worked hard his whole life, but remained forty pounds overweight. It was his second attack, sudden. At least family was with him; his grandson Jason had come over to help the old man string Christmas lights. Mack and Jodie will take food over later and then attend the wake. This is the first of probably several deaths that will reach them during the winter. The old folks just can't take the cold as well. They stay indoors in the stale air and get the same ailments over and over. And they get tired of all the gray outside.

The radio is on as Mack guides the car down the frosty road. They have come to the obituaries, and Mack turns it up, to hear about Nancy's father. He listens through several variations on "Funeral services for eighty-one-year-old Hal Lundeen of Oskaloosa will be held Thursday at ten-thirty A.M., with burial at Cedar Hill Cemetery. Visitation begins at seven o'clock Wednesday evening. The Marshall Funeral Home is in charge of arrangements for Hal Lundeen of Oskaloosa." Nancy's father is next to the last.

He feels like taking pictures. He still keeps the prints tacked to the walls of the stone house. He has four rolls' worth now, lined up like ragged banners along the light paneling. Every other day or so he stops by and stands in the cold room and looks at his collection. They aren't going to win any photography awards. Hardly any of them have turned out the way they looked when he shot them. But he's grabbed enough information to help him sort and hang them. They are divided into four groups, designated by which direction the scenes lie from Mack's home. There are the East Pictures and the West Pictures, the North and South Pictures. Underneath each print is an old business card, blank side out, bearing more information: "Thompson place," "Harold Cane's barn," "Mrs. Richie's house," "Fernmuller place." Each is a version of the same truth: an empty structure of some sort that still has enough form to be called something. Some days Mack loses track of time as he stands there and looks at these frozen scenes.

He stops now, four miles from home. A truck path leaves the county road and enters a pasture. There is no fence. Mack turns off the road and follows the track. He's pretty sure this is the Simonsons' property. The ground is frozen hard, allowing the car to enter the field with little trouble.

After a couple hundred yards, the track fades. It ends at a solitary structure, a corncrib someone's grandfather built. It edges what was a beanfield before the harvest. Where the tracks peter out, a single faint path continues, looking as if it leads to the end of everything. Mack considers putting his feet on that path and stopping only when it stops. It might take him to the beginning—the place before farmers or even Indians, the place as it was in the beginning and that it wants, deep down, to be always. Whoever gave men the idea that they could change its face and plant it as they saw fit, and make it serve them?

He takes six pictures and then drives back to the county road. He heads north as the sun climbs into the crystal sky. He passes what used to be the McDougle place. He recognizes the low slope of the chicken coop. Back in the summer, Mack had approached the deserted yard, thinking he spied blackberries. Insects shrieked from the layers of shoulder-high weeds that choked the yard and old hog pens, and breezes swirled eerily through the empty rooms of the house. But more disconcerting were the clear sounds and faces that crowded to the front of his inner senses. The McDougles have been dead twenty, thirty years, their three children routed out of this yard long ago, having established in some busier, happier town the family's new center of gravity. Yet this spot at the far end of the cornfield seems populated by ghosts, or by other beings never quite visible but always threatening to appear. Mack shivers even now, from the cold and from intuition, as the scene slips past his window.

He drives into Beulah and walks into the Lunch Hour. By now it's midmorning, and the small toasty space hums with people trying to get warm and grabbing a second cup of coffee before going back to work. A couple of the men nod to him, and he nods back. He sits not far from three women who share a table. They are middle-aged, with graying hair cropped short and decorative sweatshirts topping off stretch pants. The women around here seem to become thicker and more masculine as they age, while their husbands grow more spindly and softer around the edges.

Mack sits in a booth and asks for coffee and apple pie. From there he observes the conversation going on at the counter. Julie is pouring coffee refills, and the farmers gather round in their overalls, their denim rear ends reminding Mack of the backsides of cows at a feeding trough. His gaze travels to their faces. He sees them not as faces of people he knows but as merely faces on people. It is an odd sensation.

It's not always easy to read a farmer's face. You see the windburn on his cheeks and the cracks in his hands and know what work he does. You see the weariness in his eyes and understand that his life is not easy. But the details are hidden away, behind the handshake, the work clothes, and the slight smile that is part of his greeting, a standard hello for anyone he passes. His eyes do not speak of what calamity he's dealing with now—a market that's bottomed out or a wife's illness. His expression tells you that there's work to be done, that's all.

But when Mack looks at his own face in the mirror these days, his eyes say far too much. By now he understands that his depression does not set him apart from many folks around here; everyone has a share of it, because everyone's life has had its hard times. But for some reason, Mack had to crawl to the heart of his darkness. That's how he is different from the men at the counter.

And he has put everything into spoken words, has sat in rooms with those doctors who knew nothing, nothing at all, about the life he and all of the others have lived. He sat there and told all, offered up revelation after revelation, relinquished all of their stories with his one.

And so his face is different now from the faces of his neighbors. He looks in the mirror and sees layers of information right there in his eyes. Technically, he is no longer a farmer. But week after week, in George Dooley's small office, he delves into what it means, more than a subject should ever be explored. He has been led by people in light coats, people with smooth, sensitive hands, into the world of talking, talking, talking. He has talked, has uncovered things that can never be understood. And now his face shows all the confusion his words have caused.

He leaves the café twenty minutes later, stepping into the sharp air. The Lunch Hour sits at the end of a block. When Mack turns right and walks east, the sidewalk takes a dip, and suddenly there is

Ray Danson's barren soybean field. No matter where he turns, there is someone's land, and there is the history of his own industry. George is right: a person can survive here only by redefining everything. Mack's instincts must be redirected, his memories reorganized toward a different story and outcome.

It is a week before Christmas, and the weather is cold and bleak enough to chase everyone inside. In the middle of the workday, Beulah's streets are empty. Mack continues to wander around in the car, not yet ready to be home. All his life he has studied details: the inner workings of machinery, the texture and smell of ripening crops, the coarseness of dirt under his boots, the shade of the sky just before sundown. He needs to see other details now. He wants to see. So he parks the car on the east side of the old town square. The four streets that enclose the block are too clean, even for the dead of winter. There is little clutter of business, only smooth, empty storefronts instead. In good weather, a handful of kids with skateboards command the sidewalks, their wheels making echoes among the old, lonely trees.

The grain elevator, two streets over, towers over the small downtown. It is twice as high and twice as thick as any other structure nearby. The bank, snug at the corner of Main and Second Streets, is still the town's most beautiful building. Solid limestone up to the large front window, above it exact configurations of deep red brick. It is an opera house among the storefronts, its original name Beulah City Bank, still embossed above the arched window. Underneath, within that window, is the bank's current name, which has changed three times in five years. To avoid straining anyone's short-term memory, everyone calls it The Bank.

In the next block is Rexall Drug, the American Legion, and the post office. The post office lobby closes at four-thirty, but the door to the bank of PO boxes stays open later. Mack peers through the glass door at the frosted office window, the wall of bronze boxes, filigreed and looking just the same as when he was a kid. His family always had a mailbox at the end of the farmyard drive, and Mack had wanted one of those bronze boxes, which required keys.

The end of this block is the end of any real business. A filling station used to be here, and long after it closed the two pumps remained, quoting regular and premium prices from 1982. Some restaurant owner finally yanked up the pumps, leaving light squares on the grease-stained pavement. The pumps probably now adorn some overpriced sandwich shop in Des Moines or Chicago. Probably that sandwich shop is painted inside to look old and nostalgic, that peeling-paint, two-toned look. Here, at Ralph's old Gulf station, the outer wall, formerly a gleaming white, is bled through by its underlying rusty brick. But no one pays good money to sit there and have a ham and cheese, chips, and Coke. Even the ghosts have moved on.

He crosses the street and walks back to the square, then along its north side, past the shoe store that has become an insurance office. Then the JC Penney store that has turned into the town museum, the large interior piled in loosely organized fashion and sectioned off into rough portions of the town's history.

A bare maple tree casts shadows at the corner of the former Lee's Clothing Store. This is a friendly little spot in the summertime, when the shadows become full shade. Three or four metal chairs and a round aluminum table provide a place for several of the old men, who keep up a hoarse chatter in the quiet afternoon. If you stop to say hello, they will nod and ask how you are and keep talking, as if they don't have much time or room for anything beyond their own business, as if what younger people are concerned about has little hold on them anymore.

He walks over to the south side of the square and follows Des Moines Avenue east, into old yards and residences. On most of the streets in Beulah there is no real curb anymore. The tough grasses of dead autumn lawns fall out of their boundaries and into the light pavement of the streets. Now, with a flat layer of snow remaining, the best definition of a street is the line made by cars and trucks parked along its edges.

He goes several streets over to the community park, one block square that sits at the center of several homes and their yards. They used to have 4-H picnics here. Three large walnut trees overwhelm the set of swings and the picnic shelter. He remembers how every autumn the black, husked walnuts lay everywhere, resting under the tables and gathering in the indentations of the concrete floor.

Mack sits on a picnic table and tries to look at the houses around him as if he's never seen them before. He can hear some mom getting after her kids, her voice thin behind storm doors and windows. He sees her standing in a picture window not far from where he is. Her hands are on her hips, and she is looking down, probably at a toddler. She looks ready to yell or make a sudden movement. But as Mack watches, she suddenly laughs and bends down, out of view.

Jodie laughed a lot when the kids were little. She played with them whenever she could, to the point that Mack was sure she'd had kids just so she could keep playing as an adult. Maybe all women stop playing after enough years have passed. He can't think more about that now.

He dusts off the seat of his pants and heads back toward the square. He knows that, although he doesn't see people in the houses, they see him. In a place so small, every movement matters. People keep track of who sat at a picnic table in mid-December. He wonders briefly what the silent witnesses think of him, what they murmur to spouses or in-laws as he passes down their sidewalks.

Jodie

Rita is in a bad mood. She called Jodie at eight this morning and asked her to stop at the post office for her because she's staying in bed today. She sounds defeated. Jodie can't tell if this radical change in behavior—the staying in bed, not the bad mood—is the result of feeling bad physically or being frustrated about the car. Mack informed Jodie two days ago that Mom would be without a car, and they'd need to run errands for her.

"Poor Tom," Jodie said. "Is he working on it again?"

"No. Tom and I have an agreement. He won't figure out what's wrong until Mom's over the bronchitis."

She looked at him in surprise. "Well, this is a new strategy."

"Actually, once she's better, I'll just sneak back into the garage and fix it myself."

She laughed then, admiring the man who stood in her doorway. She'd forgotten how tricky he could be. "You know she'll figure it out after a while."

"I don't care. I'm taking her wheels away." He leaned against the doorjamb and sipped coffee. For just a moment, Jodie felt that her old Mack had returned.

So this morning Jodie has shopped for groceries, delivered pharma-ceuticals, and picked up the mail in Rita's stead. It took half the day, and Jodie has experienced a new wave of admiration for her mother-in-law. She hopes to be so active twenty years from now but dares not think that far ahead.

At the pharmacy she runs into Annette Peters, a member of Beulah's First Methodist, where the Barneses used to attend. Annette is one of the few people Jodie truly misses, now that she and Mack at-tend church in Oskaloosa. Even though they encounter people of their former church in other situations, it feels different not to wor-ship with them anymore. Annette was not only a sweet person but a conscientious friend. There was the time she arranged for a surprise birthday luncheon for Jodie, off in Pella, just a few miles down the road. Jodie went to the address thinking it was a Methodist women's meeting at someone's home, only to find that it was a home converted into a tearoom. Six other women from church were seated when Jodie entered the homey dining room, with its clean white walls and deep oak woodwork, small tables draped in white linens, and pretty lamps and potted plants giving the area a warm glow. The lunch was from a menu that changed weekly. And each woman got her own pot of tea or coffee. When the owner brought out Jodie's dessert—a decadent lemon chiffon pie—she was joined by two other women who sang

"Happy Birthday" in Dutch. Annette just grinned while Jodie laughed and blushed.

Today Annette looks tired. Jodie heard recently that her oldest daughter just lost a baby, in the third month. She wonders what other events have visited Annette's family, events that Jodie would have known about when she was in regular contact.

"Annette! How are you?"

The woman is slender, her naturally wavy blond hair tied back in the way most women deal with long hair when there's work to do. "Oh, we're all right, Jodie. How about you?"

"Fine, fine."

"I hear that Mack's doing a lot better."

"Yes, thanks for mentioning it. He is. I was sorry to hear about Katie—how's she doing?"

Annette's smile is steady. "She and Tim have done real well. It was a first pregnancy, and the doctor says there's no reason she can't keep on trying."

"Sometimes it's as if the body hasn't caught on yet. And she's young."

"Yes. They have plenty of time. You look good, Jodie."

"So do you." Their smiles linger in the pause that follows.

"You all are still in my prayers." Annette can say such a thing and not sound condescending or pitying or judging. Jodie feels pain at this renewed understanding of the friendships she has given up in the name of survival.

"We really appreciate that."

They part company, and it's a few moments before Jodie can remember what she came for and what errands are next on her list. She thinks of the birthday party, the lightness of that afternoon, and the warmth of female company. When, exactly, did she decide to forfeit all of that? Was it the shame of losses that made her withdraw? After a while, if the grief and loss keep coming, the world goes silent. No one knows what to say anymore. Taylor Senior's death was typical enough—farm accident—and he was in his sixties. But Mack giving up the farm, and then Alex losing his, and then Alex dying. A person was tempted to think that the odds were stacked no matter what. After all that, what support or help is even plausible?

She stops, last of all, at Rita's to deliver groceries and mail and visit for a bit, but not long because Rita feels lousy and is on her way to a nap. With her mother-in-law safely tucked away at home, Jodie takes several deep breaths. She tries to shake out all the negative thoughts that have plagued her this afternoon, and with that in mind, she takes Walnut Street and slows down as she passes Terry's house. The car is in the garage, the ruts in the drive half-filled with the morning's snowfall. Even though she is bundled up in old sweats and a jacket, Jodie feels suddenly voluptuous and close to shivers. She forces herself to keep pressure on the gas pedal, gliding by the small house not unlike most vehicles traveling in town when snow is on. She has never been in Terry's house, at least not since they have become lovers. She thinks she remembers dropping some materials at his door one day, some forms the school secretary had asked her to walk over one time. The memory of Terry at that time is like the memory of another person altogether. He had just moved in, had been in town maybe a month. It is amazing what new chemistry does to another person's being. Terry seems different from the guy who came to Beulah two years ago and bears no resemblance to the kid she knew in high school. Maybe he dresses differently or something. Maybe he just looks more like what he truly is, now that Jodie is paying attention.

When she steps in the door of the farmhouse, her bit of Terry happiness is shattered by music from the living room. Heavy metal something from Young Taylor's collection. Her son is stretched out on the sofa, no light on in the room, staring at the ceiling.

"Hey! Turn it down!" She has to yell this twice before the form on the sofa twitches.

"Mom, listen to this."

"No! It sounds like a train wreck. Turn it down."

"You're not really listening."

She marches across to the CD player and shuts it off. Young Taylor doesn't move; his eyes are closed. It makes her think of the way he covered his face when he was little and getting into trouble, thinking that if he couldn't see Mom and Dad, they couldn't find him.

"You can play it upstairs. Better yet, with your headphones on."

"Mom, you need to slow down."

"Yeah, I'll do that once the new maid and cook get here."

She looks at the clock and mutters Jesus's name. She can't pinpoint when she began to use it as a swear word. She'd hardly used any profanity during all her growing-up years and kept a particularly clean mouth when the children were little. But now she is uttering sacred words right and left as if she has just discovered their power. She suspects that she started using the Lord's name this way to get his attention; obviously, prayers that used the name properly had not been good enough. Or maybe this is how she tells God how angry she is at his system. Whatever, it's a protest. Supper should be ready by now. She throws open the freezer door and finds some hamburger, sticks it in the microwave to thaw. Sloppy Joes tonight. No buns. Oh well, it goes all right over toast.

Mack walks in as she is fighting the can of tomato paste.

"Hey, want me to do that?"

"No, I've got it." The phone rings. Mack is closest, but Jodie puts the can and opener in his hands and reaches for it herself.

"Jodie, it's me."

Her lips go numb. Terry's voice has become a private, important sound in her life. She sees Young Taylor's feet still at the end of the sofa, and says to Mack, pointing toward their son, "Would you tell him to straighten up the family room, please? And take his music upstairs." Mack goes to Young Taylor, still working the can opener.

"Not a good idea, calling this time of day," she says into the phone, just above a whisper.

"Oh, right. He's back home now."

"Well, my kids are here too, and most of the time the phone calls are for them."

"Sorry, Jodie, but the suspense was killing me."

"Huh?"

The phone is silent. "My note—you haven't read it yet?"

"What note?"

He laughs, nervously. "The one I stuck in the side of your purse while you were in the post office. Yours was the only car on the street, so I thought it was safe. You didn't see it?"

Jodie looks at her purse, which she set on the kitchen cabinet next to the door. The side pocket is empty.

"What did it look like?" She picks up the purse and begins rummaging through it. She looks toward the family room, where Mack and Young Taylor are picking up newspapers, talking quietly.

"Just a plain white envelope. I put it in that side pocket. You couldn't miss it."

The numbness that began in her lips suddenly rushes the length of her body. This time, Jesus's name is a true prayer.

"What?" Terry sounds irritated.

"I put Rita's mail in that pocket so it wouldn't get mixed up with mine. Terry, what were you thinking? I must have picked up your note with all her stuff."

His voice turns crackly with panic. "Do you think she's found it yet? Can you go over there and get it?"

"I'm in the middle of supper now, and Mack and the kids are home. I can't leave! And yes, she rips through her mail the minute I give it to her. Did you have my name on it? Was it sealed? She'd just return it to me."

He sighed. "No, I drew a lily on it—you know, the kind you like so much?"

"I've got to go." She hangs up as Mack wanders back in. He smiles and hands her the opened can.

Kenzie

Dear Jesus,

I'm so confused. I have so many emotions inside me now. I feel love and fear and everything else. And I pray almost every minute of the day, but the more I pray, the less you seem to be around. Oh, I know you're with me all the time, but I used to feel it more. I used to be sure. Your Holy Spirit would fill me with peace and assurance. But now I don't know what I feel.

I love Mitchell. I love him so much. I can tell that he's a godly man, someone so close to you that other people don't understand him. Just like they didn't understand the prophets—or you, Jesus. I became his friend because I thought he needed to know you and that I could help him. But it's the other way around. He's helped me so much to understand you and the world and the future and what we have to do as Christians.

I've waited my whole life for a true, spiritual friend like Mitchell. And you led us to meet each other, but everything's confused. Believing is so hard now. Maybe because I finally understand what it means. You said we had to hate our fathers and mothers. I never thought that would mean leaving Mom and Dad. But I can see what's happening, that the Tribulation is on its way and the Anti-Christ has already attacked our home. I thought you'd want me to stay and do battle, but I can see now that your ways are not our ways.

How can I leave my family? How did you leave, Jesus, when you were grown and it was time for you to start preaching and healing? Did it hurt this much? Did your mother and brothers and sisters not understand why? I know how they tried to lock you up once—they thought you were crazy. Just like people will think I'm crazy when I go away with Mitchell.

But when I'm with him, everything feels sure and true. I know that what I'm doing is the right thing. He and I can pray together and talk about your Word for hours. And he can build anything. He's so much smarter than people think. He'll take care of me. I can't believe that you sent such a wonderful man to me. I thought I was too young, that

*you thought I was a kid, just like Mom and Dad and Grandma think.
But Mary was just a teenager when you made her pregnant with Jesus. So
I guess that in your plan it's fine for me to go away. You're calling me to a
better place. I have to be in a community that loves you and only you. I
thought I could really help here, and maybe I did. But you're calling me
away now, to a real family of faith, a group of brave people who understand all the horrible things that are happening.*

*Jesus, help me do what I'm supposed to do. Thanks for bringing me
Mitchell, who can be strong even when I'm not.*

*But please, please, make this not hurt so much. I don't mind suffering
for you, but is there any way you can make it so my parents don't suffer because of what I'm doing?*

*At least Dad's home now. Maybe my leaving will make him and Mom
work together better; maybe they need the pain so that you can heal them
completely.*

*Thank you for everything. I hope I didn't sound ungrateful or like I
don't have faith. I finally do have faith. But it's different from what I
thought it would be. Everything is so different. I guess that's what it means
to grow up in the spirit.*

*Give me strength and peace. Help Mitchell as he makes the plans. We
want to do everything according to your will.*

In Jesus's precious name, Amen.

FINDING HOPE

All thy works with joy surround thee, earth and heaven
  reflect thy rays,
Stars and angels sing around thee, center of unbroken
  praise.
Field and forest, vale and mountain, flowery meadow,
  flashing sea,
Singing bird and flowing fountain call us to rejoice in thee.
  —*"Joyful, Joyful, We Adore Thee"*

Jodie

She feels nothing at all as she pulls out the Christmas tins, the ones
that get stored from year to year in the top of the pantry. They are
round or square, bearing deeply shined winter scenes or patterns of
holly or candy canes. By now she has collected about twenty of them,
and not too many years ago she and Rita filled each and every one
with homemade candies and cookies. Nearly half of the sacred family
recipes were brought out only after Thanksgiving and exploited for
Christmas and New Year's alone—the fancy confections bearing
names of ancient aunts and grandmas, long dead but coming alive for
those few weeks in the bleak winter, resurrected in sugar and nuts,
food coloring and dustings of flour or cinnamon.

This act of pulling out the tins used to feel sacred, or at least special. Today Jodie lines them up on the counter while fighting panic. She has called Rita twice, and no one answered. Unless Rita is hitching rides with Amos or someone else, she's got to be home. Her refusal to pick up the phone can mean only one thing: she has discovered the note.

Or it could mean that she's too sick to come to the phone.

The logical thing would be to have Mack run over and check on her. But if the note is the problem, that could bring disaster. Jodie would go over there herself, but she hasn't the strength to deal with Rita's wrath, which is the worst kind: courteous and full of a martyr's sorrow. Jodie will wait another ten minutes. It's possible that Rita was simply indisposed before, maybe in the shower or just waking up.

She washes the tins and sets them around the warm kitchen to dry. She will fill them with store-bought food and whatever Rita has been creating on her own. The clock indicates that the ten minutes of waiting is almost up. Jodie stares out the window above the sink. The fields are one continuous color, or a clay-induced noncolor. The wind is too cold. The sky rests on her life too heavily. She would give anything for today to be January 2.

To make matters worse, Mack is working harder than ever to entice the Christmas spirit from everyone. He has trekked to the woods and pastures three times already, gathering boughs off pines, cedars, and spruces. He has made wreaths for both doors and strung the rest around doorways and windows. Even Young Taylor is rooting through dilapidated boxes of decorations for the right bell or angel figurine to set in the middle of his dad's creations. It has been odd to watch the two of them, bent over a crippled wing or missing hook, barely speaking but apparently enjoying the process. This is a nice change. Now that Mack is busy concocting Christmas, he isn't so frantic to become useful in any other way.

Last night, unexpectedly, they made love.

She isn't sure which event has caused the most shock to her system, Terry's note landing at Rita's, or Mack's embracing her in the dark of their room. It happened innocently enough. She noticed him ratcheting his arm around as though to undo a kink. She gave him a deep massage in those muscles. He's always coming in at the end of the day with something aching. Rubbing away his minor pains has been part of Jodie's routine for years.

So she did what needed doing, and he thanked her and went to the bathroom to brush his teeth. She was settled in bed when he got there. She raised her face enough to receive the light good-night kiss, as customary as the massage. Mack kissed her on the cheek, and then took hold of her face and kissed her mouth. Then he lay over her gently, allowing their faces to linger together.

She wanted to stop, feeling, strangely enough, unfaithful. Just two days before she had made love to Terry forty miles away. It had been good, so good that she had found it even easier than before to ignore her guilt. This was costing her husband nothing, after all. He didn't touch her anymore. He would never know. He wouldn't be hurt.

But now, the hands that found the nape of her neck, then her breasts, then her tummy—these were her husband's hands. And possibly because her body had come awake in recent weeks, every touch resonated down to her deepest point of sex. Maybe Mack hadn't touched her in a long time, but he had touched her for years before that, and she'd forgotten how well he knew her specific geography. As he stroked her inner thighs and filled her mouth with his own taste, she lost all sense. The sound in her ears was of her own heart crashing.

When he moved over her, grasping both of her hands in his, she knew that she would let everything happen. It broke her heart to see the joy in Mack's face as he entered her and stayed for some time before climaxing. A few moments later he helped her come too; he really hadn't forgotten a thing.

Then he went to sleep, and she didn't shut her eyes for the rest of the night.

Tomorrow Marty and David and Sharon arrive from Omaha. All of them will gather in this house and do their best to have a holiday.

Jodie and Marty always got along well; it has cost Jodie more than she will think about to have her former sister-in-law and her niece and nephew so far away and out of touch. But to have them here at this particular time . . . she fears Marty's intuition. She fears having Rita here, full of knowledge she won't dare voice but that will color her every comment anyway. Christmas is a disaster waiting to happen, like thunderheads out of which ominous tails are beginning to form, tornadoes ready to hit earth.

Mack's boots sound on the back steps. He is returning from his walk to the end of the drive to retrieve the newspaper from its box. As he walks in, bringing the smell of cold with him, the phone rings. Jodie grabs it. "Hello?"

"Hello." Rita's voice is raspy from her cough.

"Mom, I was just about to call you."

She hears Rita struggling to clear her throat. "Did you call before?"

Jodie can't tell anything from the tone of Rita's voice. She decides to take the cowardly way out and just pretend that everything is normal. There's a thin chance that Rita was too worn out to look through all the mail. Or if she did run across the note with no name on it, she may have assumed it was Jodie's and not opened it.

"Yes, I called a couple of times this morning."

"It's the cold medicine—really knocks me out." A silence follows. Jodie pushes forward.

"I'll be over in a while, to run whatever errands you need."

"I don't need anything." The voice is distant.

"Well, there might be something. I'll stop by."

"I have something of yours."

Mack is sitting at the table, coffee in hand and newspaper spread in front of him. Jodie tries to breathe normally. "I think there was an envelope in my purse that got mixed up with your mail."

"Yes, I think so."

Jodie closes her eyes, recognizing the glaze of cold anger in the voice on the phone. "I don't think my name was on it."

"No, but it was inside."

God, just destroy me now. "I'll come over and get it." Her own voice is flat to her ears. She hopes she doesn't sound afraid.

"I'd rather you send Mack today."

Jodie struggles to put an answer together, one that will prevent all the wrong things from happening. Rita continues.

"I'll hold the note for you."

"I'll get it later then."

"I don't want to upset Mack."

She is saying that she won't tell him, and Jodie almost says, "Thank you," but instead replies, "He'll be over in a bit."

The phone goes dead at the other end. Mack looks at her as she hangs up.

"That Mom?"

"Yeah."

"She all right?"

"Sure."

"I'd better not dilly-dally over the paper then. Don't want to keep her plans hanging in the balance." He smiles and turns a page. Jodie turns away and finds some items to put into the sink. She looks at the Christmas tins and wants to scream. *Merry Christmas to each of us.* To husband and to lover, to children who instinctively worry about what they don't yet know, to mother-in-law who might just die rather than deal with this new catastrophe. To Jodie Barnes, adulteress and humbug, who hates Christmas but somehow loves two men.

Rita

At least her pneumonia has eased up. Marty, David, and Sharon are out at the farm, and tomorrow is Christmas Day. Rita has a pie in the oven and chicken and noodles on the stove. The celebration begins this evening, and she's got fudge cooling. She roams from one room to another, checking the grocery sacks that have Christmas gifts in them, making sure the nametags are on each one. There are a lot of small gifts, items she's picked up at sales throughout the year. No big gifts for anyone, but no one expects that. All the grandkids are old enough now to appreciate some money in a card. Of course, she's found them other things besides. It's just not Christmas without pres-ents to unwrap, even if all that's inside is a new pair of socks.

As if she could really celebrate anyway. In the kitchen drawer where she keeps her bills, underneath her checkbook, is Jodie's note. Jodie has not been out to get it, and Rita has been too busy cooking and wrapping to have someone drive her out to the farm. She can't take the note with her, knowing that Mack is there. The whole mess is just so awkward and painful. She's managed not to speak with Jodie since the other morning when they first discussed it on the phone.

She has read it twice. Once, when she didn't know what it was. After the meaning sank in, she read it another time, carefully. Truth be told, she took it out a day later and read it again. Written on school stationery, it was more romantic than sexual, but a person could not mistake its meaning. Every morning since, Rita has awak-ened feeling sick to her stomach. She has watched Mack and Jodie fuss and fight over the years, but she always trusted that they'd make up and keep going. Both of them were steady people, at least until Mack's illness got the best of him. But even then, he stayed commit-ted to his family. Rita's not convinced he would have gone into the hospital at all if it hadn't been for that. He really did not care about his own life back then. Watching him stumble through his days had been like observing an infant born without an immune system. You didn't know when, but you were sure that sooner or later some mal-ady would overcome the child and there would be no fighting it.

But Mack rallied because he had a wife and children. That was born into him. And Jodie just got stronger and kept them all afloat. It doesn't make sense that, after all they've weathered, she would get weak now.

This is what Rita tells herself, because it is the logical argument. But underneath that is another logic altogether. A woman gets tired, sometimes so tired that her very character crumbles under the weight. Rita has seen this happen; she remembers her own fatigue during the years when both sons were newly married and siring children and her responsibilities had grown to embrace not one but three families at the very time when she and Taylor could barely hold on to their own farm. She tries not to remember those unbearable afternoons when the quiet of her kitchen would surround her while the worries multiplied in her head. She tries to push that knowledge away now, but instead she sits on the sofa, surrounded by Christmas goodies and gifts, and remembers the women of her town.

She has known a few who carried their unhappiness like a tradition they couldn't part with. Rita decided long ago that such women would be unhappy no matter what the situation or who they were married to. But others were given burdens they could not bear: husbands who drank or beat them or simply dismissed them and defiled the marriage bed again and again. Rita figures that this is true in any place, but in Beulah the secrets have never stayed secrets. How often she had wished (though she could never bring herself to pray it) that the husband of her good friend Teresa would meet his end early. It was clear to everyone that Ted Hallowell was simply mean. When he finally did die, they all traipsed by his casket to be respectful of the dead and especially of Teresa. But the relief in her living room after the service was palpable. Teresa burst out of prison that day and hasn't stopped to catch her breath since.

Sarah James lived with her husband for forty years and had two lovers at different times. John never knew of it. And even the most righteous churchgoers stopped short of all-out condemnation. Sarah had married young because she was of age and John was there. The families had been friends and neighbors for two generations. And Sarah's father had two younger daughters to marry off as well; he would not have a grown daughter at home when she could be setting up her own household. Possibly this was why the blame people held for her did not run completely deep and true. Rather than feel sorry for herself and turn into a lump by middle age, Sarah made a life she could endure, even enjoy.

None of that matters now. Jodie is family, and she has injured the family, and Rita is so angry at her that she is afraid to be in the same room with her. And Jodie is her daughter; in every way she has loved and cared for Rita as much as a daughter would have. She is the mother of Young Taylor and Kenzie. She has become blood kin, and the thought of losing her sends streaks of panic through Rita's soul. She does not know what to do with all of this commotion inside her.

So she gets up from the couch and checks on the pies, stirs the pot of noodles. As the homemade strips of egg dough swirl in the fresh chicken broth, Rita makes a decision. She will put off dealing with this crisis over the next two days. Marty and the kids are here, the first gathering of this sort in nearly three years. Mack is doing better, and Rita is still trying to stay out of the hospital. That's a full enough plate. She will be civil to Jodie, and this adultery topic will not come up until after the holiday.

She goes to the kitchen table and writes this new request on her list of prayers: "Help Jodie and me to get through the holiday without any upset."

In a few hours, Mack comes to pick her up in the truck. He has loaded a heavy cooler into the truck bed, and in this he carefully places the pot of noodles and the pie. The sacks of presents and an additional sack of holiday cookies and candies get shoved up against the back of the truck cab, where they won't slide around. His grasp feels strong as he helps Rita step up into the cab.

"How's everything going out there?" she asks. Her son looks happy.

"Fine. They got here about an hour ago. Sharon is so tall I hardly recognized her."

"It'll be so good to see the kids." Rita nears tearfulness but sucks back the lump that's rising. "How does Marty look?"

"Good. She looks real good. She brought a friend."

Rita looks at him, and he clarifies. "A guy she's been dating for a few months. Name's Joe. Seems like a nice guy."

Rita stares at the snowy tracks ahead of them. She's not prepared for this. Her first response is protest. This is a *family* event, after all.

As if he senses her conflict, Mack adds, "And the kids seem to like him a lot."

"Really? That's good."

"Yeah. I think you'll like him. I get a good sense off him."

Rita takes in as full a breath as she can. More adjustments. More changes slapping up against them all.

They walk into a kitchen full of people; Jodie is handing dishes to any pair of hands available, and Marty emerges from the dining room. She comes across the kitchen immediately and throws her arms around Rita.

"Rita, you look so good!" The words come out close to Rita's ear. Unlike Jodie, Marty never got into the habit of calling Rita "Mom." But the affection in her voice now is unmistakable. Finally, the grasp loosens, and Rita stands back to look at her former daughter-in-law. Her hair is a different shade, lighter, and she's put on a bit of weight, which is good, because she was always so thin. She's wearing a bright holiday sweater and makeup. Just then she is pushed aside, and "little" Sharon comes forward. She is now taller than Rita, and her resemblance to Alex makes Rita draw in a sharp breath.

"Hi, Grandma! Merry Christmas!"

"Hi, Grandma!" David is standing beside his sister. He is two years older and two inches taller, long and lean like Rita's own sons but bearing the eyes and smile of his mother. Rita hugs and kisses each child in turn, aware that she's teary-eyed but not worrying about that. The room is so bright that she can hardly bear it—all her family in one place and each person smiling. Young Taylor is dressed normally for once. He comes up and kisses Rita's cheek, then takes her coat. Kenzie comes by quickly for a hug before returning to help Jodie.

Jodie calls out, "Merry Christmas, Mom," and glances across the room. Rita makes a point to smile at her and return the greeting.

"Rita, I want you to meet Joe Bernard," Marty says. A tall man with thinning blond hair and a friendly face comes forward and grasps Rita's hand.

"Pleasure to meet you."

Marty continues. "He teaches computer science at the community college where I've taken classes."

So. She met him at school. Well, that's not a bad place to meet people. Better than a bar. And he does have a wonderful face—handsome enough but full of other things too. Rita feels better right away. She had feared that she would be angry at seeing another man where her own son used to be. But at this moment it is clear that her son Alex is now part of family history. And this man has stepped in to carry on life. In fact, Rita's usual holiday blues don't feel present at all today. Two miles down the road, her husband and son lie under headstones in the rough winter ground. She can hold that thought without feeling its full force for once. It is Christmas, and her remaining children and grandchildren are here, in this house. She is glad that it's time to eat, because she feels the need to sit down. So much is hitting her senses, inside and out. She dares to identify the beating in her heart as joy.

As they pass dishes and fill the room with conversation, Rita doesn't say much. She watches each person and does her best to soak it all in. Mack was right: David and Joe trade jokes as if they have been friends for years. They gang up on Sharon, who is quite capable of defending herself. It causes Rita pain to see how healthy Marty is now; she had to get away from Alex and his alcoholism to find life. Years ago, Rita admitted to herself that Alex was tearing his family apart. But it is hard to see the truth of that confirmed in how well his wife and children are doing now, having put distance and death between him and them.

Jodie appears to have made the same resolution as Rita. She acts as if nothing horrendous has happened and talks with Rita the same as always. She and Mack relate easily today, maybe because the holiday and the houseguests have absorbed their attention. But Rita imagines that Mack looks across the table at his wife with true affection. She imagines that Jodie pats his back as she walks by on her way to the kitchen.

She imagines that they sit together on the loveseat as if they want to be there. Two hours after dinner they have all moved to the living room, where a very large Scotch pine sparkles in front of the picture window. Kenzie and Young Taylor pass out the gifts. Jodie has mulled some cider and made more coffee. She and Rita take lids off the Christmas tins and urge everyone to try this and that. The fact that half of the treats are not homemade doesn't matter. Such a thing would have bothered Rita a few years ago, but she is content that her fudge tin gets visited more than anything else.

Kenzie

It is perhaps the most important evening of her life so far. Kenzie stands in front of the mirror that hangs on the back of her bedroom door, and she studies herself more intently than she ever has. She wears a velour dress that buttons all the way down the front. It is deep purple, almost black in places. The sleeves are long and have three pearl buttons on each cuff. Mom found the dress at a sidewalk sale in Ottumwa last February. It cost next to nothing because of a seam that was noticeably crooked, what should have been a factory reject. Mom took care of that, although it meant resetting the entire dress from the waist down. It reaches Kenzie at midcalf, and so she wears her knee-high black boots, having polished them earlier in the day. She also set her hair, which she usually doesn't do. She wears the glittery earrings that Sharon gave her for Christmas. In fact, Sharon helped with her hair.

Downstairs, Dad and Joe are discussing basketball. It's weird to hear Dad talk about sports, but he doesn't often have another guy around—Young Taylor does not count when it comes to so many guy things—and her father's voice makes Kenzie's throat ache. He's acted so happy and healthy this Christmas; is it too good to be true?

She can't hear Mom and Aunt Marty, because they are off in Mom and Dad's bedroom, at the far end of the hall. Mom is going through the clothes she can't wear anymore—mainly jeans and shirts and other work clothes. Now that Marty has gained some weight, she is a mere size smaller than Mom, who has outgrown some things in the past year or two. Kenzie is sure that they are using the closed door to shield their conversation; after all, Aunt Marty has a boyfriend now.

Kenzie tries not to dwell on the fact that her aunt is sleeping with a man she's not married to. Of course, nobody comes right out and says that this is happening, but when older men and women hang out for months, they're not just dating. Mom seems so happy for Aunt Marty, and Grandma Rita acts as if this new relationship is fine with her.

It irritates Kenzie that Young Taylor has turned normal for now and the Omaha relatives act as if he's a great kid. Maybe they don't know anything about his Goth act or his getting kicked out of school. At any rate, David, who looks as normal as guys get, has hung out with Young Taylor the whole time. They sit in Young Taylor's room and listen to music, and David talks about Omaha and Young Taylor talks about Des Moines; they both talk about how lame their schools are. Their voices sometimes rise and drift across the hallway.

Sharon and Aunt Marty have shared the double bed of the spare room across the hall. Joe has bedded down in the family room, and David slept in there on the floor in his sleeping bag one night but last night fell asleep on the floor in Young Taylor's room. Kenzie offered her bedroom to Grandma Rita—none of them wanted her to spend the holiday alone at her house, even just overnight—but she is content to sleep in the living room on the sofa, in the glow of the Christmas tree. Kenzie is thankful that her own space has not been encroached upon. Sharon is really nice, but Kenzie sees right away that they are now from completely different worlds. When Sharon and David lived here, she and Kenzie did a lot of faith-related things together, but Sharon's present involvement with God is the minimum church attendance, and she has not picked up on any of Kenzie's comments meant to explore her spiritual state. Kenzie stays out among their houseguests as much as seems necessary but has retreated several times to her room. She can't manage to get to the church for her regular prayer time, so she simply prays in her room and hopes that no one knocks on the door.

But tonight everything could change. She is singing in the Christmas pageant at the Baptist church. Jenna is reading a poem, Trent is reading the Christmas story from Luke's Gospel, and Kenzie will sing a solo at the end, "O Holy Night." And after she sings, the pastor will lead the congregation in carols, and the last carol will be "O Come, All Ye Faithful," which will be the altar call. Reverend Darnelle believes that people should have the opportunity to turn to God during any service, even special holiday worship.

Her whole family will be there. This could be the night of battle, and of victory. It could be that God has brought her family to this very night in order to work miracles in their hearts. She imagines them walking up the aisle one by one, and the pastor praying with them. She imagines hugging each one afterwards, telling them how much she has prayed and how happy she is that God has touched them.

Mitchell will be there too.

He was unsure at first. Sometimes his worst battles are at church, as if Satan chooses that place to torment him the most. But two days ago he told Kenzie, "The Lord told me that you'll need my support. So I'll be there, Kenzie. I'll probably sit in the back, but I'll be singing every word right with you."

She stares at the young woman in purple, who smiles back at her from the mirror. She has finally come to the place where God wants her. And she can say with all honesty that she is beautiful tonight.

The church is full, warm, and noisy before the service begins. Then the lights go down, except for candles in the windows and dim lights over the altar. The crowd grows quiet. Kenzie's family is seated in two rows halfway back on the east side of the sanctuary. As she sits by the piano, with the rest of the choir, she looks at each loved one and prays silently for the Holy Spirit to move.

The service goes along slowly: the opening hymns, the prayers and welcome, the children acting out the Nativity as Trent reads. Trent's voice is more irritating than ever. He's trying to be deep-toned like a preacher. Kenzie notices Young Taylor and David smirking at him. She wishes Pastor Williamson were reading; he has such an intelligent yet friendly kind of voice.

Then the choir performs a special Christmas medley, and Jenna reads her poem, and Reverend Darnelle preaches a sermon that is shorter than usual. That doesn't cause him to be any less enthusiastic or evangelistic. He's possibly at his best tonight. Kenzie watches Mom and Dad, who are attentive, then Grandma Rita, who looks tired and uncomfortable. Aunt Marty and Joe are listening politely, and Sharon is not paying attention at all; she seems to be paging through the hymnal. Young Taylor is unusually focused, but on the candles to his left, and David appears to be counting the blocks in the suspended ceiling. Kenzie keeps praying.

She turns her gaze for about the twentieth time to Mitchell, who sits in the back pew near the gas heater, hair neatly combed, looking so handsome she can't stand it. He wears a dark green sweater over black slacks. He has sung with gusto through the entire service, listened to every word, and bowed his head deeply for every prayer. Twice now he has winked at Kenzie and raised his hands slightly from his lap; they are pressed together prayerfully.

Suddenly the sermon is over and the pastor says, "Before our final hymn tonight, we have a very special treat. Kenzie Barnes is going to sing for us." He turns toward Kenzie and the pianist, and Kenzie stands, feeling as if the universe were swirling around her.

She has memorized the song, but it takes all her concentration to sing, and so she reads the music in her hands, which are shaking slightly. The one or two times she looks up, it's her father's eyes that catch her. They are glistening, and he smiles at her the way he used to when she'd show a calf at the fair, leading it to the center of the circle and hoping it would come willingly rather than making her pull at its halter and reins and making a mess of things. No matter where she looked, it seemed that Dad was right there, his face saying it all: *You can do it, sweetheart. It'll be fine.*

She finishes the song, and the congregation applauds, and she's too overwhelmed to look at anybody. As the congregation stands to sing the invitation hymn, she kicks herself for not looking at each member of her family while she sang. She should have made some eye contact at least.

But the invitation has begun now, and she can't be distracted by her own performance. She sings with the choir, facing the crowd, and at every line, she looks up at those middle two rows. Through the first two verses there are no signs of response; they're just standing there, singing. Young Taylor and David aren't singing at all, but whispering to each other. Kenzie sings the third verse, her eyes glued to Mom and Dad. She shifts them to Grandma Rita. Aunt Marty and Joe are singing but look ready to be somewhere else now. Sharon reads off of their hymnal and joins in halfheartedly. It seems that the only people who might respond to the Holy Spirit are her parents and grandma.

She sings the fourth verse, willing her father to move out from the pew and walk down the aisle to the altar. She wills her mother to follow him. She pictures Grandma Rita sitting in the pew to pray. But they all just stand there and sing. Daddy's eyes are no longer glistening. Mom's eyes don't leave the hymnal.

During the last verse, Kenzie looks at Mitchell only. He sings for part of the verse, then sees her looking at him. He smiles, closes the hymnal, makes a little wave in her direction, and steps toward the door. He warned her that he might need to leave before the very end of the service; sometimes crowds bother him. But they had already agreed that she would come by his house tomorrow, after the relatives leave.

Still, his disappearing jacket signals to Kenzie that the invitation is over. Mom and Dad and Grandma Rita close their hymnals as the music fades. Everyone is reaching for their coats, which have been scrunched down in the pews during the service.

Tonight, despite everyone's best efforts, the aisle remained empty. No one walked forward to receive Jesus or ask for prayer. No one is interested in anything except feeling good for an evening, singing their favorite carols and watching the children dress up like shepherds and then having their cookies and coffee afterward.

It helps a little that Aunt Marty and Joe walk up immediately to tell her how much they enjoyed her song. They seem to mean it. Sharon does too. "That was really great—do you take voice lessons?" And then Dad scoots up and hugs her tight. He holds her for a long moment. "I'm so proud of you, baby. That was beautiful." He kisses her cheek and keeps one arm across her shoulders as others come up to lend their compliments. He looks so happy, she thinks that maybe he really did walk up the aisle, only privately, in his heart.

PART FIVE

DECISION

GIVING GRACE

Be still, my soul: the Lord is on thy side.
Bear patiently the cross of grief or pain.
Leave to thy God to order and provide;
In every change, he faithful will remain.
Be still, my soul: thy best, thy heavenly Friend
Through thorny ways leads to a joyful end.
—*"Be Still, My Soul"*

Jodie

It is immediately after the Christmas pageant, of all times and places, that Rita motions Jodie to join her in one corner of the fellowship hall. The crowd is still milling around, kids exuberant from a performance completed, standing with each other and their parents, gulping down cider, hot chocolate, and cookies. The long tables are luxurious against the discount paneling and concrete floor, their plastic tablecloths bright in reds and greens, and holiday platters heaped with treats. Three coffeepots are lined up on the table against the wall. The room is crowded and busy, and yet Rita is oblivious to everything and everyone except Jodie.

"Come talk to me," she says. Jodie expected this order last night. Even with Marty and the kids there, with bodies scattered throughout the house, Jodie waited to be summoned upstairs for a private talk in the bedroom. But Rita showed nothing but a poker face throughout the holiday.

Now Jodie starts to say, "This isn't a good place to talk," but Rita has already staked out a space near the Christmas tree. It is against the room's outer wall and therefore in drafts that seep under both the door and the south windows. Now that the children's grab bags have been distributed, no one lingers there.

So Jodie walks over to stand in front of the fragrant pine branches. Her mother-in-law holds a plate that bears her own zucchini cake as well as some chocolate–peanut butter bonbons made by the pastor's wife. She carefully cuts away a bite of the cake with her plastic fork.

Jodie considers saying something about how well Kenzie sang tonight, but she knows that it is pointless. So she waits.

"I don't know what to say to you, Jodie. I really don't." Rita looks at her food while she says this.

"There's not much you could say that I haven't already said to myself."

"You know my opinions on most things, after all these years. I don't have to tell you what I think."

The voice is so steady that Jodie relaxes slightly and takes a drink of hot chocolate from the cup that she holds in both hands. It occurs to her that Rita has chosen this place and time to protect them both. In the presence of friends and neighbors, neither one will do or say anything unseemly. Jodie sees the wisdom in this and knows that it is the only way Rita will ever operate. She is a woman above screaming matches. Everything she does is part of some larger strategy.

"You take a vow," Rita continues. "'For better, for worse, in sickness and in health.' You take what's given you."

Jodie feels heat in her face. It has been a while since she was visited by true shame. She has spent virtually all her life until recently doing her best not to do anything she would be ashamed of. Now she is rooted to the floor. From one slender branch of the Christmas tree a crocheted angel dangles close to her left eye. *God, I don't want to be here. I just don't.* But where else could she be, in Beulah? If she went running from the scene, where could she possibly end up? She drinks more cocoa, which is already growing lukewarm.

"You know that life with Taylor Senior wasn't easy sometimes." Rita is watching the pastor, who talks with one of the other men. They are examining one another's plates in the way that people always compare at church buffets.

"I know, Mom, and I don't know how you've done it. You were a farmer's wife for forty years, which is a feat in itself. Then in practically a day you lost it all." She can't bring herself to name those losses specifically. "And you just found something else to do. How can you do it—just shift gears and keep going?" She has marveled at Rita's resilience, but never out loud. It's something of a release to voice it now.

Rita looks at Jodie more deliberately than she has in years. Jodie knows her mother-in-law is more upset about this betrayal than she'll ever show. She also knows that condemnation is not the fuel that keeps Rita going. Those hazel eyes that shine from delicate nests of laugh and worry lines will always be looking for some action to take, something to make everybody better.

"Well," Rita says, "I'm a woman. And I'm old. Either one of those things teaches you to accommodate to changing situations." She isn't trying to be funny.

"I'm not seeing Terry anymore."

"He's the teacher, isn't he—the Jenkins boy?"

"Yes."

"I've known him since he delivered papers when he was a kid. He's not a bad man."

"Hardly any of them are."

"But he's not likely to take you away from all this—he has too many ties to here."

Jodie looks across the room at her husband, who is talking with the parents of Jenna Braeburn, the girl who read the poem. "Actually, he wants to take me to Disneyland."

"He said he'd take you to Florida?" Rita's disbelief is clear.

"No, the one in California."

"Do you *want* to go to Disneyland?"

Jodie looks at her mother-in-law and sees that the question is earnest. It gives her permission to ask herself, in that one, clear moment, what she really wants. "Actually, I've always wanted to see Dublin. My mother's people were Irish."

"Well, dear, Disneyland isn't really on the way, is it?" Rita gives a sudden, short laugh that makes no sound but causes her tummy and bosom to bounce. The sparkle in her eye cuts Jodie clear to the heart, and she turns away from the room to examine the various angels that dwell in the thicket of evergreen. She finishes the cocoa, down to the sweet, grainy dregs, while blinking back tears. Then Rita speaks.

"You know what?"

"What?" Jodie sees that Rita is looking toward the coffeepots. The pastor has just broken into a loud laugh. He is holding a plate in one hand, his cup of coffee in the other. His elbow is out, jabbing at Bob Franklin playfully, in case Bob has missed some punch line, and his head is cocked the opposite direction toward another man, who is adding his own comments on something.

"A banty rooster and a Baptist preacher can look a lot alike," says Rita.

Jodie stares at the scene. "He does sort of move like one, doesn't he?"

"What a silly thing—I just looked over there this minute and thought banty rooster. Must be that potbelly."

"I don't want to ruin everything." Jodie wishes she were a young bride, mourning a ruined gravy or sheet cake. More than once, Rita wrapped her in a hug and saved a culinary disaster, back when everything was so new and full of promise.

"Maybe nothing's ruined yet. But you can't expect a secret like this to stay secret."

"Have you heard something?"

"No, thank the Lord." She looks at Jodie, and for the first time her features register agony. She quickly reaches into her purse and brings out the envelope. Jodie takes it just as quickly and puts it in the large pocket of her sweater.

Mack

"I'm afraid that my family will always think of me as ill." Mack has barely greeted George today. He meant to make small talk, something like, "Don't you have a life of your own? I can't believe you're free to see me three days after Christmas." But more and more, he is impatient with this room and these hours. At the same time, he likes George more all the time, wishing that he could know the man in another capacity. But how do you become friends with the person who's been given the authority to dig around in your heart and soul? He keeps talking.

"They don't have any confidence in me, and I can't say as I blame them."

"What makes you so sure of that?"

"I fell apart. And I still take enough pills every day to kill a horse. Who knows how long they'll work, or if I'll take another dip like before?"

George just looks at him. Mack spreads his hands across his knees. "In their minds, I'll always be sick, ready to crack up." He waits while the silence laps around them. "Jodie's trying to trust me, because she's obligated. But I'm afraid I've killed whatever respect she used to have. And the kids—I've lost all credibility with them. They don't respect me—maybe they even fear me. They don't really think I have a right to tell them anything now."

"So. Prove them wrong." George has the expression today of someone who won't take crap from anyone. Mack wonders how tired George is of listening to all of *this* crap.

"How?"

"I won't pretend that you're not at a great disadvantage. The truth is, often the person who struggles the most is the very one who must prove the most. No one can fight your battles, and yet you must fight them. Another dynamic that's important to note," he says, picking at some lint on his Levis, "is the way a family can sometimes appoint one person to be the problem, so to speak, even for matters that are not his doing. A family may have a designated 'sick' one, and as long as they can believe that the family's problems revolve around the sick one, no one else has to take responsibility or initiative."

Mack considers this. "That doesn't seem to fit. They're all working hard. Except for a couple of things Jodie's said when we're in the middle of a fight, none of them have talked like I'm to blame. I just don't think they can have much faith in me—because I'm . . . weak, or something."

"Oh, I'm not talking about outright blame. Given what you've told me about your family, I don't perceive them as being malicious. But there can still be a *perception* that all the family problems would just go away if *you* got better. So that in itself puts loads of pressure on you."

"And I'm just supposed to prove them wrong."

George smiles for the first time today. "That's all."

Mack laughs, not sure what to say next. George leans forward and shifts his weight in the chair. "It's at this point that you reach down and use the strength you're not even sure you have. You look at your situation and ask yourself what you might be doing that could help in some way, and you do that. Don't make a production of it. Just take the initiative and act as if you're worthy of respect. When they see that you respect yourself and trust yourself, they'll begin to adjust."

They eye each other, as they often do when George says something that Mack doesn't quite believe.

"Mack, you've been demonstrating this sort of strength all along. You made the decision to move to the stone house, and you made choices about how to spend your time there. You took up a bit of photography, just because it seemed like the right thing to do. You took hold of the situation when Young Taylor landed at the sheriff's. You decided it was time to move home. You've done all of this on your own, and you'll keep doing stuff on your own. And the more you do, the more you'll prove that you're back. Even if your kids and wife don't respect you or trust you, my guess is that they really want to. So give them reasons."

Mack sighs.

"This is a glorious time, Mack. Life's opening up again for you. The language you use, the things that concern you, the things you're attempting—they're all evidence of getting better."

"That's hard for me to see."

"Well, that's why I'm here." George flashes a little satisfied smile.

Jodie

They're in the parking lot of the little motel, in Jodie's truck. She thinks that she'll be stronger somehow if she's not sitting in Terry's car. Of course, she also thought she could do this without crying, but here she is, her eyes and nose leaking while she wipes them with some leftover napkins from Taco Bell.

"I just think this is a decision you don't have to make right now." Terry rests his back against the passenger door, one leg tucked up on the seat. He is fairly calm and a little angry.

"Well," Jodie tries for a deeper breath, "I think we hurried into something."

"Seemed right on time to me."

"Of course. You're not the one with a family."

"Jodie, you needed this. You were about to disappear, just go away and never come back." His tone softens. "Do you really think you can go back to all of that, and it'll just be okay? Doesn't work that way. Once love dies, it's gone."

"And you're the expert because it already died on you once. You were married, what, two years?"

"I had the sense to get out before we did too much damage."

"And I'm the stupid one because I've stayed? You know, for a lot of years it worked just fine. You—" She jams a fist to her mouth, trying to let the words out in some controllable way. "You think that you understand my whole life because we've been . . . screwing around for a couple of months."

"No, I don't."

She shakes her head. "Some people can live two lives at once. But I'm—" Another tear slips down. "I'm so, so tired, and I can't do this anymore."

"Change always hurts, Jodie."

She thinks it's happening now, the flaws beginning to show. The bliss has just lifted its wings and is setting off for someone else's back-yard. *Change always hurts.* How profoundly unremarkable. The ex-pression on his face is sincere.

"Some hurt we bring on ourselves," she says.

He faces the front windshield, unfolding his leg and turning from her. "You've done exactly what you wanted to do."

"Yes."

"So just tell me what you're going to do now." The anger is alto-gether present now.

"I want—I'm going—to go home. And not see you anymore."

He opens the car door and gets out. Doesn't even shut the door but walks the step or two to his car, gets in, and drives off. Doesn't look at her. No good-bye, or sorry, or thank-you.

No matter what she does or who she's with, when she finally speaks her piece, the anger follows.

She doesn't cry for long. But she drives slowly all the way home. The land is barren, the muddy fields trickling rain, and bits of re-maining cornstalks making the place seem devastated as if by war.

This is one of those rare times when she longs for her mother the way a child just wants to be snuggled on a warm lap. Of course they talked over the holidays, and they have always talked easily enough. But years and distance have taught Jodie to handle most dilemmas without any parental guidance. And she is afraid to speak anything aloud about this mess she's made. It was possible with Rita because Rita took command of the situation; but for Jodie to tell her own mother would require strength she cannot muster. She's pretty sure

Mom would be understanding. She might even insist that Jodie come down to Galveston for a visit, to get away and find some perspective. But right now, this confrontation with Terry has already taken too much out of her. She looks ahead to the next several days and chooses one afternoon and makes an appointment with herself to make the call. In case the fallout is really bad, Mom will need some warning at least.

Mack

New Year's Day starts with a bang. Mack was looking forward to sleeping in now that Marty, Joe, and the kids have left and life has settled down, but he awakes to the furious voices of his wife and son. He puts on his robe and hurries downstairs. Jodie is standing in the middle of the family room, quaking with rage. Her attention is aimed at Young Taylor, who sits on the couch. As usual, his every item of clothing is black. In addition, his fingernails and lips are black. His eyelids are blacked clear to the eyebrows. The rest of his face is death-white.

"It is New Year's Day, and I will *not* have you sitting around the house looking like this!"

"You don't have to look at me."

"What, I just ignore you? Like that's possible."

"Yes, just ignore me. There are lots of rooms in this house. When I'm finished watching this movie, I'll go upstairs and you won't have to look at me the whole rest of the day!"

"Hey!" Mack's voice cracks across the room, and they both look at him where he stands halfway down the stairs. "Watch your tone."

"I'd rather not talk to her at all. She started it. I was just sitting here not bothering anybody."

"You're bothering me by looking like a corpse," Jodie throws in.

"Like I said, you don't have to look at me."

Mack has reached the bottom of the stairs. He is trying to calculate exactly how to approach both people. Once Jodie's eyes reach this level of snap, she has run out of patience. Young Taylor, on the other hand, is a master of perseverance and will wear out both of them if allowed to keep on in this vein.

"Jodie, why don't you let us talk." He hopes she'll take his cue and make her exit.

"I'd rather talk to Dad anyway."

Jodie throws up her hands. "Fine. Because I don't have anything left to say to this child. The two of you just go for a really long walk or something, because I've had it." She walks past Mack and into the kitchen. Young Taylor stares at the television screen, remote resting near his leg. Mack walks over, picks up the remote, and turns off the set. He ignores the colossal sigh this elicits from his son.

"We've both got the day off," Mack says. "It's been a while since we had a talk."

"That's not *my* fault. You're always busy or going somewhere else."

This surprises him. "You never act like you're interested in talking to me. I can't read your mind."

Young Taylor remains mute.

"Anything in particular you want to talk about?" Mack sits carefully on the couch, a foot or two from Young Taylor.

"Maybe." The boy looks straight ahead.

Mack sees an opportunity and decides to take the risk. "If you want a conversation with me, you'll have to wipe that mess off your face."

Young Taylor just stares at him. If it weren't such an unhappy situation, he would be comical, like a clown who has run out of the usual bright colors.

"I mean it," says Mack. "I want to look at somebody who at least resembles my kid."

Young Taylor gets up and heads down the hall. Mack follows him into the bathroom just off the family room, the one his son has claimed for his own. Young Taylor opens the cabinet and takes out a jar of cold cream.

"Does your grandma know you've got her cold cream?"

Young Taylor sets down the jar and glances at Mack, his eyes widening a bit and stretching the seams of black that surround them. "It's not hers."

Mack takes the jar and screws off the lid. A scent strikes him, and suddenly he is a child at his mother's dressing table. It seems impossible that his son and his mother can be linked by such an ordinary thing.

Mack puts down the jar. Young Taylor leans back against the sink, his arms folded.

"So take it off," says Mack.

"You do it."

"Why should I take off your makeup?"

"You're the one who wants it off."

Young Taylor hasn't budged. He doesn't look particularly rebellious, just very patient.

Mack picks up the jar. "All right, I will."

He scoops a bit of the cold cream with two fingers and swipes it onto Young Taylor's cheek. He rubs it in.

"How much does it take?"

"About that much, only all over."

Mack puts more small swipes on the boy's chin, nose, and forehead.

"There's something I can't stop thinking about," says Young Taylor.

"Yeah?"

"How is it that Grandpa would turn the tractor that short on a slope?"

Mack's heart makes a skip, but he keeps his voice steady. "It happens."

"But nobody knew that field better than Grandpa, right?"

"Why would you be thinking about that? You were only six."

"But I've heard you and Grandma talk about him turning the tractor too sharp. I've looked at that spot, and it doesn't make sense."

Mack stops swabbing the boy's face. "What do you mean?"

"It's almost like it was on purpose."

Mack is caught in midswipe. He is standing too close to Young Taylor to avoid his son's gaze. With both hands, he smooths the cold cream evenly over the kid's face. The black around his lips and eyes begins to smear. Young Taylor keeps talking.

"I mean, it makes more sense than him dumping it over by accident in a place where even Kenzie would know better than to turn like that."

"Has somebody said something to you about this?"

"No. It's what they don't say."

Now Young Taylor's face is an ever-changing greasy-gray cloud. Out of the cloud, his lips move. "And the insurance money helped us keep the farm, a while longer anyway."

Mack can't come up with an immediate answer. He feels responsible for this conversation. He somehow released the topic for fresh review when he spoke to Mom days ago. "It's not as simple as that. He wasn't losing the farm."

"But he was losing a lot of money."

"Along with most other people about that time."

"So what do *you* think?" The boy's voice echoes off the tile of the bathroom.

Mack reaches for a tissue and sees his hand shaking. "I think your grandpa was too tired to be in the field that evening. Sometimes you make mistakes when you're fatigued and not thinking straight. Grandpa was a hard worker, not the type to just give up."

"What about Uncle Alex?"

He winces at his brother's name. The memory of Alex's death is bad enough, but what Mack thinks of now is how hard Young Taylor took it. He'd been old enough to feel grief in full—he used to follow Alex around like a puppy.

"Your uncle drank himself to death. It was bound to happen sometime, but he probably didn't plan to go that particular day. If he had, he'd have used his hunting rifle."

"See, you've thought about this too."

He wipes grease off the fine-boned face, avoiding those dark eyes. "Yes, I have, and I think that Alex tried to be something he was never cut out to be." He lets their gazes meet briefly. "It's real important to know what you love and what you're good at. You have to figure it out and then live accordingly."

"What do you love?"

Mack stops rubbing off makeup and steps back for a moment. "I love my family. And I love this place." He throws away the tissue, gets another, and begins clearing away the white around Young Taylor's nose and lips. The death-pale skin of his son's face is turning a natural pink.

"Even though you don't farm anymore?"

"I've got a job I'm good at. That's enough."

"So you think you can stay now?"

"Yes."

"Sometimes I wish I could die for a little while to go see Grandpa and Uncle Alex."

Mack makes himself concentrate on the black residue under the boy's eyes. "I don't think it works that way."

"I'm pretty sure it doesn't. I almost died last summer." Young Taylor waits for Mack to meet his eyes again. "When Bobby and Dale and I went camping. We got really drunk out in the rowboat—"

Mack bites his lip and watches the tissue sweep away grime in a neat line.

"—and I fell out. It was pitch dark, and the guys didn't have a flashlight and couldn't find me. I seemed to be down there forever."

"Last summer?" Mack asks, hardly a whisper.

"Yeah. And then I started taking in water, and I tried to find the surface but couldn't. I couldn't see my own air bubbles. I thought, *This is a stupid way to go.*"

Young Taylor pauses. So does Mack, the greasy tissue still in his hand.

"And then I had this feeling that I was going someplace else and that everything would be okay. I knew that in just another minute I'd see people on the other side. But all of a sudden somebody grabbed me real hard and pulled me straight up out of the water. I thought it had to be one of the guys, but it felt like somebody a lot stronger. When I hit the surface, I could hear Bobby and Dale screaming my name—they were at least ten yards away. I tried to see who pulled me up, but nobody was there."

Mack feels a jolt of adrenaline, and tiny pinpricks along his arms and neck.

"We agreed not to tell anybody—you know, what was the point? It would have just scared everybody after the fact. And ... I didn't even tell the guys about being pulled up like that. You're the only person who knows that part."

It is now that Mack sees Young Taylor's entire face, clean. He stands back and stares. He doesn't know what he expected to find. Seething rebellion, or resentment? But all that's here is his boy, looking new and a bit pink.

"Why did you tell me this, son?"

"I thought you needed to know. Death is just another country."

Mack is still staring in amazement at this beautiful child.

"It's another country. And God's taking care of things there, the same as here. God's in charge of getting people from one place to another. You don't need to worry about it, or be afraid of it."

Young Taylor's eyes have taken on a sheen. He blinks.

Mack instinctively touches his son's cheek as if to reorient himself to a place he hasn't been to in a while. Young Taylor stares at Mack and keeps talking.

"That's why I'm not afraid of death anymore. I like hanging out with it, sort of like walking a fence line, knowing that the property you're looking at will be yours before long."

"Is that why you're always in costume? You like to hang out with death?"

"No, I just want to prove that I'm not afraid."

Mack's eyes are filling with tears. "I had a different idea."

"Stop worrying about me. I've figured stuff out without having to die."

Mack looks at Young Taylor's face, at the lips pink instead of black, and he remembers the boy as a two-year-old. He used to make a joke out of kissing people. He liked to run from person to person and make loud smacking sounds against their lips.

"I appreciate your telling me this," says Mack.

"Don't worry about me, okay?"

Mack cups Young Taylor's chin in his hand. He draws the clean, bright face to his own and kisses his boy on the lips. "I like you better with your real face."

Young Taylor gives Mack a quick hug and goes on his way. Mack watches him the rest of the day—noticing where he is in the house, following his easy movements across the bare field to the woods, going to hang out with death, or God, or the angel that pulled him up from drowning.

Mack wants to tell Jodie what he has learned. But he feels in his soul that this is not the right time. He carries his son's comfort with him in solitude, wrapping it around his mind like a quilt.

Kenzie

"I'll understand if you decide to stay."

Mitchell is standing in the middle of his barn, the finished sculpture reflecting afternoon sun from its multiple surfaces. The same light washes over him, giving his complexion a healthy, bronze glow. The top two buttons of his shirt are undone, dark hair peeking out, and Kenzie wants to rest her head right in that spot. But she stands several feet from him, her arms loaded with metal scraps. They are cleaning up, because Mitchell won't be creating any more sculptures out here for a while, maybe never again. Why he wants to be clean and orderly all of a sudden, she doesn't know. But she is here to help in whatever way she can. Staying busy makes it easier for her to cope with the many pains racing through her.

"I don't want to stay," she says. "I want to be with you. That's my calling. I just don't know how to leave without making a disaster for my family." She wasn't able to get away from the house until after lunch. Mom and Dad decided to fix a big pancake and sausage breakfast, which they didn't eat until ten-thirty. Then, because the Christmas tree was already drying out and shedding needles, Mom declared that it was time to take down decorations. That took most of the afternoon. They stopped at two to eat some leftover chili. Mom and Dad acted content to have everybody there working together, even though the day had started with a huge argument between Mom and Young Taylor. But even Young Taylor calmed down and cooperated.

So now that home is feeling a little better, Mitchell is in crisis. Kenzie has known this was coming, because of the way he acted after the Christmas pageant. She sneaked away to see him the next day, and he was silent and dark. He hardly mentioned Kenzie's singing at all. Instead, he mumbled something about how evil lived within established religion. He'd felt demons all around him in the church. He acted disappointed that Kenzie hadn't made that discernment herself.

Today, though, he seems brighter. He's been up since four this morning, he says, "putting my house in order." He has carried garbage bags out to the trash heap and had a fire going there all day. Kenzie doesn't understand why so many perfectly good items should be burned, but Mitchell says that he wants to purify the property before he leaves.

Before he leaves. He has talked about leaving since Thanksgiving, that awful night when he pushed Kenzie away. But today his actions move him closer to a real exit. Only now he wants Kenzie to leave too. He mentions nothing about her age this time, and she doesn't bring it up. Something important is happening, and all she can do is watch it unfold.

"Baby, we've talked about this," he says, tossing some rotten boards onto a pile near the barn door. "You've known for a long time that God is calling you to a different life. *We've* known it. And it's hardly ever easy to follow God's call."

"I know." She's ashamed of how weak she sounds. When he calls her "baby" she feels totally loved. But the words that follow it today are very, very hard. "Are you sure you have to leave now? I thought that maybe once the school year is over—"

"God's time is not our time. His ways are above our ways." He points toward his chest with emphasis. "I know, from the bottom of my soul, that if I stay here, I die. The enemy will overcome me. I've already called Reverend Francis's community, and they didn't have room before, but just this week a space opened up. Our place is being made ready for us."

"Do they know that I'm coming with you?"

"Yes. And after a period of counseling, Reverend Francis will marry us himself, with the whole community as witness to our covenant."

Today is the first time he's come out and said anything about getting married. In one way it's totally thrilling, but in another it's almost too scary to think about. Mitchell seems so confident that everything will work out, and Kenzie feels her own faith faltering.

"But can he do that, since I'm not eighteen yet?"

"The government's laws are not God's laws. Reverend Francis follows God and only God."

"Could my family come at least?" Now that her life's calling is more imminent, she is bothered by details and doubts.

He comes over to her and places hands on her shoulders. "They won't understand, and I think you know that." He brushes back her hair, and she closes her eyes at the tenderness of it. "All we can do, Kenzie, is follow the Lord. And I believe he'll give us the strength we need."

"You're right." She grabs another armload of scrap. They work into the evening, and Kenzie leaves just in time to eat supper with her parents. Mitchell says that he will likely work through the night. He wants to pack up the house and be gone after dark tomorrow.

"Pack up as much as you can carry," he says. "Tomorrow at midnight, I'll drive down to just below the timber, south of your house. You can meet me there."

"Do you want me to come over tomorrow?"

"No. I've got matters to take care of in town. It's better if you spend the day getting ready." He stops her as she heads for the gate. It's dark, and just a few stars show from behind a veil of clouds. He holds her and kisses her hard on the lips. She hangs on to him a long time before moving away and down the road.

Once home, Kenzie stands in her bedroom and tries to slow the thoughts speeding around in her head. She doesn't know what to take. She'll have to decide tonight and somehow sort through everything tomorrow during the day, with everybody around. Well, Mom will believe her if she says that she's reorganizing her room; she does that every few months anyway. Mom understands reorganization and will leave her alone. If anyone sees her getting her suitcases out of the hall closet, she'll just say that she's storing some old clothes and books in them for now.

Supper is uneventful, but every little comment or movement makes Kenzie want to rush out of the room and cry. She keeps saying to herself, *God will give me the grace I need. Jesus goes with me, wherever I go, and I will never be alone.* She wants to say something meaningful to each member of her family, but words will not come. The time has passed for making appeals or getting their attention. It is truly time to leave.

But she falls apart when she goes upstairs later and sits on her bed. She cries so hard that she worries that someone will hear her and knock on the door. She soothes herself by writing a long prayer to Jesus. She copies several Psalms into her journal and prays them for herself. Then she gets the suitcases from the hallway, with no interruption or detection, and places them on the bed. She starts with her closet, sorting clothes and shoes. She goes downstairs and gets several garbage bags from the kitchen. Mom is watching television by herself.

"Where's Dad?" Kenzie doesn't know why she should ask this now; she will no longer be here to follow her parents' every move and worry about its consequences.

"Over at Grandma's working on her car."

"Mom, I'm cleaning out my room."

Mom looks up. "Getting sorted out for the new year?"

"Yeah, I guess. If I label some bags and boxes, can you take some things to the community closet for me?"

"Sure."

It is one in the morning when she falls exhausted into bed. She has sorted through her closet and dresser and most of her bookshelves. She has her trunk and desk to go through, but they'll have to wait until tomorrow.

In the corner are several piles of books and various other things. She's decided to give some of them to Bekka and some to Janelle. She won't need them anymore, and at least her friends will have something to remember her by.

Rita

Can it really be January? But, yes, Christmas is packed away, and Rita has just turned the calendar to its new page. It's as blank as can be, and she detects some failure in her system. Usually the month is penciled in before she even turns the page. She writes in birthdays and anniversaries, deadlines for insurance payments and the like. When she feels so inclined, she includes events listed in the church bulletin, but she doesn't participate as much as she used to, so the months are automatically freer.

And Mack got her car running last night. It didn't take that long, which irritated her, and she said so.

"Mom, you never know about these things. It could have just as easily taken me a day or two to get to the bottom of it."

"Well, thank you. It'll be nice to have transportation again."

Her son looked as if a comment was on the tip of his tongue.

"I do appreciate you and Jodie carting me around. You've been a lot of help."

"No problem, Mom."

Their conversation hasn't been as easy since the afternoon Mack brought up his father's death. She can't yet forgive him for such disrespect. But she can't fault him for the way he looks after her. She's decided that it's best not to bring up that discussion. He hasn't either, so maybe he's realized how wrong he was. Life will carry on. And now that she has her wheels again, she can freely mark up the month of January.

She is at the kitchen table doing just that when someone knocks on her front door. Through the frosted glass, Rita can see a person's shadow. Nobody knocks on her front door anymore.

But there it comes again, this time with a woman's voice. "Mrs. Barnes? It's Reverend Maynor."

The pastor of the Methodist church. Rita goes to the door. When she opens it, Alice smiles. "Have I caught you at a bad time?"

"No. Come on in." Alice wipes her feet carefully on the small rug in the entryway. Rita shows her to the living room.

Alice is close to fifty, and divorced. Slightly overweight but always looks healthy. She preaches out of books of the Bible that the former pastor, the ancient Reverend Sipes, didn't seem to know existed: Amos, Ruth, Obadiah, Titus, even the Song of Songs with all the racy stuff. It's hard not to like Alice, because she's so down to earth. But she's unpredictable too, and Rita wonders what has brought the woman into her house.

They chat for a few minutes about the holidays, the weather, and the pathetic state of the town's streets, which is a regular topic this time of year. But after a few minutes, Alice sits back against the sofa.

"Rita, I'm telling people about a special service we have coming up. It'll be at the church in Oskaloosa two Sundays from now, in the evening."

"What kind of service?"

"Well, it's sort of a grieving service."

Rita sits up a little. "You mean a memorial?"

"Not really. We're not mourning the death of people necessarily." Alice watches Rita's reaction to this. "It's more like we're mourning a way of life that's gone."

"I'm sorry, Reverend, but you've lost me."

The pastor scoots forward on the couch, her corduroy skirt draping past her calves. "This service is for families who have left farming over the past several years."

Rita struggles to comprehend, and Alice keeps talking. "You see, a number of people around here have gone through huge changes. They've lost farms or simply decided to leave farming for one reason or another. But it's hard to just leave a whole lifestyle and go on as if nothing has happened. And so what the church here and in Oskaloosa would like to do is hold a special service that will help those families say good-bye to the former life and look forward to what comes next."

"Well," Rita says, smoothing the doily on the arm of her chair, "I don't know why you're talking to me. I've lived here for years, haven't farmed since 1990 or so. I switched lifestyles some time ago." She adds a slight laugh to that.

"I know, but the rest of your family is still moving through this transition." Alice tries to meet Rita's eyes, and her voice grows soft. "Rita, there's been a lot of loss in your family. And nothing anyone can do or say can lessen that, but I really think it's time that your faith community support you in a more tangible way."

"The faith community around here has outlived its usefulness where our family's losses are concerned." Rita straightens up even while she feels that her body is caving in on itself. "You're still pretty new here, and you don't know the history, but I don't have a lot of fond feelings for some of the church folks around here."

"I do know that. I wasn't here, but the same kinds of hurts happened in the town where my parents farmed."

"Then you'll understand that these kinds of things are best kept in a person's family. Nobody else can really help."

"I don't agree. I've seen what happens when people are allowed to share their grief in a place where they are supported."

"Honey," Rita gets up suddenly, pretending to stretch out her knee. "We're doing all right. I really appreciate what you're trying to do, but I don't care to participate."

"What about your son and his family?"

"You'll have to ask them, but I doubt they'll be interested either."
The pastor gets up and slips on her coat. Rita stands politely as she
does so. "Please don't think that I'm being ungrateful."

"I'd never think that, Rita."

"Good. I hope the service accomplishes what you want it to."

She watches Alice go down the walk. Her own heart is pounding.
She feels invaded, just as she did the day Mack said all that about his
father.

"People have no right to dig up hurts." She returns to the kitchen
and her calendar but is too agitated to sit down. She says to the refrigerator and telephone, "I wish to hell everybody would stop trying
to help me!" She opens the fridge to survey her dinner options but
closes it after a moment, instead microwaving leftover coffee. Once in
her chair in the sitting room, she searches through channels and finds
a movie. She stares at it for two hours, hardly aware of the plot or the
dialogue.

HOLDING ON

Though vine nor fig tree neither their wonted fruit should
   bear,
Though all the field should wither, nor flocks nor herds be
   there;
Yet God the same abiding, his praise shall tune my voice,
For while in him confiding, I cannot but rejoice.
                   —*"Sometimes a Light Surprises"*

Mack

He can't remember the last time he and Jodie ate alone in the farmhouse. Usually at least one of the kids is around. It's early afternoon,
and they're having a late lunch. While defrosting the freezer, Jodie
found some round steak that had been in there a while, and so she
has thawed it out and made them pepper steak. Young Taylor is running around with Eric. They dropped Kenzie off at Bekka's in town.
She was carrying boxes and said she needed to see two or three other
friends and would be back in the early evening. So Mack and Jodie sit
in the quiet while the freezer drips onto towels they have spread
across the linoleum.

The outdoors is drippy too, with a cold constant rain that has
begun in the past half-hour to make tiny tapping sounds against the

windows to signal the temperature dropping. As raindrops turn into
sleet, Mack hovers over his plate of warm food, happy that his wife
sits across from him in the sweater he bought her for Christmas.

"Good steak, sweet."

"Thanks." She nudges hers with a fork. "So Mom is happy, I'll bet,
now that she's got her car back."

"Oh, yeah."

"Did she figure out what you did?"

"Nope." He laughs.

"We dodged that bullet, didn't we?"

"Uh-huh."

"You know, she wants us to get marriage counseling." She looks
up to see his response.

"She harping at you about that? She cornered me a week ago."

"I think it's probably a good idea."

He stops chewing. "You do?"

She nods, taking a steak knife to the meat on her plate.

"Well . . . sure. It's fine with me. I didn't want to drag you through
any more than necessary. And it's worked out pretty well with this
guy I'm seeing. You want me to set up a time with him?"

She keeps looking at her food. "If you like him, yeah. I'd rather not
see a complete stranger."

"Have you been wanting to do this? You should have told me."

She lets out a careful breath. "I hadn't really thought about it until
lately."

He reaches for her hand and squeezes it. "Let's do it then. Whatever you want." To his surprise, she pulls away. She covers her eyes
with her hands. He stares at her while several moments go by.

"Mack, I've really screwed up."

A knot pulls tight in his stomach. She stays hidden behind her
hands.

"What?"

"I really have. And it's all my fault, and I don't want to tell you
anything."

No. No, please. He works hard to swallow and then decides to get right to it. "Are you about to ask me for a divorce?"

"No. But you may want one anyway."

"God, Jo, what's happened? Just tell me."

"I've been with someone."

There it is. Jodie's face is in her hands again. He notices, in an odd second of coherence, how red and chafed they are.

He can't utter a word. After a long moment, he brings a fist down on the table. Jodie flinches, but speaks again.

"It's not been going on for long, and I've already ended it."

He sits there while silence pulses around them. Finally, he manages, "I guess it was too little too late."

She remains quiet, and the words spill out of him.

"All I'm trying to do here, to get myself straightened out, is to be here for you and the kids the way I should be. But I guess I just didn't get well fast enough, did I?" The last sentence rips out of him. If he didn't feel so out of breath he would raise his voice. But this is like a dream in which he tries to run but can't, tries to take a swing but his arm will hardly move, tries to cry out but there is no sound.

"I just said that it wasn't your fault."

"But if I'd been any kind of husband, I don't imagine we'd be having this conversation, would we?" He gets up from the table and stares out the window above the sink. She seems small, just feet away from him, huddled over her dinner plate. For the first time in their years together, her size and softness make him want to hurt her. It isn't softness after all, but cunning and looseness. She's taken that softness elsewhere. Another man has loved the comfort of her body. Mack hears oceans roaring in his head.

"Who?"

She doesn't answer.

"Huh? Who is it?" He doesn't wait for a reply but steps closer. "What I want to know is why you waited until now. You had the perfect opportunity back when I wanted to die anyway. But then it was all this 'Oh, Mack, I love you, and me and the kids still need you and there's so much to hope for!'" The force of his words makes her lean away. "Why wait until I've let all those doctors take me apart and put me back together again?"

He draws back and watches her. She won't look at him. "Do you have any clue in your head how hard I've worked over the past few months? You could have just divorced me a while back."

"And have you kill yourself and then everybody would blame me anyway." Her voice is surprisingly strong. Any fear or sorrow of moments before slips aside now, and her features come alive. "I didn't have the luxury of making a choice back when you were suicidal. I had to concentrate on helping everybody survive."

He is exhausted suddenly, and slumps into the chair nearest her. "Jo ..." His mind gets cluttered, the way it so often does when he needs to make a decision or think hard about something. Jodie isn't looking at him, but she isn't moving away either. "Jo ..."

"Like I said, I've already ended this mess. It was a stupid thing to do. I just wanted something—" She is working hard to form sentences. "I just needed something for *me*, Mack. I needed a break. Needed to feel different, or something."

"You needed a break from me."

"It's more than you. I'm just so tired. No matter how much I sleep, I'm so tired I can hardly walk or talk."

Even as anger pounds his gut, he is compelled to search for something to repair this disaster. "That's how I felt when things were so bad. Maybe you're depressed too. Maybe you should talk to George yourself."

She's crying, her face once again hidden behind her red hands.

"We're all having a rough time." He wants to stroke the hair back from her face, but now that feels like something he needs permission to do. He senses an awful new reality descending over them. His relationship to Jodie has changed, more than he's suspected or is ready for. The kitchen is now a strange room, and he wonders if he should take himself away from this house. Only this time it will have to be farther than the stone house. This time it will be a gigantic move. The whole world will shift.

"I guess we've got to figure out what to do now." How many times in nineteen years has one of them said this? When both vehicles were broken at once or one of the kids needed surgery or a hailstorm shredded their profits for the year. They had taken turns saying this. Now this sentence is but an ugly punch line. All the other problems solved still add up to this. Mack believes, though, that this problem will not be solved. This is the one that will take them down.

"If you want a divorce, I won't fight it. You're right. It's time for you to do things for you now." His voice breaks, but he recovers. "We'll need to agree about what to tell the kids."

"I'm not asking for a divorce."

"When did you start seeing this guy?"

"A couple months ago."

"So, the way things have been lately with us—that's not good enough."

"I don't know, Mack, I don't know. I can't think right now."

"So am I the last to know? Has the whole town been laughing at me?"

"Only one other person knows, and it's somebody who's not going to talk."

"Please tell me he's not one of our friends."

She pauses a long time, and he thinks of Ed, who has been close to both of them for years. It wouldn't be like him to betray a friend or cheat on his wife, but who can predict stuff like this? A few minutes ago, Mack wouldn't have suspected Jodie either.

"If I tell you who it is, you have to promise not to go over there. You've got to let me deal with this, not cause a scene."

He leans back against the cabinet, gripping the metal lip of the countertop. "Okay."

"Terry Jenkins—at the school."

He is slightly relieved that it's someone outside his own circle. But the image of the social studies teacher brings on immediate nausea. A younger guy. Somebody without bags under his eyes, who can still make it happen twice in one night.

"Don't talk to him," she says.

"You've told him it's over?"

"Yes."

"You won't see him again."

"I'll have to see him—we both work at the school."

"Maybe you should work somewhere else now."

She moans, head in her hands.

"You feel something for him?" He hates himself for opening this door.

"How am I supposed to answer that? You think I'd just screw around with someone I had no feelings for?"

In Mack's mind, the complications are multiplying. Even if she has ended this, can it stay that way? Maybe they should all move away. But does he really want her to stay, after this? Is he being too kind? His wife has cheated on him. And lied, and left him without letting him know.

"You do what you have to do." He walks out the door and into the yard, giving room to his anger. He wants to hurt her, knock her off the chair, jerk her up by her hair, make her sorry, make her beg forgiveness, make her hate Terry Jenkins.

But he gets in the truck and drives away. He doesn't act like a kid and spin his tires. He is still a man, a grown man. He is big enough to let her go. He only wishes that he hadn't come to care so much about his life again. He wishes he hadn't already made plans for what he might do this year and next.

He has to work harder to drive, because the roads have begun to get slick. But even while he maneuvers the next few miles, a new sensation registers. He can't bring his thoughts to rest on what has just happened in the kitchen; it's a pain he can't come at straight on. But at the center of him is motion, a stirring of something like hope. He knows that he will have to drive for a while and maybe get out to walk and endure all the hurt that's in him. He will need to take time and pay attention.

And then he will follow his son more closely and talk to him more readily. He will even talk to George, with Jodie or without her. He will go to church some more and listen to his daughter sing.

Jodie is part of the picture but not all of it. Still, he will do everything he can to keep that part.

Jodie

She hears a car in the drive, and even though she's sure it wouldn't be Mack returning so soon, she hopes that it's him. But when she goes to the door, Bekka is standing there. Her older brother waits in the drive, his car idling loudly. Bekka's eyes are wide.

"Mrs. Barnes?"

"Hi, Bekka. I thought you were bringing Kenzie home."

"She left my house an hour ago, walking. I thought she was going to her grandma's."

Jodie doesn't know what to say, or why Bekka is on her step looking scared.

"Mrs. Barnes, this will probably make Kenzie really, really mad, but I need to tell you something."

Jodie is not used to seeing Bekka intense in any serious way. The girl is pulling something out of her school bag.

"This is Kenzie's journal. She left it by accident." She looks distressed. "You know, earlier, she gave me some of her things, some books and stuff she didn't want anymore. And I guess she accidentally packed this with them."

"Oh, well, thanks for bringing it. I know she'll get worried when she finds it missing."

"I read some of it." Bekka looks close to tears. Jodie guides her to a kitchen chair and sits in the one next to her. The girl keeps talking. "I can't believe I never figured it out."

"Figured what out, honey?"

"She's running away."

Jodie pulls back and laughs automatically. "Oh, no—Kenzie's fine. Who told you that?"

Bekka opens the journal to a page and points to a handwritten paragraph. "She and Mitchell Jaylee are leaving for this retreat place near Kansas City. Did she come home yet?"

Jodie reads the paragraph at Bekka's finger. She can barely make sense of it. Mitchell's name appears several times. "Bekka, what does she have to do with this guy?" Her mind flips through any reference she has of their neighbor to the north. Hardly anyone ever sees him.

"I didn't know she had anything to do with him. But we haven't been hanging out much. I thought she was spending more time here, now that Mr. Barnes is back home."

"No. We hardly see her until suppertime."

"I didn't read much more—it's private, you know? But she wrote this yesterday. Do you know where she is now?"

Jodie is on her way upstairs, Bekka right behind her. They enter Kenzie's room, and both of them gasp. The bed is made, and the shelves and dresser top, the desk, and every other surface is spotless, with only a few items remaining on them. Jodie throws open the closet door to find just a few clothes hanging there. Against the wall are several garbage bags with big labels on them; some are for the community closet, others are for Bekka and whoever wants them. The dresser is empty, and the bookshelves are nearly bare.

"Dear Jesus." Jodie runs to the hall phone and calls Rita, hoping Bekka is right and that Kenzie is there. No one answers.

"I can call Janelle and anybody else I can think of. Maybe she's giving them some stuff, like she did me." Bekka pulls out her cell phone and begins punching in a number.

"Good. And call the Baptist pastor, all right? I'm going over to the Jaylee place."

Bekka looks frightened. "You think you should do that? By yourself, I mean? You want Regan to go with you?"

"Just call everybody and then go home, all right?" She leaves Bekka in the upstairs hallway and runs out to the car. There's enough ice on the road to force her to drive slowly to Mitchell Jaylee's. The drive is empty, the doors locked and curtains drawn. No one is in the barn or the yard. She stands in the drive and feels weaker than she's ever felt. Her little girl is with some older guy in a car, heading far from here.

In the truck, heading to town, the panic turns into rancorous self-indictment. She yells at her reflection in the rearview. "If you hadn't been running around the county acting like a whore.... How could you miss something this big? What good are you to anybody?"

She drives into town, to Rita's house; the garage is open and the car gone. Of course, now that she's mobile, God only knows where she is. Jodie goes inside, using her key to the back door, and calls the sheriff's office. They reach Jerry on his radio, and he instructs Jodie to go back home, and he'll meet her there.

She nearly plows into Mack at the intersection two miles from the farm. He appears to be on his way home. She jumps out of the car and shouts at him. He puts the truck into park and rolls down the window.

"Have you seen Kenzie?"

"What's wrong?"

"Have you seen her?"

"No—what's the matter?"

It takes a moment for her to explain and for him to comprehend. When he does, he shifts the truck back into gear. "Go home," he barks. "Go home and wait for Jerry. I'm going to Jaylee's."

"I was there already. It's all locked up."

"Just go home."

Through the next hour, Jodie feels as if she is watching bizarre scenes from some fictitious life. The whole sequence of events is surreal. When Jerry arrives, she shows him the journal page and tells him what she knows, but she barely understands any of their conversation. It's as if she is merely an observer, watching things fall apart. When Mack returns from the Jaylee place, his face is stone-white, and he shakes his head before she can ask him anything. Jerry comes over to both of them.

"State Patrol's looking for them. Mitchell's van will be easy to pick out. Can't be traveling too fast either, in this weather."

"His place is all cleaned up, stuff packed away." Mack's voice is hoarse.

"She's been dating him?" Jerry is still doing his best to get information from both of them, taking notes.

"Oh, no," Jodie says. "At least, we had no idea. This is all a complete shock."

"He ever call over here, or give her rides home, anything like that?"

"No. She gets rides with her friends from school, or her brother—" She turns to Mack. "Did you see Young Taylor? He went over to Eric's."

"No. Did you call over there?"

"No, I didn't think."

He picks up the phone and walks into the living room with it, stretching the cord around the doorway. She can tell by his responses that the kids aren't at Eric's house. Mack heads for the door. "I'll look some more."

Jerry grabs his arm. "Mack. Just stay here, all right? You can hardly see straight. I've got Stan and Donny both out there, plus the guys in Oskaloosa and the State Patrol. He won't get far without somebody seeing him. And—" He measures his words. "It appears from what Kenzie wrote that they've both been cooking this up. It's not a kidnapping or an assault. Mitchell doesn't have anything like that in his history, you know that."

"I know he's half nuts."

"Diagnosed bipolar a few years ago."

Mack and Jodie stare at him. Jerry shifts weight to the other hip, looking more authoritative than usual. "They used to call it manic-depressive." Jodie thinks that he probably knows every secret in Beulah and beyond. She wonders if he has noticed her comings and goings with Terry. The sheriff keeps talking.

"He goes off his meds from time to time—but he's never bothered a soul around here. I've known him since he was a kid, and I'm tellin' you, he's not the violent type. So just get all those ideas out of your

heads. It won't help a thing for you two to work yourselves into hys-
teria."

Mack pulls away from Jerry and goes to the family room. He sits
on the couch and stares out the window, hands clasped in his lap. He
doesn't speak to Jodie or look at her. Was it just a little while ago that
she made that horrible confession? Why, today of all days, did she do
that? Why tell him at all? What good has it done? She looks at her
husband, in his own universe, sitting on their couch, and suddenly
she's sick to her stomach. They need to find Kenzie together. They
need to handle all of this together. But because of what she's done,
the whole process is crippled now. She hurries to the bathroom and
vomits. When that is over, she cleans up and walks back into the hall.
Mack is standing there.

"Did you know anything about this?"

"What?"

"Her hanging around Jaylee?"

"No! Bekka didn't even know about it."

"Because if I find out that you knew and didn't tell me—"

"Mack, I didn't know anything. Nobody knew anything." She
stares at him, and the rage in his eyes continues to flame. "You think
I wouldn't tell you something like that—about our own daughter?"

"I don't trust you to tell me anything anymore. Anything could be
going on in this house! I committed the sin of getting sick—and I
come home and I may as well still be in the hospital. You cut me
off—" He fairly hisses this, moving closer to her so Jerry won't hear.
"You cut me off, no discussion, no warning. So, no, I don't think
you'd tell me something like this. I don't trust you, Jodie. I don't trust
you!" He leaves her in the hallway.

She goes back into the bathroom, this time to cry. It has finally
happened. She has finally killed her family. She has done the one
thing that will cause everything to fall apart.

Mike Williamson, the youth pastor, calls, alarm in his voice. He
will keep calling kids from his house, hoping to raise some information. Somebody must have seen Kenzie sometime today. Then the

house is quiet, sleet and wind hitting the windows. It's dark outside. They wait, not talking much, in the family room and kitchen. The phone rings at five-thirty. It's Jenna Braeburn, one of the older girls in Kenzie's youth group.

"Mrs. Barnes? I'm sorry to bother you, but Kenzie and I are stuck at Wal-Mart, and I tried to call home but my stupid sister is online and I can't get through. Would you mind sending somebody to get us? My car just spins around in the parking lot, and I'm afraid to drive."

Jodie feels faint and sits down. Mack shoots off the sofa.

"Are you girls okay?"

"Yes. Kenzie wanted to buy my birthday present. My birthday isn't until next week, but we decided to go shopping today. I guess that wasn't such a great idea."

"That's all right." Jodie is motioning to Mack and Jerry that everything's fine. "Kenzie's dad will come out in the truck and get you, okay? Just stay where you are. Can I talk with Kenzie?"

She hears the phone changing hands. "Hi, Mom. Sorry about this."

"It's all right." She fights to keep her voice normal. "Dad's coming to get you, all right? Just stay right there. Do you hear me?"

"Sure, Mom. Thanks."

She puts down the phone. "She's with the Braeburn girl at Wal-Mart. Their car's stuck."

The sigh that fills the kitchen issues from all three of them. Mack puts on his jacket. "Thank God." He heads for the door.

"Well, that's easier than what I was expecting," Jerry says as he grabs his own jacket from the back of a chair.

"Maybe it was just a daydream or something." Jodie looks at the journal, which is still on the kitchen table. "Just something a kid would write in her journal."

"Jaylee's gone, though. That's a fact." Jerry puts on his cap. "I think you'd better talk to Kenzie and find out for sure what's been going on."

"Oh, I intend to. I'm sorry we caused all this commotion, Jerry."

He waves at her. "I'm just happy it's turned out this way. You and Mack come talk to me if you find out anything about Mitchell. If he's been involved with Kenzie, that's a whole other problem. She's only fifteen, right?"

"Not quite fifteen." Jodie doesn't get up but watches Jerry disappear into the night air, where the silver lines of sleet are now illuminated by the yard light.

She picks up the journal and reads the first few pages, then closes it and puts it down. Her daughter's dreams and longings break her heart. And she can't bring herself to enter a place that is so private, so absolutely true.

Rita

In midafternoon the Ford dies halfway between the Glen farm and town. Just the way Rita has imagined it would, all those other times when it didn't after all. She turns the corner at Miller's Mile, and the engine slows down and just stops. At that very moment, a gust of wind catches the car, rain with it. Rita leans into the front windshield, and she can see that the rain is tapping the glass and hardening as it slides down. It is three in the afternoon, but the countryside has fallen dark as the weather moves across it.

"Well, this is just fine." She grips the steering wheel and hears her own breath gust inside the car. During the seconds when the wind lets up, there is a massive silence around her on the road. She looks at her watch, at her hands in their gloves. She tries to stare down the road in any direction, but the windshield is fast becoming a glaze. The Glens are the only people who live on this stretch, and they are a mile behind her. Another two miles lie before her.

Rita has not been truly afraid of much in her life. She is a person who gets out of her chair and does something when the situation turns grim. But the only options now are to stay in the car and pray for someone to happen by—not likely on this road at this time of day—or to start walking. Just the thought of the cold air makes her lungs hurt. The time at the hospital taught her a new sort of fear. She remembers the sensation of not being able to get her breath, of coughing and coughing and not being able to clear her throat and gulp in air. The doctor preached hard at her upon dismissal. "You can't afford to get so much as a cold, you understand that? Take care of yourself or you'll be back in here."

So she sits in the car, the cold creeping in and beginning to nip at her cheeks and legs. A mile or two isn't that far to walk, in good weather. Her arthritis makes it painful, but she could do it. But she can tell that the temperature is dropping quickly, and the worn soles of her shoes will not keep her upright on a sheet of ice. It wasn't that many years ago when Frank Darling's wife tried to walk across a field to home when her car got stuck during a snowstorm. It was after dark, and she never found the house. Her body was found a quarter-mile from the barn the next morning. Nancy Darling knew those fields like the back of her hand. But zero visibility and cold have a way of wiping the map clean and confusing a perfectly good mind.

Rita tries to start the car. She tries to at least get some juice to come on so she can run the heater. But the alternator light flashes weakly, then goes out. She pulls her coat tighter. "Lord, you'll have to send someone out of their way." Her prayer sounds tiny in the lonely car. "Please do that."

She waits and waits. Her watch tells her that an hour has passed. She can't see out any of the windows now. And she is truly cold. She thinks of Alex, out in that drafty garage with his radio on, working on his truck, too drunk to know that it was time to go in. She figures that the cold didn't bother him at all. His death was probably as easy as death gets. In some ways, he had died before that anyway. Something in his soul had given up. That bothers her almost more than the drinking did.

"Lord, I'm calling on your help," she says, loudly. "You've got me in a situation I can't get out of on my own. Please send help soon. Amen." She's not necessarily blaming the Lord, but she's out here because she was delivering medicine and groceries to the Glens, both too old and feeble to get around, even together. She's out here for the right reason, but maybe her timing was off today. Maybe if she'd skipped her TV story that came on after lunch . . .

As the space outside her car grows darker, her memories become clearer. How white her son's face was, almost the color of the concrete floor of the garage. He looked peaceful. She tried to move his body, but it was so stiff. She couldn't move his fingers, his neck. He was heavy as lead. She had to leave him and walk to the house. The handle of the back door was so cold she could feel it through her heavy gloves. The door made a great crack when she pulled it open and went inside to make the phone calls. So disrespectful to leave Alex out there in the garage, frozen into a position of uncomfortable sleep.

Something thumps the window, right near her head. She looks out and sees Alex's dark eyes staring in at her. "Lord," she says, tears rumbling up, "is this heaven? I expected it to be warmer."

The car door comes open, ice crackling with it, and two slender forms lean down to look in at her. "Grandma, are you okay?" The person who has bent down to get closer to her pulls a scarf away from his face. Young Taylor's cheeks are rosy from the cold, his thick lashes harboring tiny droplets. "We nearly slid into you."

"Young Taylor, what are you doing out here in this ice storm?"

"Eric's taking me home. Decided to go the back way, because there's a pileup on the main road."

"Pileup? Anybody hurt?"

"No. They're trying to get one guy out of the ditch, and everybody's hanging around, blocking traffic."

"This car just stopped. I've been out here for an hour. Didn't think anyone would come by."

"Normally, nobody would," says Eric, leaning closer. "But we can pull you home. How's that?"

"Please do."

"Grandma, get in Eric's truck. The heater's running."

"Who's going to drive this one? Somebody's got to steer."

"I'll drive it. Let me help you out."

"No. I'm fine. I'll just scoot over."

"You sure?"

When she moves to the passenger side, Young Taylor gets in. He tries to start the car and gets nothing. Eric's jumper cables are not in the truck, but he does have a chain, so they hook up the car that way. Young Taylor hops back in. "It's a lot warmer in Eric's truck."

"I'll be home in my warm house soon."

It takes them fifteen minutes to get to Beulah, with Young Taylor steering and Eric pulling as gently as he can. When they get to the main road, Young Taylor angles the wheels toward Rita's street. She puts her hand on his arm.

"No. Don't take me home."

Young Taylor honks at Eric, and both vehicles stop. "You want to take the car to Tom? He can probably get to it tomorrow."

"No, take this car to the dump."

Young Taylor laughs and looks at her. "You serious?"

"I am absolutely serious. Take us to the dump."

"We'll take you home first. It's just four blocks."

"No, take me to the dump too." Her voice quivers.

"Grandma, I think we should just take you home. We can do whatever you want with the car tomorrow."

"Young Taylor, you haul this car to the dump right now! Don't back-talk me or act like I don't know what I'm talking about."

"Okay. We'll go to the dump, and then Eric and I will take you home in his truck. Okay?"

"That's fine. But this car goes to the dump."

Young Taylor hollers out the window and gives Eric the plan, and they cross the main road and head for the junkyard. Rita can feel her grandson looking at her every few moments. Maybe he thinks she is going crazy. No matter. What do young people know about life? And this one has been running around for nearly a year now, looking like Halloween, so he has no room to talk.

"Dump's the best place for this piece of junk," she mutters.

"I never thought you'd do it," says Young Taylor. "Take it to the junkyard. You've really liked this car."

Rita feels the tears burn in her throat again. She feels the words come up too, like bad food: "He should've known better than to buy me a Ford." All the men in her family line up on the hood in front of her: her son frozen dead, her other son out in the woods, her grandson with black eyeliner, and Taylor Senior, handing her the car keys. "I told him all along that I wanted a Chevrolet."

Jodie

Their relief is short-lived. Mack brings Kenzie home, and Jodie can tell from their faces that he hasn't said anything to their daughter about the journal or their frantic search. The moment Kenzie sees her journal on the table, she grabs it and looks from one of them to the other.

"Why is my journal here?"

"You left it at Bekka's, with the books you gave her."

"Oh." She turns toward the staircase. Jodie moves to intercept her.

"Tell us about Mitchell."

Kenzie stops cold. "Have you been reading this?"

"Just tell us about Mitchell."

"You don't have any right to read it—it's private! I can't believe you did that!"

Mack has moved closer to her. He motions toward a chair. "Just sit down here and tell us what's going on."

"No! I don't have to tell you anything!"

"Sweetheart, we need to know if you're involved with somebody." Jodie keeps her voice as gentle as she can.

"Sit down." Mack has a hand on her arm.

She sits and folds her arms, wrapping up tight as if to protect herself from both parents. They sit down on either side of her.

"Have you been seeing Mitchell?" Jodie doesn't know how else to put it.

"We're good friends."

"So tell us about it."

"You won't understand." Kenzie starts to cry. "You'll never understand. That's why I wasn't going to tell you."

"You were going away with him?" Jodie decides to keep talking until Mack jumps in. He sits across from her, eyes fixed upon their daughter.

"We didn't do anything wrong. He wouldn't do anything wrong. He's not like that."

"What exactly have you done?"

"Nothing! Like I said. We just talk."

Mack speaks up. "But you were planning to go off with him, weren't you?"

Kenzie doesn't say anything. She looks at her hands. After a moment, she nods. "There's this place in Kansas. It's a community where Christians work together. They share everything, and—" She stops, as if suddenly too exhausted to say more. "I knew you'd think it was crazy."

"When were you going to do this?"

"Tonight."

"That's why your room is all cleaned out." Jodie finds it hard to breathe. Now that Kenzie has confirmed her fears, she doesn't know where else to go with this.

"He's already gone." Mack's voice is harsh. Jodie stares up at him. Kenzie looks at him too, tears still on her cheeks.

"What do you mean?"

"His place is cleaned out, and the van's gone. The sheriff's had people looking for him all afternoon."

She jumps up from the table and is upstairs before they can stop her. They hear the door slam. Jodie slumps against the kitchen wall. She looks over at her husband.

"Did you have to say that?"

"The sooner she faces up to it, the better off she'll be."

"Just because you're mad at me doesn't mean you should be cruel to her."

"I'm not being cruel. That son of a bitch Jaylee is the one who's cruel. Do you think he ever intended to take her anywhere? He's odd as hell, but I don't think he's stupid enough to take a minor out of state."

She knows he is right. She also knows that she cannot ease her daughter's agony. Some things cannot be borne by others, ever.

"Are you going to go up there?" Mack asks.

"No. I'll wait a while. She needs to be left alone."

"It appears that we've already left her alone way too much."

"Don't start, Mack."

"I'm not starting anything. Whatever craziness she's gotten mixed up in started long before now. I'd better not find out that ... that bastard has—" He turns away and brings both hands to his face.

"I don't think anything has happened." She knows that she should touch his shoulder or at least move closer, but the distance is just too far. "I'll find out. She'll talk to me later, and I'll find out, but I don't think anything like that has happened."

Mack is wiping his eyes. He clears his throat. "I'll talk to her too."

"We can do it together." She climbs the stairs then, and stops in front of Kenzie's door. She can't hear anything. Jodie slides down the wall and sits there in the hallway, waiting for an entrance.

FINDING HOME

I can see far down the mountain,
  where I wandered weary years,
Often hindered in my journey
  by the ghosts of doubts and fears;
Broken vows and disappointments
  thickly sprinkled all the way,
But the Spirit led, unerring, to the land I hold today.
Is not this the land of Beulah?
  Blessed, blessed land of light,
Where the flowers bloom forever,
  and the sun is always bright!
                    —"Is Not This the Land of Beulah?"

Kenzie

She decides that, even though they know about her and Mitchell, she
will leave at midnight anyway. Since they've found her, maybe they'll
stop looking for him. And he told her he would be away today, taking
care of business. That's why his house is all closed up. But if there's
any way possible, he'll be down by the woods later. And she will go to
him. Her suitcases still wait in the coat closet by the front door.

Mom has not left the hallway, and Dad is downstairs; she can hear his movements in the family room. Maybe she should just talk to them, act like she's fine now, so they'll leave her alone and go to bed.

"Jesus, why did you let everything get so complicated?" She tries to pray, but can't. She glares at the journal, which now lies on her bare desk. How could she be so stupid? And how did her most prized possession get mixed up with the giveaway stuff?

Mom taps on the door. For the third time in an hour. Kenzie walks over and unlocks it, but turns her back before Mom can look at her.

"Kenzie, talk to me about this, okay?" She follows Kenzie to the bed, and they both sit on it. "Sweetie, I really want to understand what's been happening. Dad and I are just concerned—we're not mad at you."

"Yes, you are. And you're mad at Mitchell, who's my very best friend. So you may as well be mad at me."

A shadow rests on them. Dad is in the doorway, the hall light behind him. It's seven o'clock and dark outside. Kenzie scoots across the bed and sits against the wall. Dad moves her desk chair close to the bed and sits on it. He and Mom don't look at each other.

"We're not mad at Mitchell or you," he says. "But we need to know . . . what's happening with you. That's all."

"Even if I explained everything, you wouldn't understand."

"Try us." Dad's voice is steady, but not edgy the way it gets when he's controlling his temper.

"Well, he's really gifted. He's an artist. I bet you didn't know that." Her parents shake their heads.

"And he has such a heart for spiritual things. We read the Bible and pray together all the time. I've grown so much since I got to know him."

Dad's jaw is working nervously, but Mom is making a little smile.

"And sometimes he is so full of ideas that he doesn't sleep for two or three days. He reads all night or works on his sculptures or just makes all sorts of plans for the future. I've never met anyone like that."

Mom sits cross-legged, there on the bed, and tucks hair behind her ear. "How long have you two been friends?"

"A few months. Since before Halloween."

"So you talk? And you pray, stuff like that?"

"Uh-huh."

"Do you . . ." Mom is thinking hard. "Do you feel romantic toward him?"

"It's more like a calling."

"What calling?" Dad asks.

"To work for God together."

"That's what you were going to do at this retreat place?"

"Yes."

For a moment, she thinks that the conversation is over. She has answered their questions, and nobody's getting mad. But Mom's eyes are working still, and she then does what she is so good at doing— getting to the point.

"Kenzie, have you been having sex with him?"

Thank you, Jesus, for helping us stay pure. "No, Mom."

"You haven't?"

"He's kissed me a couple of times, that's all. We want to stay in God's will."

"You know," Dad says, and clears his throat, "there's a reason Mitchell stays up for days at a time."

Mom finally looks at him.

"It's God's Spirit," Kenzie says.

Dad rubs his hands together slowly, the way he does when he's working out something in his head. "I think there's more to it than that. He has a condition that makes him swing from highs to lows. It's a chemical thing in his brain."

"How would you know?" She can feel demons at the door.

"Well, because someone who knows him told me. And Mitchell doesn't always take his medicine—"

"I don't want to hear this, okay? You think that everything gets solved with some stupid pill!"

"No, I don't."

"You're the *king* of pills! You don't know anything!"

"Kenzie!" Mom's eyes flash.

"I'm just trying to do things the right way, Mom!" If she hadn't cried so much already, there would be tears coming now. She's glad there aren't, because she has to be strong. "I pray and pray, and it doesn't make any difference. You just don't care! You don't have faith! Nobody in this family cares anymore! You just pop pills and argue and—" Well, maybe she didn't run out of tears after all. She gets off the bed to head for the hallway and the bathroom, but Dad takes hold of her, and just like that she's on his lap. And just like a little girl with no strength at all, she is crying into his shirt, and he is saying over and over, "Baby, baby. We're all right. Everybody's all right. Baby, baby..."

The rest of the evening is quiet, full of tears and sighs. She can tell that Mom and Dad are both hurting a lot; they hardly ever cry in front of her or Young Taylor, but they weep too a little, and stay close by. Mom makes hot chocolate, and they are at the kitchen table drinking it when Young Taylor comes in, full of a strange story about Grandma. Dad just stares at Young Taylor and manages a question or two.

"So she's home? She's all right?"

"Yeah."

"And where's the car?"

Young Taylor shrugs. "She made us leave it at the dump. Said something about wanting a Chevy. I don't know—you go talk to her."

"She coughing a lot?"

"No. I think she got scared, though, sitting out there on the road."

"Well, good. Maybe she'll stay put for a change."

"Maybe we should just get her a better car." Young Taylor seems to notice then that something's wrong. "What's up?"

Mom pulls him down to the remaining kitchen chair and goes for another cup. "Nothing. You have supper?"

"Grandma made me eat soup with her."

Shortly before midnight, Dad walks Kenzie down to where she is supposed to meet Mitchell. He didn't want to at first, but probably he thinks this is the easiest way to confront Mitchell. Then Kenzie thinks it's probably not such a good idea. She wants to go by herself, promising to say good-bye to Mitchell and come right back. Of course, Dad won't go for that. Mom says that maybe she should come along, but Dad waves her off, almost as though he's mad that she'd suggest it. Probably fathers need to take charge of stuff like this.

They wait a long time, but Mitchell never comes. She tells herself that he must have found out that people knew, and so he stayed away. But that doesn't even matter now. She is tired and kind of relieved that she doesn't have to take such a big, awesome step this minute, this day. She wonders if Jesus has intervened, through Mom and Dad and even the mistake with the journal, and saved her from what looked right at the time but really wasn't. In a strange way, when she and Dad walk back into the house and she goes upstairs, she feels as if she is returning to her real self. This is too confusing to think about—who has she been lately, if not herself? And haven't her prayers been true, her time with Jesus exactly what it should be? But she pushes all of this away as she crawls into bed, her head aching from all the crying and trying. Dad kisses her good-night, and Mom comes in and lies down beside her. She doesn't remember when Mom gets up, only that she is alone when she awakes for a moment and sees that the clock says four A.M., and she feels perfectly safe.

Jodie

She and Mack have been talking, off and on, for hours. Kenzie is spending the day at Rita's, helping her clean out kitchen cabinets, because Rita saw a mouse two days ago and won't rest until the whole place is ravaged. The two of them are without transportation, and Kenzie is calm, though not talkative. Mack and Jodie decided that a day with Grandma might do her good, although Grandma has no idea that she almost lost Kenzie to some cult off in Kansas. Young Taylor has uncharacteristically taken his hunting rifle and Ed's dog out to the fields in hopes of bringing home some rabbits. He still won't eat any form of pork but has apparently rediscovered the value of killing his own food.

Jodie is cleaning house like a mad woman, Mack trailing behind her, doing what he can. And the whole time they talk. They yell or cry or stomp out of the room. He has set up an appointment for them to talk with George, and now she doesn't want anything to do with it. She says she has broken things off with Terry, but he suspects she hasn't. They talk at each other, over and around each other. It is a prolonged battle, brimming with strategy and failure.

"I'm trying to do what you need for me to do, Jo."

"How can you know what I need? I don't even know what I need. You think you can just fix things. That's always been your problem. You're your mother's son. Just fix things and expect people to shape up."

"Maybe I used to be that way, but not anymore. Nothing's that simple. I'm not trying to make it simple."

"Just give me space, Mack."

"And let you leave without trying to put us back together?"

"I don't have the energy to put anything back together."

"That's why we need to keep our appointment with George."

"It would be you two against me."

"What?" He drops the pile of newspapers he's gathering. "What are you talking about?"

"You've already got this relationship. I'm the new one. And I'm the one who's been sleeping around. I know where this is going."

"Jo, it's not like that. This guy is real professional. He'd never stack the deck. He wants to help both of us."

"But, see—" She slaps the dust rag on the back of the sofa. "See, what you don't get is that, no matter what anybody says, you're the person who needs help and I'm the person who has screwed up. Because you're the one who went to the hospital, and I'm the one who stayed home and let everything go to hell. I'm the one who didn't hold things together in the first place. See, Mack, it's *my job* to make sure you and the kids are okay. And I couldn't do it. I just couldn't do it. So I'm already guilty."

Mack gets up and heads for the door.

"Where are you going?"

He doesn't turn around. "I can't."

"Can't what?" The old impatience rises in her, this inability to deal with her husband's unfinished sentences.

"I can't be in this room right now." He is through the kitchen and gone before she can pull him back with more questions.

But his words repeat in her mind: *I can't be in this room right now.* When has he said this before? She knows he has said almost those exact words, but not recently. She picks up the dust rag again and stares out the window, where Mack is coming into view. He is walking to the old barn, the one that houses all their leftovers. He will rummage around for an hour or more, finding things to chop into kindling or patch up in some way.

Then she hears those words of his, from deep in her memory. *I can't even sit in the same room with him.* It was what Mack told her the Sunday he walked out of church, halfway through the service. One of the deacons was their banker, and after months of battles in the man's office, after the notices and warnings and refusals had built up into a wall no human could climb over, Mack had said that he could not sit in that church with that man. He had left before the offering plates were passed—a part of the service painful to them, a family who had given to the church always, without fail, until recent months—and he had never gone back.

I can't be in this room right now. Jodie feels a hammer strike that hard thing inside her, that core of strength that has, over months of coping, turned into coldness. She realizes suddenly that Mack did not say what he actually meant: *I can't be in this room—with you—right now.*

So this is what she has become: the banker. The caretaker of other people's troubles, the one who in the end turns tired and angry and fi-

nally greedy, the one who stops hearing others' sorrows and simply col-
lects their property. The one to whom the debts are owed, debts that
cannot possibly be repaid. She has piled up Mack's debts, all the pains
his pain has caused her, and she has kept the books, and he can see that
pile of debts between the two of them, and he knows that what she de-
mands of him is impossible. She needs a bookkeeping sort of justice.
She is the banker, and she can foreclose whenever she wants.

Jodie feels the hammer strike again, like a judge's gavel, against her
tired, rigid heart. She tries to stop thinking, but instead imagines, in
acute detail, the devastation in her husband's spirit. The accumula-
tion of defeats. The constant inability to do enough or be enough.
And the loss of the one person, his wife, who could have, with a look
or a few words, rendered those defeats less deadly. Jodie begins to
tremble. In light of this great, awful sin, this gathering and keeping of
debts against her husband, her adultery of recent days seems almost a
small thing.

Mack

As his family troops out the door and gets in the car, Mack fears that
he is leading them to a place from which they will not return whole.
After Reverend Maynor came by a few days ago and invited them to
the special church service, Jodie didn't say a word about it, but Mack
brought it up with George. And George, the master of deadpan, displayed enthusiasm on the spot. A grieving ceremony, yes. A chance to
make the good-byes formal. What an excellent idea. And Mack called
the reverend and committed his household to the evening, without
asking anyone else's permission. This is not the way he usually does
things, but when Jodie and the kids gave him incredulous looks, he
did not defend himself but took another tack altogether.

"Would you all do this for me? I feel like it would help." Asking for
help is not his habit either, but it won over Kenzie, who, even as
wounded as she is, still wants to be helpful. Young Taylor shrugged,
and Mack took that as a yes.

He has feared all day that Jodie will back out at the last minute. If she goes, it will be only for his sake, and these days he cannot measure the depth or intensity of her feelings toward him. He no longer assumes that she is committed to his well-being, and this has wiped out his equilibrium. Somehow, he stays in the house. He even sleeps in their bed, although he doesn't lie down until she is asleep, and he does not touch her. It stirs up all of his anger to be so close to her. His stomach churns acid, and he doesn't sleep for hours at a time. But they have decided that the last thing their daughter needs right now is seeing her dad move to the spare bedroom. Plus, Mack fears that if he walks out of their bedroom he will never again find its entrance.

He doesn't know how he keeps going about his business, putting in full days at the shop and dwelling in the farmhouse every evening, taking care to talk with his children. It's all he has, these moments full of awkward questions and answers or superficial comments about the day, but he just keeps talking and listening and trying to read these people who have managed to wander so far from him and each other.

It's as if his soul has its own agenda now. He goes through the motions of love and acts as if things will get better, which, as recently as a few months ago, would have felt hypocritical. But the efforts don't seem hollow to him. They are steps he must take, regardless of any immediate reward or relief. So he steps into each day and just keeps stepping.

Now the four of them step into a cold afternoon in mid-January. Mack notices the sky without really studying it. In the back of his mind float masses of chalky gray. He is ready for the sun to shine again, ready for color and the smell of soft dirt. The fields are still bright and expansive from the snowfall of two days ago. Even without direct sunshine the land's surface is as smooth and white as frosting on a wedding cake. In fields where corn stood during the past year, perfect lines of tan stubble push through the crust of snow and mark the memory of harvest.

In a land of long straight lines, Grace Methodist of Oskaloosa offers a large room filled with roundness—oval windows and pews that curve to hug the front of the sanctuary. The old wood shines. The gently shaded stained glass tints the air with combinations of color that suggest holiness and perfection that reside not out in the elements but in people's hearts. When summer was laden with heat and maturing crops, the sanctuary air brushed silkily across bare arms and necks, and the polished wood of pews, altar, pulpit, and piano tickled a person's nose with the memory of resin, sawdust, linseed oil.

Mack and Jodie first came here to worship summer before last. It was a shift away from the friends and enemies of the tiny Methodist congregation in Beulah. The pastor serves both congregations. Reverend Maynor, with losses of her own behind her, has been ordained for five years, the last two of them served here. She lends a soft strength to the community in the way the church gives curves to the straight-edged fields beyond its property.

Now, in the dead of January, the dried-out Christmas greenery has been removed from windows, ledges, and railings, but still there is the scent of cedar. It is a golden room in the middle of a cold blue landscape.

Kenzie hasn't said much to either Mack or Jodie since the night they found out about Mitchell Jaylee. For the first time in her young life, Mack senses true defiance in his daughter. It doesn't present itself as open anger, only quiet obedience that seems to have no spirit left, and Mack approaches Kenzie as if she were a new acquaintance.

He and Jodie talked to the youth pastor at the Baptist church, who was almost as upset as they were, ashamed at not having figured out that something was wrong. Pastor Williamson showed them a video that Kenzie gave him to watch, apologizing for not having jumped on that issue immediately. Mack and Jodie watched about fifteen minutes of it, while Kenzie was out of the house. Reverend Francis struck them as most definitely crazy if not criminal, but they don't yet know how to suggest this to Kenzie. Pastor Williamson has offered to work on this part of it, and they are grateful.

They are also relieved that the situation with Jaylee did not go further. After talking with Kenzie, Pastor Williamson is convinced that there was no sexual relationship, although it certainly seemed to be heading in that direction. Mitchell hasn't been seen in Beulah since the day he and Kenzie were to run away together. Jerry has tried to contact Reverend Francis's compound, but no one will return his calls, and given that Mitchell is a grown man, Jerry is not compelled to bother law enforcement officials two states away. This would not be the first time Jaylee shut up his house and disappeared for weeks at a time.

Now Kenzie and her mother sit mutely in the pew, a foot apart. They look shut down, and as Mack observes the other people who are gathering, the fear races through him again. He has no right to drag them through this, not now.

Rita is homebound, after yet another trip to the emergency room. Not from pneumonia but a fractured shin. She slipped on her own back step, taking out garbage that Mack would have hauled out if she had just waited another twenty minutes. He is slightly grateful, though, that she is unable to be with them this evening. She's shown no interest at all in the service, and he has run out of fight or patience where she is concerned. Amos cornered him earlier today, when Mack stopped by to take the two meals Jodie put together for her, and asked if Rita would like company, and Mack said, yes, she'd probably really like that.

Young Taylor does not sit with them but takes a place in the very back pew, close to the door, in case he needs to make a fast getaway, Mack guesses. He wears all black but no makeup. Mack turns in the pew once or twice to be sure he's not slipped out. The second time, Young Taylor, his arms stretched along the pew back, raises a forefinger in acknowledgment.

Ed and Lacy are here. They sit in the pew just behind Mack and Jodie. Of course they would be here, as they are always close by. Several members of Beulah Methodist are present; Mack doesn't know which "grieving families" they are connected to, but he does notice Jon and Annette Peters and remembers that Jodie used to go places with Annette. What Mack hasn't expected, though, is to see the

Lesters, Masons, and Kernbetters, neighbors who have farmed adjacent acreages during the past twenty years. The Masons were good friends of Rita and Taylor Senior. They smile at Mack and Jodie and sit a few pews away.

Three other families are making formal good-byes to farming. Two of them Mack and Jodie know, having followed their tragedies at a distance even while their own unfolded. The third couple live in the next county, and their loss is the most recent: they auctioned off their goods not quite three months ago.

Reverend Maynor has some opening comments, but they are short. The congregation sings a hymn, and a deacon offers a prayer. The man has likely never prayed at this type of service before, and he sounds a bit unsure. He keeps his thanks and requests general, but does say at the end, "Lord, help our hearts heal tonight," and these words cause a shift in Mack's thinking. It is a personal, painful request, and he is unaccustomed to bringing raw emotion into a church building. By now, such pain comes up as normal when he sits in George's office. But the public feel of this church makes him wonder what in the world he is doing here, and he dreads what may happen next.

"I've asked a few of you to come prepared tonight," the reverend says, smiling, "just to get things going. I'd like for us to spend some time telling stories. They can be any stories at all, but the important thing is that they are your stories. So Julia is going to start, and then I think a couple of others. Then we'll open it up to whoever wants to talk."

The stories do come, one after the other. To Mack's surprise, only a few recount hard times—droughts, accidents, or sick hogs. But there are many more stories of kids, cats, and even calves, stuck in trees or muddy stream bottoms, of hilarious chases after persnickety livestock, of poison ivy making the rounds through three families in a week, of parties of women sweating in one another's kitchens, putting up pickles, green beans, corn, and applesauce.

He didn't expect the stories or the warm, at-home feeling their telling brings. He didn't expect to cry from laughing and for that to feel good. He didn't expect any laughter at all, just some Scripture readings and admonitions to praise God and trust his providence. They have been sitting here for more than an hour now, and no one has read any Scripture at all.

Their neighbor Dave Kernbetter, who is going on seventy, clears his throat and begins to speak.

"Young Taylor was three years old and somehow got into my sweet corn patch. I guess he'd been in the truck with his mom when she brought lunch out to Mack and Taylor Senior, the next field over. I could see the adults standing around the truck with the hood up— always something breaking on the equipment—" Chuckles around the room confirm this. "Anyway, I guess while they had their heads together, Young Taylor got away and got into my field. But I didn't know he was anywhere around.

"So I'm chopping weeds out of my rows, and I see some stalks moving like there's an animal comin' right for me. I've got my old dog Patch there with me, and usually he'd take after anything that didn't belong there. But Patch just looks back at me, confused." Dave stops while a laugh rumbles up from his gut. His wife Mary is shaking beside him and wiping her eyes.

"Then all of a sudden I see this little brown head of hair and a totally naked kid underneath it. It was hot as blazes, and I guess he'd been just wearing a diaper, but he must have lost that a few rows back. But—oh yeah, he did have his sneakers on. So there's Young Taylor, movin' ahead straight as a plowhorse, red as a little beet. He looks up at me, and I say, 'Young Taylor, what are you doing here?' and I reach down to grab him, but he takes out and runs east, away from me *and* his folks. So all I can do is run after him. But a little guy with no clothes can travel pretty fast, you know." The whole room is laughing itself to tears. "I caught up to him and grabbed him, and he screamed bloody murder all the way back to the truck. And I'm tryin' to figure out how I'm going to explain how come he's got no clothes on."

Mack doesn't dare look back at Young Taylor. He hears little sobs beside him and sees Jodie pull out a tissue, her face red and bright from laughing. She leans toward him suddenly. "We could never keep a diaper on him."

Mack smiles and squeezes her shoulder. "Nope. We almost got him a leash after that, though."

Reverend Maynor stands up, in the center aisle, the pulpit behind her. "We've remembered the history so many of us share. The good and bad times. Most of these memories have to do directly with your farms. You'll always have those memories and those stories. They will be part of you forever. But for the families we are honoring tonight, there will be no new stories connected with that livelihood."

The room falls silent, as if she has mentioned something they have all agreed will not be spoken aloud. She is not daunted by this.

"The difficulty you face is that the life you had as farmers—all the wonderful and tragic moments that came with it—is over. This is the part that is not so easy to talk about. I remember when my daughter died in a traffic accident, six years ago, at age seventeen, I felt for months afterward that if I admitted out loud that she was gone for good, I would lose everything I had of her. I was afraid that the moment I said good-bye, all the memories would fly out the windows and doors and never return. I lived in fear of losing my memories. As you know, if you've lost a loved one, memories can be so vivid and close that they are almost like objects in the room with us."

Mack thinks of Alex sitting by the stream in the dead of night, and of his father's boots in the museum.

"But the truth is, putting your grief into spoken words will not steal the rich history you have built. And until you put your grief into words, until you truly grieve and say good-bye, you won't be able to build new stories for yourself and your families. This is another reason we're here this evening. We're here to celebrate your families as the farm families they have been. But we're also here to say good-bye and help you move to the next part of your lives."

She asks then that people speak, one at a time, and briefly, of what they must say good-bye to. Nearly a minute goes by, and the pastor remains steady. Finally, Adri Bart speaks up. She is in her early fifties and looks as plain and strong as farm women tend to look. Her voice does not waver, but her hands shake slightly where they grip the pew in front of her.

"What I miss most of all is the spring planting. The world just feels new when it's thawing out from a long winter. Now we hardly ever hold the soil in our hands." She sits down quickly, and others rise, one by one, and speak.

"Harvest is what I loved most. When you can pull in a good crop, nothing in life feels better. You've got the proof right there that you did a good job."

"Now that we're in town, we've got a smaller garden spot. I hate not having half an acre to do with as I want. My favorite smell is green beans when I'm cooking them with ham and putting them up. I used to count jars by the dozens. Now I don't put much away at all. It doesn't feel the same, with that little garden patch."

"Working with the hogs, believe it or not. I had hogs ever since I was seven years old. Used to show a sow every year at the fair. Then I'd cry when we'd sell her come winter."

"I miss having the whole family around. It was so hard the day Frank got a job in town to bring in more money. I had three little ones at home. He worked in town during the day and farmed at night. I hated seeing him work to exhaustion. I hated that he didn't enjoy the farming, since he was always too tired to do it. But I really hated that he wasn't there with me during the day. I missed carrying lunch out to him or just going out to where he was and listening to him talk about how things were growing."

"The hardest for me was when my wife had to work outside the farm. The kids were in high school, and she took a job at the nursing home. Harder work than the farm, and the pay was hardly enough to matter. Life felt different after that."

Mack feels his heart throbbing, moving words to the front. But he's been putting things into words for months now. He knows they will come out and yet he won't be destroyed. He clears his throat. A few people look at him, but some look at each other, understanding what he has been through.

"What's been hardest for me is farming without my dad and brother. Dad's been gone ten years, but I'm still not used to that. And as you know, my brother died a couple years ago, not long after we sold everything but the house and a few acres. I haven't farmed for a while now, but I still miss working with both of them."

A long silence follows Mack's short speech. He feels tears in his throat, but nothing gets so far as his eyes. Since that day with George, when he stated how God had forsaken them, the tears have not been so easy to come. He wrestles now with bigger, deeper things that don't show themselves so freely.

A few more people speak, and Mack ventures a peek at Jodie's stone face beside him. Young Taylor says nothing, but that isn't a surprise. Kenzie sits slumped beside her mother, not seeming to connect to any of this. Maybe she will be able to later, with the pastor she knows better. But Mack aches for his wife to speak. He wants to know if the worst of all this for her is really him or if her grief includes the sorts of things people are naming now.

"Anyone else? I don't want to rush anyone, but I feel as if we're winding down." Reverend Maynor searches the room with patient eyes. Mack sees the eyes rest on Jodie. He sees Jodie look back at the minister, her head coming up just a bit.

"I just . . ." Jodie says, her voice abrupt, "I just don't know what I'm part of anymore."

It feels as if the whole room turns then and focuses on Jodie. Mack wonders suddenly if any of the people here know about Terry Jenkins. He looks for judgment in the faces around them, but all he sees are eyes that seem as hungry to hear Jodie speak as he is.

"So much of living out here is being part of everybody's life. We're all in this together. We're dependent on the weather and the market. Hardly anybody goes through something that everybody else doesn't go through. I used to belong to all that. I was part of the seasons changing and the neighbors working. What am I part of now?"

A tear slips down her cheek. Her whole body is trembling. "I don't know what I'm part of now. And I don't know who my family is." Her hands come up then, to cover her face, and she rocks. Mack hears Lacy begin to cry behind him.

He will remember forever how the room seems to collapse as his wife's sobs fill the arched space above them. How she makes sounds that he's never heard come out of her before, and how Kenzie suddenly slides close and clings to her mother. And then Lacy comes up too, scooting around Mack to gather both Kenzie and Jodie, and by then the room is weeping. He thinks that he weeps too, but mostly he is riveted to the sight and sound of his wife. He doesn't move, but allows her to be comforted by others. For the first time since all the hard times began, this does not feel like failure to him. He watches others stroke her hair and grasp her shoulders and speak soothing things to her, and he knows that this is meant to be. At some point he notices Ed sitting beside him. His arm comes down on the back of the pew behind Mack. Mack can't tell if the wetness on Ed's face is tears or sweat, but the grief is plain.

When the weeping subsides, Reverend Maynor reads two Psalms. They sing two hymns, easy ones that are old and second nature and require nothing but the heart and tongue to remember them.

Then each of the four families is presented with a small cloth bag filled with corn. This represents all their lives' harvests. The second is an empty scrapbook, leather-bound, a place in which to collect new memories and stories. Reverend Maynor has written a blessing, and she asks the families to stand, and she blesses each one. It is a lot like a baptism. After the blessing, they sing the Doxology, and the congregation comes forward to add good words, handshakes, and hugs. By then, the tears have dried and the mood has shifted. The air, though warm from the gas heater in the back of the room, feels light.

Rita

Rita's alone, on her couch, her bum leg resting on pillows on the coffee table. She hasn't done a useful thing for two days now. Jodie has helped deliver all the pill bottles to the neighborhood, and Mack picked up mail. It hurts too much for Rita to stand long enough to make soup for her folks. This is miserable.

Mack came by at noon, as he promised. He was pleasant enough, but his mind was on other things. He offered to take Rita to the church service tonight, but didn't push it when she declined. She quickly shifted the topic to asking about Jodie, Kenzie, Young Taylor, things at work. His answers were no different from a thousand other answers on other days.

Her TV remote had stopped working, a real inconvenience. She can get to the bathroom in just a few steps. But the crutches hurt her underarms, and changing channels by hand had become a burden. So Mack replaced the batteries. He got her fresh water, putting the little pitcher on the TV tray next to her. He washed the few dishes in the sink and reheated the lunch Jodie sent. Rita has to admit that her grown-man son is pretty good with the details. Taylor and Alex were fairly worthless when it came to anything inside the house, but Mack, maybe because of Jodie, has learned how to put a plate in front of a person and clean up the little messes that aren't that important but irritating all the same. He followed Rita's instructions wordlessly and with no resentment that she could see. She hopes he'll be this nice a decade from now, should she live that long. This is part of why she takes care of so many old folks—hoping God will notice her good works and provide the care she needs when she can't do for herself anymore. She has watched the light go out of too many faces as the years stole mobility and memory and simple pleasures. When she thanked Mack for his help, she meant it.

It is evening now, and she nibbles on the ham sandwich and carrot sticks and apple cake Jodie sent. Her leg is throbbing again, and she changes positions to ease it. Of course the doctor gave her pain pills, but they remain in their little bottle by the water pitcher—all she needs is to lose what little clarity she has to narcotics.

She got bored with television an hour ago, so now she stares at the blank screen and notices that the landscape hanging on the wall above it is tilted. It's too high for her to reach; even Mack would need a step stool to get up there and fix it. But he's gone now—and with the whole family off to this grieving service, probably no one will stop by later tonight. So Rita gets to look at this crookedness for the livelong evening. She tries to picture a person tall enough to reach and make the adjustment. Amos is shrunken up—and she wouldn't trust him on a stepladder anyway.

Another image comes to mind then, of Joe, Marty's new friend. Huh. She hasn't thought of him much since Christmas, has decided not to get too attached until they make it official—if they ever do. But that Joe, he could reach right up there. He towered over everybody at Christmas.

Maybe she should take a little more initiative. She picks up her notebook and turns to a blank page, writes "Dear Joe," and stops. He's new to the family and probably wonders if they like him or don't. She should have written him a note right after the holiday. Well, that's one oversight easy enough to correct.

Dear Joe:

Happy New Year—I hope it has started out well for you. I'm at home with a busted leg, but other than that, things are fine.

We really enjoyed having you visit us for Christmas. It was so good to have Marty, David, and Sharon with us, and we appreciate that you spent precious holiday time here in Beulah. We didn't hear much about your family. I hope the holiday was good for them too.

As you must know, our family has had its struggles. That's not so unusual for any family, but we did seem to pile up more than our share over the past few years. We've managed to deal with whatever comes. And we value helping each other through hard times. I've told Marty this, and now I'll tell you the same: No matter what happens, you can always come home to us. We'll do whatever we can to help.

It appears that you and Marty are pretty serious, and I think that she and the kids do well by having you around. So I hope things work out for all of you. And if you stay with them for the long haul, you'll automatically become part of the Barnes clan. That's not a threat, just a promise!

Please don't be a stranger. Beulah's not big and busy the way Omaha is, but we'll treat you well when you come to see us.

Most sincerely,
Rita Mae Barnes

She folds the letter and sets it where she'll remember to give it to Mack tomorrow. He needs to get her stamps too—better yet, stamped envelopes, because she's on her last envelope or two. She's let herself run low on a lot of things lately. No matter how hard she works to keep everything organized, one thing or another gets neglected. She considers turning this concern into a new prayer request, but her notebook landed on the kitchen cabinet somehow, and she is unwilling, for now, to go get it.

Mack

On the way home from the service, Jodie begins to cry again, not the sobs of before but steady, rhythmic sighs. No one speaks. Mack glances in the rearview mirror and sees that Young Taylor has his arm around Kenzie's shoulders. Kenzie looks tired and sad. Young Taylor's face is calm. His eyes meet Mack's in the mirror, but he says nothing.

They get to the farmhouse, and Jodie takes hold of Kenzie, and they walk together inside and upstairs. They go to Jodie and Mack's bedroom and shut the door. Mack taps on it and is told they are fine but need some time. He walks downstairs and finds Young Taylor at the kitchen table, having a bowl of cereal.

"I need to go see how your grandma's doing. I won't be long."

"Want me to come?"

"No. I'd rather you stay here with Mom and Kenzie. I won't be long at all."

"Okay."

Mack is surprised at how tired his mother looks. He's also angered at how little she wants to hear about the service.

"I thought you'd be interested," he said.

"I'm glad it went well. Sure it did good for some people."

"I think you would've liked it."

She shrugs and asks him to move her tray closer. She pours water from the Styrofoam pitcher. "I don't need some preacher telling me how to move on."

Mack wants to say, "I'm not so sure about that," but knows that tonight mercy is called for. He promises to come during his lunch hour tomorrow.

At the corner of Main and Walnut, he turns north. Three blocks later, he pulls into the drive of a small house near the school. He sits there, with the engine rumbling, and sees the curtains at one of the front windows part. Terry Jenkins looks out at him. Mack can't tell if Jenkins recognizes him or not.

He doesn't know what he planned to do, coming here. He promised Jodie that he'd let her handle it. But of course that's not enough. The man in the window has wronged the man in the car. Eventually they must face each other and settle something.

Eventually. Not this evening. There is too much pain welling up in the house where Mack lives. Anything he starts here with Jenkins will not end easily. Mack has never been a violent man, but he fears that violence waits low inside him for the few times in life when it's truly needed. He imagines hurting Jenkins, actually harming him physically. Jodie's sobs in the church have released a new level of anger in him. He wants someone to pay for all that's gone wrong. Even though Jenkins is a little part of it, it would be easy to kick the life out of him tonight.

He pulls out of the driveway and goes home. It's either a cowardly decision or a very wise one. All he knows for sure is that he needs to be home, not in jail, or not trailing in later with bloody knuckles.

He sees Kenzie at the kitchen sink when he pulls up. But by the time he walks in the door her feet are disappearing at the top of the stairs. Young Taylor sits in front of some demonic-looking video, a skinny, death-white kid rising from the ground, his teeth black. Young Taylor munches a sandwich. "Hey, Dad."

"Hey."

"How's Grandma?"

"Tired, but okay I think."

"Cool." There is the same emaciated kid, dressed in robes, chanting "disposable teens" over and over.

"You consider that entertainment?"

"Yes."

Mack goes upstairs and knocks on Kenzie's door. In a small voice she grants him entrance. She is on the bed.

"Is Mom still in the bedroom?" he asks.

Kenzie nods. "She wants to sleep."

"That's probably what she needs." He sits near her on the bed. "I know the service upset her, but I think it was good that she went. I'm glad you were there too. That meant a lot to Mom."

"She'll worry about me now, won't she?"

He looks at his daughter, seeing again the agony that glowed out of her the other night, after they had waited and waited for that son of a bitch Jaylee to show up in the woods. She was so sure he would come, and then so inconsolable as Mack walked her back up to the house. She wouldn't look at him, but the yard light had shone in her eyes, and he was sure he'd never seen so much pain in one person.

That night Kenzie's face had brought another terrible memory out of storage. Back when they decided to sell the farm, Mack had arranged for Buddy Humbolt, the auctioneer, to come out and work on the list of goods to be sold. The evening before Buddy came, Mack saw Kenzie carrying something down toward the creek, right at dusk. He waited until she was back at the house before going to investigate. At about ten-thirty, with flashlight in hand, he found the stash at the base of the old cottonwood. Her bicycle, covered up with grass and branches. A box filled with other treasures—some of her favorite books, the doll Rita had made her when she was five, a photo album. Kenzie was ten then and didn't understand that her most personal belongings would not be sold along with the machinery and acreage. Mack returned to the house, choking back tears, and did his best to explain.

No. He didn't do that. He told Jodie, and she had the conversation with Kenzie. Just one more difficult job that got dumped into his wife's lap.

Mack thinks of all this now as he tries to look into his daughter's eyes, which stay focused away from him. "Mom and I both know you're going to be all right. She's worried about me mainly, but I'm doing a lot better now too." He rubs Kenzie's knee and smiles at her, willing her to look at him. She does, but with no return smile.

"I guess it was dumb to talk with Mitchell so much."

"Your heart was in the right place. We don't think you're dumb."

"I just really thought he wanted to know Jesus." A little tear has entered her voice.

"Maybe he does, but he'll be better off learning about Jesus from someone else. Maybe you and Pastor Williamson can pray for him to find the right person to help him."

"Like that does any good." Her voice is lifeless.

"You don't think it does?"

"Hasn't done this family any good." He sees darkness shift over her countenance and feels a strange relief. Better to get mad at God early and get it over with.

"Oh, I don't know about that," he says. "We can't always see how things are working."

"You think things are working?" Her eyes accuse him.

"Here and there, yeah. I'm not giving up."

"You're not?"

"No. I won't give up, I promise." He grasps her hand, and after a second or two, she squeezes back, feebly.

"Do you think you can sleep too?" He wants to cuddle her the way he did when she was little, but such expressions have to be rationed out now, in her almost-grown life.

"Sure."

"I'll see you in the morning." He leans over and kisses her forehead, stroking her cheek lightly with his hand. She turns her head to return the kiss but otherwise remains still, as if her thoughts and emotions have had a paralyzing effect.

He goes downstairs to say good-night to Young Taylor, who has turned down the TV and is reading a magazine, rolling an empty pop can under his bare foot.

Their bedroom is quiet and pitch black. Jodie hasn't left a light on, as she used to do when she was first in bed. He can hear her sleep-breathing clear across the room. He undresses, down to his underwear and T-shirt, and crawls in beside her. She budges slightly, from habit, to make room for him.

"Mmm," she says in her sleep.

"It's just me. Kenzie's in bed, and Young Taylor's reading. Mom's okay, just tired."

Her breathing changes. She is awake, barely.

He props himself on one side, facing her back, and leans over to kiss her cheek. "Is it all right for me to do that, sweet?"

He feels her head nod against the pillow. "Yes," she whispers, hoarse from crying.

He nestles as close as he can, spooning his shape against hers, her fine hair in his face. He strokes it once or twice, then lays his arm over her side. After a moment, her breathing grows deep again.

Kenzie

Dear Jesus,

It feels strange to even write in this journal now. It's not private any-more—who knows how many people have read it? Maybe I should burn it—but I need to think about that before I really do it.

Who are you anyway, if you're not the person I've been talking to? I don't know what to believe. Were you with Mitchell and me, or not? Did you hear all our prayers? And those miracles that have happened in Rev-erend Francis's ministry—where did they come from? Mom says that he's probably not a bad guy, just misled. If you let people be misled, what else will you let happen?

Pastor Mike says that he understands why I would feel like the Tribula-tion is already here. But he thinks you're more patient than that—that you want to give all of us plenty of time to find grace. He says that the Book of Revelation is true but it's hard to say how it will work itself out. That you want us to concern ourselves with living in faith today instead of worrying about tomorrow and the End Times.

Well, I'm sure this is the End Times. But I won't argue with Pastor Mike about it.

Mom says she understands about falling in love, even if it's with the wrong person. She says that Mitchell left me behind because I'm not old enough, no matter what he says. She says he would have been arrested if he'd taken me to Kansas.

But I know that Mitchell's not afraid of the government or getting ar-rested. I still think I'll see him again, but I don't know if I'll go with him, even if he asks. I feel like the time isn't right, that's all. Mom says that she and Dad need me here, that just having me at home makes life happier. Even Young Taylor said it would be a waste for me to hook up with some guy right away—he says I have too much talent to not go to college and do a lot of interesting things first. He's never complimented me like that be-fore. And he doesn't talk to anybody unless he really means it.

Bekka has been really sweet to me. At school she cornered me so I had to talk to her, and I said, "I don't want to talk—this is all so embarrassing," and she said I shouldn't be embarrassed because falling in love is so out of everybody's control, and she has this theory that we have to fall in love with several people before we can tell we've found the right one. She thinks that I might fall in love more than some people just because I have so much love in my heart. Then she told me about some really dumb stuff she did to impress this college student who worked for her dad two summers ago. So we laughed about acting stupid around guys, and I feel okay with Bekka now.

Dad tries to hang around and talk with me more. He says he gets tongue-tied because I'm growing up so fast and he feels like he doesn't know what to say that I'd be interested in. He says that he's glad I remember to pray for all of us, because sometimes he gets busy and forgets.

So, I don't know where you are now, Jesus. I don't know what to say or if you're really listening or if you'll ever touch my life again, or even if you ever did. I guess I'll keep writing prayers to you anyway, just in case.

But it feels really lonely, not praying in the same way as before, not having the faith I used to have.

If you're there, please help me sometimes. And maybe let me know, if you're close by, that it's really you.

Mackenzie Barnes

Jodie

She has been a weepy mess for three days. The whole church service thing unhinged her completely, and as she walks through each task of her day, her limbs feel so loose and unmanageable, her mind so unsteady, that she is glad Mack is still here. Part of her had hoped that, after she confessed her unfaithfulness, he would leave and that part of life would be finished and she and the kids could get on with the business of refashioning home together.

But he is still here. He lies down beside her at night, quiet and un-
moving. He has ventured a couple of times to kiss her cheek or rub
her back, but he doesn't try to talk or do anything. If she looks into
his eyes, the grief inside them lays her low, so she doesn't look.
Maybe anger would be easier to deal with. At this point in her life,
forgiveness is simply confounding. She can't make sense of Mack, certainly not of the kids. In a jolt of mild horror, she realizes that the person she relates to best right now is Rita. She stands at the kitchen
sink, which seems to be the still center of her whole life, and scours
the cooked-on grease of the skillet, trying to rub away this new
thought. She hears Mack walk in from the dining room, and she turns
to face him. There is a bigger matter they must deal with this evening.

"You need to go get Young Taylor," she says.

Mack stiffens. "What's happened?"

"Nothing, yet. But you'll never guess where I just found him."

He waits. She reaches for the dish towel and dries her hands.

"I was coming back from town, and I glanced toward the cemetery,
and there he was." She makes a helpless motion with her hand.

"At the cemetery?"

"Yes! On a lawn chair right at the graves. It was so ridiculous I had
to pull over and look. He's at your dad's grave, lounging like he's at
the beach or something. It's hardly twenty degrees today."

"He's wearing a coat, isn't he?"

"Of course—jeez!" The calm on Mack's face makes her want to
slap him. "But that's not the point. He's out there *sitting in the cemetery.*"

"Maybe he's just visiting."

"He's never gone visiting before. You don't think this is something
to be concerned about?" She turns back to the sink and plunges her
hands into the water, too mad to keep looking at her husband. Here
they've had one child about to run off to some cult, and now the
other is grave-sitting for no apparent reason. She spouts out words
while fishing silverware from the bottom of the murky sink. "I'd just
like for one person in this family to be okay."

"Why's that, Jo?"

She turns toward him again, the dishrag dripping onto the floor. Mack has moved closer, and he talks quietly. "Why should we be okay? Our situation isn't okay. It hasn't been for a long time."

She is without an answer. She tries to process what he's just said.

He leans back against the cabinet, folding his arms in front of him. "I'm not so sure it's right to expect everybody to be okay. I'm just happy that we're trying to cope."

"Well, the coping in this family hasn't been too constructive."

"No, it hasn't. But we're still here, aren't we?" She can feel his eyes studying her. "You know, I don't wake up anymore and ask myself, 'Do I feel happy today?' A lot of days, that's still too much to ask."

"So what do you ask yourself?" She has turned back to the sink and is looking out the window.

"Well, it depends. If I get up feeling really rotten, I ask, 'What's the main thing I need to do in the next hour?' And I don't take it any further. If it's a better day . . ."

She's looking at him now. She wants to read his face and know that what she's hearing is not just a lot of bull.

". . . if I'm not feeling so rotten, then I ask, 'What's one thing I want today that's possible?'" He meets her look, and she sees nothing false in him.

"I still want you to go find out what our son is doing in the cemetery."

"That I can do." He puts on his jacket but turns to her before walking out the door. "Come out there yourself in, say, twenty minutes."

She can't think of a reason to refuse. "Okay."

She watches the back of him as he walks out to the truck. It is the most familiar sight in the world, and she wonders if it is so familiar that she's tired of it and wants it out of her life. She has him memorized whether or not she wants to remember every detail of his face, every small habit and posture. Maybe the only place left to go is further in, past the stuff she knows. Lately he says things that seem to

point to some place deeper, a spot with which she's not so well ac-
quainted. She wonders if it's possible for there to be parts of Mack she
doesn't know at all.

At the other end of her situation is Terry, to whom she has not spoken for nearly a week. She has picked up the phone several times and
put it down again—yet another indication that her personal drama is
on a par with bad moviemaking. She and Terry haven't seen each other
since the day in the motel parking lot. The grief over this seems out of
proportion to the situation itself. She no longer has sex once or twice a
week with this man she found so attractive and exciting. She tries to
think about it in merely those terms: the sex has stopped. That is not
all, though—she has lost as well the smiles and looks in code when
they happened upon each other at the school. Because she is no longer
with him, he looks better than ever; she wonders if she really did rush
her decision to break things off. She and Mack are existing together,
but she can't imagine that there will ever be the excitement between
them that she has rediscovered in another bed.

The fact is, though, that Terry let go easily once she told him they
had to stop, and if her thoughts linger upon him, she fills up with
anger and hurt. She had hoped he would fight for her a little bit.
Maybe she was merely sex to him. Was he more than that to her? Of
course—the attention, the laughing together, the amazing warmth
they generated. That went beyond sex, had to. Whatever was there,
Terry is not fighting for it. He avoids her. She imagines that he flirts
with the second-grade teacher, who is younger than him. Yes, it's that
easy for him. He has no attachments, no regrets. Even if it's not that
easy emotionally—and she does believe he's hurt by her leaving—to
move on is simply easy for him in a lot of other ways.

And she knows a deeper truth. It wasn't that difficult to give her
body to Terry, but she never gave him her heart. Not that she with-
held it or saved it for Mack or anyone else. She's misplaced her heart,
or maybe she's locked it away. Or maybe it is hiding on its own. Until
it comes back, anything with Terry or Mack or any other man is
doomed to fail.

She shakes her head as Mack puts a rusty lawn chair into the truck bed. As he leaves the driveway and heads toward town, her sadness follows him. They have lost so much, and both of them are old and tired. He expects for life to heal; she looks for a balm that she believes, more all the time, does not exist. She has to admire Mack's willingness to keep going. In fact, he is turning out to be more of a fighter than she believed him to be. Not that long ago, he was willing to give up his life and all of them. Was ready to say good-bye and leave them with unanswerable grief. Jodie wonders now if what she has really resented was his weakness. In fact, she knows, deep down, that the only reason she told Mack about the affair was to see how he would respond, to find out how much she really mattered to him. Dear Jesus, what kind of a manipulative person has she become?

She can't think more about any of this. She is learning how much she can think in a day, and it's not much. So she does mindless work and thinks for a few moments, and then she stops herself and finds more mindless work. She has devised her own way of coping, after all.

In the back of her thoughts, an old hymn scratches up memories of things she used to build her life upon. She tries to replace these unbelievable words with her own, with something she is more likely to trust. No such words are forthcoming, and so she allows the hymn phrases to tumble around some more. For the first time, she notices that the chorus ends not in answer but in question.

Is not this the land of Beulah? blessed, Blessed land of light,
where the flowers bloom forever, and the sun is always bright!

Mack

He pulls into the narrow drive of the cemetery, at the bottom of the hill, where he can look up the rise and see his son. Sure enough, Young Taylor is stretched out on a lounger. He's having a smoke. The color of the cigarette tip matches the sky beyond, those ancient, fluid fires above the spent fields. Mack turns up the track that leads to his father's and brother's graves. As he gets closer, Young Taylor makes a slight motion with his wrist, and in that second he becomes a snap-shot of Alex, the younger Alex, before the hope left. Mack parks the truck and walks over.

"Hey, Dad."

"Hey." Mack looks around. "How did you get out here?"

"Eric dropped me off." He wears a down-filled denim jacket, an old red scarf at his throat. His ears match the scarf. A small blanket they used to take on camping trips is wrapped around his legs. He looks to be here for a while.

"I think there's a wool cap in the truck—you want it?"

"No." Young Taylor takes a drag. It's one of those clove cigarettes. He holds it toward Mack. "Want one?"

Mack shakes his head. "You know those are twice as bad for you as the regular ones."

"Yeah, but they burn twice as long, so I only smoke half as many of them." He studies Mack for a second or two. "You're not going to tell me to come home, are you?"

"No, no. You've got a pretty nice view here." Mack scans the rows of headstones, the cut marble and granite, the older, milky rectangles leaning over and barely readable, the occasional angel raising its wings above the dead grass.

"Quiet too," says Young Taylor, resting his head against the chair. The tinted sky reflects against his face. "Once a person ends up here, he's through talking."

"Is that why you come out here?"

"It just feels like a good place to be. Hard to say why."

Mack stares at Young Taylor's silhouette. His son doesn't move at all, except to bring the cigarette up and back, in a slow, thoughtful motion.

"Is it okay if I sit here with you?"

"Sure."

Mack gets the lawn chair out of the truck. He notices that his son is directly on top of Taylor Senior's grave. The family Taylors stacked one on the other. It doesn't strike Mack as disrespectful, but fitting. He positions his chair on top of his brother's resting place and sits down. It feels a little bit as if he and Young Taylor are waiting in line, just one layer up from death.

"It just makes me think bigger, when I'm here." Young Taylor turns to Mack when he says this, to see if his dad is listening.

Mack nods. "It can't help but work on your perspective, can it?" They sit quietly for several minutes, while the sky in front of them shifts its colors and changes shape. Beyond the hill and its resting dead lie fields that look more dead still. Mack knows that looks are deceiving, that even now the world beneath their feet is heating up, preparing for spring. He sits there on the slope and imagines movement far below, the anxiety of seeds waiting for their time, the sluggish awakening of worms and beetles.

He feels energy waken inside him as well, other things biding their time, sentences about to form, even the conversation that emerges now, phrase by phrase, between him and his son. He looks across at Young Taylor's still profile and is filled with wonder that they are here, underneath this dramatic sky and sitting atop centuries of gains and losses. The two of them hold the present moment, with all of its dreams on the verge of bursting out.

He realizes that he is breathing hard. He laughs a little, giving vent to the pressure that surrounds him, the noises and textures that fasten him to this place at this moment. He wants to reach over and touch his son, to steady himself, but instead he speaks.

"Probably every person should come sit here from time to time."

Young Taylor grins at him. "What a world that would be."

Mack laughs. "I don't suppose it will happen anytime soon."

They settle back, as the earth tips forward. Mack feels the solitude gather at their feet and shoulders, and he knows that he can stay as long as it takes to do whatever is needed.

After a moment or two, he hears a familiar sound. It is the cold clatter of a car engine, and Mack gazes hopefully down the road as Jodie's dust rolls toward them.

ACKNOWLEDGMENTS

This story could have been set in just about any farming community in the United States. I chose Iowa because it's but a few hours' drive from my home in Chicago, thus making research possible, even affordable. I chose Iowa also because of its mythic character in the American landscape; the Iowa farmer has become an archetype of strength, independence, faith, and fruitfulness. To explore loss as thoroughly as possible, I wanted to delve into the heart of what has been lost—not just a family farm here and there, but a core belief, an icon.

I chose Mahaska County because, when I drove around the state nearly five years ago, I was drawn to that area. I don't know if, statistically, Mahaska County is any worse off or better off economically than other counties. Clearly, a lot of people are doing just fine, and the crops there continue to grow and thrive and offer harvests year after year. But in Mahaska County, as well as in similar counties all over the nation, the rural community has had to deal with the forces that shape Mack's story.

As far as I've been able to ascertain, there is not, nor has there ever been, a town in Iowa by the name of Beulah. Beulah, Iowa, is fictitious and at the same time very much like many tiny towns throughout Iowa, Illinois, and other farm states. I had already decided on the generic surname of Barnes for the family in this story when I discovered, in Mahaska County, the small town of Barnes City; it has no connection to the story of *Dwelling Places*.

My thanks to the academics and journalists who have written so eloquently about farming in America; their statistics, stories, and descriptions helped me flesh out this fictional tale. Thanks to the counselor for a farmers' hotline in Nebraska who could lend detail to the pain and depression faced by so many who are caught up in frightening change. Thanks to the former farmer willing to talk about the difference between "before" and "after," and to the rural pastor who mentioned a service she'd witnessed once that celebrated a farm family who had had to move on. Thanks to the café and motel owners, the fellow diners and guests, who stopped to chat with this city girl passing through, who provided color and language to the story, though they were unaware of their help. Thanks especially to Brent Bill, who helped me get the farming details straight, and to Charlie Cooper, who lent similar expertise to the scenes involving a therapist. Thanks to my husband, Jim, who not only endured my repeated trips out of state but came along once or twice and provided photo images for my research.

I am ever grateful to my agent, Kathryn Helmers, who found a home for a story whose subject matter is not highly sexy or marketable, and to my editor, Renee Sedliar, and the entire Harper San Francisco team, who were willing to make a home for *Dwelling Places*.

This is a story of loss, but of faith too. It is certainly not every farmer's story, but the journey of Mack and his family is the same one required of any of us when life is not what we expected, and when the songs and prayers we have memorized since childhood no longer make sense.

Vinita Hampton Wright
February 2005

For more information on Vinita Hampton Wright, her publications, speaking engagements, and workshops, go to:

vinitahamptonwright.com

Or contact her at:

Vinita Hampton Wright
9347 S. Eberhart Ave.
Chicago, IL 60619
vinitawright@sbcglobal.net